STAR SHEPHERD

R.R. VIRDI

BOLIDE
PUBLISHING LIMITED

STAR SHEPHERD

© R.R. VIRDI 2019
Cover Art by Sarah Anderson

All rights reserved. No part of this publication may be reproduced, distributed, or transmitted in any form or by any means, including photocopying, scanning, uploading to the internet, recording, or other electronic or mechanical methods, without the prior written permission of the publisher and/or author, except in the case of brief quotations for reviews.

This is a work of fiction. Names, characters, businesses, places, events, and incidents are either the products of the author's imagination, or used in a fictitious manner. Any resemblance to persons, living or dead, or actual events is entirely coincidental.

First published in 2019 by Bolide Publishing Limited

http://bolidepublishing.com

ISBN NUMBER: 978-1-912996-07-0

TITLES BY R.R. VIRDI:

The Grave Report
Grave Beginnings
Grave Measures
Grave Dealings

The Books of Winter
Dangerous Ways

Monster Slayer Online
The Goblin King

Anthologies
The Longest Night Watch
Stardust Always

CONTENTS

STAR SHEPHERD

BOOK 1 OF SHEPHERD OF LIGHT

CHAPTER ONE

NOT THAT GOOD A FRIEND

No man could truly enjoy his drink with a gun pressed to his side. Star stiffened and kept his eyes on the acrylic glass. The thought of being shot made it difficult to appreciate the subtle spices in the brandy.

The barrel of the weapon pulled away from his side, just enough to alleviate the pressure.

Star had no delusion it was no longer trained on him. He raised his eyes from the transparent counter, eyeing the back of the bar.

Rows of black shelves hung along the wall. Electric blue light illuminated the panels holding the bottles of alcohol. A lone mirror sat opposite the bar, reflecting the soft lighting to make the place feel larger than it was. Halogen red strips arced along where the walls met each other and the ceiling—an added bit of visuals that did nothing to enhance the otherwise dismal black of the surrounding furniture and paint.

"You know, Star, there's only so many places to look before you'll have to look at me." The man's voice was made of smoke and whisky.

Mostly whisky, Star noted. But he recognized the voice and turned to greet the gunman. "Zheer." Star inclined his head.

Zheer had a face made from sharp edges and weathered skin done no favors by a complexion that needed to see more light. He ran a gloved hand through his brush of black hair. His eyes carried a mischievous gleam that did nothing to soften the cold, iron grays that drowned out the tinge of blues. "You weren't exactly hard to find, you know?"

Star exhaled in relief, moving his glass from side-to-side with his index and middle fingers. "Who says I'm hiding?"

Zheer held up a finger with his free hand. He stowed the bulky revolver into the folds of his heavy, olive-toned canvas coat. His hand emerged from the clothing with a stark white piece of paper.

Star arched a brow. "Really?"

Zheer shrugged. "I look like I'm going to carry 'round a lens?" He flipped the paper around, holding it an angle so only Star could view it. "*That,* and the mighty princely sum below it says you're hiding."

Star's mouth twitched before breaking into a lop-sided smile. "It's not hiding if you're running, is it?"

Zheer mimicked his expression before stowing the sheet. "You're wondering if I'm here to collect."

Star's brow raised higher. "Are you?" His fingers drummed along the counter.

It consisted of thin films of clear carbon and printed

titanium weaves as fine as hair. The metal gave the counter the slight silvery sparkle under the bar lighting. And it wasn't easy to break in fight.

Shame.

"I might have had a terrible temptation to." Zheer turned to look ahead at the far end of the bar.

Might have.

Star mirrored Zheer, staring down the way. "I take it if you've found me, not long before men of a more officious nature end up here."

Zheer grunted, reaching out to snag Star's drink. He took a swig and slammed the glass down harder than necessary.

The bartender, a man made of whipcord muscle and knotted wood, gave him a look. His thin lips pulled down to one side in what could have been the start of a disapproving frown. The dark-featured man held the stare before busying himself refilling another man's drink.

Zheer exhaled through his nose. "Government and corporations are after you. Expect trouble of the private, well-armed, and not-so-nice, and law-abiding kind."

Star rolled his eyes. "Corporations *are* the government last I checked."

Zheer waved a dismissive hand. "Think they used to call that semantics. Still, for the money they're offering, won't be long till more than just those bodies will be after you. We're talking citizens, less than savory sorts. Heck, Liberation Movement folks will be after you. Separatists—extremists too. You know what they're like. Always crowing on about how the government and those that serve 'em are dogs needin' to be put down. They're just as ruthless and maybe crazier. You're going to need friends and one heck of a corner to hide in."

Star pulled his drink back, swirling the amber fluid around without wanting to take a sip. "So, question is: Are you friend, Zheer?"

Zheer clicked his tongue. "Not as good as one as I should be. Showed up just in time to tell you to get what you came for and run."

Star plunked his glass down, fishing in his pockets for a sliver of metal. He pulled free a thin card of palladium, stamped with its weight and the name of the company that had printed the currency. "Ought to cover my drink *and* yours."

Zheer stared at the card. "Yeah, and several more of mine to come." He raised a brow, and gave Star a knowing look. "What'd you do?"

"The right thing. Isn't that the sort that always lands you in the most trouble?"

Zheer nodded more to himself than Star. "Yeah, that's about the way it goes. But I should've been clearer." Zheer's eyes hardened. "What'd you steal?"

Star rose, eyeing his surroundings without turning his head. He counted thirty-two people cramped within the place. That was enough hands to start a good deal of trouble should the need arise.

His stomach twisted and let him know it may come to that. "Who says I stole a thing?"

Zheer recovered the drink, tipping it back until it was drained. "I say. I'm not stupid. It's known around some of the circles that you went to Autumn—backwards world if ever there was one—and then the government quarantines the place. Next thing the galaxy over knows is the whole world's declared a threat. Military hammers it from orbit till it's nothing but glass and dust. Now, in all of that, there're rumors of one little ship making it off world."

Star said nothing. When a place was so far out the way of well-traveled routes, someone was bound to think it was backwards. All it made them was wrong for thinking that.

"And I've got a pretty good guess as to what that ship looks like. Tell me if I'm wrong, eh? Double Y-frame, sleek little thing retrofitted to be lighter, more efficient on fuel—faster. That sound about right so far?"

Star ignored him, staring at the only entrance to the bar. It was just wide enough to fit two broad-shouldered men at the same time. Convenient if he needed to get out. Not so much if a group of people were looking to get in. His lips pressed together.

"Thing's damn near military, minus the fact I know it's not much in the way of weapons. Those ships weren't ever popular for much but smuggling, and in your case—shepherding. How am I doing so far?"

Star's teeth ground against each other. "Annoyingly, like you're heading to a point I may not want to hear."

Zheer grinned. "Leaving a planet ain't a crime. So, makes me wonder what got the government so hot on Autumn to waste it like it did. The planet was some kind of threat. Putting a price on you is pointless unless you walked away with something you shouldn't have." Zheer's grin slipped, replaced by a cold glare that made his face look like a porcelain mask.

"Maybe I didn't. Maybe I'm doing my job, shepherding. Maybe I'm taking something somewhere it belongs, and that rankles the powers that be." Star matched Zheer's stare. "What I'm carrying doesn't belong to anyone. It belongs to everyone." His look hardened enough to make the metal card seem brittle. "Remember that."

Zheer lifted his hands in a gesture of resignation. "I will. I'll make certain they mention that in your eulogy."

Star moved from the counter, heading toward the exit. A hand closed on his wrist. He turned his head a fraction, enough to look at Zheer.

"Might want to sit back down." Zheer nodded toward the entrance.

Star followed his look and hissed.

A group of men entered the bar. They moved in unison, walking with the posture and pacing drilled into them through years of military service. Each dressed in the same crisp, black uniform. Silver buttons ran down the middle, pinning one half of their coats over the other all the way up to their high collars. A single copper bar, half the width and length of Star's thumb, was pinned to their breast of their coats.

"Men like that might take notice of a man like you—wanted and all—especially since you're standing when everyone else is sitting." Zheer nodded to the stool.

Star averted his gaze and took his seat. "Well, this is going to get bad and fast."

Zheer tilted his head in a way of agreement. "Yeah, sort of expect that with you." One corner of his mouth pulled up in what could have been the start of a smile.

Star glowered. "Won't take them long to make me out. They'll likely have lenses with my face brought out to the best resolution the government can produce."

Zheer nodded. "Not long at all."

Star exchanged a glance with him. "Don't suppose you have a plan? One you're willing to share with an old friend? Maybe make my trip last a lot longer than stopping right here."

"And how long is that?" The light in Zheer's eyes intensified.

"All the way to the end?" Star hoped more sincerity than grit and alcohol colored his voice.

Zheer shook his head. "No. Sorry, but like I said, I ain't that good a friend. But I can help you find the man to take you there and back again." His face broke into a wide smile like he was pleased with himself.

"Is it too much to hope that that man's here and in a disposition to want to help me?"

Zheer's laugh came in a muffled series of light puffs through his nose. "Call it a bit of luck in your otherwise shitty day." He jerked a thumb to his side, gesturing down the counter.

The man Zheer pointed at was in his early thirties at first glance, wearing a simple white shirt and black pants. He kept his hair longer than finger length, swept back. The rich black of it caught the blue lighting from the bar and seemed a deeper color. His face could have been carved from maple wood. It was all chiseled edges and angular cheek bones.

"And he is?" Star turned back to Zheer.

"A pilot. The sort you need. Has no love for the fine

gentlemen who just entered this establishment." Zheer shot a quick glance to the uniformed men.

"I *am* a pilot."

Zheer coughed. It didn't sound any less condescending than if he had laughed. "He's better."

Star weighed the decision. "And he's got no love for the military—government?" He eyed Zheer askance.

"None." Zheer shook his head. "I know what you're thinking. He's looking for work. Good work, mind you. I'm betting you've got that. And, yes, he'll be wanting to lay low and out of sight of the military if he can. Means you've got a pilot with a semblance of the same goal as you—only, better than you."

Star scowled. "Semblance doesn't mean the same. You've got a point though. He won't need too much convincing?"

"Oooh, I'm thinking not much now." Zheer gestured with a glance to the pilot.

One of the military men put a hand on his shoulder, turning the pilot away from his drink. The uniformed man had a generous amount of flesh in his face that should have burned away during his training. His sloped brow and thick lips did him no favors either. The button-like eyes set deep in his face only added to his near-comical appearance. He leaned close to the pilot. "Have time to help the military? It'll be a public service."

The pilot blinked. He had sharp, hooded eyes the color of rum under a bright light. Their glow seemed dulled, likely by the drinks he'd been consuming. He looked up to the man in uniform. "Did my fair share of service. Lot of it public. Some, not so much." He waved his hand dismissively, turning back to the bar.

The military men exchanged glances that morphed into the same look. Their brows furrowed, jaws hardened, and eyes narrowed.

If looks could kill. Star brushed aside his long coat with a swipe of a hand. He reached to his waist before Zheer leaned over and clamped his hand on Star's wrist.

The man with the button eyes grabbed hold of the pilot's shoulder, digging his fingers into the meat between his neck and the joint. He grunted and spun the pilot around. "Let me clarify." The soldier cleared his throat. "Not helping us, in even the smallest of capacities, can be construed as obstructing a government investigation."

The pilot blinked slowly, as if he struggled to remember how. "Construe it how you want." His mouth moved like it was too much effort to speak, the way Star would expect from someone who'd spent his time drinking hard in the bar. "I don't even know what it is you want."

The soldier held out his hand. Another placed a thin sheet of translucent acrylic material onto his palm. He brought it forward, raising his hand to ensure the pilot could see it. The button-eyed man pressed his thumb to one corner of the sheet. It flickered internally with white light before dissipating. An image materialized above the card in full color. The density and brightness of the pixels made the three-dimensional portrait appear opaque.

The pilot stared at the photo, almost looking through it. He teetered in his chair, not far enough to fall but enough to startle the soldiers by him.

Two of them moved to his sides to steady him.

The pilot took no notice, keeping his gaze fixed on the image. "And?"

Button-eyes looked to the picture, then the pilot. "Look familiar?"

He looked familiar to Star. Awfully so.

A dark-featured man stared back from the lens's display. He had skin like warm sand and eyes a few shades darker, much like the brandy Star had been enjoying. Dark brows edging on the thick side and thicker hair worn past ear length, swept back. His nose was on the thin side—aquiline. A few days' worth of stubble lined his hard jaw. The man's cheekbones weren't quite as pronounced as the pilot's.

Zheer exhaled through clenched teeth. "Well, that's you done, isn't it?"

Star pulled up the collar of his coat, retreating into it. It was a small hope that they'd only probe a few patrons before moving on. His ribs twinged as Zheer's elbow bounced off them. He peered out from the confines of his long coat. "What?"

Zheer nodded to the scene.

The pilot held his stare on Star's image. His gaze flicked in Star's direction for a microsecond that went unnoticed by the soldiers.

The brandy from earlier felt like it had risen from his stomach to congeal into a cold cube blocking his throat. Star swallowed it.

"No. Never seen 'em before. Why?" The pilot's face was a neutral mask that could have given lessons in stillness to steel.

"Look harder." The button-eyed soldier pushed the card closer.

"What's he done?" The pilot held his stare with the soldier, but Star felt like the glare was meant for him.

Question of the day. Star lowered his head, keeping his eyes fixed on the conversation.

"Stolen government property." The soldier's voice hadn't wavered. They'd likely been fed the lie and told to repeat it until it was a reflex.

Star's fingers curled, tightening until they balled into fists.

The pilot's mouth twitched. "Serious crime. Can't help you, though. Done my best; never seen the man."

The button-eyed soldier sighed in resignation, the strength leaving his shoulders. "Fine. Can't be helped. I'll need your citizenry identification card to log that we've questioned you, to follow up if need be."

The pilot's lips pressed thin. He raised a hand, upturning it while digging into his pants with his other hand. A black card emerged from his pocket pinched between his thumb and forefinger. He handed it over.

The soldier plucked it from his grip, swiping it through a groove in the lens that was barely wide enough to accommodate the card. Star's image flickered like the display had lost its ability to render it properly. His features morphed into the pilot. The soldier's eyes darted over the text scrolling through the air beside the image. "Ahiko Kohiba. Age: thirty-five. Occupation: unemployed. Former status: navy—pilot, honorably discharged."

Star gave Zheer a look.

"I told you he had problems with them. I don't know much of what; I didn't ask. I reckon he's got more cause to hate them than you. He knew 'em better, after all."

Star's look intensified. He imagined his glare as shards of glass stabbing Zheer. "That's trouble I don't need. There's 'not fond of the government,' and there's being one of them. That kind of fallout, whatever it is, always leads to complications."

Zheer shrugged as if it were inconsequential. "Sometimes a man's needs outweigh the luxuries. He's the best. He's here. He's looking for work. Those are all things you need. Not to mention the fact I'm the one who called him here on account of knowing you'd need a hand." His face remained neutral, but a hint of light entered his eyes.

Star stared at him nonplussed.

"All the help I could offer. Don't make a liar out of me, Star. Promised him a good job is all."

The button-eyed soldier handed Ahiko's card back. His surly demeanor sobered, and he stepped to the counter beside the pilot. "Didn't know you were one of us. Sorry for the attitude; you know how it is."

Ahiko's face tightened for a moment. The silent expression made it clear to Star that the pilot knew exactly how it was. Ahiko's fingers drummed against his glass, their speed picking up by the second.

Zheer leaned closer to him. "Did I mention our boy has a temper?"

Star stared.

"No? Well, now's the time to let you know. And I've got one of those feelings."

Star rose from his seat, cursing himself.

Ahiko hiccupped, raising his glass to his face. He looked over the edge like he was searching for something. The pilot got to his feet and thrust the hand holding the glass toward one of the soldiers.

Alcohol splashed over the soldier's face, beads peppering his dark, umber skin. His fingers went to his eyes. "Ackh." The soldier's features tightened as he rubbed his face. The other soldiers rushed the pilot.

Ahiko struck an open-handed blow against the button-eyed soldier's ear, driving him sideways. "I know how it is. I know how y'all *discharged* me too!" he slurred.

Great. A drunk. Star doubled his pace, rushing to Ahiko's aid. He lashed out with an open hand, hooking his fingers around the collar of the man's uniform. His biceps strained as he pulled the man close. Star twisted at the waist, pulling the soldier down at an angle. He released his grip.

The man stumbled off-balance and careened into a circular table a couple of feet off the ground. He toppled it over. A multicolor assortment of drinks splashed over a group of men sitting on their knees. Glassware *thunked* onto the ground, clattering before rolling away undamaged.

The men looked at the wet splotches on their clothing before glaring at the fallen soldier. They set on him in a drunken frenzy.

Star looked over his shoulder for help.

Zheer stared over the edge of a glass, flashing him a wink before tipping the drink back.

Bastard. Star turned to face a soldier rushing him, arms outstretched. He shot a glance to Ahiko.

The pilot teetered against the bar like he had forgotten how to stand properly. His back collided with it, bending further than normal. He rode the momentum and tumbled onto the counter. Ahiko's foot snapped up, the tip connecting with the underside of another soldier's chin.

The blow lifted the man onto the tips of his toes before he sank back to even footing, rocking on his feet. He collapsed into a heap a second later.

Star lurched forward as a soldier grabbed hold of his coat and hauled him close. He slammed an open hand into the man's face, digging his thumb into the corner of one of his eyes. His fingernails raked the skin around the soldier's brow.

The soldier screamed, releasing his hold and stumbling back to paw at his face.

Star covered the distance between them, grabbing him by the shoulders and shoving him into a group of patrons engrossed in their own world.

They weren't pleased by that. The drunkards took hold of the soldier, raining blows down on him.

Ahiko staggered forward like he was losing his balance and proper use of his legs. He lumbered into a soldier, grabbing hold of him for support. Ahiko fell backward and dragged the solider along with him. He released his grip, letting the other man's forehead crash into the counter.

Star blinked at the drunken pilot's movements. There were discordant bursts of energy throughout his stumbling that made it appear like he was in complete control.

Ahiko slumped against the counter before falling to his bottom.

Star reconsidered his thoughts about the pilot's control. He caught movement out of the corner of his vision.

The button-eyed soldier held the display lens up for everyone in close view to see. Star's face stared back at him.

His eyes widened as he realized what was about to happen.

All eyes turned to the lens, and the reward displayed below.

Ahiko hiccupped, staring from the image to Star. "Hell, maybe I should've turned you in." He looked to the soldier. "Turns out I have seen *that* man."

Star reached for his gun.

CHAPTER TWO
A BIT OF MISCHIEF

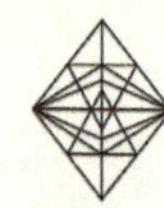

The button-eyed soldier screamed and jabbed a finger at Star. He drew his sidearm, a sleek pistol with a barrel just large enough to slip over a pen. The entirety of the weapon barely protruded from the soldier's grip. It was too compact to store projectiles.

Shit. Powered weapon.

Star pulled his hand free, pointing his index finger at the soldier.

The man froze, staring at Star's hand.

"Bang." Star lowered his thumb. His mouth pulled to one side in an uneven smirk.

The soldier's mouth moved soundlessly. His stare flicked to the lens then back to Star, confirming it was the same man.

Star shrugged. "You wouldn't shoot an unarmed man, would you?"

Ahiko looked at the lens. His mouth twitched. "For

that kind of money, I reckon everyone in this bar would." The air felt like it had been filled with a flammable gas. One spark and the bar would ignite. Star felt it was in his best interest to give it that light.

He inclined his head toward the lens. "Says I'm wanted alive. Bounty's no good if this"—he patted himself—"is all holey-like." Star gestured to the soldier's gun before turning around to address the entirety of the bar. "So, question is, who's wanting to collect on the biggest payday of their lives?" He hooked a thumb over his shoulder to the military men who had gone still. "Them, who, truth be told, ain't much in the way of sharing? Or the lot of you?" He gestured at the patrons.

The bar's occupants exchanged looks. A single, silent message hung in each of their faces: the allure of reward money.

One of the soldiers drew his sidearm, training it on the closest person. The tip of the weapon quivered. His eyes widened as the patron he aimed at rushed him.

Match struck. Kaboom. Star turned to Ahiko, tensing the muscles in his legs.

A trilling shriek, like the cry of dozens of birds, cracked through the bar. The irradiant blue shot lanced past the charging patron and into the wall behind him. Debris plumed into the air. Smoke rose from the impact point.

An incoherent cacophony of noise erupted throughout the bar. Occupants leapt to their feet, many grabbing the nearest thing they could reach to use as a makeshift weapon. Others pulled their own firearms.

Star inhaled sharply and ran toward Ahiko. The

movement set everything off.

"Need 'em alive!"

"Warning shots! Don't be killing civilians."

"Heck with 'em."

"Split him each and every way; still more than any of us earn."

High-powered screeches and dull, percussive blasts peppered the shouting. Wood, stone, and designer glass showered the patrons.

Star doubled over, crossing the distance and coming to Ahiko's side. "Two choices: stay here, might be you die; come with me and might be you live."

"A mite too many mights in those choices. I prefer just to be, to be honest." Despite the situation, an amused glimmer hung in Ahiko's eyes.

Star swallowed the curse fighting to make its way out of his mouth. An electric wail filled his ears just as the space between him and Ahiko flashed. A palm-sized portion of the counter had liquefied, composite materials bubbling.

The pilot eyed the spot before looking up at Star. He held his hand out for support. "Might be I want to live. Let's go."

Star hauled him to his feet. His chest cried out as a pair of arms wrapped around him, squeezing him tight enough to build an ache in his ribs.

The button-eyed officer thrashed, wrestling to take Star to the ground. "You crazy?"

"On account of starting a ruckus in a bar full of military men looking for me…yeah." Star wriggled in the man's grip, snapping an elbow behind him. The joint throbbed as it connected with the soldier's temple.

The button-eyed man staggered back.

"Come on—" Star scanned the brawl, searching for the pilot.

Ahiko had vanished amidst the chaos.

He swore and barreled through a soldier and civilian grappling one another. Someone tumbled to the floor in front of him. Star stopped, grabbing hold of a table that had managed to remain upright in the chaos. He swept at a glass, hooking it with his fingers and sending it hurtling behind him.

Every bit of mischief, no matter how small, goes a long way when things get difficult.

A pained cry echoed over the commotion of the brawl.

Star smiled. He placed his hands against the back of a civilian, shoving them into a group of people embroiled on the ground.

The man stumbled over them, crashing onto the group and joining the fray in inebriated rage.

Star shambled past the remaining people, all of whom were too fueled by their anger to notice him weasel by. He slipped through the exit and into the corridor. The air at the side of his head hissed. A bolt of neon blue arced by, its screech rattling his eardrums. The blaster bolt washed over a section of the aged and unvarnished steel comprising the corridor. "Tch." Star looked back into the bar.

The button-eyed soldier stood atop a stool, struggling for balance. He sighted in on Star for another shot.

Star looked to his right. Translucent paneling ran along the length of the corridor, providing a window out to space. He didn't know if the panes could take a blaster bolt without compromising their integrity. And he didn't want to find out.

A tawny ball hung in the near distance, dominating the view. The planet's coloring was peppered with the sort of red that came with rust. A world of sand and iron.

His collar went tight around his throat and pulled against him. Star lurched against the wall as another warning shot sailed by.

Ahiko stared at him. "This job of yours, it pay?"

Star nodded. "Where'd you go? Hell, where'd you come from?"

Ahiko ignored him. "I *was* hiding outside the entrance for my own safety. Saw my would-be employer standing in the middle of the hall waiting to be shot. My need to be paid outweighs yours to be stupid. I saved you, so"—he shoved Star—"let's go."

Star staggered a few steps before breaking into a run down the hall.

Ahiko trailed several feet behind and to his left.

"You're awfully spry for a drunk." Star fought to swallow air faster than it left his lungs.

Ahiko brushed aside the comment with a wave of his hand. "Where's your ship?"

His panting increased, each breath making his lungs feel like dry rubber being stretched too far. "Second hangar. Closest I could get it to the recreation arm." Star willed away the fatigue building his legs, cursing his heavy boots. Jarring tremors raced up his shins with each step.

Another flash of blue wailed by.

Both Star and Ahiko yelped in unison, recoiling from

the path the shot had taken.

"Thought the bounty specified alive?" Ahiko wasn't at a loss for breath despite running. His words had lost their slur.

Star eyed him askance before turning back. "I thought so too." The path continued with an opening on the right leading to another corridor. Movement caught his eyes through the clear paneling ahead. He lashed out with hand, clawing at Ahiko's shoulder. Star's fingers dug into the pilot's clothing, and he pulled him in his direction.

Ahiko went along with the motion with more grace than a drunk should have been able to manage.

Star committed the oddity to memory before juddering to a stop. He looked over his shoulder to find the bar brawl had spilled into the hall behind them. Several soldiers and civilians struggled to break free. Some would likely pursue him. He turned to face ahead. The movement he had noticed in front of them came in the form of a trio of men.

They were similarly dressed as the soldiers in the bar. Star sighed.

One of the men had the face of a pinched rat. His wiry, red hair was cut short everywhere but the top. It only served to accentuate his narrow and long features. A transparent card sat pinched between his thumb and first two fingers. Star's face rotated slowly in the holographic display. The man's eyes looked like dull slate, a hint of darker gray colored them as they widened. He glanced at the card once more before gawking at Star.

Ahiko capitalized on the soldier's stupor. He pivoted, snaking his hand below the card. The pilot slapped the bottom of the device and launched it up before the soldier's face.

The rat-faced man blinked.

Ahiko thrust both his palms into the soldier's chest, driving him back.

The other two men caught their friend under his arms, helping steady him.

"Run!" The pilot jabbed his fingers into the eyes of one of the men supporting the rat-faced soldier. Ahiko shoved the man with a quick blow from his palm, causing the entire trio to collapse under the weight of each other.

Star heeded the pilot's words, breaking into a sprint and rounding the corner down the path the soldiers had come from. Hollering echoed behind him. He didn't look back. Last thing he needed was to turn and catch a shot to the face.

His mother had always warned him not to stick his face into things. That was how you lost an eye, or worse.

A streak of blue hurtled by, affirming his mother's warnings.

"Alive, dammit!" The shout barely carried down the hall to Star's ears.

Something the size of a pebble impacted his upper back with enough force to cause him to falter a few steps. He pawed at it, reaching for whatever had struck him. Cool metal pressed against his finger tips. Something crackled like miniature lightning, and the muscles in his hand spasmed.

He jerked his hand away from the thumbnail-sized piece of metal—the shock tack—embedded into the thick leather of his coat. Fortunately, it hadn't burrowed deep enough to wedge its prongs into his skin. Star pulled the collar of his jacket up to cover the exposed skin of his neck and head.

The last thing he wanted was an electric brain tickle courtesy of the government. He figured things up there were scrambled enough considering the trouble he'd willingly signed up for.

"Atch!" Ahiko fumbled, causing Star to glance at him. The pilot's movements lost their coordination, his feet dragging like he was drunk again. He tumbled against the steel side of the hall.

Star slowed as his mind raced, feeling like meteor shower. He imagined bright streaks bombarding his vision as tried to sift through the thoughts.

Three soldiers and more were coming.

A silver hexagram sat fixed to the back of Ahiko's right triceps. The device shivered in place, and light pulsated from the spot where the taser met the pilot's skin.

Great.

If he lingered any longer, he was likely to catch one of those. Leaving meant Ahiko would end up in custody for assaulting soldiers.

The fingertips on his left hand tingled. His heart felt like it was caught in an iron-cold grip, struggling to beat. Star's balance wavered more in his mind than actuality. His thoughts drifted to the planet of Autumn.

Not again.

Star reached into his coat, plucking a sliver of transparent plastic composite free. He knelt by Ahiko and jammed the card between his skin and the device. Wriggling the material several times, he pried the taser loose. A quick snap from the card pulled it from Ahiko's arm. Six pin-holes wept small beads of blood.

"Come on." He grabbed the pilot under one of his shoulders, dragging him along.

Ahiko babbled incoherently.

"Yeah, sounds about right for where we're at." Star slipped the pilot's arm around himself. "Move. Doubt they'll be able to ready and code any more of those to shoot soon."

Another fast-moving object pelted his coat.

Color me wrong.

Star picked up his pace, pulling Ahiko along until the pilot found some semblance of strength in his legs.

He pushed himself free of Star. "First left." Ahiko nodded ahead, sprinting toward the turn. His body hunched forward like he was still suffering from the effects of the taser.

Star followed the unintentional example and doubled over enough to lower his profile. He trailed on Ahiko's heels, tearing into the turn after him. A hard *plunk* informed him another taser had smacked into the metal siding of the hall just behind him.

How many do these guys have?

The end of the hall broke into a room exuding a gaseous fuchsia light. It washed out of the mouth of the room and toward them.

Ahiko pointed to it. "We'll lose 'em there. Parlor's got more ways out than in depending on how you're counting."

Star had no idea how someone could count an entrance differently than an exit, but he didn't argue the point. He pumped his legs and closed the distance between the pilot and himself.

The pinkish glare throbbed around the mouth of the entrance almost in rhythm with his own heartbeat.

Star pulled ahead of Ahiko, peeking over his shoulder on instinct.

The soldiers had turned into the hall and leveled their weapons. Their tasers had vanished in place of blasters. Fortunately, they didn't fire, showing more restraint than the button-eyed officer in the bar.

Shooting into a busy parlor was generally frowned upon. It didn't do favors for the government's image either.

Star barreled through the entrance, wincing as the staccato flashes of bright lighting assaulted him. A pinkish-purple hue fought to burn itself forever into his vision. He raised a hand to block what he could, rubbernecking to find a way out. A dull ache manifested in his shoulder as Ahiko brushed past him harder than necessary.

"This way!" He grabbed Star's coat and hauled him to the left.

The parlor was a far cry different than the bar. An endless rows of rectangular machines lined the place. There was no telling them apart to his eyes. Each was the same garish purple made worse by the overall pink-tinged lighting. Simple white screens tumbled through countless images trying to align them once stopped. Slots dominated the scene, ringing out in discordant chimes and clinks without stop.
It was a place of jarring colors and lights refracted over polished metals and pooling over smooth glass. The parlor made the bar look like a relic of the past.

Star broke free of Ahiko's hold and ran alongside him. "I'm not seeing a mess of ways out. Only a way of messes to lose your money."

Ahiko scowled and turned right, dashing through a new row of slot machines.

Star followed behind and glanced at the entrance. He found it a small relief the soldiers hadn't barged in yet. His chest felt like he'd caught a sack of bricks, stopping him short in place.

His relief vanished.

Star stared ahead and into the face of a soldier whose uniform sported far more bars than the previous ones.

The officer's face carried more lines than it should have. A mixture of hard living coupled with being in his later years, evidently. He gave Star a level-eyed look, appraising him without showing any obvious signs of losing his temper.

Star inclined his head in a way of silent apology, brushing past the man.

Ahiko's eyes widened. He nodded in a direction as a prompt to Star to follow.

He did, falling in line with the pilot.

An incomprehensible scream rang out over the commotion of machinery and gamblers.

Star turned a corner, trailing Ahiko. He managed to catch a glimpse of the scene unfolding behind him.

The trio of soldiers from earlier barged into the parlor, flagging down the officer. They didn't bother approaching him before raising their hands simultaneously. Three images of Star flickered above their lens displays. The officer registered it faster than Star imagined possible and turned to the nearest machine.

He pulled a card from his pocket, inserting it into the slot.

The entire row of machines died.

All manner of folk rose from their seats, rounding on the officer before processing who he was. They grumbled in discontent before resuming their seats. Star's face spread over their screens in black and white. The effect rippled through the entirety of the slots in the parlor within seconds. The clamor of angry customers followed, growing by the second.

Ahiko released a long, low whistle. He gestured around the parlor with his index finger. "Notice something? Awful lot of men and women in uniform."

Star glared.

The pilot shrugged. "What'd ya think when you docked here? Terizen Station is a military hub. Soldiers come here to unwind, spend money"—he waggled his brows—"have what needs scratching scratched."

"I was thinking I needed a reprieve from being hunted, and this was the only place I had to do so."

Ahiko ignored his rebuttal, hustling down another row.

The parlor's clientele were quicker on the uptake than Star favored. They rose to their feet, swarming them.

Ahiko shoved a woman, looking to be in her late years, into a small line of people.

Star groaned. Necessity outweighed niceties he supposed. He lurched to the side as someone wrenched on his coat. Without looking, Star slammed his forearm down, breaking their grip. He pulled back on one of their wrists and sent them to the ground.

The row flooded with more people, squirming to tear past one another to get at the pair.

Ahiko looked back to Star, face breaking into a mischievous smile.

Hell's got him so happy?

The pilot elbowed someone Star couldn't make out before shoving hard against one of the machines. It rocked slightly. He kicked out, driving his heel into it. The machine wobbled again before he pushed it over.

The mass of people on the other side moved out of its path.

Ahiko seized the opportunity, clambering over the fallen machine and plowing through the tight-knit group.

Star copied the pilot's process, going as far as toppling two machines in quick succession. He bounded onto them and drew a thunk of protest from their cheap metal frames. His hands went out, clawing at people's clothing to drag them into one another or out of his way. Star placed his hands together like a stiff shovel and thrust them between a pair working to block his path. They parted enough for him to ram through using his shoulder to widen the gap.

Ahiko increased the distance between them, running without bothering to wait for Star.

He couldn't fault the man as much as he would've liked to. Not when he wasn't their target.

"Who gets the reward?"

Star couldn't pinpoint the voice. He didn't bother, giving silent thanks for greed and curiosity. The question broke over most of the screaming, enough to bring a lull to it. People clamored as Star rushed through the confusion.

Shouting filled the place once more. Customers voiced their concerns to the nearest military official who would listen. They overwhelmed the soldiers in a money-driven fervor, pumping their fists and getting too close for anyone's comfort. The scuffle reminded him of a lesson he'd once learned: The only thing worse than the promise of money is wondering if someone else will get the reward for your work.

A screech comprised of electric chittering drowned the sounds coming from the mob. Screams followed.

Star kept his gaze fixed ahead. He saw no point in turning to catch what had been shot. It was a needed distraction that would keep the crowd's attention on the military.

Ahiko raced up a flight of stairs, moving fast enough that it looked like his feet were barely touching the ground.

Star swallowed another string of curses over the weight of his boots. Acid burned throughout the muscles in his legs, urging him to stop. The same dry heat racked his lungs and made them feel tight. He buried the pain and pushed on, making it to the top.

A similar scene filled the second floor. Throngs of people embattled with each other and soldiers spaced between, all of whom were trying to organize the chaos. None of them seemed to notice the similarities between Star and the image flaring across every screen in the parlor.

It was a truth of the universe when people got mad enough, all they saw was everything wrong around them and not what was right in front.

Star pulled on his collar and set after Ahiko. He

picked his way through the mess of people, nudging the occasional person with enough force to rile them a bit more. Things played out as expected.

A person would lash out at the spot Star had been, striking someone else. Pockets of the crowd erupted into worse fighting.

Star repeated the process until he'd broken free of the thicker cluster of people, searching for the pilot who'd vanished among the mass. "Dammit." He leaned to the side, peering past the remaining people.

Ahiko was nowhere to be found.

Star huffed, working to calm the beehive of activity in his mind. He'd told the pilot where his ship was. Nothing indicated the man had been stopped or caught. His best course of action was plowing ahead and hoping Ahiko would find him at the hangar.

An open exit into a corridor hung a mere hundred feet from him.

Good enough.

Star pushed clean of the few patrons blocking his path and rushed forward. He left the parlor behind, embracing the dimly lit path. The simple corridor was a welcome relief to his eyes. Somehow, the dull metal lining managed to reflect soft orange and muted browns coming through the glass paneling.

Star subdued the urge to look out into space. He demanded more from his legs, boots rattling the loose sheets of metal below his feet as he raced on.

The path split three ways ahead.

He scanned the horizontal beams running across where the corridors met. An antiquated placard sat over what he figured was a defunct screen. A messy scrawl indicated the path to the hangars. Star picked up his pace and turned left. With luck, his pursuers would think he still lingered somewhere within the parlor.

Metal work and faint lighting blurred along his path.

Running became a mechanical process. Pain and fatigue washed away under the repetition of scanning signs and picking his paths through the halls.

Damned time.

Star came to a path blocked by a pair of doors with teeth like gears meshed into one another. He fumbled through his coat, fingers rifling in one of the larger pockets. Hard plastic brushed against his fingers. He pulled the translucent card free. A spider web of platinum ran through the plastic. Star held it up before a circular lens the size of his thumb nail.

A conical beam of turquoise light filtered out from the scanner, thinning until it was spread wide enough to cover the width of the card. It danced over the material, registering it. The scanner chirped and flashed the same color as the light.

Metal groaned and shuddered as a plume of gas puffed out from the sides of the doors. They slid open to reveal the corridor leading to the hangars.

Static crackled over his right ear. Star looked up at the wall-mounted box hanging a foot above him. The honeycomb mesh sported a few finger-sized holes like someone had jabbed at the device in frustration.

"Terizen Station hangar bays abide by the following rules: All weapons must be holstered and battery cells removed. If you are in possession of projectile weap-onry, please remove all ammunition. Discharging weapons within the hangars is a category three offense.

Capital punishment will be levied. No exceptions."

Fine by me.

Star placed a hand against the angled walling for support, allowing most of the strength leave his body. He lumbered forward at a leisured pace and allowed his body a reprieve from the running.

The doors huffed behind him before shutting.

Star hobbled to the first pair of signs displayed opposite one another. The one on his right read "Hangar Two." He approached the shuttered gate.

It was of similar design to the entrance he'd passed through moments before.

He repeated the process of displaying his card.

The familiar beam projected and spread over his pass. It vanished. The lens did not flash, instead adopting a solid red.

He blinked. "That's never good."

Something the size of his little finger pressed against the back of his hips. "It's good for me."

Shit.

CHAPTER THREE

AND I HOPED TOO SOON

Star fidgeted.

The barrel of the gun jabbed deeper into his back. "I wouldn't, lest you're wanting to give me cause to shoot you."

He frowned, fighting to recognize the voice. "I'm taking it this is on account of the ever-so-high bounty I'm worth?"

"It is."

"I've said this far more than I ought to have today, but last I checked, I'm wanted alive." Star turned his head a fraction before the barrel ground against his body, making it clear to remain still.

"Alive. Blasters don't kill outright, though. Not when aimed at your hips. It'll hurt. It'll burn the wound shut too. There's a reason they issue us these."

Military. Great. He pegged the voice as well. "You were back in the bar, weren't you?"

The button-eyed soldier grunted in what Star took as affirmation.

"I noticed a distinct lack of shinning metal bars on your uniform. Enlisted?"

"Not for long. I turn you in, and with what they're offering, I can collect on more than just money. Likely I make enough friends with the right people to become an officer." The soldier's voice came out deeper than before, quivering noticeably.

Star didn't think that was how promotions work. He deigned to keep that thought to himself. Aggravating a man with a gun to his back didn't seem prudent. "Sounds like you've got it all figured out."

"More than you, Shepherd."

Seems like.

Star turned his face a tad more, pressing his cheek against the cold metal in front of him. His gaze turned down the path he'd come from. He couldn't help shaking. A smile forced its way across his face, and laughter made its way out.

"Even with you making a fool of me back there in the bar, I still got you."

"Yeah, you did. Didn't get the pilot though, did ya?" Star's smile widened.

"He didn't." Ahiko stood to Star's side, staring at the pair. "You know, it's a nicety to buy a man a drink before jamming your piece up against his rear much like you're doing now." The pilot waggled his brow before nodding to Star.

The soldier stammered, pulling the gun from Star's back. He jammed it against his hips like he was unsure of what to do. "Move, and I'll put one through him."

Ahiko rolled his shoulders. "Not much of a bother for me, is it? Let's say I let you walk with the wanted man. Am I of the right mind in assuming you'd forget about me"—Ahiko pressed a hand to his chest—"and the raucous misunderstanding not so long ago?"

The soldier nodded. "I'm already forgetting."

Star glared at the self-serving pilot. "Well, you're fired."

"Don't recall being hired proper. Touch odd firing someone for something he didn't agree to in nothing more than some words exchanged."

Star blinked, trying to make sense of what the pilot had just said. He looked to the soldier to see if he'd understood it any better.

The military man stared more through Ahiko than at him.

Guess not.

The pilot took a step closer to them.

Star fidgeted as the blaster pressed against him for effect.

"I'd stay where you are, Kohiba. I'd prefer to bring in the Shepherd without a hole."

Star nodded. "I'm of that mind as well on account of my health remaining wholesome. And not the kind he's itching to do."

Ahiko's grin pulled more to one side. "Fair enough"—he inclined his head—"soldier?" He left the question hanging in the air.

"Creed Benson, and not looking for anymore issue with you, *former* Captain Kohiba."

Captain? Star turned his gaze back to the pilot.

Ahiko shrugged. "And I'm not looking none either."

He held up a finger. "Except for the rather large one hanging before us all."

Creed tilted his head to the side. "What's that?"

"Greed, Creed. What says you get Star Shepherd over to where you're planning? At least, not with interference. See, the people on Terizen are eyeing him much like you are. They want a piece. I've got the feeling that your fellow soldiers do as well. How fond are you of sharing? Don't see how one man splits so many ways. And the funny thing is, people split easier than money from what I've seen." The pilot's eyes glimmered.

Star tried to swallow the knot forming in his throat, but it remained fixed in his place. If the pilot kept it up, Star was likely to be shot, and the former captain would follow. The thought Ahiko might catch a bullet brought Star a measure of comfort.

"I assume you have a suggestion, Kohiba?" Creed eased the weapon away from Star's back.

"I'm the *me* and he's the *you* in that assumption"—Ahiko nodded to Star—"meaning it's best not to assume, unless you want to be the *ass*."

Star imagined Creed's eyes spinning nearly the same as his were.

"But as far as you're wondering, yes, I have a suggestion." Ahiko slapped a hand against the scanner. "Hangar's on lockdown behest of military authorization. That about right?"

Star watched Creed bob his head in agreement. *A little less attention on me, a tad more on the pilot if you will.* Star sucked in a breath, pulling his stomach toward his spine in an effort to thin his profile. He pressed himself further against the wall and managed to inch away from the weapon more.

"I recall that what's locked can be unlocked, and that upstanding members of the military carry cards to do so." Ahiko gestured to the scanner with a tilt of his head.

Creed raised a brow at the pilot before eyeing Star. "And?"

"And I'm looking to get off Terizen. He's got a ship, one wanted and likely to fetch an extra sum if you bring him in with it. Also means you won't have to share with no one." Ahiko flashed a smile.

Creed rummaged through a pocket with his free hand, pulling free a card similar to Star's. A secondary web of precious metal hung suspended between the plastic. It was made of glittering black particulates. He tossed it toward Ahiko.

The pilot caught it and placed it against the scanner. "Could've done that yourself."

The hangar bay doors opened.

"Could have, which is when you might choose to pull something funny and make off with my prize. You want off Terizen, fine by me. We'll fly out together. But that's it. You're not taking the Shepherd or the ship." Creed ground the barrel against Star to make a point.

"Don't suppose nobody could take Shepherd? I'm fully able and willing to walk myself down to my ship and be out everyone's hair." Star gave the soldier a toothy grin. His answer came in the form of being shoved through the opening. "No, then."

The hangar was a cavern of cold silver panels and grates. One thing served to break the monochromatic view. The clear paneling showcasing a blanket of black looking like diamonds had been sewn into it. Prismatic gaseous bodies hung in the distance adding a bit of mystic and color to the dark expanse.

"Move." Creed shoved him again.

Star found slight relief in the distance between the weapon and his backside increasing. He glanced out of the corner of his vision without turning his head. Ahiko had come a few feet behind him to his side.

The pilot whistled in appraisal, nodding to the ship ahead. "Heckuva bird. She do anything other than sit and look pretty?"

Star ignored the comment.

The double Y-frame stood true to its name, resembling the letter. Its proportions weren't evenly distributed. A near-straight hull made up most of the ship's six-hundred meter length, curving slightly downward as it reached the bow. Its thrusters hung below the stern, angled downward to the sides much like the wings of a bird in flight. A simple design with elegance that spoke volumes over everything else. It reminded Star of a bird of prey.

"Nice paint job." Ahiko sounded like he was speaking more to himself. "That polar silver looks a bit too much like white. Has a nice sparkle to it though." The pilot leaned in closer to Star. "Don't suppose ole Creed will let me keep the ship when he's done collecting on you, do you?"

Star's teeth ground together.

"Think I'll sell the ship." Creed chuckled. "Bound to fetch a nice price."

His fingers dug into his palms as he balled his fists.

Star imagined bashing the soldier's head a few times against the hull of ship.

"Shame." Ahiko clicked his tongue against his teeth. "Would've liked to keep her. Have to scrape off the red stripe running along her sides and wings. Bit tacky"—he nudged Star—"don't ya think?"

Star amended the imaginary scenario to include the pilot's skull as well. Maybe he'd be able to perform a percussion solo with both of their noggins.

"She looks fast." Ahiko had returned to speaking in a tone clearly meant for himself.

"She is." Star didn't know where the pilot was going with the questions, but something didn't sit right. His stomach roiled like his drink had consisted more of tainted water than cheap liquor.

"Mhmm. That makes it easier." The pilot rubbed his chin.

Star eyed him. "Makes what easier?"

"My job. The one you didn't hire me for proper, afore firing me rather improperly, truth be told."

He stared at Ahiko, trying to sort through the tumbled tongue-twister. "I can't tell if you're insane or wholly aware of what a pain in the ass you are—truth be told, so long as we're telling truths."

Ahiko grinned. "Now you're getting it."

Creed shouldered his way between them, still keeping the blaster leveled on Star. Its tip hovered between his ribs and kidney. "I've got a bit of truth that needs telling. I'm not particularly fond of either of what you two are saying. Anything funny, and I'll—"

The pilot waved his hand in a lackadaisical manner. "Heard ya right the first time. You'll shoot the Shepherd. No skin off me if you do. Though, reckon it'll be a bit off of him. He might take that personally."

"Just might." Star nodded to the ramp leading up into his ship. "She doesn't open up for anybody. Not that kind of girl." He waggled his fingers. "You going to let me coax her into letting us onboard?"

Creed eyed him. The soldier's mouth twitched like he was searching for something clever to say.

Star felt they'd all lost that game the moment Ahiko had shown up.

"Nothing funny." Creed narrowed his eyes.

Star tipped two fingers to his temple in a simple salute. He turned to Ahiko. "You know, I finally think I understand you."

The pilot arched a brow.

"How'd you like to help me pilot this bird?"

Ahiko's brow rose higher. "You offering me a job?"

"I am." Star gave him a look.

"Like hell you are." Creed moved the gun from Star's side and turned toward Ahiko.

The pilot ran a quick hand through his hair in frustration. "Well, shoot." He surged to the side, ramming Creed with his shoulder. Ahiko turned and shoved Creed again and sent the soldier toppling. "Move, Shepherd. Get her open."

He didn't need the shouting. Star clambered up the ramp and slammed a palm on the underside of the ship. A panel fell open. He jabbed a finger across the segmented screen, keying in the combination.

Supersonic chirping rang out as a lance of blue lightning struck the air a foot from the panel. The space around the ship's hull shimmered a faint violet and dissipated almost as fast.

Star whipped around, eyeing the fallen Creed.

The soldier aimed the blaster at him.

Damn.

The ship's hatch opened with a smooth, gaseous hiss.

"Go!" Star waved a hand to Ahiko, ushering for the pilot to run.

The man obeyed the command and ran up the ramp.

Creed's blaster flashed.

Star hadn't registered the bolt, only its trilling cry. His abdomen spasmed as searing heat radiated through the tissue. One of his hands pressed against the wound on instinct. He winced and fell to a knee.

Creed rose to his feet, steadying himself. The blaster remained stable in his grip.

Of all the things not be shaking. Star grimaced, stilling his quivering body as he met Creed's eyes. Talking wasn't an option. He settled for something more satisfying. Star tapped a finger to the panel he'd used to open the entrance hatch.

"Don't. Next one will go through one of your knees." Creed leered.

Amber light flooded the hangar. An automated voice blared over a low, droning siren. "Detection of discharge, hangar bay two. Security is en route. Please remain where you are. Repeat: Detection of discharge, hangar bay two. This is a category three offense. Terizen station security and local military have been alerted."

The soldier snarled and whipped about, searching for the source of the speakers.

Star welcomed the distraction and dragged two

fingers along the security screen.

The ship's thrusters groaned in discontent.

Oh, don't give me that. He pounded the base of a fist against the hull.

A lengthy whine built in the propulsion, increasing in volume with no sign of stopping. Loose metal paneling around the hangar vibrated and threatened to tear free. A metal cart rolled a few inches before the hurricane-like force hurtled it unceremoniously against the far wall.

Creed raised an arm in front of his face trying to brace against the storm.

Star waved at him with a two-fingered salute. The pain from the wound hadn't subsided, but he managed to dredge up enough words for the soldier who'd made his trip to Terizen unpleasant. "Nothing personal, it's just personal is all. I'm not overly fond of being shot. Figure it's best to return a favor done. How'd you like to be shot into space?" Star tilted his head toward the mouth of the hangar.

Creed struggled to level the blaster at him.

Not being keen on seconds, Star tapped the console above him.

The thrusters answered in kind and picked up in intensity.

Creed's feet left the ground as he tumbled through the air. He crashed to the side of the door leading into the bay. The soldier clawed at the lip of the entrance, trying to pull himself to it.

It had closed during the alarm sounding, a safety precaution to lock down the area.

Star turned and hobbled up the plank into his ship.

The ambient lighting hadn't registered his entrance. Star grumbled, leaning against the bare metal walls of the narrow corridor. A screen sat on the inside paneling around the hatch. He jabbed a finger at it, shutting the entrance to the ship. A low groan escaped his lips as he leaned back. The burned tissue in his midsection refused to stretch. Every movement made it feel like steel hooks raked across his innards.

"You fine, because you don't look fine? I'm askin' because it seems like something someone in your employ should do." Ahiko stood to his side, a few feet further up the incline leading into the main hub of the ship.

Star could barely make out his silhouette in the darkness. "It'd behoove that someone in my employ to fetch a medical kit so their employer doesn't leave them unemployed on the account of dying. It's bad for one's financial affair." Star grimaced and swallowed a hiss trying to make its way out of his mouth.

"Right, and the lights. Hard to do any of that in the dark, which, it needs pointing out, is where you've been keeping me on why you're wanted by the authorities."

Star glared at the pilot.

"I'm taking your silence as a request to shut up and go find that kit?"

He imagined Ahiko was smiling. The pilot could have benefited from a straightening that came from the punching sort. "Yeah, not so much a request, as much as it is an order from your new employer. That is…depending on how long you're wanting to be employed for." He exhaled and removed his hand from the wound. Bothering to make the retort to Ahiko had only served to aggravate the injury.

"Right. Might help if this place weren't on the dark side." Ahiko banged a fist on a panel.

Star grunted in agreement. He leaned toward the panel he had used to shut the hatch. Three of his fingers swiped horizontally along its top.

A gentle thrum ran through the ship, preceding the burst of white light. It carried the intensity of a neutron star.

Star shut his eyes and welcomed the warm red of the inside of his eyelids in place of the jarring light. The optical assault weakened enough for him to take a peek. "Hate that every time."

Ahiko stared back at him, blinking hard as if trying to squeeze the discomfort clear from his eyes. "Well, that's a touch too bright."

"A touch." Star couldn't argue the fact.

"Seems like a waste of power too. How much fuel can this thing sling anyhow?"

Star averted his gaze. "Enough."

"For?"

"Till we get to where we need to."

"Which, I should point out, is easier when that information is shared and all. Especially so with the pilot, on account of me needing to know where I'm heading." Ahiko's face remained neutral, but his eyes shone.

Star waved him off. "Right now where you're needed is up front and piloting. Don't bother talking back. I'll fetch the kit myself. Go."

Ahiko's mouth twitched as if he were going to argue, but he caught Star's look and swallowed the reply. He nodded to himself and sprinted ahead.

A staccato of chirping peppered the air like screaming hail. Sounds like slapping wet clothing tinged each burst of shrieking lasers.

"That sounds bad!" Ahiko's voice echoed through the ship.

Star ignored him, gripping an overhead railing and using it to haul himself forward. He lumbered into the main hub, a circular room with a series of corridors leading out of it.

The whole of it was made of bare metal and carbon composites. Star hadn't found the time for decorating between being hunted and shot at.

A set of thin slits ran along the curved wall to his right. Each slit was wide enough to slip his fingers between. He hobbled over to the first one, jamming a hand in and wrenching with more force than necessary.

The panel exhaled a light puff of air before slowly rolling open as if to spite his urgency.

Star grumbled and rummaged through the storage bin. His fingers brushed a smooth can that rolled out of his grip. He fished for it, wrapping his hands around it. Star plucked it free and extended its slender nozzle of a tip. His eyes shut on reflex before he lifted his shirt and depressed the button at the back of the can.

A glacial breath washed over his abdomen. He released a high-pitched note. The wound numbed, and unseen grains of sand rushed across his skin to replace the pain. His breath came in ragged gasps. The can fell from his grip, rattling on the floor before rolling away.

The ship shuddered as its thrusters screamed louder. It hadn't drowned out the sound of the blasters impacting the shielding.

Ahiko came into view from around the corner. He leaned out of the corridor leading to the cockpit. "I'm as much for a show as the next man, but that's not the show I'm wanting to see right now." He nodded to Star's exposed midsection. "Especially since there's another one of the explosive kind happening outside. Might want to come take a look. Seems important since they're shooting at us."

Star grunted in an effort to clear his throat. "And let me guess, you find yourself mighty important and allergic to being shot?"

The pilot grinned. "That about sums it up." He receded into the hall.

Star pushed off of the storage lockers, smacking the base of his fist against the open one. It retracted as he set off after Ahiko. He turned the corner and hobbled down the hall. The windows of the cockpit brought to light a scene he'd feared.

A torrent of miniature comets bombarded his ship only to meet resistance in the form of flaring violet.

"How long's that shield set to hold? Impressive, by the way." Ahiko leaned against the console, eyeing their surroundings.

"As long as we don't go anywhere."

Military personnel had swarmed the hangar. Each was clad in a zero-environment suit in the event Star decided he was no longer content with sitting in the hangar. Terizen Station security were mixed along with the soldiers, dressed similarly and tethered to secure railings and pillars. They carried an assortment of weaponry from military lasers to outdated projectile launchers.

Each got the job done—painfully so, as far as he was concerned.

And I'm painfully concerned. Star pressed a hand to his side and weighed the situation. He knew the barrage wouldn't cease until the personnel outside collapsed the ship's shields.

Ahiko strapped himself into the pilot's seat, shooting Star a glance. "I'm not one to point out things that aren't under my purview—"

"Then don't." Star collapsed into the seat beside him, running through the auxiliary checks. He allowed Ahiko to take care of the primaries. *Man's going to keep talking anyhow.*

The pilot's fingers danced overhead and in front of him in a mechanical process that managed to carry an inherent grace. It was the sort that could only come from decades of practice.

Star noted Ahiko didn't have to look at what must have been an unfamiliar ship console to him.

The pilot navigated it with an uncanny sense.

Ahiko shot Star another look before nodding toward the hangar exit. "And I know it ain't my job to say—"

"It's not." Star finished running his checks. "But I've got the feeling you're going to anyway."

"You know me so well and in so short a time. I'm nursing a serious worry as to what will happen when we head out that way." Ahiko inclined his head toward open space.

"Cell reserves will hold the shields enough for small arms fire."

"And how is it they're holding up for this long?"

The pilot stared hard at him.

Star averted his gaze. "Is it a problem?"

Ahiko shook his head.

"Good, then take us out."

The pilot's brow furrowed. "We're still held under the lockdown."

Star held out his hand. "The military card you pocketed. I noticed you didn't give back to ole Creed."

Ahiko quirked a smile. He pulled the card free from a pocket and handed it over.

Star took it without looking and slipped it into a slot near the far right of the console. He thumbed a switch to the side, waiting for the device to read the card.

Ahiko stared past him to the box. "That a stripper?"

Star nodded. "It is. Will pull every sort of code and authentication from the man's card it can before wiping it. That's our way out. Transmit code to the hangar bay's automation system and force open the lockdown."

"Which is when I take us out and into what—I ought to point out—is going to be a larger mess. Terizen Station has defensive weaponry. The funny thing about that is what's defensive's always been a matter of perspective. Same things used to protect 'em will be turned on us to render us into none too similar to your bounty image."

Star held his look. "We'll be fine."

Ahiko's mouth twitched, and he looked out the window like he didn't believe Star.

He pushed aside the pilot's doubt and keyed in a command on the stripper box.

The transparent barrier ahead quivered in disdain as if it didn't want to heed his order. The amber lights strobed erratically before dying out to be replaced by a sea of angry red. Baritone alarms sounded.

"Unauthorized departure. Hangar bay two depressurizing. Warning."

"Well, at this point, seems safe to say I'm going to be joining you on them wanted lists."

Star eyed him. "You almost sound like you want that."

Ahiko slapped his hand onto the T-shaped lever near the center of the console. "I'm not one to commit to anything halfway." A twinkle formed in one of his eyes. "Think they'll make the bounty as pricey as yours?"

There was something terribly wrong with that man. Ahiko shouldn't have been walking unassisted, much less flying after how the man had been drinking. And Star had made him his pilot. There must have something equally as wrong with him for doing so.

The barrier receded into the right-hand side of the hangar wall. Station and military personnel were yanked into the air by invisible hands. The only thing keeping them from joining the endless expanse were their harnesses. They twisted and twined round one another like leaves caught in a storm. A soldier managed to squeeze of an erratic burst of laser fire that skirted over the ship's shielding. The impacts prompted a series of angry purple flares.

Ahiko released a triumphant, rolling howl and flicked a trio of switches.

The ship juddered as the landing gear retracted, suspended only by its thrusters.

"Into vasty nothingness we go!" Ahiko slammed the lever forward.

Where he hoped they'd stay without issue.

His ship quivered once almost in anticipation before launching out of the bay. He struggled to see anything more than the black tapestry of space and sequined stars.

Ahiko's cry picked up.

He's going to kill us.

The pilot smacked his hand against the bare paneling running along the side of the console.

"Don't bang her."

Ahiko threw a hand to his forehead in salute. "Aye-aye. Besides, I like to know the name of a gal before that happens. Seems proper."

Star rolled his eyes. "*The Last Leaf.*"

Ahiko grunted and pursed his lips. "Odd named girl." His expression sobered, and his eyes widened as he rubbernecked.

"What's wrong?" Star's heart doubled its pace.

"Remember those defensive weapons I mentioned earlier?"

Star's heart sunk into his gut, the spasmodic throbbing refusing to calm. "I do."

"They're getting offensive."

The air in front of *The Last Leaf* erupted into light that pulsed without stop. It was like watching never-ending hail strike the surface of a lake through an amethyst lens. The shields flared as the silent onslaught took place.

Star noticed the lack of irradiant colors cutting through space. "Station's armed with projectiles?"

Ahiko gave a quick jerk of his head that Star took to be an affirmative. The pilot's hands blurred in response to the situation.

"Bit antiquated, no?"

Ahiko glared at him. "See how I'm busying myself with the sort of work that'll hopefully lend to our survival? You asking questions isn't conducive to me doing that successfully. I'm defending and keeping this leaf from falling out of the sky. How about you do the task you seem all too prolific at and offend—greatly so."

Star arched a brow.

"She's got weapons, don't she?"

Star gave Ahiko a level look. "You want me to open fire on a station filled with civilians? I may be the wanted man, but I'm thinking your priorities are a little muddled. How keen are you on raising your bounty to match mine? Because that's the way to do it."

Ahiko's mouth twitched, and he turned away from Star. The pilot pulled back on the throttle, sending the fingers of his left hand pecking across the console.

The Last Leaf slowed and the bow tilted up.

Star's fingers dug into the side of his seat. "Oookay. I think this is the proper time to be discussing just because the ship *can* do something isn't an invitation for you to go about doing—"

Space tumbled outside of the cockpit. Stars spun across his vision, becoming the only point to orient himself. They blurred to the point he worried his sight was slipping. Star's universe changed orientation every second. His view shifted through six different directions.

The Leaf tumbled as purple-hued light strobed in defiance of Terizen Station's attack.

"So far, so good." Ahiko's composure was holding better, Star noted.

A palm-sized monitor wailed.

"I spoke too soon. I have that habit." The pilot sighed and took note of the display. "Shield's running on cells? And they're near gone. How'd they hold so long back in the hangar?"

Star developed a case of deafness and hooked a thumb to the right of the cockpit. "Take us out of here."

"Can't. World of problems with your plan, Shepherd." Ahiko kept his gaze fixed ahead.

"Let me guess, you'll do me the kindness of telling them to me."

Ahiko slammed the lever up.

His harness tightened around him as the ship accelerated. Star rattled in place, trying to keep his head from tearing from the rest of him. He thought it was a good enough plan for the moment.

"Don't know where we're heading. Your fault, by the way. Wanna take a stab at what happens when you do tell me? No, don't bother. I'll save you that. I have to slow down long enough to set us up. And in the meantime—" Ahiko jabbed a finger at the screen displaying shields.

"Not much left."

The monitor chirped in distress before silencing.

Ahiko's eyes went wide.

Star's mirrored the pilot's.

"I'll need to amend that. We've got nothing." Ahiko's eyes narrowed.

"Your look says it's worse than nothing."

Ahiko exhaled. "It's worse than nothing. We're

tagged."

"What?"

"One of those old *projectiles* you seem to frown on happened to be a ship tracker. Made it through—yes, you guessed it—when the shields piddled out. We go anywhere, and the military is following."

Star grimaced and looked out the window. "Put her down before we're put down."

"And before the military's birds catch us. By the by, they've sent some to meet us."

There's my hopes becoming issues. And I hoped too soon.

CHAPTER FOUR

A TAD DISCONCERTED

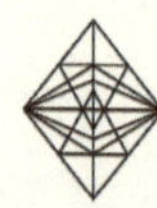

"I'm not keen on having a dog fight out here. Likely they've called the nearest hub for more military. This ain't a great start to our adventure, Shepherd."

"Azzip's mostly sand and rock?" He glanced at Ahiko.

"Right. And?"

"And those rocks are magnetic, right?"

Ahiko's eyes grew larger as he caught on. "Works for me. It's temporary though. They'll find a way to dig us out. Won't hide us for long."

"Even shortly so is better than not hidden at all, especially in this case."

"I can get behind that. Putting her down on Azzip." Ahiko throttled back and adjusted the controls.

The Leaf twisted, bringing the sandy-brown planet into view.

"Wanna know the odds of me putting her down?"

Star glanced at him. "Hopefully better than the ones of you shutting up. Been praying for that, and it ain't happened yet."

Ahiko smiled. "Better."

Shrapnel bounced off the hull and skittered over the cockpit window having bounced off the hull.

"We're still being shot at."

Ahiko ignored him, sending the ship into a drunken weave toward the planet. "Touch odd."

"What is?"

"We're outpacing fighters…" Ahiko broke contact with the view ahead to stare hard at him.

Star shied away from the look. "Lucky thing."

"For the short time I've known you, you seem to be getting by solely on lucky. A lot of it. Uncannily so."

Star cleared his throat and gripped his seat as the planet closed in. "Bit too fast."

Ahiko ignored him.

The rattling intensified.

"I'm fearing for my ship, myself, and your wellbeing, pilot. Not necessarily in that order."

The blackness of space was ripped from his gaze and filled with hot orange and soft browns. Flames washed over the ship's bow as they broke into the atmosphere. *The Leaf* shook harder.

"Company." Ahiko glanced up to a monitor.

Star gave him a silent look, the message clear.

The pilot nodded and throttled back. "Let him come say hi before I wave 'em bye."

"That doesn't sound like a—" Star stopped short as the pilot scowled at him.

"My job's getting us out of the trouble you're so

great at getting into. Might want to add that to my description."

Star inclined his head. "Noted."

The flames intensified, drowning everything from sight but the hellish trinity of colors that came with them. They gave way to a palette of countless browns. A sea of copper and bronze grains with hints of wheat thrown in.

Monoliths of red stone protruded from the ground like jagged teeth.

A hailstorm of metal struck *The Leaf.*

"Those sound awfully like bullets."

Ahiko's lips curled. "I'm awfully certain those *are* bullets. Here's hoping that's all we see and hear. Don't want a close look at a military fighter, believe me."

"I do. Find us a place to lose them and put down."

He nodded, grunting before accelerating towards the red rocks.

Star hissed and turned away from the view. He wasn't fond of their rapid approach.

Metal pinged the ship without stop, threatening to build to a crescendo he felt would end explosively.

Star turned back to peek out of the window.

He regretted it.

Ahiko flew the ship toward the largest and closest of the protruding stones.

Star swallowed and bit back what he wanted to say; he didn't find it wise to distract the pilot given the circumstances. His head snapped to the side with enough force he knew he'd be massaging the spot for days to come.

The ship rocketed past the first stone at an angle.

Star struggled to keep his body from being shaken apart.

Ahiko sent *The Leaf* pirouetting through the first pass of rocks. "Picking up nothing but garble a ways ahead. Good sign."

Star eyed the pilot as if he were crazy.

"Means more of these—a lot more. Your plan. I'm just seeing it through. After all, someone has to."

Star resisted the urge to reach over and unbuckle the pilot.

The world tumbled without end. Seas of sand became granulated skies, and an ocean of soft blue took their place as the spinning continued.

A thunderclap swallowed his thoughts and jarred him from his reverie.

"One bird down."

Star shut his eyes.

Another thunderclap.

"That's two. Oh—"

"Oh?"

"Nothing."

Doesn't sound like nothing.

"Birds pulled back."

The pressure holding Star in place eased. He figured Ahiko had throttled back a touch. "That's not a bad thing." He didn't understand why the pilot sounded concerned.

"In the immediate, no, not so much. But they'll be touching down. Likely in the nearest town, which, I should point out, is a while away. A long while."

"Focus on the here and now."

"Fair enough, Shepherd. Now we're here." Ahiko

nudged him with an elbow.

Star opened his eyes to find a canyon skip by underneath.

It was the color of rich clay and old sangria all muddled together. Endless rows of jagged stone spires dotted its surface. Some of the formations jutted out from the canyon walls, giving it the appearance of a heavily fanged maw.

Star frowned. "None too inviting of a place."

"Doesn't need to be inviting. Just needs to be enough of a mess for us to find the tag and wrench it free. That is, before they find us." Ahiko maneuvered *The Leaf* around the canyon for a second pass, throttling back to nothing. He positioned the craft over the opening. "Now's the tricky part."

"Oh, now's tricky, is it?"

The pilot flashed him a glare. "If you're not wanting your ship to kiss one of them rocks, then yes, I'd say this is tricky." Ahiko brought *The Leaf* down in sporadic drops.

The ship seesawed past the stony protrusions as it sank.

Star considered holding his breath for the descent. A look out of the window made him reconsider. He didn't think any man could hold out for that long without it becoming permanent. Star eyed Ahiko. "Do me a favor?"

The pilot shot him a quick glance.

"Hold your breath till we're down, for luck's sake."

Ahiko followed his example and looked down the canyon. He turned back and glowered at Star. The pilot shook his head before returning to bringing the ship down.

Star leaned back, counting the seconds in his head. He found the confines of his mind a much needed reprieve from the hectic chase on Terizen Station. A jarring impact rolled through the ship and into his spine. His eyes remained shut. "Tell me that wasn't you banging my ship into the canyon."

Ahiko released a delicate cough. "No. That was the canyon banging into your ship. Besides, I'm a gentler touch than that. At least until I'm asked not to be."

Star groaned. He had the feeling the pilot was rather amused with himself. Star hoped he kept his amusement to himself and away from the console.

The shaking lessened while the noise from the thrusters echoed through the canyon. It was like listening to a tsunami pass through a tunnel.

Star's world rocked like he'd been swept up in the storm. He feared the seat would be torn from its mounting as the ship vibrated with renewed vigor.

Like a switch had been flipped, the raucous noise subsided. The rumbling followed suit.

"That's us down. You'll note we're in one piece, and there's a lack of people in military uniforms around us."

"And I'm also noting a none-too-subtle hint that you're wanting thanks for doing your job?" Star opened his eyes, letting his head loll to give Ahiko a sideways look.

"Notably, jobs pay. I'm not seeing any of that yet." Ahiko matched his look, flashing it back.

Star grumbled and unfastened himself from his seat. "Plenty of that at the end of the road." He rose and craned his neck, peering up into the canyon.

Rusty reds and clay browns towered over them as far as he could see.

"Problem with that is that the end of the road is often the end. Hard to get paid when it's all said and done."

"It's a mighty deep of a hole." Star pursed his lips, ignoring Ahiko's retort.

"No mightier than the hole you've dug yourself and, by hiring me, myself into." Ahiko unbuckled the seat harness and came to his side. "We should be good for quite a spell with all this magnetic rock though." He nodded outside. "Come on. I'll need a hand finding that tag and prying it loose."

Star inclined his head in silent agreement. He led the way to the main hub. Reaching the central common room caused a knot to form in his stomach. He grimaced through it, staring at the multiple passages leading from the hub.

"It wouldn't be too much to hope that you're happening to be carrying some weapons along with whatever it is you've stolen?"

Star shrugged. "Some. And might as well make this clean and clear now. I've stolen nothing." He jerked a thumb to the storage containers he'd plundered earlier. "Middle one. Fingers in—no wiggling 'em about—smooth pull."

Ahiko sauntered past, slipping his thumbs through the belt loops of his pants. He tugged on them as he approached the storage locker. His hand went to the groove, and he did as Star said. He released a low whistle and fished inside, pulling free a pistol formed from black composite material. "Rather old-fashioned."

Star moved to the locker as well, reaching in. His fingers brushed against something like worn sandpaper. He tightened his hand around the grip and drew the weapon.

The revolver made a brick feel light in comparison. Strips of textured white tape had been wrapped around the grip to provide a better grip. Sweat and grime had yellowed the outer layer of the tape. The cylinder looked like it could house a dozen rounds, each thicker than his thumb. No amount of polishing would restore the dull metal's luster. It failed to catch the interior lighting, despite the brightness.

Star frowned at the weapon before holstering it at his hip, making sure his coat would keep it from view. "I'm hoping we won't need these."

Ahiko arched a brow and stared at him sideways like he was crazy. "You ever been to Azzip?"

Star shook his head.

"How's that possible for a shepherd?"

"We ferried people and cargo. Never made a habit of staying on ground long enough to get used to the smell of the air and the folk. Open space is home." A hint of longing touched his voice. He noticed and buried it.

Ahiko arched a brow. "*Ferried.* Past tense."

Star's mouth twitched, and he fastened a single button on his coat near the waist. "Shepherding's an old tradition. Some done it so long, before we took to space, that the name stuck. Since then, job's stuck. Not many of us left that carry the name and the job." He cleared his throat and turned to leave.

Ahiko fell by his side. "And in all that time you've

never learned much of the worlds you stop by on. Explains why you need a pilot—a good one."

Star gave him a level look.

"Taking people from one place to another is a job needing more navigation than fancy flying. I do fancy." The pilot smiled.

Star snorted and rolled his eyes as he thumbed a switch above the ramp. "It's only fancy flying till it goes wrong. Then it's called a funeral, and with what I'm paying you, it'll be none too fancy at that."

The pilot's smile slipped.

Star did a short jog down the first ramp leading to the exit hatch. He ran a finger across the screen, opening the way out.

A low-powered whine sounded off.

Ahiko glanced around the ship before turning to face him. "What was that?"

"Security measures. In the event someone I'm not keen on tries to get inside her"—his lips twitched—"they're going to be stuck wondering why their ass is glued to the ground and the world's spinning."

The pilot glanced around once more before giving him a level look. "Which is why you weren't too concerned when Creed was ushering you to your ship at gunpoint. All you had to do was let him try to access it on his own, and I'm assuming even with military override, he'd have been left a tad stupefied."

Star grinned.

"And the same if I had tried." The pilot's look hardened.

Star's smile widened. "Consider me an equal opportunity protectionist."

Ahiko's lips pressed into slits, and his eyes followed as he stared at Star. "You're not as funny as you think."

Star put a hand on the hatch frame, pulling on it as he stepped out. Heat washed over him, threatening to dry his skin instantly. It was the sort of warmth that came from sitting just close enough to a fire to be uncomfortable. "I think I'm funnier than you know." He lumbered down the ramp, eyeing the surrounding stone walls.

The canyon drop would deter most people, even pilots, and it left only two ways for people to come after them. It was a bit of good and bad in the situation.

He turned to look behind him and past the ship.

It was the same as in front. The canyon's path continued far beyond where he could see in either direction. Smaller stone formations and low ridges ran along the canyon ground. Some portions of the wall protruded further than others, breaking up the line of sight.

He sighed and moved to the side of the ramp.

Twin bars hung from a panel higher up on the ship near the thrusters. They were fixed in place with small sheets of metal running between them.

Star moved over to the ladder, grabbing hold of one of its side and hauling himself onto it. He whistled to Ahiko as the pilot exited.

The man nodded and jogged the short distance to him. Ahiko followed him, clasping the ladder and climbing behind.

Star's hands smacked against the top of one of the thrusters. He fought for grip, straining the muscles in his upper back and arms to haul himself up. Releasing a heavy breath, he clambered atop *The Leaf.*

Ahiko joined him. "Tag's bout no bigger than the size of your palm. They're built along the lines of a giant beetle. You'll notice a metal hump sticking out somewhere along her hull. Getting it loose will be the pain."

Star grunted in acknowledgement and set off in search toward the left side of the ship. He gestured for Ahiko to take the other half.

The pilot moved off in silence.

He scanned over *The Leaf* best he could. Nothing matching Ahiko's description came into view. Star passed a pair of vertical body flaps that came to his waist. He leaned at an angle to give them a quick once over. No tracker.

A series of piercing whistles sounded.

Star turned to the source. He caught sight of a waving arm. *Let's hope the rest of him is attached to it. Wouldn't be surprised. Man's got a habit for recklessness.* His lips pursed together as he mulled over the thought. *Then again, I'm not much better.* He resolved to keep the realization to himself.

He made his way over to Ahiko. The pilot was hunched near where the hull met the starboard wing. Star came to stand behind him, looking over his shoulder. He spotted what the pilot had.

An object, true to Ahiko's description, sat embedded in the hull of *The Leaf.* The black metal stood out in sharp contrast against the ship's color. A series of finger-like tubes ran out from its sides, plunging into the metal of *The Leaf.*

"How deep do those run?" Star thrust his chin in the direction of the tracking device.

"Not deep enough to be a pain. Just far enough to be a hint of trouble. Pulling out's never easy." The pilot shook his head more to himself as he muttered something below his breath. He drew his pistol, looking over it favorably before stowing it. "Shooting it won't work. Besides, your ship's harboring that oddity about keeping her shields up indefinitely so long as she's immobile." Ahiko gave him quick stare.

Star ignored it, raising both brows in a silent question.

The pilot shrugged. "Cutting's our best bet. Though, with what, I don't know. Torches are no good. They can't muster the sort of heat needed to get through, otherwise the thing would've burned up on reentry. We'll need something industrial, ship-maintenance grade. Bound to be something near 'round shipyards."

"We're in a canyon. Getting to a shipyard, much less civilization, isn't going to be easy." Star frowned, cradling his chin in one of his hands.

"Best we get walking then. Canyon's long, but not so much we can't make it out in a few hours. After that, it's just a matter of getting our bearings." Ahiko rose to his feet, rolling his shoulders free of what looked like stress.

Star mimicked him, going as far as cricking his neck to the side. "Let's make the long walk ahead a bit shorter, hm?"

Ahiko arched a brow.

Star ignored him, turning and heading back to the ladder. He climbed down faster than some would deem safe and made his way to the panel before the hatch. His fingers moved without thought, freeing the screen and entering a command.

The Leaf's underside released short puffs of compressed gases as the belly opened. Twin curved panels pulled away from each other as a motorized hoist descended. A cage of silver metal alloys hung suspended by a series of clamps. The hoist touched down on the ground with an impact that sent sand and other particulates leaping into the air.

Star walked over to the cage with a hand outstretched.

"What's in the box?"

"Simple crawler. Not fast, but handy for this terrain. We'll make better time on it." Star placed a hand to the side of the contraption and felt around for a lever. He found it and wrenched.

Metal ground and squeaked.

He stepped to the side just as the front portion of the cage fell to the ground.

The crawler lived up to its name. A low-sitting vehicle comprised mostly of high density composite plastics and carbon, its body reminded him of a lengthy and segmented insect. Its front was sharp and angular, giving the headlights the appearance of bug-like eyes. The machine looked as if it hadn't finished its time on the assembly line. It lacked a final coat of paint, covered only in a dull, gray uniform primer across its body. Each of its six wheels were larger than his head, sporting ridged tread thicker than his fingers.

Star stepped into the container, moving to the side of the crawler. He stepped onto a running board and mounted the machine. His thumb brushed over a pad of metal cubes sporting dotted marks. He pressed them in a sequence he had committed to memory.

The crawler thrummed to life with a little quiver that

rolled up his spine. Star grabbed hold of the horizontal bars, twisting one of them. A guttural rumble sounded before quieting altogether. He maneuvered it out of the cage, slapping his left hand against the metal contraption as he exited.

The fallen grate rose back into place as the hoist shuddered. Within a handful of seconds, the container had risen back into the belly of *The Leaf.*

Star tilted his head to beckon Ahiko.

The pilot made his way over, eyeing the spare seat behind Star. He paused and gave him a look. "I never was much for being behind. Sure I can't drive?"

Star twisted the accelerator and rolled forward half a dozen feet.

Ahiko swore and ran the short distance to the vehicle. "Right, right." He waved a hand. "I'm getting on. It behooves me to tell you that you're full of drama."

"We're stranded in a canyon, on the run from the government with a tracker on my spaceship. Drama found us. And if you keep sassin', you'll be hoofing it on foot." Star kept his expression neutral, trying to keep a lopsided smile from breaking across his face.

The pilot's mouth twitched like he was on the verge of replying. Ahiko looked past Star down the length of the canyon. His mouth remained shut.

Glad to know that's possible.

Ahiko hopped onto the seat behind him, placing his hands on the U-shaped bars on the side. "What little I saw of the surface is saying we need to head thataway." He gestured to the right wall. "Azzip may be a hot ball of dust and rock, but it's well inhabited. Precious minerals and water ain't too much of an issue with a government friendly station in orbit. We'll find something sooner than later."

Star agreed in silence and eased the crawler forward before increasing its speed. The machine shuddered as if disagreeing with the notion of accelerating.

Something rattled around the canyon like small stones rolling against glass.

Star kept his look fixed ahead. "You hear that?"

"I did." Ahiko's voice had deepened and dried like he'd swallowed some of the sand around them. "Could be nothing more than wind and stones falling about the place."

Star's gaze shifted to the canyon walls without turning his head. "Could be. Could be more."

The walls stared back at him with no answers as to what had caused the noise.

He exhaled and accelerated.

The sound returned, growing louder. It was like hail battering hard stone, and it stopped as soon as it had come.

Star looked over his shoulder to the pilot.

Ahiko's eyes scanned the higher points of the canyon. "I'm beginning to find that noise a tad disconcerting."

"A tad." Star kept his gaze low, looking over the small, stony mounds and piles that littered the canyon floor. *If I were waiting somewhere to ambush somebody...*

The rattling picked up, drowning out the sounds of the crawler and his own thoughts.

Hunched shapes materialized from behind the rocky formations. It was like watching the stones come to life. They were heavily bundled under patterned cloaks of patchwork browns and muted oranges. Lengthy staffs stuck out from under the clothing, all of which were leveled at Ahiko and him.

Star looked back to the pilot. "I'm more than a tad disconcerted by that noise as well…"

CHAPTER FIVE

AND THE HORSE YOU RODE IN ON

Ahiko's hand blurred at his side, pulling free the slim pistol.

The staffs whirred with the sound of electrical power. Orange light bled between the exposed sections in the black metal. Their cylindrical tips glowed the color of an angry, giant star.

The pilot froze.

Star weighed the situation.

The robed figures were inhumanly still, making the rocks beside them seem more animate as the wind stirred loose pebbles and grit among them. Their weapons stayed just as motionless.

They didn't shake one bit, meaning they'd done this before and had no quarrel doing it again. It wasn't a reassuring sign.

He flexed his fingers, slowly raising his hands to his waist.

The figures closed in a step.

Star raised his hands higher, eyeing the robed group.

Veils obscured any facial features that could be used to identify them. A lining of white mesh ran over their eyes. The honeycombed design must have allowed them enough vision to coordinate their efforts while preventing outsiders to peer in.

"There's another inconvenience in our long list of what's been a rather too-short trip." Star's hands reached over his head.

"If this is to be the standard, might be I point out that this is too short a list for how many more there're bound to be over what's a long trip." Ahiko glanced at him out of the corners of his eyes.

Star inclined his head a fraction as way of conceding to Ahiko's point.

One of the robed figures broke from the tight-knit grouping and jabbed a staff toward Star. "Quiet."

His mouth twitched. "I can do that." He tilted his head toward the pilot. "Him, I ain't that sure about."

Ahiko sputtered.

"See what I mean? Even when he's wordless, he's got to run his mouth." The air left his lungs as pain blossomed through his solar plexus. The world slipped to the side as he fell from the crawler. A red flash tore through his otherwise blackened vision. His lungs felt like they'd been gone over by a rolling pin. Star dropped to one knee, gasping in ragged breaths.

"Get up!" The voice shook like more than one set of lungs drove it. It sounded like it had emanated from a cavern of stone and grit. A rough, booming thing.

Star coughed several times and turned his head to

watch Ahiko.

The pilot had eased his pistol back in place and held his hands outstretched in a non-threatening manner.

Placing a hand against his thigh, Star pushed himself up to a shaky stand. He eyed the robed figure that had driven the staff into his body. "Don't suppose I can ask what this is all about?" He cracked a weak, crooked smile.

People love smiles and those who could be calm, charming. He didn't need to rile up more trouble than necessary.

The robed figure growled.

Maybe he wasn't as charming as he thought. Star's smile slipped.

"Take the crawler. Bind them. Move!" The figure ushered the others with an arm hidden beneath the oversized folds of their robes. "And the horse they rode in on. Find a way in. If not, peel it apart panel by panel. Salvage and sell."

Star's stomach did somersaults. "You want the crawler, fine. All yours. I'm asking here, nicely so, don't touch my ship. We're not here by choice. And we didn't aim to cause you any trouble. Let us be on our way, promise you no issue."

"Issue's already brought up. You're here." The grave-voiced figure motioned again. Several robed members rushed to obey, coming to Ahiko's side before surrounding Star. They pulled slender cords from under their clothing, lashing the ends together before grabbing hold of the men's wrists. The material reminded Star of a snake, dark and scaled with a design much like their meshed eye coverings.

Star doubled over as they forced him down. His hands were pulled behind him. The cord brushed against the hairs on his wrists, smooth and cool despite the desert heat.

Not metal then. Maybe something softer? Something I can cut. He looked to the jagged surfaces of the stone around.

One of his attackers must have caught his looks. "Don't bother. Carbon allotrope. It'll hold up to lasers, heat, and even cutting."

He pursed his lips. It wasn't ideal, but it wasn't impossible to deal with.

Another of the robed figures mounted the crawler.

Star wished he'd shuttered the machine before being forced off it.

The assailant pawing over his device throttled it forward, beckoning one of their compatriots to mount the backseat.

"Search 'em."

Star was kept in his doubled-over position as a series of hands rifled through his pockets. He managed to catch sight of Ahiko being subjected to the same.

"Now hold on… I'm not fond of being fondled without my say so. And saying so, you ain't got it." The pilot squirmed and yelped. "Oi, there's places you ought not to be sticking fingers and hands without an invitation!"

Star groaned as they plundered his personal effects.

One of the figures relieved him of his weapon and snaked his identification card.

He caught them doing the same to Ahiko.

"Bring them home." The figure in charge made a circular motion with their hand.

Star's view of the world vanished. The clay and sandy tones were replaced by a film of black cloth. The base of the black sack closed around his throat, stopping short of choking him. His lower back spasmed as something the size of a fist jammed into it. "Argh."

"Move." The voice was accentuated by a hand shoving Star forward.

He did as ordered, not wanting to complicate things. *Cool. Calm. Collected.* Star recalled everything he could. The fellas were misshapen, hunched. There was a reason for that. Powered staffs were odd. Impractical too. Military wouldn't use 'em. Neither would private security. Resistance fighters was a possibility.

He shook his head to clear the train of thoughts. No, he was overcomplicating things. He had to focus on what he knew, not what might be. They were on Azzip, though that wasn't worth much. Everyone out this far found their way here eventually. Some just ended up staying permanently—and not by choice.

Star swallowed, hoping that wouldn't be their fates. *Go this far, can get us out further. Somehow.* A slow, rhythmic hum broke him from his trance.

It was a tune that rolled easily enough off the tongue. The notes flowed consistently until they broke once into a deeper drone. The basso tone leveled back into the smoother sounds from earlier.

Star pegged it as Ahiko's voice. *Even tied and bagged, man can't shut his mouth.* He walked on, pondering what he could in the hopes of finding a way to free themselves. His head throbbed as if the earlier rattling were occurring inside his skull. The surface of his skin pricked with a heat that was digging its way deeper into him. His thoughts muddled until sifting through them became impossible.

He squinted at the black cloth blocking his view. Desert heat and light, black mask. It meant they knew what they were doing. The goal was to keep Star and Ahiko dehydrated and mucked about in the head. They'd have a hard time focusing and wouldn't be able to see worth a damn. He exhaled. The fatigue and disorientation built as sweat plastered his hair to his skull and brow.

Star walked until his legs felt like they were made of stringy glue about to come undone. His chest harbored more sweat and dust than air. He coughed, jarring his aching skull. The black in front of him blurred.

He sank to the ground, his knees impacting the coarse sand and sending a jolt up his legs. Star tried recounting the last time he'd eaten properly, much less drank.

Don't think the bar counts. Been running lean since Autumn.

The strength fled him.

Another impact rattled his body, reverberating through his skull.

The blackness passed from in front of him to within him.

***

A sporadic burst of clacking tore Star back to cold consciousness. The abysmal tapping sound echoed through his skull, feeling as if it were coming from inside him and not the world around him.

His eyes fluttered open as he pressed a hand the side

of his head. Cold beads of moisture licked the skin of his palm.

The world around him was painted in shades of darker browns and reds than earlier. Shadows muted the otherwise bright colors. The only remaining visible splotches of the stones from before came from the flickering orange lights washing over the rocks around him.

A cavern, likely carved into the canyon walls, unless it was natural. Star was certain there'd be a train of these crisscrossing through the place. It would make it easier to move around without dying under the sun. It made ambushing people easier as well.

His lips curled as his vision fought to steady itself. Star opened his mouth to speak, racking his throat for what little saliva he could. The tissue felt scraped raw. Star rasped, trying to make some semblance of coherent sound. His throat disapproved of the idea as it seized and burned.

One of the robed figures came into hazy view. Their clothing stirred from a wind source he hadn't identified. The colors seemed to blur.

Hell, maybe it's me. Head's still reeling.

A hand grabbed the back of his neck, moving up along it until it cradled the base of his skull. Their palm engulfed most of his head. Each of their fingers felt thicker than two of his own together.

"Drink." The cloaked figure pulled a leather skin into view. Something sloshed within it.

Star's lips trembled, and he leaned forward as best he could.

They pressed the skin's spout to his lips.

He sipped. The fluid clung to his tongue and the inside of his lower lip. It had the consistency of syrup with a sharp, citrus taste that carried a hint of a bite. Star fought the urge to drown himself in the drink and possibly choke. He pulled more of the sappy drink into his mouth, letting it coat his throat. A modicum of relief followed.

The figure watched him in silence.

His head stopped aching, and his vision steadied further. Star cleared his throat. "I'm assuming this is the home mentioned earlier?" He quirked a brow and directed his stare at the white mesh over the figure's eyes.

Their head shifted in what he took to be them matching his stare. The white mesh held level with his eyes. "One, yes, you fainted. The heat got to you. Could have been worse."

I'm thinkin' worse has already happened.

"Stay here. Shazhan will want to speak with you." The figure rose, leaving the skin by Star's side.

"Yeah, you bring Shazhan, and Sha's mom while you're at it! I'd like to have a word with 'em both on the utter lack of hospitality we've been shown." The voice rang through the cavern.

Star's skull panged upon hearing it. He let his head loll to the side to stare at Ahiko. "I'm of the opinion that you didn't shut your mouth the entire time they dragged us about."

The pilot lay on the ground opposite him several yards. His bindings had been removed and redone to have his hands fixed in front.

Star's wrists were fixed in the same fashion.

Ahiko gave him a weak grin. "Dragged you. I held onto my pride and walked." His grin widened in what looked like self-satisfaction.

Star aimed to free him of that delusion. "Pride is meaning capture by folk of a rough disposition, being stripped unarmed, and bound? You held onto that for certain."

Ahiko frowned. "I'm regretting my employment with you."

Star ignored the pilot's lament. "What'd you figure out so far? No more foolin'. Tell me what you've learned."

Ahiko gave him a blank stare that came off as a practiced look. "I was captured same as you; don't know what you're getting at."

"I'm getting at the fact that you weren't captured same as me. Not that I recall, at least. You made a point of how I passed out. You didn't."

The pilot's mouth twitched. "And?"

"And, I remember you humming. Didn't strike me at first what for. You're former military. Am I wrong in assuming—and I don't think I am—that the tune was more than just that?"

Ahiko's flat look broke. His mouth pulled to a corner. "You're smarter than you look, know that Shepherd?"

He grunted.

"Was counting steps. Taking it that you heard the change in tune?"

Star nodded. "Marker of some kind? Every certain number of steps, makes counting 'em easier?"

Ahiko bowed his head in agreement. "Short of it is

this, it's a long walk from the ship." The pilot's mouth moved like there was more to say, but he remained silent.

"But?"

"*But* I know the way back. Assuming we get out of here." Ahiko looked around as if trying to get his bearings within the cave.

"Didn't you make mention of why not to assume?"

The pilot frowned. "It bears pointing out my advice is somewhat temporal and not always applicable to situations."

"I'm guessing those non-applicable situations almost always involve yourself."

Ahiko's frown deepened.

Star pushed the pilot's wordplay and complaints from his mind. He looked around the cavern now that his aching head had settled.

The orange lights from earlier were cast by wide cylinders with a quarter of their shells exposed. Fiery light and heat radiated from the openings. Cheap wire grating covered the heating coils and filaments. The large devices rested upon single legs that split into a tripod configuration as they neared the ground.

He noted a distinct lack of wiring, indicating something cell-powered—temporary. Possibly because it was mobile or because they couldn't get rutting power out here.

The facts told him more about his captors, enough to raise questions that made it increasingly difficult to identify them.

Star exhaled, rubbing a hand against his brow. *Think.* The carbon cords still bound his wrists together, and it was the same for his pilot. Cutting them wouldn't work. Carbon was temperamental though. It didn't hold up well to repeated trauma. Great thing for stopping a bullet—once. He looked around and smiled.

The stony surroundings offered no end of hard surfaces for him to work with.

Star glanced at a rock the size of his head sprouting from the ground. It had a conical tip and widened near the base. *Damn near perfect.* He looked around once more.

The cavern was empty.

It was likely one of many, no doubt. A room to leave those they captured. He noted several dark halls leading out. But 'out' didn't mean out somewhere better. Weighing the risks, he felt it best to tackle the immediate problem. He brought his hands overhead. The cord dug into his wrists, reminding him of their strength. Star aligned the band as best he could with the tip of the stone. He brought his hands down, slamming the cord against the protrusion.

A *clack* rang through the space. The cord shook, sending a slight tremor into his wrists. The carbon held.

Star frowned, eyeing the material.

A basso rumble floated through the cavern. The heavy chuckle shook small pebbles and dust. "It's industrial-grade flexy carbon. Not going to break that easy. Keep it up for another year or so, it might chip." Another robed figure entered the room.

Star's chest tightened, and adrenaline rushed to renew his strength and senses.

The stranger stood at full height, not hunched like the members from earlier. They were roughly a head taller than him. Their robes looked at the point of tearing from the girth of their shoulders.

Star swallowed and raised his hands in a gesture he hoped would bring a measure of calm to the speaker.

The figure inclined their head. "I've got a feeling you've been doing a lot of hand raising of late."

Star felt they were eyeing him through the mesh.

"More than you know." Ahiko raised his hands more in a gesture of resignation.

"And what makes you say that?" Star pulled away from the stone, arching a quizzical brow to their captor.

"I'm Shazhan." The figure's hand went to the front of their robes, clinching them tight. Shazhan tore the clothing free from their body and head.

Ahiko sucked in a sharp breath.

Star felt the need to do the same.

Shazhan could have been made from the stone around them had it been painted a taupe gray dusted with ash. The creature's skin mirrored craggy mountains.

The blockage in his throat cleared, leaving him able to speak. "What's an Elan doing so far out into human-occupied space?" Star regretted speaking a second later.

Shazhan's chest rumbled. "Surviving—barely."

The Elan wore another set of clothes under the robes. A loose, brown cloth tunic and a pair of pants to match. They didn't do much to hide the creature's bulk. It was built with thick slabs of muscle that could have shamed the largest of men. Its mass was supported by a powerful torso and a set of hips that were nearly as wide as its shoulders. The creature's legs were hinged the other way, which was how they were able to hunch down so low and move fine.

The Elan's head was noticeably larger than his own. The area around its eyes were recessed and lined with small black mottled portions of skin that looked like pebbles surrounding amber lenses.

Star looked around the cavern. "Pardon me for saying so, but this doesn't look to be much in the way of surviving…," he fumbled, searching for the right title.

"*Barely*. And I'm male."

Star's lips pressed together for a moment. "Wasn't on my mind."

Shazhan titled his head, eyeing him intently. The Elan waved a hand as if the matter were no conse-quence. "I've got questions for you. The look on your face says you have some for me as well."

Star nodded.

"You came to our land, brought the military as well, not a great start." Shazhan stared at Star before turning his gaze to Ahiko.

The pilot shrugged.

"I did. Didn't mean to, for what it's worth."

Shazhan spat on the ground. "Nothing's what it's worth. Why are you here?"

Star fidgeted, racking his brain on how to answer. Truth might set a man free, but sometimes it sure as hell condemned him. Lying didn't do one many favors either. So he settled on a partial truth. "Didn't have much of a choice. Was forced here. If you let us go, believe me, we'll be heading far and away."

Shazhan shook his head. The shaking made its way to his chest which vibrated like he was restraining another chuckle. Whatever it was, he swallowed it and cleared his throat. "I'm sure you will be. Although, I don't have much reason to let you go."

"Tit for tat. How'd a bunch of Elan end up near the backwater edges of human territory? Makes sense closer to the other end, borders the Minoan system. Planets are more developed and tend to cross over into your space. See the mixing there, but here? Too far to be an accident. Too much of a bad choice to be intentional." Star made a point of looking around the cavern to accentuate his claim. "This ain't exactly comfortable living."

"No, no, it's not. Came here decades ago by way of necessity. The short of it is my people were on a diplomatic mission. Some of your kind led us here and stranded us."

Star swallowed. *Great, and he's already soured to humans.* "No fault on me and mine, though." He nodded toward Ahiko.

"And I'm not blaming you. We're here; we're getting by. Not much welcome in the towns, if you can call them that. Got by for a time doing labor. Ended up shouted out into the hills and canyons by your government. Locals had no problem." Shazhan released a dark laugh.

Star gave what he hoped seemed a genial wave with one hand. "Government problems seem to be going around. And seems the government's going around creating problems."

Shazhan reached into a wide pocket on the side of his pants. "I know. Next question." He removed a lens and activated it. The device flared to life, revealing a familiar image. Star's face revolved slowly. A hefty sum hung below in a static display, and a bright gleam entered Shazhan's eyes. "What are we going to do about this?"

CHAPTER SIX

A SIMPLER SOLUTION

The air froze in his lungs despite the warmth radiating from the devices around him. He looked to Ahiko for help.

The pilot must have found himself suddenly entranced by something on the other side of the cave. He turned away from Star's gaze and stared at the far wall.

Well, he's fired…again.

"The reward they're offering for you is enough to get my people home. It's awfully tempting." Shazhan gave him a look that made it clear he wasn't exaggerating.

"Might be. Though, I can't but wonder why you've not done so already if it's that tempting. We're still here." Star smiled. "Unless you're harboring a severe distaste and distrust of the government—and rightfully so. They've already dumped you here. Why not leave you here and keep the reward, right?"

Shazhan blinked.

"You know a bit of my truth. Tell me a bit more of yours, and maybe I'll tell you a tad more of mine. You might want to hear it.

The Elan squinted, looking away to one of the halls before turning back. "What do you want to know?" He squatted before Star, crossing his arms and placing them over his thighs. The action didn't look particularly straining for the creature.

"Why'd the government haul you out this far to leave you to dry? Doesn't sound like the best way to sow diplomatic ties with the official reps of another species."

"It's not. And, it's complicated." Shazhan looked over his shoulder before turning back.

Star held up his hands. He inclined his head toward the bindings and gestured to the lens. "Complicated, I get."

The Elan's thick, ridged lips wriggled. "Suppose you do." He sank to the floor, folding his legs under him. "The Elan don't hold much territory in the Minoan system. But we're left to our own. No one wants what we call home, and we're grateful for it. We catch some of the outfall of your folk though."

Star folded his lower lip and chewed.

Criminals and the like often fled into the Minoan system, ending up somewhere in what little the Elan owned. Most passed by. Some lingered and caused trouble.

"And your folk have been getting tired of it?" Star kept his face neutral.

Shazhan lowered his head in what was a clear yes. "Decided to send word to your people, find a way to come to some semblance of an agreement." The Elan's face scrunched in what Star took to be disdain.

"Bad idea there. Should've asked the folks stranded in your neck of the woods how our government can be. They're under the yoke of"—he rubbed his thumb against his first two fingers—"and money makes men walk along the rich's talk."

Shazhan bowed his head in agreement. "Indeed. They didn't much care for us being ambassadors. We were tricked, stranded—our ship and technology likely stripped. We've no way home."

Star frowned. "And your people?"

The Elan shrugged, straining his tunic at the edges. "Likely told that we died on our journey. Any number of lies could have been sent and believed."

He nodded. It wasn't a stretch to believe what Shazhan had told him. The only problem with it was what the Elan intended to do.

Star's mind raced. A solution to Shazhan and his people's problem lay within arm's reach. The only thing they had to do was turn him in and the ship. With that, they would be able to return home. If the government didn't just take what they wanted.

There's always that chance though.

They hadn't done so, however.

A plume of dust leapt to the air as the ground shook. The air reverberated as invisible drums echoed through the cavern halls. Loose, minute stones trembled above, breaking free to shower the trio.

Star looked around for the source. He turned to face the Elan, eyes widening.

Shazhan stared back, giving him a clear look that he

had no idea of the cause.

"I'm getting one of those feelings tickling me the wrong way." Ahiko squirmed on the ground, working to right himself.

Star got to his feet and held out his hands toward the Shazhan. "I don't ever want to know what tickles you the right way." He shot a quick look to Ahiko before turning back to Shazhan. "But he's right. I'm harboring a knot in my gut that says it's trouble."

Shazhan stared at Star's binding, then back to him. "Trouble you might have brought down on us all." Shazhan's face hardened.

Ahiko groaned. "He brings it on everyone." The pilot's following words were drowned out by the reports of thunder.

Star shut his eyes, exhaling slowly and vanquishing the thought to throttle his pilot. "Maybe so. Seems only right, then, that I be the one to help you sort it, no?" He arched a brow.

The Elan's lips pressed together like he was mulling the thought over. "Trusting humans hasn't gotten us far." He waved a hand to the rumbling cave around them. "It's not much of a place to be or like."

Star sighed in resignation. *I thought as much.*

The cavern shook harder. Another echoing boom rolled through the network of halls around them.

A robed figure, an Elan he wagered, hobbled into the room. Their hunched weight was supported by a cane fashioned from a branch nearly as thick as Star's arm. Most of its bark had been removed from time and use by the look of it.

Sometimes the simple things do best for folk.

The robed Elan snapped their wrist, sending the cane *thwaping* into Shazhan's leg. If he had felt it, it didn't show.

He turned to regard his cloaked compatriot. "What is it?"

"Military." The speaker's voice carried more grit and dry sand than Shazhan's. Star felt it was the sort of thing that came with advanced age.

The cave grew colder despite the heating apparatuses around him. Star fidgeted and looked to Ahiko.

The pilot shrugged, his face a neutral mask.

Didn't take them nearly as long as I'd hoped.

Shazhan eyed the newcomer. "What are they doing?"

The robed Elan sagged under their clothing. They hunched further, placing more of their weight on the cane and sighed. "Dropping charges. Few scouts atop the canyon saying it's nothing much to worry about. They're making more noise than making craters." The Elan stopped and peered at the ceiling. "Still, bit irritating how loud they are. Not to mention the shaking."

Star bit down on his lower lip. He wasn't sure of what to make of it all. His attention fell on Ahiko, whose eyes were wide.

The pilot's head tilted toward them like he was trying to focus hearing from one side. "Are they flying over?"

All eyes turned to Ahiko.

Shazhan grunted at the pilot, drawing his attention. "Why?"

Another crash of thunder—louder than before—resonated through the room.

Ahiko gestured at the ceiling with a thrust of chin.

"That's all the *why* you need. Tell me."

The Elan with the cane bowed in affirmation. "Yes."

Star motioned to the pilot. "I take it that you know what this means? And that it's a bad thing."

"Sonar charges." Ahiko's face tightened. His eyes remained fixed on the quivering cavern ceiling.

The explosions grew louder, as well as more frequent. *Storm's coming.*

"They're dropping charges that have more bang than boom, if you catch my meaning." Ahiko glanced at him.

Star didn't, but remained quiet.

"They don't do much in the way of blowing holes as much as they do of making noise. Ships fly overhead picking up the feedback. Makes it easier for 'em to get an idea of what's below."

The pair of Elan exchanged looks. Shazhan rubbed the underside of his chin. "They're mapping out the canyon?"

Ahiko inclined his head.

Shazhan faced Star. "They're looking for you and your ship." He turned to his fellow Elan. "Not us."

The pilot squirmed and wriggled further away. "Not looking for me neither."

Star glared at him.

Ahiko gave him a hapless grin. "I'm nursing the temptation to tender my resignation."

Star's glare could have made glass shards seem dull in comparison.

The pilot rolled his shoulders in a mild shrug.

"This complicates things further." Shazhan's voice had grown distant and hollow.

His stomach felt compressed by an unseen hand at

the look the Elan had given him. It chilled his blood and marrow.He'd seen that look more times than he'd have liked to recall. It never boded well and never had.

Shazhan reached behind his back. The sound of metal scraping against glass managed to screech out under the basso drumming around them. He drew a slender blade with a width no wider than Star's index and middle fingers together. The chisel-tipped weapon was an inch longer than his own hand. It looked to be comprised of seven different materials, each a jarringly different color than the next. A prismatic sheen flowed through the blade.

Star swallowed.

"Don't have many options ahead of us." Shazhan stared at him directly, but his words seemed aimed at the Elan by his side. "Our people come first."

They always did. It was about how every problem started as well. Putting some above others, leaving some to drown. It was what got them in to this mess in the first place.

Shazhan pointed the blade at Star. "Could turn you into the military, collect on that reward. I'm not willing to trade the dreams of tomorrow for the temptations of today, however. Doing that means being stuck here with you till they come. Means my people could find more trouble." He shook his head. "I've got a simpler solution. We leave, and we leave the military with what they're looking for." Shazhan raised the weapon over Star's head.

Ahiko thrashed. "Consider my nursing nursed, I quit."

The blade fell.

CHAPTER SEVEN
A USEFUL GUEST

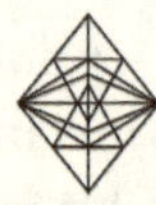

Shazhan brought the tip of the weapon against Star's bindings. The carbon resisted the impact. A wisp of smoke sprouted from the point where the odd metal met the cord. Electricity crackled and the blade passed through the carbon, severing the bonds.

Star remembered how to breathe and stared at the Elan. He waited in silence for an explanation.

It never came.

Shazhan adjusted his grip on the weapon, taking care not to contact the blade with his fingers as he handed it in a pinched grip to the Elan by his side.

The robed figure accepted the weapon with a similar, delicate hold.

Star committed the action to memory.

Ahiko extended his hands to the approaching Elan. They cut the pilot free.

He muttered a barely audible thanks and rubbed his wrist. "Since we're not being filleted or turned into the military, I figure it's best we go." Ahiko jerked a thumb toward one of the halls.

Shazhan nodded, extending a hand to Star.

He took it and pulled himself to his feet. "You going to tell me why you're letting us go?"

The Elan's mouth spread wide in what must have been a grin.

Remind me to never ask him to smile.

"You're free to go *now*. Didn't say a thing about you going free." Shazhan chortled, ushering them with a hand.

Ahiko glowered at him. "Remind me to teach you why you don't go around questioning fortuitous happenstances." He looked around at the numerous passages leading out of the place. "Where to?"

The robed Elan lifted their cane, pointing to the third tunnel, nearest the center of all eight. "Leads us deeper below. We'll be safe there—for a time."

The pilot flung his arms overhead in a melodramatic manner. "Never thought I'd be one to say this, but deeper ain't always better. Sometimes a man falls in too far to pull out of trouble."

A heavier blast shook the cavern. Head-sized chunks of stone fell free from above, crashing to the ground with enough impact that Star whispered a quick prayer of relief he hadn't been struck.

Ahiko whistled, eyeing the stones and rubbing the back of his head. "Going deeper seems a mighty fine plan. Reckon it's a good thing I suggested it." He gestured to the tunnel. "Come on. Doesn't do any favors for my wallet or my way off this planet if my employer dies."

Star followed the pilot and the robed Elan. "Funny, that. I thought you terminated said employment."

Ahiko grinned. "Brief review of a recent change in circumstance has me realizing it's in my best interest to quit my termination and reemploy myself in your employ. Good? Good." The pilot's speech had picked up in pace by the word until Star felt the insides of his ears were spinning.

Star waved a hand to brush off his comments. He glanced to Shazhan. "Are you coming?"

The Elan shook his head. "My responsibilities mean shepherding my people to safety." The light in his eyes burned brighter. "All of them. I think you know a bit about that."

Star lowered his head in acknowledgement. He stopped, gesturing for Ahiko to go ahead. "I'd be a poor guest if I didn't stay and help."

The Elan shuffled past him, going to one of the nearby heaters. "Guest? Inviting yourself in are you?"

"Invitation was done on account of you bringing us here, I feel. Fair's fair. Consider it working my way out of being a prisoner into useful guest." Star flashed him a smile.

Shazhan snaked an arm behind the heater, grabbing hold of one of the polearms from earlier. He grunted, hefting the weapon, looking up to the ceiling as if contemplating.

Another crack of thunder jarred the cavern.

Star glanced in the direction of the sound. "I'm not the sort of man to tell another what to do in his own home, but—"

"But you're about to. I'm of the same mind." Shazhan beckoned Star with a wave of his hand. "Come, you'll be needing your weapon." He turned to address the pilot. "Any way the military will be able to scale the canyon walls?"

Ahiko's face pulled into a frown. "Too many ways, each a problem. It's why we ought to stop yammering and move. The sort of company that's coming isn't looking to make friends. And they've got no cause for keeping you and your people alive. Only one they're looking for is him." He nodded to Star.

"He's right. Best get your people further under-ground." Star gestured to the tunnel Ahiko and the robed Elan moved toward.

Shazhan rumbled, and the noise reverberated around them despite the booming of the charges. "Some, yes. Others will stay and fight. We're not giving up what little we've got left. Means too much. Figure you understand that much."

Star bowed his head.

"Go." Shazhan waved a hand to the other Elan and Ahiko.

The pair moved down the tunnel without another word.

Star fell in step with Shazhan as he guided him into another tunnel. "If the military's coming down here, they're looking for a fight. Don't expect they'll play fair. Much less be granting mercy to a gaggle of aliens. No offense."

Shazhan grumbled, placing a hand against the tunnel wall. "None taken. And don't think we'll be any fairer."

He rapped the butt of his staff against the stone to his side. Shazhan walked on, scanning the path ahead.

The echoing blasts grew louder.

"Glad to hear it." Star followed closely, watching for any signs of movement. "Never was one for a fair fight. Among the most unfair things in life I've noticed.

Shazhan grunted in what could have been agreement.

A fire built in Star's calves as he adjusted his footing. He grimaced and dealt with the steep incline best he could. One of his hands went to the wall for support. "Not much good if the long walk tires us out before the military gets here."

Shazhan moved without showing any signs of fatigue. "Then don't tire." He led Star up the tunnel, rounding the corner ahead to the right.

Star exhaled and buried the string of obscenities that came to mind.

The thundering sounds ceased.

Shazhan walked as if he hadn't noticed or cared.

Star did. "Can't tell if that's a good thing or a bad one."

"Bad." The Elan led him down the new path, stopping outside an opening on their left. "Only reason for them to stop is that they've found a way in. With the network we're harboring in the canyon, wasn't much of a surprise. And you're worth enough of a sum that they'll be sending a frightening number of people our way." Shazhan glanced at him.

Star met the look.

"Last chance to turn and run." The Elan's face remained neutral, but his eyes took on a faint light. "Any other man would've gone by now."

The alien was appraising him. Star measured his next words. "Maybe. The way I see it is like this: You've had a handful of chances to turn me over. Could've killed me and left me for them."

"Thought crossed my mind more than a few times. Still mulling it over."

Star suppressed the shudder. "But you haven't done so. I could turn and run, save for the fact my ship's grounded. You know that. If I don't help out, could be the military sweeps you over and comes after me anyhow. I run and you win; all you have to do is hang by my ship to take me again."

Shazhan ignored him, turning back to the opening in the wall. He lumbered in.

Star followed.

"You seem to have an overinflated sense of self-importance, Shepherd. You're worth something. Doesn't mean you're worth something in a fight. What makes you think you'll make much difference?"

Star bristled. "Maybe you're looking at it the wrong way. They're less likely to turn your people into ash and all if I'm along. Wanted alive, remember? They could have glassed the place by now."

The Elan paused, furrowing his brow. "True." He gestured to the small room around them.

Various pieces of clothing and items littered the hole in the wall. It was the sort of mess one would expect a group of raiders to accumulate over time.

Star arched a brow. "Belongings of former guests of yours?"

Shazhan grunted, batting the side of a wooden trunk with his staff. He bent and flung the antiquated storage container open. "Grab it; make yourself useful. I'll be down the way ahead." He turned and left.

Star approached the trunk, leaning over to eye its contents. His revolver lay atop a mixture of clothing and other handheld weaponry. He retrieved the gun, giving it a once-over. It checked out well enough. Star slung it into the holster hanging off of his hip.

Cold static snaked through his fingers, racing up to his elbows.

He took a deep breath and stilled himself. There was no telling what would truly happen in the coming moments. He'd take it a step at a time. Worrying too much never did much good. It only stole one's calm and judgment. What happens, happens. And he'd take it all in stride.

Star's thumb brushed over the revolver's hammer. He released his breath and left the room, turning to look for Shazhan.

He stood several dozen yards away, engaged in conversation with another of his kind who had chosen to remain cloaked.

Star crossed the distance in long strides. His left hand remained glued to his weapon as he covered the ground. A gentle heat built in his ears as he neared the pair. He worked to listen in on their discussion.

"—like insects scuttling through our network. Sixteen sections already reporting contact." The cloaked Elan slammed a fist into the wall.

"Contact, funny choice of word. Violent?" Shazhan kept eerily still.

The robed Elan bowed his head. "Understatement if there ever was one. I don't know the count. Not sure

I want to. If we survive this, there'll be many days tending to the dead and their rights."

Lead weight fell into Star's stomach, settling and weighing him down. The current situation wasn't his intent, but he couldn't shake the feeling he'd dragged the Elans into it. He pushed aside the fact that they had kidnapped him.

There was plenty of fault and blame to go around. Always was. Solve this problem first, and maybe there'd be a way turn something bad into something good.

"Enough of our people have gone deeper. All we've got to do is hold out. We buy them some time before we do what needs doing." The robed Elan's voice carried a weight of finality.

Shazhan nodded in agreement.

Star came to their side, eyeing the both of them. He had heard words with the same tone back on Autumn. And he remembered what followed. "Do I want to know what that entails?" His thumb trailed over the lines of his gun faster than before.

The robed Elan turned to him. "Finish what you brought down on us. Have half a mind to finish it now." He brushed aside his robe. A shorter variant of the polearms from earlier hung on his belt. It was the length of Star's arm. The Elan pulled it free, leveling it toward him.

Star's thumb froze. He kept still, not wanting to provoke the alien into something worse. "I'm thinking half a mind's an overestimation. Especially if you plan on shooting the one man keeping you alive. I die, military's got no cause for letting any of you live."

Shazhan placed his hand over the tip of his comrade's weapon. "He's right. Don't much like it, but it's the truth. Now's not the time nor place for us to be fighting."

A series of trilling cries echoed down the tunnel. The electric shrieks picked up in until they sounded like a single cry.

The Elan looked down the hall. "Though that time's coming—fast." He pointed ahead.

Blue lights flashed across the walls. They grew closer. Star's gripped his weapon. "Here they come."

CHAPTER EIGHT

THREE HEARTS TO GIVE

Three men came into view wearing fatigues along the same pattern and color scheme as the Elan. They could have passed by unnoticed were it not for the tips of their weapons. The barrels of their blasters flickered with a few remnants of angry crackling light.

Seems the guns have a shorter temper than the men behind him. Wonderful.

Each of them rocked to a halt and trained their weapons on the Elan, paying Star no mind.

The Elan reacted in kind, leveling their polearms at the soldiers.

Star cleared his throat.

The blasters pointed in his direction.

Not my brightest moment.

Star kept his hand on his gun underneath his coat while raising the other in a slow manner.

The soldier on the left stepped forward. He looked

to be in his late twenties, solidly built along an athlete's line. He was a shade darker than the stone around them with eyes to match. "A human? What are you doing here?" His gaze flicked to the Elan before returning to Star. "Prisoner? Wouldn't surprise me."

Star pressed his mouth. He looked at Shazhan and his comrade. He could escape under the guise of being a captured man in need of rescue. But how long would that last? And at what cost? It was a poor thing and a poorer man that'd screw over those that'd done him a favor.

"Something like that." He grinned, his mouth pulling more to one corner.

The soldier tilted his head as if he hadn't heard him properly. "You have an identification card on you?" He shot a quick look at the Elan, his jaw hardening. "You stay still."

Shazhan and his companion bristled in unison, but they hadn't fired.

Small blessings. His mind blurred, searching for a way to turn the situation to his benefit. Asking for a card meant they didn't know who he was at first look. There was a small chance they didn't know who they're looking for, just that they were looking for someone.

Star feigned reaching into the right side of his coat. "Sure do."

The soldiers turned their attention from him.

Star snapped his empty hand in the direction of the closest man. "Here, catch."

The soldier's weapon turned as he shifted to retrieve the unseen item on instinct. His free hand flailed in momentary panic before he realized what had happened.

Star drew and pulled the trigger. The revolver bucked as a cylindrical bolt of white light screamed out from the tip. It hammered through the soldier who had asked for his identification, passing through the wall behind with ease.

Twin lances of fiery orange whistled past his left shoulder, striking the remaining soldiers. A pair of fist-sized holes hissed smoke from the center of their chests. The heat from the weapons cauterized the wounds instantly.

The muscles in his forearm and wrist went cold. His fingers numbed. The weight of the gun seemed to double as his hand shook. Star swallowed and holstered the weapon. A heavy weight fell on his shoulder, sending his heart lurching before it beat twice as fast.

Shazhan gripped Star's shoulder tight before releasing the hold. "You did well." He tilted his head, regarding Star. "You're shaken. Don't be. Maybe you've never killed before; maybe you have and couldn't swallow it well. Now's not the time for thinking. It's the time for doing. Understand?" The Elan's gave him a knowing look.

"More than I'd like." Star's throat ached, but he grunted to clear it.

"Good." Shazhan accentuated the word by clapping a hand to Star's shoulder.

He staggered to the side, fighting to regain his balance. Star rubbed the spot before nodding ahead. "They came from that way. What are the odds any of your people are left?"

The Elan grimaced. "Hard to say."

Another staccato of lasers sounded off down the

hall.

Shazhan's face hardened as he shambled past. "If that's a sign, I'm saying we're about to find out." He picked up his pace and lumbered into the hall.

Star grabbed his left wrist with his right hand, stilling the quivering arm. He looked over his shoulder to catch the remaining Elan staring at him intently. The creature's face may have been obscured, but Star felt the weight behind the stare. It was a look of judgment and trouble. "You've got something to say. Best get it out now before we get into a worse situation."

The Elan stepped toward him. A heavy rumble blew out through its veil. "You've already made things worse. Shazhan's granted you safety—for the moment. You're going to have to earn that with me. I get any moment—a speck of one—to put my people over you, I'm taking it. Understood?" The alien lowered the tip of his weapon so it pointed below Star's chin.

Star lowered his gaze to the weapon before meeting the Elan's eyes. "Better than you know." Star pushed the tip of the staff away from his face. "I rather fancy being alive. Not going to let someone like you take that from me." He inclined his head, gesturing to the Elan's waist.

The creature lowered its head, staring at the revolver leveled at its waist.

Star smiled and pulled the gun back. "I think it's best we save the guns and wrath for those itching for it, no?"

A chittering of electric screeches echoed around them.

The Elan grunted and moved off in the direction Shazhan had.

Star tightened his hold on the revolver before easing it. He sprinted down the hall after the Elan. An electronic symphony screamed ahead of him, an inter-mingled racket of screaming lasers and droning blasts. The sounds galvanized him to run harder.

His fingers tapped against the pistol's trigger guard as he passed through a bend. Orange motes of light pulsed above him. Each was no bigger than the tip of his thumb. Every burst illuminated a slender protrusion of metal beneath it, wedged into the stone around him.

The light didn't have the strength to be useful in guiding people through the place. He caught sight of the Elan who had threatened him. Star came to his side, nodding toward the bend ahead. His chest heaved like he'd run miles instead of yards, his breathing audible even under the barrage of howling weaponry. "How much farther?"

"Not far." The Elan increased his pace. "Listen to the noise."

The sounds were edging on deafening despite their rocky surroundings. Tangerine-colored skies and cherry leaves flashed through Star's mind. The sounds of lasers and screams peppered the image, tearing him from it and back to reality.

"If you can't keep yourself calm and together, let me do us all a favor and shoot you now." The Elan's voice hardened, and he shot Star a sideways look.

"I'm fine." Star drummed his fingers against the revolver.

The Elan grunted as they rounded the final bend. He gestured to the opening of the tunnel.

Orange globules tumbled through the air and out of

sight as they passed the mouth of the tunnel. Bright blue lances cried back, streaking in the opposite direction.

It was like watching a coordinated light show. The entirely too lively screams, accompanying the sound of weapon fire, reminded him otherwise. He raised the revolver, taking it in both hands as he advanced toward the opening.

The Elan to his side did the same. He lifted the staff, holding it chest-level with both hands, sweeping it from side to side. "Looks bad." The Elan's baritone refused to be drowned out by the firefight.

"And it's going to get worse. Looks can be deceiving and all that." Star brushed a thumb against the revolver's grip. He picked up his pace, leaving the Elan behind. His heart rate matched the ballistic barrage of lights hammering across his vision. He felt the discordant color-show would burn itself into his corneas the longer he stared.

He forced himself to take another step, breaking the lip of the tunnel to enter the domed cavern.

Stalactites of muddled orange-red quivered in place, threatening to break free should a stray blast impact one. The same blinking lights from the tunnel dotted portions of the walls. Multiple tunnels led into and out of the cavern. Small stone humps and dirt mounds littered the cavern floor. Some appeared natural formations; others were clearly fashioned as protective barriers one could crouch behind.

The Elan knew this day would come eventually. Glad they prepared for it.

A palm-sized portion of stone wall to his left

exploded. Debris showered the side of his coat, pelting the tough material and jarring him out of the reverie.

Star sprinted toward the source of the orbs of orange light, taking care to stay out of the Elans' firing paths. He increased his pace as he approached a waist-high mound of dirt and stone.

The Elan behind it ceased firing and turned their weapon on Star.

Star's heart lurched, and he grabbed hold of the surface and clambered over the stone. A hard tremor rattled up his boots to settle in his ankles. He threw up a hand. "I'm not with them!"

The tip of the glowing staff thrummed with bright energy itching to be discharged. "I'm supposed to take your word for it? Way I see it is we capture you and then the military comes knocking. Coincidence?"

Star smacked the bulk of his revolver against the Elan's weapon. He reached out with his free hand, enclosing his fingers around the creature's loose clothing. He leaned back, pulling with his weight. "Get down."

The Elan sank more by choice than Star's effort. They crouched below the tip of the stone ridge. "Well, that's something. Could've let me stay fixed on you and have me a nice target."

"Could have. Wouldn't do for proving my intentions and winning hospitality, would it?"

The Elan shook their head.

Lasers screamed against the stone to their backs, hammering against the surface in hopes of blasting through.

Star gripped his weapon tighter, muttering to himself.

The Elan rose, releasing the stored energy in an angry ball resembling a miniature sun.

Star took a series of short breaths, steeling himself. He braced against the wall and pushed off the ground. He twisted, scanning the far side of the cavern.

Three men stood in the corner on the left.

Star sank to his knees, burying the details in his mind. He drummed his fingers along his weapon before springing to his feet. Star spotted two armored men. They were close to the center tunnel at the far end. He fell to his knees again, breathing deep.

The Elan stared at him. "You going to do more than jump and look?"

Star met the creature's stare.

A pair of blue lances struck the side of the Elan's head, stunning the alien.

Star rocketed to his feet, barreling into the creature and driving it to the ground. He pawed at the burning wraps around the Elan's face.

The creature coughed and brushed aside Star's hands. "That hurt." The Elan pulled the head covering free, running a hand along the marred side of its face. "Think my wife will notice?" He brushed his fingers against blackened bits of stony skin. It looked like someone had charred the surface and ran a blade across it. Parts of the Elan's face peeled away under his touch.

"Yeah, I've got a feeling she'll notice." Star extended a hand more as a gesture than actual aid. He couldn't have hauled the creature to his feet no matter how hard he tried.

The Elan grunted. "That's a problem. I already took one to the heart earlier." He patted the center of his chest. "I promised her that a long while back. Now I go and ruin her face."

Star arched a brow. "Don't worry too much. Way I hear, your kind's got another three hearts to give."

The Elan frowned. "Don't remind my wife that." He grunted again, pushing off the ground with the butt of his staff.

Star pursed his lips. "You could stay down."

"Could, but my people are in trouble. Could you?"

Star shook his head. "No, but I aim to be a damn bit smarter than you about it." He stood, glancing to the remaining corner of the cavern.

Another three men stood there, staggering their shots. *One. One. Two.* He counted the blasts hurtling by to the other mounds. The first man fired, then the second. Then the first and third fired together. Star tallied the total and played through the scene in his head.

Salvos of blue and orange lights howled and hummed overhead.

Star exhaled. *Aim with your eyes, not your hand.* He sighted in on the far right corner of the cavern. *One.* He squeezed. Light erupted from the barrel, striking a

man above his breast as he appeared from behind cover.

A scream told him all he needed to know.

One. Star fell to a crouch.

Blue light streaked by.

Two men remained. He hoped they weren't aiming for him when there was plenty else to shoot at.

He rose, leveling his revolver to the same corner. Star traded glances with a soldier pointing a blaster at his chest. *Shit.* Star fired in haste, sinking to the ground as the laser went overhead.

No pained cry followed. The shrill sounds of weaponry persisted.

He shook his head, muttering to himself and trying to reestablish his count. "Aw, hell." Star wrapped both hands around his gun, taking a pair of breaths. He rose and fired three shots in succession before collapsing.

Star glanced at the numerous Elan further back in the cavern. Most huddled behind cover in pairs, taking turns in firing their staffs. He totaled their numbers at eleven including the one by his side.

Flashes of blue dominated the air, overtaking the dwindling orange balls.

He inched along the ridge, peeking over it. Star narrowed his eyes as men fanned out along the various protrusions.

Dozens of soldiers poured in from the tunnel near the far wall. They stormed the cavern, unleashing a torrent of bolts toward the Elan and him.

Star replied in kind, sticking the barrel of the revolver over the ridge and firing blind.

"I'm noticing you haven't bothered to reload that thing. Curious." The Elan flashed him a look.

Star glanced back. "Funny, I noticed the same about yours." He gestured to the staff with a thrust of his chin.

"Run on cells. We get our use out of them." The Elan's gaze fell on the revolver. "Looks rather old. Doesn't act like it though."

"No, it doesn't. You complaining?"

The Elan shook his head. "No, just questioning. We're the first place of civilization—if you can call Azzip that—on the way from Autumn."

Star stared, burying the intensifying noise of lasers drowning the humming blasts from the Elan.

"Rumors reach us just fine out here. Especially to my kind. Some of us are sympathetic to the resistance. Some of our people joined. Easy way off the planet."

Star's gaze deepened. "If you've got a point, best get to it before they get to us." He jerked a thumb toward the soldiers.

"Point is, I've heard stories about what the people of Autumn were trying to bring about. Heard they've succeeded too."

Star swallowed; the revolver felt heavier in his hand. He raised it a fraction in the direction of the Elan.

The gesture didn't pass unnoticed by the creature. "Weapon shoots something awfully like what I heard about. A brilliant light. That's what they called it, isn't it? The Light." The Elan stared at the barrel of the weapon. "Don't blame you. With what's going on, nobody would notice if you shot me. But you look like the kind of man who's got problems with getting blood on his hands."

Star's hand shook, but he kept the weapon trained on the Elan's chest. He shook his head. "Problem's not in spilling it. It's in washing it off. Don't clean easy, no matter how hard you scrub. As for The Light"—he waggled the revolver—"this ain't that."

Just a piece of it.

The stone vibrated to their side, shuddering under the barrage of fire.

"You going to kill me?" The Elan remained motionless. "If you don't, I've got a feeling they will. Might be a kindness."

"Maybe I'm just not that kind." Star lowered the weapon. He turned and peered over the mound. "There's too many of them for me to count now."

The Elan frowned. "Maybe you should have learned to count to a higher number."

Star scowled and looked over his shoulder. He sucked in a breath through his teeth.

A handful of Elan lay exposed from their rocky cover. They were stiller than the stone around them.

Star amended his mental tally of the Elan pairs from earlier. His frown deepened as the odds worsened. The look on his face must have spoken volumes.

The Elan to his side grunted, drawing his attention. "What's the problem, besides the obvious?"

"I don't see Shazhan. Had reason to believe he's important to your people, no?"

The Elan matched his frown. "He is."

Is. Present tense. He's holding onto faith his pal's alive. Star's thoughts turned to Ahiko. *He should be fine. Man's got a habit of getting by.*

The absence of firing lasers pulled him back to reality.

Star exchanged a quick glance with the Elan.

"Any survivors who intend to stay that way, throw your weapons out from your cover and stand up." The voice had an authoritative ring to it.

Star cupped a hand to his mouth. "No, thank you. Rather comfortable here with a nicely sized hunk of earth and stone keeping me from you." He tapped the barrel of his revolver against the mound. Hollow thuds rang out through the otherwise silent cavern.

Countless blue streaks lanced overhead. "Come out or you die, Elan."

His mouth twitched. They didn't know who exactly was behind the particular rock he hid behind. It was a problem, and a boon. "Seems you've overlooked a simple fact. If I stay behind this fine rock, you can't kill me."

"We're not aiming at you," called the voice.

Star blinked. *What?* He turned his attention to the mounds behind him. One of the Elan had broken cover, holding their hands above their head.

A bolt struck the Elan where a human's heart would be. The second laser impacted his ribcage. The alien collapsed to the ground.

Star's scream buried the sounds of their weapons. "Stop!" His hand snaked out, ripping the staff from the Elan beside him. Star lobbed the weapon overhead. It clattered against the ground. "I'm coming out. I surrender."

CHAPTER NINE

FOR THE DEAD

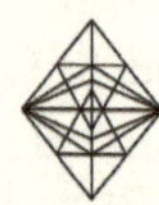

He glared at the Elan next to him. "Stay down, stay quiet." Star loosened his grip on his gun and let it hang from his index finger inside the guard. "Take it you know how to use one of these, antiquated as it is?"

The Elan nodded and took it.

Star exhaled, inching one of his hands out of cover. He hoped they wouldn't touch. He waved and prayed the gesture would placate them before he stood. His limb remained intact. Star rose, eyeing the swarm of soldiers.

They stared back, some tilting their heads and flashing each other puzzled glances.

"I figure you weren't expecting me." He hooked a thumb to his chest. "Surprise?" Star offered them a lopsided grin.

Every soldier's face hardened in unison. They bore the same frown.

They must've taught that to each other. He felt they ought to be taught how to smile a tad more.

Star let the thoughts die as a pair of soldiers exited the mouth of the tunnel near the far side of the cavern.

They were clad in slim-fitting armor fashioned from poly-metal and plastic blend that had the problematic characteristic of being laser proof. Projectiles were useless. The material was finished in a flat black that turned away even the brightest light without reflection. Their faces were hidden within a pair of close-fitting helms sporting a pair of circular lenses where their eyes would be. A third lens sat between them.

The men hefted rifles as long as his forearm and leveled them at targets behind them. They looked like nothing more than slender barrels protruding from a sleek, rectangular base form-fitted to the man carrying them. The rest of the soldiers snapped erect, turning on their heels with mechanical precision.

Ain't that a trick…

Slow claps echoed out from the tunnel ahead. A figure came into view as they neared the mouth of the tunnel. He stood a few inches over six foot and with the perfect posture that came with long years in the military. The man could have been carved from cold marble. His face was stark—angular edges that only bolstered the severity of his face. Hints of gray threaded his dark, cropped hair.

Star had seen blocks of ice warmer than the man's eyes. They radiated cold, calculating intellect.

The dirt and debris refused to cling to and mar his immaculate white ensemble. His tailored coat had padded shoulders with golden stripes running over them. A cape hung from one of his shoulders, calling attention to its crimson coloring. Much like his coat and pants, it was immune to the grime and dust in the cavern. His black boots caught and reflected even the smallest bits of light.

Star's hand went to where his revolver usually rested. He exhaled and reminded himself that he didn't have it. His gaze hardened. "You."

The cold-faced man ignored him, placing one of his hands to his hip. A single holster hung from his side.

Star couldn't make out the weapon inside.

"I am Admiral Killian Cain." He seemed to be addressing the entirety of the cavern. The admiral stared past Star like he was of no consequence.

It helped putting a name to the face he itched to put a hole in. A big hole. His fingers curled into a fist. Star held his stare on the admiral.

The admiral didn't return it. He walked past him, stepping over the bodies of several fallen Elan. Killian Cain's eyes were fixed to a mound near the opposite side of the cavern. "You've given me quite the problem, Shepherd."

"No more than you gave me back on Autumn." Star's fist tightened.

Cain made a sound like he paid him no mind. The admiral moved around one of the rocky coverings. He gripped his weapon, pulling it free and training it on something behind the mound. The revolver was an identical match for Star's, save the wrappings around the grip and the dull color. Cain's handgun matched the polished black of his boots.

Star had a feeling the gun fired the same as his.

Admiral Cain gestured with the weapon. "On your feet." He backed away from the mound, keeping his gun trained in place. "Gently now. Sudden actions prompt equally sudden responses. We don't want that now, do we?" The admiral flashed Star a quick smile.

Star gritted his teeth.

An Elan rose from behind the stony protrusion, casting a wary look around their surroundings.

Star pursed his lips and looked around the cavern without turning his head. Shazhan was noticeably out of sight. The Elan didn't seem like the kind of man to leave his people behind. Not without a plan at least, which meant something was up. And what usually went up came down. Star exhaled and counted numbers silently in the hopes of keeping calm.

The Elan stared at Admiral Cain.

The admiral averted his gaze, keeping the revolver leveled on the alien. "Now, we have a problem." He swept his free hand in a wide gesture aimed at soldiers. "One that needs to be addressed. That man is a fugitive." Cain jabbed a finger at Star. "Star Shepherd is accused of felony grand larceny from the state. Given the nature of his theft, it amounts to treason, in fact."

The Elan released a grunt that shook the bindings obscuring their face. "Seems like your problem is with him, not us."

Cain shook the gun. "Quite. But by harboring a known fugitive—given the bounty, how could you not have known—you've made it your problem. And sadly, worsened mine." The gun steadied, its barrel trained on the Elan's face.

The alien took a step back.

"You see"—Cain looked at Star, keeping the weapon steady—"I'm not trying to make my point with the alien. I'm trying to make it with you, Shepherd."

Don't. Star took a step towards the pair.

Cain's weapon bucked. A blast of carmine light struck the Elan's face and drove it back. The alien warrior fell to the ground as the garments over its face smoldered and hissed. A sound like crackling fire emanated from the Elan's body.

An incoherent scream came from Star's side. The Elan next to him got to their feet, squeezing their finger into the trigger guard of his revolver. Their roar echoed through the cavern as they trained the weapon on Admiral Cain.

Star wished the Elan had loosed their shot.

The two men clad in black armor fired. Torrents of opalescent laser fire cut the alien down. Steam hissed spitefully from the cauterized wounds.

Star tried to lock the muscles in his throat as an acrid stench clung to his nostrils, refusing to let go.

Cain holstered his weapon and pointed to the revolver in the Elan's hand. "I believe that's yours, Shepherd."

Star eyed him, then the Elan's corpse. "Seems picking up guns near you is hazardous to a man's health."

"Only if they point them at me. Go on. After all, it's the only souvenir you have left of Autumn." Cain's hand fell on the butt of his revolver.

Star caught the simple gesture as he kneeled to recover his weapon. He brushed aside his coat, holstering it.

"Good man. Now"—Cain steepled his hands

beneath his chin—"Shepherd, what am I supposed to do with you?"

He opened his mouth to speak, stopping when the admiral waved him off.

"You and I both know you're worth something alive, and no, I don't mean the monetary value. You're bringing that ship somewhere. I'd like to know exactly where."

"Funny thing, I'm having trouble remembering. My memory's not what it used to be. Something does come to mind, though. Someone looking awfully like you killing countless innocents on a planet you had no cause to be on. Heard the same man ordered the glassing of that world." Star's gaze hardened. His fingers flexed, and the temptation to draw his weapon deepened.

"Shame. I'll have to jog it." Admiral Cain stepped over the body of the Elan he had shot in the face. He circled the mound, heading to another near the far right corner of the cavern backside. "Oh, do come out. You're wasting my time and yours."

A basso cry shook loose stone free from the rocky cover. An Elan surged to its feet, rounding the protrusion and pointing a staff at the admiral.

Killian Cain drew, pivoted, and fired.

A neon-washed lance of red rocketed through the Elan's chest. The alien fell to its knees, glaring past the admiral to Star.

Star averted his gaze as the Elan collapsed against the ground. Dead men, living ones, and all the aliens between seemed to find ways to blame him. He didn't need that weight, unsure if he could keep carrying it. He cleared his throat. "That supposed to make me talk?"

Admiral Cain raised a finger and waggled it. "Tsk. Tsk. Don't bother lying to me, Shepherd. I saw the sort of man you are on Autumn. I know you care, even about them." He nodded to the fallen Elan. "And you know I always get what I want."

Star's fingers tingled, and the itch to grab his weapon grew. "Not always. I know I slipped that noose you were keen on tying around my neck on Autumn."

Killian Cain's face stretched tight. "I'll tie it tighter this time."

Star matched the admiral's look. "You'll try."

"Trying gets a man nowhere, Shepherd. Doing is all that matters, and I plan on doing many things. The question is, will you be alive to see them done? There's no need for you to die. What I want—what the Oligarchy wants—is The Light and the location you're delivering it to. You're only necessary to provide that information. After that, you're free to go." Cain gave him a smile reserved for predators.

Star lowered his gaze to the Elan by his side. "Yeah, I'm seeing what that freedom's worth. Pretty sure he won't be worrying about anything ever again."

"Don't be pedantic. You're not one of them." Cain waved the revolver at the nearest Elan corpse.

"I'm not one of you, either."

"You could be. You could be." Cain seemed to be speaking more to himself than Star. "Your situation doesn't have to be defined by the choices you've made, Shepherd. You can shape it by the choices to come. Decision's in your hands." Admiral Cain gave him a thin smile.

Star looked past the admiral to the robed figure

shambling into view in a tunnel opposite the one the soldiers had entered from. "Hard to choose when the government makes its choices based on the whims of a few people telling the rest what's best for us." He nodded to the approaching Elan. "Seems like they didn't get much choice."

Shazhan emerged from the mouth of the tunnel, surveying them with a neutral look. His eyes had lost some of their light from earlier. He raised a hand. "Voices carry in here. The shepherd is right: My people didn't get a choice. Seems fitting to take yours." The Elan glared at the admiral. A sliver of cylindrical metal tipped with red protruded from the alien's grip.

Star's heart lurched before doubling its beat. *Aw hell.* He turned in place, prompting the soldiers to train their weapons on him. His eyes turned to the cavern ceiling and the motes of blinking lights. The Elan weren't messing about in their planning. He took a step back.

The soldiers bristled, several of them slipped their fingers in the guards to fire.

Star looked back to the Elan.

Shazhan put his free hand to his throat and clutched it. "*Hall shalla.* For the dead."

And we're about to join 'em.

Shazhan's thumb fell on the button.

A brilliant flash of light washed over the ceiling as the world around Star exploded.

CHAPTER TEN
UNCANNY HABITS

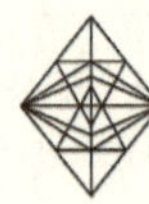

Stone and earth broke free, raining down around the cave. Stalactites hurtled toward him with the intent of pulping his body.

Soldiers darted and dove to avoid the downpour, scattering into the various nearby tunnels.

A streak of red light blasted a head-sized hole at his feet. Star leapt to the side and staggered, avoiding a falling piece of stone the size of his torso. It shattered, pelting his leg with smaller rocks. He pushed it from his mind and hurdled a mound in front of him.

An incoherent snarl cut through the sounds of the disintegrating cavern ceiling. Red light flashed over the rocky cover. It strobed without stop.

Star scuttled forward, keeping his profile low. He looked to where Shazhan had safely retreated back into the tunnel he'd appeared from earlier.

Another burst of light blew apart the ground before

him.

He snarled, brushing aside his coat and ripping his revolver free. Star aimed over his shoulder without looking. Another mound blocked his immediate path as he shuffled past debris and raining stone. He fired without stop, hoping to dissuade Admiral Cain and any lingering soldiers with the barrage of light. Star scrambled around the side of the protrusion and raised his profile. He'd made himself a bigger target.

Another lance of red howled over his head and confirmed his thought.

Star doubled his pace, spasmodically jerking the trigger.

The Elan receded into the tunnel, ushering him with a wave of their hand to hurry up.

He followed the alien's advice, running until the muscles in his legs seared with heat. Star peeked over his shoulder and spotted the two black-clad soldiers lingering by the opposite tunnel. He fired in their direction.

The bolt of light went wide, striking a section of the cavern far above them to their right. Unperturbed, they fired back.

A kaleidoscopic beam of energy hammered into the lip of the tunnel ahead, collapsing a portion.

Shit.

Another ray cut a swath through the ground beside his right foot.

Star leapt and rushed toward the opening, lunging to one side in an effort to avoid the debris littering the tunnel. Electric pain racked his left ankle as he clipped a stone and stumbled, his knees absorbing the jarring impact. He staggered forward and reached out with a blind hand, fingers closing around cloth.

Shazhan clasped his arm and hauled him upright, dragging Star along several more feet through the tunnel. "Almost took a nasty fall. Come on, let's move."

Beams of energy peppered the tunnel. Its mouth collapsed behind them.

Star's chest burned, feeling tight. Exhaling hurt just as much as sucking in a breath. He pushed aside Shazhan's hand and steadied his pace, enjoying the reprieve. "Was worried you'd go and do something stupid like that."

Shazhan released a baritone grunt. "You're welcome. I didn't have to come back and save your hide. My priority was getting the ones who couldn't fight to safety."

Star looked back at the tunnel's entrance. "Those who stayed behind, they knew what they were signing up for. They were planning on holding that ground no matter what."

Shazhan nodded. "And you made it out; be grateful for that." The Elan increased his pace.

"Believe me, I am." Star slipped the revolver into its holster and lurched forward. Another pang went through his ankle. He hissed and suppressed the pain. "Where to now?"

"Below."

Star furrowed his brow. "Deeper we go into the canyon, the deeper we're into trouble. Won't be easy fighting our way out if reinforcements show up. If the admiral survived that—" Star turned to look back again. "Did he?"

"Saw him taking shots at you for a moment. After that, saw nothing. He's probably buried. Good riddance." Shazhan turned down a path to the left, placing a hand on the tunnel wall for support.

Star stumbled after him and worked to keep his balance as the path sloped down more than he had anticipated. His fingers dug into the crevices along the stone walls for grip. "How long do you think you can last—honestly?"

Shazhan let out a low rumble but said nothing. The Elan took a right through a short bend before descending down another lengthy path.

Star huffed a breath in irritation and adjusted his pace to keep up without risking a fall. "Are the rest of your people down wherever we're headed?"

Shazhan remained silent. He paused, looking up to the ceiling and placing an outstretched hand against a wall.

"What are you doing?" Star looked around the narrow passage in case anyone had found a way through the blockage they'd left behind.

"Listening, you should try it." The Elan pressed himself closer to the stone.

Star bristled and placed his hands to his hips. "If I listened, the Oligarchy would have their hands on something to keep common people down for good."

Shazhan's body quivered, and a deep chuckle left his mouth. "Common, that so? You've got a stolen ship the government wants and a cargo so precious they're barely letting word out about it. They're willing to throw money and as many bodies as they need after you. Don't think that's common."

Star frowned.

"Come on." Shazhan waved a hand. "We'll get you below, then we'll get you out."

"Out? What happened to keeping me as leverage?"

Shazhan rounded another bend and grunted. "Look what good it's done my people keeping you at all. More trouble than you're worth. Turning you over won't bring us anything but misery." A silent question hung in the air after the Elan had finished speaking.

"So…what good am I to you?" Star's fingers twitched. A thought crossed his mind, begging him to take up the revolver just in case.

"You're not." The Elan stopped.

The twitching grew.

"You've got an uncanny habit of being bad luck for anyone around you. That being said, I've got the urge to let you loose and hope you bear some of that ill fortune on your government."

Star's hand froze. "You'd let me go?"

The Elan bowed his head. "My home's under attack. The last of my crew and people who ventured into your backwards system are dying. All for taking you. You think the military will stop that if we hand you over?"

He shook his head. "No."

"I've got a lot of cause to hurt your government. Note: not your people. My kind's learned well enough that your system doesn't care much for men and women like you. You're the nails. I want you to be thorns in the sides of those using the hammer." Shazhan took off down another bend.

"I can do that." Star took lengthy strides, falling in step behind him. "I've got more than enough reasons to hurt them."

"Sounds like. One condition though."

Star's pace faltered. "What's that?"

The Elan braced against the tunnel wall as he turned a slight corner down another path. "Last decline and we'll be there." He exhaled and hunched, keeping his head from brushing against the low wall. "I know what my people know, Shepherd."

Star swallowed. Word had spread too fast for his tastes—though that was bound to happen with what he had set off with. He shook his head clear and waited for the Elan to continue.

"What is The Light? Why's the government after it? I'm not stupid enough to believe that little gun's all there is of it. Your military's got enough firepower to keep the people down and quiet. A pair of fancy pistols won't change that."

Star bristled but kept quiet.

"You've got them scared. I want to know why. They've got you all in chains, and they're content with it. What have you got that can change that, Shepherd? They've got their money piled in the center of the galaxy for the wealthy, the powerful, and the connected. People like you are left to drift and fend for yourselves in the backwaters. You've got no chance of moving up or on." The Elan grunted as he stepped over a small, uneven hump in the sloped ground.

"True." Star left it at that, letting the Elan go on with his rant. It gave him longer to ponder.

"How do you mean to fix that?"

Star rolled his shoulders and looked past the alien. "I don't. I'm just bringing what I can to the people who can. I'm a delivery man, nothing more."

The Elan grumbled. "Doesn't answer my question."

"No, it doesn't." Star gestured ahead to an opening. "That it?"

Shazhan grunted in what he took to be an affirmative. "Is it a weapon, Shepherd?"

"The most dangerous kind. The kind that sets people free. The kind that keeps others from holding any power over them. It's the sort of thing that lets a man be independent and make his own choices, right or wrong. The Light's going to change a lot, and the powers that be aren't too happy about it." Star grinned.

"I can live with that." Shazhan bent further and eased out of the tunnel's mouth.

Star followed, stepping through and pausing.

The cavern could have housed rows of industrial carrier ships. It went on for miles and looked equally as high.

He blinked several times.

"It's a funny thing how much distance you can cover when twists and turns go down. Most people lose track of that when they're stuck talking." The Elan's face stretched into a wide smile.

Star gawked at the scene around him.

Countless Elan rushed past, clutching staff weapons. Bundles rested fastened across their backs. A smaller assortment of items hung from cords tied to the larger packs.

It's an exodus.

A single structure dominated the cavern. Its front was of hexagonal design formed from a tungsten-colored metal. The forward half of the ship sprouted from the wider octagonal base that ran the rest of its length.

It was simple, efficient, and damned big. But it got the job done when transporting endless people in comfort and safety. The vessel looked like it could withstand an armada.

"Epyon-class. One kilometer long. Less than half that in height. Almost just as wide. Tough birds." Star pulled his gaze from the ship. "Where'd you get it?

"Piece by piece. Sold and scraped what we could of our own ship, save for the core. That's lying around here as an insurance policy for something like this moment. All in all, fetched us a good sum, but good's not great. Rest came from doing what we planned on doing to you. Kidnap, scavenge, and sell. Do it for long enough, curry some favor with the local powers, and you can get yourself a transport ship." Shazhan motioned to passersby, urging them to hurry.

"Uh-huh." Star scanned the ship before turning his attention to the mass of Elan swarming the cavern. "This place is too big to be natural." His gaze flicked to both ends of the area before settling on Shazhan. "How'd you get the ship in here? Hell, how do you plan on getting it out?"

"In by bits, out as a whole. Trust me, my people have been working long on this. Honestly thought we'd have more time"—Shazhan sighed and looked around the cavern—"but it's as ready as it'll ever be. Time we followed suit and did something more about our fates than hide and scrabble for loot. I'm not letting someone else take our home away from us. Not again." The Elan's hands balled before releasing.

The world shuddered.

Specks of dirt and stone peppered his coat. Star raised a hand, squinting as he looked to the ceiling. Plumes of dust and former cavern shook free. He frowned, glancing at the Elan. "How stable is this place?"

Shazhan grunted and shambled toward the ship, beckoning him to follow. "Enough. The rest of my people worked on this day and night." The Elan headed toward the closest of six ramps extending from one side of the transport vessel.

A hollow boom sounded above them like a drum. Another beat followed before erupting into a frenzied percussion that felt as if it'd shake the cavern apart.

"They're going to bury us at this rate." Star raced toward the ship.

Shazhan shook his head, turning to bark an incoherent order to another Elan bustling by. "You, maybe. Not us."

The cavern shook harder.

"What's that mean?" The pit of his stomach roiled. Star glanced at the walls as the drumming dulled. He followed the various sources of softer thumping within the stone around them.

"It means we're leaving. You've got other priorities." The Elan tugged on Star's coat to get his attention. "There." Shazhan waved a hand to far left corner of the cavern. "See that? Tunnel down there leads you to a reservoir system beneath the canyon. Follow the waterworks. They'll take you close enough to what little civilization there is on Azzip."

Star arched a brow. "What's close enough?"

Shazhan moved to help a shambling member of his

race, placing a hand on their back and ushering them forward.

Star watched rows of Elan rush up the ramps into the ship for what he hoped would be the journey to take them home. He extended a hand toward Shazhan.

The alien took it, gripping him gently. "This is where we part ways, Shepherd. Nothing personal, but I hope to never see you again." He released his hold, turned, and marched toward the rest of his people.

"And I hope you make it home."

The thumping throughout the canyon rock reached a crescendo. Portions of the walls erupted with a thunderous roar. Stones of all sizes tumbled the ground.

Star brought an arm over his head as he rushed toward the tunnel Shazhan had pointed to.

The familiar sound of laser fire screamed around him. A trio of beams peppered the path before him.

So much for them giving up.

He slowed his pace, ripping the revolver free and firing blindly.

"Hit them back. Keep people clear and heading toward the ship!" Shazhan came to Star's side, falling to a knee as he leveled his staff toward the gaping holes in the cavern wall. "Bastards must have been blowing their way through the tunnels and walls to get here." The Elan loosed a pair of orange blasts toward an opening harboring a pair of soldiers. An orb struck the lip of the hole and splashed over it. The second ball of energy impacted the sidewall, blowing stone free.

Orange light washed over the opening to better illuminate the men within. They shielded their eyes with their hands.

Star spread his legs, adopting a shooter's stance. He fired twice at the man on the right side of the crudely formed tunnel. The first bolt of light struck the soldier's shoulder, sending him against the tunnel wall for support. Another shot impacted his side right where one of his kidneys would be. The light burned through the area without resistance, and the soldier crumpled.

The remaining man glanced at his colleague before turning to fire with renewed vigor. He unleashed a sporadic burst, sweeping the rifle across his field of vision. Half a dozen streaks raced toward them.

Star spat and dove to the side, recovering to a shaky stand as a blast cut through where he had been standing. The remaining shots went wide of their intended targets, a few striking the hull of the ship. Star spun and loosed a shot in the approximate direction of the tunnel. The blast struck the edge of the tunnel, sending a plume of debris into the air to obscure the soldier's vision.

Star used the moment to look around and assess the scene.

A double thunderclap boomed over the sounds of weapon's fire. Two more tunnels appeared as former wall fell to the ground. The process continued, soldiers coming into view within the newly blasted openings.

"Like damn roaches, but with explosives. Have to hate that kind!" The voice carried notes of amusement despite the situation.

Star turned to his side, blinking.

Ahiko stared back at him before stepping past him to raise a military rifle. He had likely plucked it from a corpse. The weapon resembled a tube slotted with various sized holes along the bulk of its body. A smaller nub of a cylinder protruded from its front and served as the barrel. The stock was nothing more than a padded piece of metal. It was designed to be light, functional, and cheap to mass produce. That didn't buy a man aesthetics or comfort.

He buried his questions, grateful his pilot had survived.

Ahiko released a controlled burp from the weapon, spewing a triplicate of energy lances toward one of the fresh openings. He repeated the process, firing in multiple, controlled bursts.

A dizzying amount of fire answered back.

Star let the strength leave his legs, falling to the ground and pressing himself flat. The air around him hissed as superheated blasts zipped by. He pushed aside the crisscross of fire being exchanged, tunneling his vision on where Shazhan had pointed earlier.

Just get up and run. It's that simple. Up. Run.

Fingers dug into the meat of his shoulder.

Star jerked, clasping a hand to the one squeezing him. He turned to find Ahiko staring at him.

"You got a plan?" The pilot pivoted, releasing another trio of shots before turning back to face him. "This isn't going to go in our favor." He nodded to the ship.

Star followed the gesture.

"Those Elan who can't, or won't, fight are nearly done boarding. Not enough numbers to hold this off. We've got to think about us." Ahiko's face twisted into a snarl as he fired another salvo. Angry puffs of steam vented from the rifle's holes, prompting the pilot to swear and toss the weapon to the ground.

Star scrambled to his feet, jerking a finger to a spot down the hangar. "Path out of here." He broke into a run.

Ahiko came by his side, panting. "No good." The pilot winced, and his breathing intensified. His pace faltered as he gulped down air. "Too far."

Star's face tightened. Ahiko had a point. The longer the pair of them remained exposed, the better the chances they would catch a blast that would put them down for good. He managed a weak shrug.

The pilot's brow furrowed as he took a series of deeper breaths through his nose.

Star didn't push for a better suggestion, instead taking the reprieve to fire his revolver without thought. Flashes of light strobed in the corner of his vision.

A deafening sound, like storm winds through an amplifier, filled the hangar. The noise grew with no sign of stopping.

Star slowed his pace and cupped his free hand to one of his ears in hopes of muffling the screaming. Hurricane winds buffeted him, threatening to rip the weapon from his hand and his coat along with it. He glanced at the ship.

The Epyon-class vessel roared into life. Halogen white lighting flared along the ship's hull and across its bow. Thrusters along the base of the ship screamed louder as they smoothly propelled the ship dozens of feet higher. The landing gear retracted.

Every soldier within eyesight redirected their fire on the new threat. A jarring array of lights cut through the air and hammered the ship.

The space vessel shrugged off the barrage like it had

been pelted with nothing more than stones.

A muted scream graced his ears. Star turned to Ahiko.

Sweat beaded the pilot's face, and his strides grew shorter. The pilot opened his mouth, jabbing at the ship.

Star shook his head and motioned for Ahiko to shut his mouth. The effort in talking would only tax them further.

Ahiko made a circular motion with his index finger along the side of his skull before pointing at the ship.

Star bobbed his head in agreement. *Damn crazy, that's for sure.* He didn't see what they aimed to do in powering up their ship within the canyon. *Got no way out…unless. Aw hell.*

The Elan validated his fears. Rows of elongated barrels along the front of the ship swiveled to take aim. Paneling along the bulk of the ship parted, and cannons extended from the openings.

They meant to blast their way out.

He shot a glance to the pilot.

Ahiko's wide-eyed stare matched his. He flashed Star a look, mouthing something drowned out by the ship's noises.

Star had an idea of what he meant. He scanned the stone wall closet to him.

Various tubes and duct work ran along it. Translucent piping made from aerospace polymer pumped clear liquid from somewhere below the hangar. It was wider than both men put together.

Star pointed frantically at the water duct system.

Ahiko shook his head.

He upturned his free hand, jerking a thumb down at the ground.

Recognition dawned in Ahiko's eyes, and he gave Star a hapless shrug.

Star took it as a sign of resigned agreement, and they raced toward the pipe-works. He set his sights on the main body of the largest duct and fired. A torrent of water rushed out from the fresh hole. He fired in quick succession until countless portions of the tubing had been blasted away. Streams of water spewed furiously, widening the gaps.

A salvo of ear-splitting energy blasted around the entire hangar. Stone seemed to evaporate under the power of the ship's lasers. The firing blew through feet of solid rock with easy, creating a thunderstorm of dirt and boulders.

The soldiers were the worms buried under it all.

Rocks of all sizes crashed to the ground. Men were pelted by smaller stones—driven to the ground by larger ones. A boulder flattened a soldier into the metalwork of the hangar.

Star fired along the top of the severed piping, tearing apart the section responsible for the suction. He looked over his shoulder and into the distance above. The ceiling seemed so far off to him—a problem he didn't think the ship would be concerned with.

"Get in!" Star gestured to the now-empty pipe, waving a hand to accentuate his point.

Ahiko couldn't have heard his cry but understood his frantic gesturing. The pilot placed a hand on the edge of the pipe and slipped in.

Star glanced over his shoulder, spitting as the ship rose higher.

The Epyon-class ship's cannons aimed at the ceiling.

He stowed his revolver, following Ahiko's example and grabbing hold of the pipe's edges. Star hauled himself inside as every bit of weaponry on the ship screamed in unison.

I'm sick of worlds exploding around me.

Blinding light flooded the hangar.

Star sank into the pipe.

CHAPTER ELEVEN

STIRRING THE POT

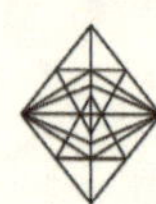

The duct work rattled like it would come free.

Star slid along the wet piping with little resistance. He hoped the drop ahead wasn't a nasty one.

Grains of dirt and stone brushed across the back of his head, some making their way down his collar. He squirmed.

Hollow groans echoed from the world above.

A palm-sized portion of his head throbbed as something crumbled against his skull. He winced and shifted his hands above him, interlocking his fingers to form a makeshift shield. Debris rolled down the pipe behind him, bludgeoning his fingers and any other exposed bits of skin.

Star set his jaw, gritting through the pain. A warbling cry came from ahead. He tensed his muscles, bringing his arms in close and readying himself for the landing. The pipe angled into a light bend that jarred his back as he passed through. A bend ahead gave Star little idea of what to expect at the end of the piping. Instinct told him to shy away from the downward turn.

He mimicked Ahiko's earlier scream as he passed through the bend in the pipe and sank. His arms flailed like windmills as he plummeted, the broad of his back smacking against water. He broke through the surface by a foot before rising to the top. Star stared up at dark, unmarred stone, and blinked. "You okay?"

"Apart from being stranded on a backwater world, captured by aliens, shot at by the military, and whatever the hell just happened?" A loud splash tinged Ahiko's rant.

"Yes."

The pilot groaned. "I'm wet; that's how I am."

"You're wet and alive. The latter takes some precedence and ought to be appreciated."

"I can think of a few situations where it'd be appreciated if the former were given precedence." Ahiko sounded amused with himself.

Star shook his head and treaded water as he scanned the area.

The immediate portion of the Elan waterworks looked to be a single channel of water a couple of meters wide. Half a dozen pipes, similar to the one he and Ahiko had fallen through, hung along the walls around them. The mouths of the polymer tubes sat a few feet beneath the surface of the water. Dim lighting illuminated small patches of the underworks.

Star glanced down the stream before fixing his gaze on a pipe ahead. A handful of seconds passed before he confirmed they drew nearer to the water siphon.

"Slow moving current. Likely this water comes from the canyon itself. Whatever cut through it must run below it. Betting there's more streams like this networked around here."

"That's good—why?" Ahiko stared.

"Means there's likely a series of paths for us to navigate. Shazhan told me there's a way to the nearest town through here. Now I know he wasn't lying. Moving water means it's moving somewhere. Means there's a way out. And we could be down here a while, bit of a nicety to know we won't die of dehydration." His mouth quirked to one corner.

Ahiko grumbled incoherently before swimming to a narrow latticework made from various scrap metals. Splotches of rust mottled portions of the makeshift walkway. Ahiko grabbed the metalwork, hauling himself atop it. The interwoven bands flexed under his weight.

Star followed him and clambered onto the wobbly surface.

"Where to?" The pilot glanced at him before looking ahead.

Star exhaled, running a hand through his hair, shaking the excess water free. He trailed his finger through the air along the same path of the current. "Shazhan didn't really tell me which way exactly."

Ahiko narrowed his eyes. "And that ain't exactly a way I'm willing to risk my life on. Could be we end up stuck down here forever."

"We will be if we don't decide." Star leaned back, easing some of the stiffness from his body before shrugging. He took a step, the latticework below bending in tandem. A low breath left his lips as he steadied himself and walked forward.

Ahiko followed him in silence.

Star moved along the path, letting the minutes slip by uncounted as he watched the slow-moving current. He found a modicum of solace in observing the water take its time in going along.

There was a time he could live like that—move along space at his speed. All he had to do was carry things from one end to another like a wave. Then he got the bright idea of signing up to carry a bit too much.

Star exhaled and dragged the back of one of his hands across his eyes, wiping away some of the water. The simple action pulled him away from his thoughts.

The metal path went around a sharp bend. He crept forward, peering around the corner. Star pulled back and flashed a look to Ahiko.

The pilot opened his mouth to speak.

Star closed the gap between them, placing a hand over the man's lips. He shook his head. With his free hand, he gestured for the pilot to keep his voice down.

Ahiko inclined his head.

Star pulled his hand away, shooting a glance behind them before looking back.

"What is it?"

"Soldiers ahead." Star pressed his back against the wall, taking steps to peer around the corner again to reassess the situation. He cupped a hand to the side of his face and hoped it would muffle his voice enough. "They look out of it, bit beat. Odds are they figured the same as we did and got down here while they could. Only refuge I could think of when the damn ceiling was coming down on us."

Ahiko's lips pressed together like he was weighing the situation. "How sharp are they looking right now?" He arched a brow.

Star leaned around the corner before snapping back. He shook his head. "Sharp as bricks. Don't seem to be looking for anything but a way out."

"Good. Means they won't be keen on finding us. We just need to get by them without starting a fight." The pilot gave him a level look.

Star brushed off the statement, looking around for a way to slip past the military. He glanced at the stream of water. His reflection stared back. The weak lighting within the underworks made it difficult to stare through the surface of the water.

That works.

He sank to his knees, dipping his feet into the stream as slowly as he could.

Ahiko shot him a look that said he thought Star was crazy.

Star ignored him, easing himself into the water to minimize the noise. He let himself sink under the surface. The world distorted, and Ahiko nearly vanished from sight as Star fell further. He hoped the pilot caught on fast.

Water rippled as Ahiko passed through it to fall beside him. The pilot raised two fingers to his forehead in a mock salute before swimming past him.

Star put a hand to the wall, pushing off it to force himself further below. He undulated forward and kept his gaze flicking from ahead to the surface of the water. His lungs felt stretched as he neared the soldiers.

Voices cut through the silence, coming through the

water garbled.

Star stopped, bringing a hand over his mouth out of instinct. The pressure in his chest built.

Ahiko hung a few feet ahead, glancing at the surface and back to Star. Several bubbles flitted out from his nose.

Star's eyes widened, and he fought the urge to exhale and suck in a breath at the same time. He buried the feeling and crossed the distance to Ahiko.

The pilot stared at him before shooting another look at the surface.

A lance of blue-white energy cut through the water a foot from them. Several more beams arced by.

Star clamped a hand to Ahiko's mouth as the pilot pressed one to his. Both men exchanged frantic looks before staring at the surface.

The laser fire subsided.

Star released his hold as Ahiko did the same to him. He reached into his coat, ready to pull the revolver free.

The pilot shook his head and jabbed his index finger to the space above them. He pulled a hand close, forming an edge with it and making a cutting motion in front of his throat.

Star understood the nonverbal cue and kept his weapon in place. A pair of invisible hands kneaded his lungs, stretching them like dough. He shut his eyes for no other reason than as a mental aide to help him endure the mounting agony in his chest.

Another exchange of muddled waters reverberated above.

Star kept from sighing in relief, easing himself forward in hopes of leaving the soldiers behind. He looked over his shoulder to find Ahiko keeping a leisured pace with him.

A bolt of energy speared through the water, crackling by his left ear.

Star exhaled.

Laser fire riddled the water like a storm of javelins.

Ahiko surged forward in an adrenaline-driven frenzy.

Star followed his lead, doing everything to block the lead weights and fire stringing his muscles. A trio of lasers cut off his path. He stopped, exhaling the last remnants of air. The sides of his skull felt caught in a vice-grip that had no intention of relieving the pressure. He relented, using what little strength he had to claw at the water around him. Star swam toward the surface with one hand and reached into his coat with the other.

The laser-fire stopped.

He didn't. Star burst from the water, his lungs screaming. He ripped the revolver free and fired as he was still drawing. The first round sailed harmlessly past the four soldiers in view. Light bloomed across the wall where the bolt impacted, passing through the stone with ease.

The soldiers jerked their weapons in Star's direction.

He fired again without aiming, hoping the erratic shots would send them running.

The soldiers scattered along the narrow grating.

Star sucked in a deeper breath than before, his lungs finding relief in the extra portion of air. It was short lived.

The soldiers turned, spreading their grouping along the latticework. Two men knelt and trained their weapons on him.

Hell.

Star turned, tearing at the water as he pulled himself below the surface. His legs burned with effort the harder he pumped them. A pair of beams passed by his left shoulder. He clamped his jaw to keep himself from inhaling out of shock. Star covered another foot before rolling, clasping both hands to the revolver.

Another bolt of energy rocketed by.

His finger hammered against the trigger, pulling in more jerky reaction than smooth control. He couldn't imagine the scene above water. Countless rounds flashed through the surface to pepper the walls and grating around them. He exhaled, the pressure returning throughout his chest. Star squeezed out a trio of shots before breaking the surface.

He swallowed as much air as he could, spinning in place and bringing the revolver around to where the soldiers had been.

Crumbling bits of stone fell from the wall. The latticework sported a series of fist-sized holes, and portions of it were collapsing under their own weight.

Star noticed a distinct lack of soldiers. He looked over the area, clenching his jaw as he mulled things over. The soldiers had been closer to the bend Star and Ahiko had rounded earlier. He fired at the corner, driving a round of light through the stone.

A yelp echoed back, followed by a barrel protruding from around the corner.

He twisted, not bothering to plunge below the water as he swam. A single shot tore through the air above him. His arms felt like they'd fall from their sockets if he continued the effort. A second shot never came. Star didn't feel like taking the gamble and instead increased his pace. He swam toward a break in the path ahead that led to the right.

Ahiko leaned out from the wall ahead, waving at him.

Star came to the corner, reaching out with both hands to grab the metalwork.

Ahiko grabbed his wrists, helping haul him onto the woven structure. "They let you go?"

He shook his head, doubling over and placing a hand against the rough stone wall for support. "End of the day, they're people too." He coughed several times before he was able to continue. "I gave them enough hell to make them reconsider. I'm not worth dying over. Think about it."

Ahiko mirrored him, leaning against the wall. "Fair point. Most of 'em went through a ringer fighting the Elan. If I were in their shoes, and it's worth noting I sort of am, I'd want to be out of here and heading home." Ahiko gave him a sideways look.

Star waved a dismissive hand and holstered his revolver. "I'm noting that we're alive and in need of a direction. You have an idea?"

The pilot frowned, tugging at his shirt. "None. But there's bound to be more folk down here, and if we keep moving around sopping wet, we're going to get their attention."

"You don't seem like the kind of man bothered by the spotlight."

The pilot shrugged. "I find it problematic when that light's accompanied by a laser." He pointed to his face. "High-energy blasts and this mug don't get along on account of me needing a pretty face to match my wits."

"Think you've got a higher opinion of your looks and wits than is reality." Star brushed past him, moving down the path.

Ahiko let out a resigned sigh. "I've got half a mind to turn back and take my chances with them."

Star didn't bother looking at the pilot, imagining the man hooking a thumb over his shoulder in the direction of the soldiers. "That's about as much mind I pay to those sorts of concerns. All you have to do is turn around and start walking. Maybe you'll make it halfway down the passage before they shoot you."

Ahiko grumbled to himself.

As much as he wanted to push it away, Star had to admit the light barbs eased the weariness plaguing his body and mind. He needed a few uninterrupted minutes to set himself straight. The way things were going, he didn't think he'd get that chance.

Star led the way in silence, occasionally shooting glances over his shoulder to ensure they weren't being tailed. He took it as a small relief that they weren't.

He needed to focus. He'd been pushed and pulled too many ways to keep things in sight. Star took a breath to settle himself and thought on where he wanted to go—needed to be, knowing he'd get there.

He stopped to heed his own advice. Star counted the seconds as he inhaled, reminding himself to do the same on the breath out. He turned and looked at Ahiko after composing himself. "You're former military." It wasn't a question.

The pilot inclined is head.

"What are we likely to find once we hit the surface?

How's the military going to be looking for us?" Star resumed walking, keeping his pace measured. The idea of skulking around the underworks longer than necessary didn't appeal to him. However, every moment within the dark passages was another without the greater military presence above them. That wouldn't get him any closer to delivering his cargo though.

Ahiko rubbed a palm against his chin. "They'll be running aerial patrols—A-stars, fast little birds that can cover a lot of sky in no time. With how many troops they've got combing this place, fair bet to say they've got a carrier in orbit. Could be worse."

Could be.

"So, odds are soon as we hit the ground, a patrol could spot us?" Star kept his voice neutral, hoping the pilot wouldn't pick out the tinge of worry trying to creep in. The path ahead forked three ways, and the possibilities weighed heavier on his mind than he would have liked. He clenched his fingers, reminding himself to breathe.

"There's a chance. Azzip's a big place though. If I were a bettin' man, and I am, I'd wager they're keeping tight around the canyon. Word's bound to have hit some pilots that troops made contact in the tunnels. Makes sense anyone trying to leave would pop out somewhere around here."

It did, meaning their best bet was getting out somewhere along the bottom of the canyon. Town be dammed. It wouldn't be good if they were put down before even getting back to the ship.

An invisible hammer struck the core of his mind. "The ship." Star smacked the base of one of his fists into the wall. "The Elan captured us along the bottom of the canyon."

"Right…" Ahiko frowned, arching a brow.

"Means they've got passageways leading out there. If they're raking the dunes above the canyon, we'll keep low and scuttle to the ship. Has to be a pain for them to ping us down here in the rocks, right?" Star stared at the pilot, hoping Ahiko would agree with his reasoning.

Ahiko tilted his head and pressed his lips together. "Could do. Still have one problem though: the tracker."

Star's heart sank into his stomach.

"Got no way of cutting it loose." Ahiko gestured to Star's side. "That gun of yours might do the trick."

He arched a brow. "Might?"

"You drop the shields to cut on your bird; that thing would tear clean through that tracker." The pilot shrugged.

And likely through the ship. Star had no way of controlling how far the blast would go.

"As much as I might love something hot and temperamental in my hands, not the touch we're needing right now. Sometimes a little finesse goes a long way." Ahiko raised his brows twice as if trying to nudge Star into acknowledging the joke.

He didn't, choosing to turn and eye the split paths ahead. The passages were perfectly identical to him. It was never that simple, though; otherwise, why have three ways to go? Something gripped his shoulder, wringing a bit of water from his coat. He glanced at Ahiko.

The pointed to a stream of water. "Path on the right,

current's picking up."

He was right. Star missed it at first, but the surface of the water moved noticeably quicker than the paths to the right. "Bound to be a reason for that."

"A simple one too. Often is." Ahiko narrowed his gaze on the path. "Downhill? Only reason I can think of. Not much use to the Elan making water hard to get to?"

Star grunted in acknowledgement. The reasoning made sense to him. If they had made the path themselves, common sense would have dictated creating a place for the water to pool. It would be easier to collect.

And easier to go bad. Stagnant water wouldn't be as clean. Then again, what the hell did he know about what Elan could and couldn't handle? He settled for Ahiko's appraisal.

"What do you make of that, then?" Star pointed between the middle and left paths. Water slapped into the furthest passage before brushing aside and resigning itself to filter into the middle way.

"Water would still make its way down if it were level, which is what I'm guessing the middle way is. Likely the left's heading up an incline. At least enough of one that this slow-moving stream can't do anything about it." Ahiko's eyes widened for a second.

Star caught the look. "What?"

"I took a mess of turns and downhill tunnels to get to that hangar. Means we've got to be heading up, for a while at any rate, to get back to the same level we were on before Shazhan let us go." Ahiko moved to the end of the latticework, pressing down on a simple metal girder running between both sides of the tunnel. The pilot hopped onto the beam and flailed as he tried to keep his balance.

Lacking better ideas, Star followed him and stepped onto the girder. His ankle protested the action and tightened. He winced and made a mental note to proceed slower. The metal surface had held up better than the latticework, meaning less rust to provide some form of traction. His boots skidded as he took another step.

Ahiko hissed to get his attention. "Up and down, not so much forward. Easier to keep your balance. That, or you could just take another swim and cross." His mouth split into a wide grin.

Star nursed the urge to stuff that mouth with his fist. He shut his eyes for a moment and breathed. It wouldn't do to pummel his pilot. Employer-employee relations tended to suffer when the former kicked the latter's ass. Star took the pilot's advice, taking higher steps that didn't reach out as far. His balance improved, and he crossed the beam.

Ahiko clapped him on the shoulder before turning to walk toward the passage they'd chosen. "Been meaning to tell you something, but I wasn't wanting to make things worse for you."

Star stayed silent, staring at him.

"It's a good bet there are more troops down here." Ahiko gave him an apologetic shrug. "You said Shazhan told you a proper way to get down here. That means the military's got an easy way in too. They're not messing about in searching this place. With what's going on above, you can be damn sure people are skulking through here and not just to get away from that collapse."

The man had point. Star slipped out of his coat, pressing it to the stone beside him and busied himself in wringing it dry. Most of the water would shed off the material as they walked, but the simple busywork kept his mind from dwelling on what Ahiko had said. Droplets beaded and raced across his hand as he squeezed one of the sleeves.

"Star?"

He ignored the pilot, grabbing his coat by its mantle and snapping his wrists. The jacket sent drops of water onto the mesh below and the wall. The coat had been good to him. While the water wouldn't do anything to ruin it, he wasn't fond of putting through anything more than he had to.

Some things were more than just clothes; they were memories. He slipped an arm into a sleeve, shrugging his way into the rest of it.

"Shepherd." Ahiko thumped him on the shoulder to get his attention. "Now's not the time to be getting lost in your head. Considering what you've dragged us—notably, me—into, maybe your brains not the best place to be."

"Maybe not, but for all the trouble it's brought me, it's gotten me out of it all just the same." He pulled the front of his jacket, tightening the material around him. It was out of comfort more than anything else. "Let's go, and hope you're wrong about more troops being down here."

Ahiko blew out a breath and kept pace beside him. "I don't make a habit of being wrong."

Everyone was wrong some of the time. Some people went through most of life being wrong most of the time.

And there wasn't anything wrong with that. It just was what was.

"First time for everything." Star knew that to be true. Nothing remained static, no matter how much a man wanted something to. One could either dig their heels in while the world and life changed around them, or they could find a way to take charge best they could. "If you *are* right, then we'll deal with 'em."

Ahiko let out a delicate cough that seemed forced. "You seem a touch too confident about that."

"It's that or being afraid. The latter doesn't do much in helping a man think clearly." Star needed to hear himself say the words aloud as much for him as to bolster Ahiko. He didn't mention that, however.

Star paused to drag the soles of his boots across the wall to his left. The path's incline grew steeper, and the soles of his shoes failed to grip as well as before. He ground his feet against the waterless passage floor before setting off.

Ahiko had an easier time making his way up, moving beside him with his hands in his pockets. The pilot didn't seem perturbed by the slippery surface.

Star chalked it up to the man's military experience. As much as he complained, it was likely more a personality quirk than being bothered by anything. He made a mental note to take less of the pilot's crap as it would be nothing more than attitude for the sake of it.

Some men just had to stir the pot.

The passage stayed blissfully empty as the slope increased. He hoped the trend continued, but his left hand rested on his revolver. The habit was new and not one he'd grown entirely fond of.

The weapon had come to fit comfortably in his hand, familiar. Its weight had become reassuring. Star didn't know what it meant, likely something he was overthinking.

He took a series of breaths to still his mind. It worked, and Star set his focus on the immediate problem: getting back to *The Last Leaf*. He followed his chain of thoughts, addressing the problems ahead of him.

The tracker had to go, and getting to a town would be near impossible. Industrial cutting equipment, however, had more uses than just chopping up bits of ship. "Ahiko, the military was blasting open new tunnels when we were above."

The pilot nodded, his brows furrowing.

"Besides explosives, what are the chances they'll have something a little less impactful on them? Something along the lines of cutting equipment?" Star smiled.

A hint of a light shone in Ahiko's eyes. "Very good odds. Any deployment of this scale has engineers paired with infantry. It's fair to say there's a handful down here to clear any blockages or sealed doors. They'll be carrying portable cell packs to power plasma cutters."

Star's smile grew. "And am I right in guessing those'll cut through our tracker?"

Ahiko's grin was answer enough. "We'll have to keep our ears open more than our eyes."

Star quirked a brow. "Why's that?"

"They make a helluva lot of noise. Loud crackles, like a fire tearing through a bunch of dry twigs. Lots of snaps and pops. With these tunnels, you're bound to hear them before you see them."

Star committed that to memory and moved up the incline. If the engineers were paired with infantry, it meant they could find themselves in another fight. He wasn't keen on that happening. He'd endured too much of that of late.

"I need to ask you something, Shepherd."

Star glanced to the pilot, gesturing with a thrust of his chin to go ahead.

"As much grief as I've been giving you—"

Which has been a lot.

"Truth is, I'm committed whether I like it or not. You've pulled me in, and there's no climbing out."

Star knew where this was going.

"I'm going to see this through till I'm paid. And if that's going to happen, you need to be straight with me, here and now. Where are we headed?" Ahiko stopped, crossing his arms and staring at him hard. "I was asked to blindly follow when I was in the military. I'm not going on in life the same way. I want to know, Shepherd. All of it."

CHAPTER TWELVE
PICKY BLESSINGS

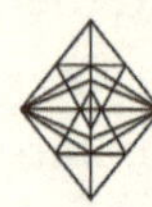

He sighed, his coat feeling heavier around his shoulders. Telling the man the truth might ease the weight. Star felt it was worth the shot. "Near about to the other side of the galaxy."

Ahiko didn't say a word.

"A good deal out of the way too. Away from any trade and shepherding routes." Star blew out a breath, debating how to break the bad part to the pilot.

"You beating around the bush isn't reassuring. Hope you know that." Ahiko gave him a thin smile.

"Slaydus. That's our destination."

The pilot sputtered before trying to swallow the noise. He ended up choking, racking his throat to clear the self-caused blockage. "The hell's wrong with you?"

Been wondering that myself.

"Slaydus ain't a planet. It's an overgrown ball of green next to nowhere. Nothing there but trees and sky."

Star stared at him. "I was paid to deliver cargo there; that's where I'm going. You asked. I answered. You not liking the answer isn't my problem, unless you're thinking of firing yourself again?"

Ahiko shook his head and ran a hand through his hair. "There's more to this, Shepherd. Military on you, claiming you've stolen their property. It doesn't sit right with me. They've told their fair share of lies, so I'm not inclined to believe them hands down. But this ain't that simple either. You've got something they want, whether or not you took it from them. And Slaydus may be dead, but someone's going to be there to take their cargo. No way they're letting you drop off it cold." The pilot's voice sounded distant, like he was talking to himself and trying to rationalize it all.

Star left him to his thoughts, moving ahead until the incline leveled off. The latticework to his left was a tighter knit than the previous ones. No rust tinged the surface of the metal bands. He stepped onto the walkway, testing its ability to hold its weight. It did a better a job than the previous meshes.

"I want to know who."

Star looked over his shoulder. The pilot had caught up and stared him in the eyes. He figured Ahiko had the right to know. "Liberation Movement." The words fell with a heavy weight that nearly echoed through the passage.

The pilot's mouth moved soundlessly. He winced before shaking his head and cradling his temples. "You're trying to start a war, you know that?"

Star leaned a shoulder against the wall. "I'm trying

to stop one before it starts. There's the difference."

"Depends on who you ask. Liberation Movement's a bunch of ornery crazy folk thinking they can take on the military, the Oligarchy. There's a reason a handful of families are in power—because they have that power. They've got the money to buy what they want and who they want, and that gives them a say on how to run things the way they want. You think a bunch of civilians are going to fight and change that?" Ahiko rolled his eyes.

"Don't know what will happen, truth be told. I know what I believe, though." He tilted his head back, staring at the ceiling.

Ahiko groaned.

"They've got the right to live their lives the way they want. They're not hurting anybody, but they're being kept down by fuel prices and energy costs. You know it too. What options do people on the outer edges of the galaxy have? Join the military or try to get by on their own, which ain't allowed. What's the fuel at right now?" Star turned and glared at the pilot.

Ahiko didn't answer.

"And how much has it gone up since the last annual adjustment cycle?" He arched a brow, waiting for an answer he knew wouldn't come. Star couldn't blame Ahiko. He knew he had the pilot on the point, and the man couldn't admit it.

"Enough." The muscles in Ahiko's throat visibly strained, making it clear he had fought to get the words out. "And you're changing that how? What have you got that can break the Oligarchy's grip? They *own* every fuel and mineral market in the galaxy. *Every one.* Ain't one resource a man can call his own without them snatching it up and taxing you for it. That's if you're lucky. It's their rules."

"And ain't that a shame. Maybe it's time for someone to change 'em. Liberation Movement's got a way to change that. They just need what I've got."

Ahiko arched a brow. "And what's that?"

"Waiting aboard *The Last Leaf*. It's called The Light. If you want to know more, I'll have to show you. Words won't do. Now, come on." Star waved a hand as he pushed off the wall with a foot. He didn't wait to see if the pilot would follow. After what he'd told him, he figured the man might have to sit a moment and stew.

It wasn't easy processing that much information. Especially the scope of it all. He'd left Ahiko with as many questions as answers he'd given. Star had pulled the man into a life on the run, at least until the job was done. But if they made it out of here alive, Ahiko would have a chance to vanish if he wanted. Star would make sure to offer the man that much.

Seemed proper to him. If it came to that, he'd finish the journey alone. He'd started it that way. He could end it that way.

Star hoped it wouldn't come to that. Sometimes an extra hand went a long way. He looked back to the pilot.

Ahiko stood rooted in place, his gaze turned to the ground. He looked lost in thought.

Star could've left him there, so long as he didn't stay stuck forever. A man could drown in his own mind. Sometimes the worst thing a person could be stuck with was their worst selves. Everyone had nasty habits in letting the bad drag them down away from the good.

He felt the need to pull the pilot away from that.

Star cleared his throat loud enough to jar Ahiko out of his stupor. "You okay? I know I'm asking a lot of you, but you wouldn't have been on Terizen if part of you wasn't up for this. Am I right?"

Ahiko gave him a hollow, distant look. Seconds passed before something hard and hot filled his eyes. It was a thing of iron resolution and heat. "Didn't ask for this"—he ran a hand through his hair again—"but I'll take the chance to stick it to certain powers that be."

Star took those powers to be the military. Zheer had told him the man had had a fallout with them, but he didn't know the terms. He'd only caught the mention of an honorable discharge. That sort of thing only happened when someone wanted a man out of the way without causing a lot of fuss. He figured Ahiko had been forced out by backroom politics. Star felt there wasn't a need to press the man for more until he was ready to open up on his own.

"Well, that's what I'm offering, Ahiko Kohiba: a chance to get back at a whole mess of people who've wronged too many to count. That includes you. We pull this off, it'll shake the foundations of a galaxy. Are you in?" He extended his hand toward the pilot and raised a brow.

A slap echoed out as Ahiko's hand clapped against Star's. The pilot wasted no time in exchanging grips and shaking. "Almost as good a payment as anything else. Though, we're still getting paid, right?" He gave Star an oblique stare.

"Handsomely." Star broke the shake and turned to move away.

"Nothing better than when the money matches the man." The pilot chuckled to himself.

Star groaned. The pilot needed to take his overly high opinion of himself down a notch before someone else did, forcibly so.

He counted it as a small blessing that Ahiko kept his mouth shut as they progressed down the length of the passage. The way had remained blissfully simple, keeping straight as much as one could hope for. He'd grown weary of the earlier twists and bends. It made finding a way out all the more difficult.

The sound of steady trickling drew his attention. He turned to look at one corner of the passage. Water streamed from a portion of the wall above, pooling into a lengthy furrow that bisected the path. It ran perpendicular to them and carried the water to the left of where they stood. The source of the water interested him more than where it led.

He gestured toward it with two fingers, making sure the pilot took note. Star leaned to the side and eyed the wall. Water flowed in a continuous, smooth torrent from a hole that had to have been bored into the stone by precision tools. He figured the opening had been made by the Elan to circumvent more of the canyon's natural waterways.

It meant there'd likely be a good deal of water above. If there was any chance of more soldiers being around, the noise and cover could come handy.

He pulled his revolver free and took aim to the side of the opening.

"We're starting fights with walls now? You've got a terrible habit causing trouble with everything, you know that?" Ahiko nodded to the wall. "That includes the inanimate. What, he look at you funny?"

Star ignored the pilot's quip and fired. Stone parted, widening the opening by the size of a man's head. Water rushed to fill the gap and race into the channel. Star repeated the process mechanically until the hole was nearly as wide as his torso.

Ahiko stared at the furrow before turning to Star, his face making it clear he understood the idea. "Water level's up to about our necks if we get into that."

Star inclined his head.

"It's making a bit more noise than before too. Just enough to let us move about with no fear of being heard."

"If you can keep that mouth of yours in check, yeah." Star fought to keep his face neutral.

Ahiko's eyes narrowed. "Fair enough." The pilot's face hardened, and he shut his mouth.

A garbled sound echoed down from the path on the left. Star and the pilot exchanged quick looks before moving toward the source of the noise. Sharp crackling cut through the passage, making it impossible to make sense of the warbling sound.

Star tilted his head in the direction of the noise.

The pilot cupped a hand to his mouth. "Sounds dead on." He waggled his index and middle fingers, miming a pair of legs walking. His fingers stopped as he made a fist and tugged it.

Star didn't know what the gesture meant for certain, but he had an idea. It spoke volumes that Ahiko had barely talked. He meant to act quickly and quietly. Star had no issues with that. He lowered his head, gesturing for the pilot to take the lead.

Ahiko passed him by, edging toward the channel of water. He flashed Star a look before sinking to his knees. A sigh escaped his lips as he eased himself into the water, taking care to minimize the noise.

Star leaned and squinted to get a better look down the passage. The crackling sounds echoed down the way, but the path remained dark. Odd. He would've thought something that loud would have made as much of a scene to go with the noise.

Ahiko hissed through his teeth, beckoning Star with a jerk of his head.

Star kept his hand on the revolver as he entered the channel the way the pilot had. There was no point in rushing things now that they found what they needed. A gentle throb filled his skull as water encircled him. His thoughts went to his coat, but he suppressed the flicker of annoyance in having it get wet again.

Comfort and ease were luxuries—and not ones he'd signed on for. He repeated the mantra to himself as they slogged through the furrow. Minutes passed before Ahiko stopped in front of him. Star froze, leaning to look past the man. The air in his lungs felt like it had crystallized into ice.

A pair of soldiers, clad in black armor, stood at the sides of an engineer. Fortunately, their backs were turned to Ahiko and him.

The man at the center was close enough to Ahiko's description to warrant taking a chance at subduing them all: a middle-aged, dark-skinned fellow with a shaved head. He wore the same sandstone gradient clothing as the soldiers from earlier. A hefty, cylindrical pack hung from his back. A simple, flexible tube ran from it into a lengthy rod in his hands. The crackling sounds emanated from the device's tip. A heavy, black shield sat to the side of the cutting tool, obscuring the light emanating from it.

Star didn't like the idea of engaging the armored soldiers. He wasn't sure if he'd managed to kill any of the ones before. The revolver shook, forcing him to tighten his grip to help settle his nerves.

Ahiko swallowed, gesturing to the two armored soldiers with a finger.

Star remained silent.

The pilot pointed at the revolver then to the guard to the left. He extended his index finger and thumb like a mock pistol.

Star quirked a brow and bowed his head in the direction of the remaining guard.

Ahiko held up a finger. He pointed to the guard closest to him before flashing another finger. He repeated the motion to the man closest to Star before raising two fingers.

First. Second. At least, I hope. He nodded and kept his concerns to himself. It was likely Ahiko meant to deal with his target before Star did. The man had no weapon, but he had to have had some semblance of training in the matter.

Ahiko pointed below, sinking his weight until the water touched his nose. He crept out and motioned again to Star.

He got the hint and swallowed as much air as he could before submerging. His gaze stayed fixed on the surface of the water. *Man better know what he's doing.*

Ahiko's hand slapped against the water as he sunk beneath the surface in a smooth, controlled manner.

Star put both his hands to his weapon and sunk his weight until his bottom touched the base of the channel. The tip of the revolver aimed at the edge. He had an idea what the pilot was planning.

Ahiko flexed his fingers like he was anticipating a hands-on fight.

Star took note of that, playing a mental scenario in his head of going from his target to Ahiko's.

One of the guards broke over the edge and peered down. He pointed his weapon to the spot where Ahiko sat.

The pilot surged from the water, grabbing hold of the man's ankles and dragging him into the channel. Ahiko held the man in a bear hug and refused to let his grip be broken by the thrashing.

Another figure loomed over the water-filled furrow.

Star fired twice. The rounds struck the armored soldier's torso within a microsecond of each other, washing over his midsection and driving him back. He spun and focused his aim on the man in Ahiko's grip.

The pilot pushed the armored man toward him.

Star fired without pause. Each blast impacted a portion of the armor, sending the man spiraling into the wall. The light flared against the black protective gear then dissipated as if it were absorbed. Star looked at his weapon and then eyed Ahiko.

The pilot pounded a fist to his chest, opening it and splaying his fingers wide before dragging the hand across his torso.

His assumption was correct: Their armor possessed

the capability of dispersing the energy from his revolver. They were most likely unconscious from the impact.

So long as they were out of the way. If a man got too picky about their blessings, chances were they wouldn't get any more.

He rose and placed a hand on the edge of the channel.

Blue light flashed, striking the surface of the water by him.

Star ignored the bolt and eyed the engineer. "Don't. Just don't."

The engineer quivered in place, the cutting torch dangling at his side from a strap. The slender pistol shook in his grip and he pivoted, training it on a spot beside Star.

Star glanced to his right and found Ahiko leaning against the furrow, staring at the engineer. He faced the engineer and fixed him with a look. "You shoot my pilot, I shoot you. Not good odds."

The gun shook harder in the engineer's hand.

"We've got no cause to kill you." Star raised his free hand. "Breathe."

The soldier followed his advice, taking a series of short, ragged breaths.

"Slower. Think. If we wanted you dead, we'd have shot you already. Way I remember it is that you shot at me." Star lowered his gaze to the spot the engineer had fired at. "I haven't shot back."

The man's hand stilled a tad.

Star hoped it was because the engineer had calmed and not because he was taking aim.

Thoughts raced through his mind like a meteor shower. A wrong move could set the engineer off in panic, and that often led to worsening a situation. The more questions you fed a man, the more they tended to overthink things. Sometimes it was easier to let him know what to expect. Star eased his open hand to the edge of the channel, taking a grip. "I'm going to pull myself out now."

The engineer blinked several times. He nodded a moment later.

Star clambered over the edge and straightened himself. A gentle splash prompted him to look to the source.

Ahiko climbed out beside him.

Star eyed the engineer, watching to see if the unexpected action caused the man to grow twitchier.

It didn't.

He exhaled a long breath through his nose as quietly as he could. "I'm going to put my weapon back in my coat, okay?"

The engineer didn't say a word.

Star took it as a sign to go ahead. He brushed aside his jacket, holstering the weapon. "It'd make me feel a mite comfortable if you were to show me the same courtesy."

Ahiko frowned at him, the look saying what he'd done was stupid.

It was a possibility, but sometimes trust went further than a shot ever would.

"This is the part where you lower you gun." Star inclined his head, eying the holster at the man's hip.

The engineer took a moment longer than Star would have liked, but he stowed the weapon. "What do you want?" He glanced to Ahiko before settling on Star.

"That cutting torch of yours and a way out of here, if you've got that that is." Star arched a brow. "Do you?"

"I do, but I need this." The engineer grabbed the torch and raised it. "There's something behind there." He hooked a thumb to a steel door behind him that looked fashioned out of portions of a ship hull.

"What's back there exactly?" Star took a step forward, keeping his right hand in the air, fingers splayed.

The man shook his head. "Not sure, but it needs to be checked out."

That it does.

Star noted a hint of effort in the man's voice. His words came out a bit too clear and smooth, like they were practiced. "Could've sworn I heard a touch of accent in your voice."

The engineer's mouth twitched.

"You're not from the inner circle of planets, are you?" Star took another step.

The soldier shook his head.

That's something.

Star pulled his hand to his chest. "So, you're like me then. We're both from out of the way, blue collar working men. Let me guess, you joined the military to get out, see the galaxy—grab a touch of better schooling. That about right?" Star took a pair of steps closer.

The man nodded.

"I can understand that. All I'm asking now—person-to-person—is that you tell me a bit more about what's behind that door. The way out would be a nice touch too."

The engineer swallowed and shook his head like he were in disagreement with himself. "Yeah, fine. Was ordered along with a handful of others to scurry over the place. Do a sweep." An outer-circle accent flooded his voice as he dropped the practiced tones. "Did my job. Looked around with them two"—he nodded toward the channel—"found nothing till we came 'round here."

Star took another step. "And?"

"Was odd, that's what. Got blips of something leading us this way. Readings were like a drive core for a ship, but not any I've ever seen." The engineer's lip pulled down into a frown. His brows followed, knitting together.

Star had an idea as to what the core had come from. And he hoped to hell he was wrong. He thought about what Shazhan had told him earlier about scraping their Elan ship.

"I got muddled results. Soon as we got to the door, I scanned again." The engineer's frown deepened. "Got something radioactive coming from in there."

Star matched the man's expression. "Radioactive—nuclear?"

The man shrugged. "Possible, can't figure out why I'm reading a drive core, though."

"Something along the lines of alien—Elan, maybe?" Star dropped the caution and closed the distance.

The engineer backpedaled until his back was against the door. "Could be, why?"

Star glanced to Ahiko before pressing a hand to his face. "Shazhan told me they'd left their core lying around as an insurance policy for something like this." Star gestured with a hand around him. "What good's a core lying around?"

Ahiko's eyes seemed to double in size. "Given their fondness for blowing up bits of their own caves and canyons—"

Star rounded on the engineer. "How hard's it to rig a core to blow?"

The man stammered, at a loss for words.

"How hard?" Star's voice echoed through the passage.

"Nothing you couldn't do with a bit of time. Wouldn't be too hard to build a dirty bomb, add in the right materials and all." The man shrugged, clearly unaware of what Star was hinting at.

He grabbed the engineer's collar and pulled him close. "And that about fits the readings you've been getting, right?"

The man's eyes widened. He turned and looked to the door. "There's a dirty nuke right behind us."

CHAPTER THIRTEEN

HELL OF A GAMBLE

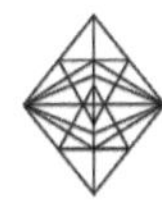

Star loosened his grip. "How big is that boom going to be?"

The engineer's mouth moved without sound as if he were trying to remember how to speak.

"How big?" Spittle left Star's mouth.

"No way to be sure. Likely bet it'll take a sizeable chunk out of the canyon. What, with all the magnetic ore buried in this place, it'll play hell on any scanner in the region. Good odds that interference will blanket the area. Any ship in space with an eye down here won't see shit." The engineer's chest heaved, and sweat beaded his forehead.

Star reached out and grabbed the torch, giving it a gentle tug. "I'm going to need this, and you're going to need to tell us how to get out of here."

The man hesitated.

"Now!" Star ripped the torch from the man's grip,

reaching out to unbuckle the power-pack. His fingers worked the clips that held the harness to the engineer's back and shoulders. The pack slipped from his body, falling into Star's grip. He tugged the pack via the straps and released a small grunt of effort.

"A few minutes down that way"—the engineer pointed down the passage ahead—"there's a makeshift service lift. Thing's cobbled together from scrap metal, ship parts, and an actual lift system. Rickety, but does the job. There's a fair share of them throughout this place. That one leads out to the canyon floor. Good bet it's one of the ones the Elan use to get in and out of this place."

Star glanced to Ahiko, and they exchanged a nod. "Works for us." He clapped a hand to the engineer's shoulder in what he hoped was a reassuring gesture. "Now, you've got a couple of choices. You can stay here and hope that bomb doesn't go off. Or, you can warn everyone you can and get the hell out."

The man stammered.

"Don't think. Do. Pick, man, and move!" Star shoved him by the shoulder and turned in the direction the man had pointed. He slipped the pack onto his back, fastening the buckles. The weight wasn't as bad as he'd thought. Most of it settled along the center of his back and wasn't any more than an extra twenty pounds. *It all adds up, though.*

Ahiko broke into a jog ahead of him.

Seeing the pilot take off with a renewed sense of strength galvanized Star into sprinting after him. The wet clothing acted like a second skin lined with lead. Acid burned his tendons and sinew, but he worked to bury the pain.

Pain meant he was alive. Pain could push a man forward as much it could drag him back.

Molten metal clung to the insides of his chest, biceps, and legs. He let the heat fuel him and drove himself harder. Every breath raked the lining of his throat as he drew closer to Ahiko.

The pilot had the grace to shoot a quick glance over his side and notice him. He kept quiet, however.

Star understood. He had little energy and adrenaline left to fuel himself. The passageway blurred into a charcoal smear as he ran harder. He didn't know what would give out first: his muscles or his lungs.

Ahiko's pace slowed ahead, and he made a weak gesture to something coming up on their right.

Star looked in the direction the pilot had pointed. A break in the wall illuminated by light filtering down from somewhere. *I'll take that as a sign.* The simple fortune invigorated him to ask a little more of his body.

The pair of them came up to the exposed section in the tunnel wall. It was exactly as the engineer had described. A rudimentary lift crafted from various bits of ship pieces and machinery. The platform was metal landing without any sort of cage or rails to secure the occupants. A pair of levers sat to one side. It wasn't difficult to gather what they did. Six heavy-duty chains ran along the wall up and out of sight, most likely the mechanisms to drive the lift.

Star followed Ahiko onto the platform. Both levers were marked with arrows indicating their direction. Star lumbered over and grabbed hold of one. He wrenched the rod upward, eliciting a series of resigned clicks from the contraption. The lever locked into place.

Metal rattled like it would come loose from the machine coming to life. The floor jerked as if it intended to shake them off.

Star fell to all fours, using it as a reprieve to rest and keep his balance.

Ahiko mirrored him.

The lift groaned and ascended, dragging itself upward. Bits of metal screeched as they scraped against the wall.

Star noted long gashes in the stone around them. The lift had been crudely fashioned into the chasm, likely having taken bits of the wall along with it during earlier uses. A low murmur caused him to turn.

Ahiko lay on his back, a forearm pressed against his head. He grumbled beneath his breath.

"What's wrong?" Star eased himself onto his bottom, not going as far to lie down. He didn't think he'd be able to get back up if he did.

The pilot waved a lazy hand around their surroundings. "Hell, what's right? Nothing." He sounded like he were speaking more to himself, trying to work through the series of difficult circumstances. "Just thinking aloud is all."

The lift shuddered. Star eyed the walls, noting that the elevator coasted upward without contacting the stone. He turned his gaze up and squinted. Bits of untouched rock crumbled and fell free to pelt the metal patchwork they rode on.

Another shake—deeper than before.

The sound of an approaching thunderstorm echoed down from above, amplified by the elevator's chamber.

Ahiko pushed off a hand and rose. "That don't sound inviting."

Star sighed. "Inviting ain't the choice of word I'd use when concerning us. We've been none too welcome wherever we've gone."

"Think that's got more to do with you than me. I only just joined this ride. Still harboring a bit of regret on that one." Ahiko let out a light snort.

"Me too."

The pilot blinked and looked at him. "What was that?"

Star shook his head, fighting not to smile. "Nothing." He took a cue from Ahiko and pushed off, getting to his feet.

Another quake rolled through the earth, jarring the lift.

Both men yelped and fought not to fall to their sides.

"What's going on up there?" Ahiko placed a hand to his brow and gazed toward the ceiling.

"I don't know, but it can't be worse than what we're leaving behind."

Star's comment sobered the pilot, who lowered his hand and took a breath to steel himself. Ahiko faced him with a thin smile on his lips. "Since meeting you, I've felt like I've been going from the frying pan into the fire. Getting worried I'll soon be ending up in someone's belly—for good."

"I'm not. You're likely to give any and all parties a serious case of indigestion. Stars and skies know I've got trouble stomaching you at times." Star kept his face neutral as a wounded look crossed the pilot's.

"You know, Shepherd, some might consider

employment with you a hostile work environment. I oughta sue." The smile on Ahiko's face deepened, becoming something a bit more genuine.

Star let out a laugh that racked his lungs and morphed into a short cough. "You go ahead and do that. You'll get about what the government gets out of me." Star spat.

"If that's what you're paying, you can keep it. Downright unhygienic." Ahiko shuddered.

A wave of light filtered in, larger than the scant illumination earlier. It grew by the second as the lift slowed its climb.

Stone shook like it'd been struck by a colossal hammer.

Both men staggered as one corner of the lift struck the cavern wall, digging in and refusing to let go. Chain links went taut on one side, and the platform jerked to an angle. The makeshift metal panel dipped, working to upend both men into the stone and send them below.

Ahiko and Star fell flat, grabbing onto the higher side of the platform.

Star grunted as an unrefined edge of metal dug into the soft flesh of his palm. Another shake nearly caused the material to slice through skin and meat. He winced, setting his jaw until his teeth ached.

The lift rose as if it were suspended by a drunken puppet master. Bits of chain ground and quivered as they tightened. The inevitable came. A link snapped, sending the platform seesawing and jarring the other chains.

Star loosened the grip of one hand, rolling to his side and glancing up.

A ledge stared back at him.

Helluva climb, but possible. He looked to the far corner that dipped lower than the others. One misstep and his own momentum could carry him to the edge and off. Ahiko followed his gaze and glanced to him.

"I don't know what you're thinking, but I'm already not a fan. I may have the looks of an angel, but I sure as heck can't fly. No way I'm falling." The pilot kicked his legs against the platform, sliding up and gaining a bit of relief in his hanging position.

Another chain vibrated in a manner that would lead to a single outcome—breaking.

Star nodded to it. "We can sit here, holding on until this breaks and get a free ride down."

The pilot glared.

"Or we can take a leap of faith." Star jerked his chin to the ledge above.

Ahiko's brows shot up, and his eyes widened. He gave him a look of silent condemnation.

Snap. A second chain broke and tilted the platform further.

Star took a breath.

Sometimes all a man needed was a crazy leap to get to where he was going.

He tucked his knees to his chest and released his grip. Star slid across the metal base, using it to build momentum. He slammed his legs into the platform and pushed off, rocketing up with a jump. His body sailed by the edge and he lashed out with a hand.

Hot agony streaked through his fingers as he managed to grip the ledge. The small digits strained from the impact and weight. He could feel the joints and sinew stretch. Star shifted his weight and swung his other hand up, clamping onto the stone shelf. He screamed, using it to wash away his pain and fatigue as he hauled himself up. His fingers throbbed from smacking and dragging across the rough stone.

Ahiko cursed below, scrambling to keep from falling.

Star reoriented himself and leaned over the edge, extending an arm. "Let go and jump toward me!"

The pilot flashed him a look before glancing at the failing chains.

Another rumble rippled through the ground. The chains shivered under the added stress.

"Last few yards; don't overthink this, man. Jump!" Star motioned with his hand, trying to pull the pilot out from his fears. Sometimes a man grew too occupied with all that he could do, should do, and the things that might never happen. In that, he forgets to just do anything at all. Star aimed to make sure his pilot remembered that. "Dammit, Ahiko Kohiba, get to your feet!"

The man did, his eyes snapping wide as if Star had slapped him. He shook his head and swore as if he were trying to rally himself. Ahiko placed his feet against the platform and pushed up to a crouch. He released his grip and ran, springing after a few steps.

Star leaned further, stretching his arm toward the pilot. Ahiko's fingers clasped around his wrist, squeezing hard. He held onto the man, ignoring the pain building in his shoulder. Star inched back, twisting and using every bit of his body he could to pull the pilot up. "You're hefty for a small guy." Star tugged harder.

"It's my wit and good looks, they're a ton of baggage

I just can't shake."

Star ignore the pilot's retort, using his other hand to push against the stone and add to his efforts.

Ahiko's free hand slapped against the ledge, his fingers digging in against the loose layer of dust and sand. He gripped the stone and pulled himself up.

Star climbed to his feet, using the muscles in his back to help draw the pilot along. He let go as Ahiko stumbled forward.

Both men doubled over, placing hands on their knees.

Star turned to get an idea of where they were.

A narrow path ran ahead through the canyon, breaking into another way. Howling winds cut through the chasms, echoing as they passed. The sky boomed like an invisible drum beat.

Ahiko's breathing eased a tad, and he straightened himself, looking ahead. His chest heaved as he pointed down to the break. "What's that look like to you?" He stopped to catch another breath. "About a few hundred yards?"

Star shrugged. "About."

"Think I saw a chasm like this off of the main canyon when I flew us over. Tried to clock as much of the features as I could." He winced, placing a hand against his lower back as he leaned and sucked in a breath. "Most of the canyon runs pretty near as straight as can be. Little breaks like this stood out."

Star stared at him in silence, unsure of what the pilot was getting at.

"Means we're likely not that far from your ship."

Star took the news as it was. Not far didn't mean close enough. There would be enough distance to cover to make it a pain. Star shrugged under the weight of the cutting torch and pack. They felt heavier given his recent exertion. He'd have to bear it and go on.

He rolled his shoulders and trudged forward, glancing to the pilot. "Which way after the break?"

Ahiko jerked a thumb to the right. "We're ahead of your bird, if I'm right."

"I'm not fond of when you are, but this time I hope so." Star moved on, leaving the pilot with a befuddled look on his face.

The rumbling spread through the canyon. It carried a sweeping wind with it. Stone and dust rained from atop the chasm, showering them as they broke into a jog. Darkness flooded the canyon, prompting the pair to look up at the source.

A starship screamed into view, several thousand feet above the canyon. Its mass drifted by in low atmosphere speed as it blotted out the sun.

Star put a hand to his forehead and eyed the ship. Epyon-class. *Son of a bitch.* The sight jarred him into realization. He whirled about to Ahiko. "What are the odds that ship's visible to anything out in orbit?" He raked the lining of his throat and hoped the pilot heard his scream.

Ahiko frowned, putting both hands to the side of mouth. "Damn good! It's above the canyon. Ain't nothing hiding it now." The pilot's cries were muffled, but audible.

Nothing hiding it now, but the mother of all bombs going off would do a fine job of that.

He lumbered forward as best he could. Fatigue and stress had done their number on him. He asked his body for more, but it refused. Star resigned to the fact and pushed on at a pace he could manage.

A cascade of red light streaked through the sky, screaming toward the Epyon-class carrier.

Star nearly stopped upon seeing the crimson beams cut across the horizon. Fear of the bomb galvanized him into keeping his momentum going.

The lances of energy impacted the Elan's ship, washing over an invisible barrier in angry waves of tonal red. Light flared in defiance of the shield before fading. The Epyon-class vessel turned the broad of its bulk to face the direction of the incoming fire. Viridian beams of light arced through the skyline, heading out of the atmosphere. The Elan ship fired without pause, peppering distant space with an endless salvo of green.

Red blasts answered back and struck the bulk of the starship. The shields shimmered a shade of soft lavender before vanishing.

Star found it a small relief that the vessel remained intact. His pace remained measured despite his body's protests. He and Ahiko neared the mouth of the break into the main portion of the canyon. Carmine light flashed above, strobing across the stone walls. Sand and debris hammered the path and his body. He lifted an arm to protect himself from the worst of the bombardment.

It felt like being a damn ant caught in a rainstorm, going unnoticed by heaven on high, still getting hammered by the downpour.

Star rounded the corner and looked to Ahiko for direction.

The pilot turned right, heading down the main

canyon way.

Star followed behind in hopes the pilot knew what he was doing. In his experience, Ahiko made his way through his life through uncanny luck more than skill. *Same could be said of me, though.*

Ahiko scanned the skyline as he put more distance between him and Star. A hand went to the pilot's forehead as he watched the battle above.

Star mimicked the action, glancing toward the ship.

A volatile exchange of light filled the horizon. Lasers passed by each other to sail onward to their targets. Some lances struck each other, blossoming into thunderous splashes of energy across the sky. Red and green strobed in a near-hypnotic display.

A lone thought kept him from being rooted in place. If they didn't move, there'd be a hell of a light show to overshadow the one they watched. He grimaced, ignoring the feeling in the back of his knees. The tissue felt like rubber bands stretching to the point where they'd snap. Thin streams of heat lined the sinews as he ran harder. Every breath of air felt like it was sending handfuls of sand to grate against his lungs.

Shrill cries tore through the drumming barrage of laser cannons. Streams of closely grouped lances rocketed into the forward section of the Elan ship. Lavender light cried back, sparking in retaliation as the shields appeared to wane.

Pushing something up against a wall left people with no choice but to fight back. It made them desperate. And desperate folk tended not to think clearly. They were sort of people that'd nuke a canyon to get clear.

Star put both hands to the sides of his mouth, letting

the torch dangle free at his hip. "Ahiko!"

The pilot glanced back.

"Run, don't stop. Don't think how tired you are—run!" Star smacked his hands together, miming an explosion, before jerking a thumb to the scene above.

Ahiko turned to look ahead and increased his pace.

Star did the same. Every step made it feel like the cutting torch ignited parts of his insides. The lining along his chest and throat burned with the acidic tinge of bile and dryness. *A bit farther. Eyes ahead.*

The exchange between the ships tugged at him, beckoning him to watch. He shut his eyes until the urge passed. When it did, he opened them to find a silvery-white ship dominating the view ahead. *Like a damn mirage. I'll take it, though.*

His body felt like it was held together by cheap glue ready to come undone under the heat and stress. He pushed anyway, deciding he'd fall apart on his own damn ship, and not this forsaken ball of hot dust.

A cocktail of anger and hope fueled him.

Rage was a hell of a thing. If a man got angry enough, he'd push himself harder than ever before. If he was given a hint of hope along with the anger, something else would come out of him.

Star gave himself over to the anger at being hunted. The searing heat and ringing bells racked his skull every time he thought of Admiral Cain and Autumn. And he clung to the hope that he'd fulfill the promise he made not so long ago.

Raw emotion flooded him, driving him toward *The Last Leaf* with his mind fixed on one thought: run. Star's feet hammered against the unforgiving ground of the canyon. Rogue blasts from the ships struck along the surface of the gorge, sending bits of stone leaping into the air, crashing to the ground in his path.

Dammit.

Ahiko had made it to the ship, taking cover near the rear hatch.

Star raced the last dozen yards and planned out the best course of action. Someone had to cut the tracker free. But the man to take them out of here was Ahiko. He shook his head, trying to keep self-preservation from dictating his decisions. Preemptively starting the thrusters would save them a bit of time. He'd have to climb up, start cutting the tracker free, and hustle back before Ahiko took off. It was doable.

I hope.

Coolness washed over him as he passed into the shade of the ship. He found no respite, however, shambling by Ahiko, onto the ramp to access the panel. Star jabbed his index finger against the screen. The ship quivered as Star entered another series of numbers. The hatch hissed, sliding open. He gestured to the pilot as *The Leaf's* thrusters roared to life.

Ahiko gave him a quick look then glanced at the ship. He raised a single brow.

Star gave him a thin smile and clapped the pilot on the shoulder.

Ahiko bowed his head a fraction before slipping into the ship.

Star stepped off the ramp, smacking a hand onto a rung on the ladder. He clambered up and convinced himself this would be the last bit of effort for the day. A part of him knew it was a lie, but the comforting lies were the easiest to believe in his experience.

He pulled himself onto the wing, finding his balance. The urge to turn and watch the battle grew. Star wasn't looking for a reminder of Autumn. Not if he could help it.

Tangerine skies, washed with strawberry, blurred through his mind. Bands of red light had sailed through the horizon and struck the ground, spreading out like waves to encompass the earth.

Star shook his head clear of the memory and plodded forward across the ship's surface. He made his way to the spot from earlier, kneeling beside the tracker. The smooth rod of the plasma torch sported a single toggle switch in the center of its mass. He flipped it, eliciting a web of crackling energy from the tip of the device.

Nothing happened.

The sound of the battling ships grew.

If that ain't a sign to hurry. He smacked a hand blindly against the power pack. His fingers brushed against a textured knob. Small bumps ran along its outside, almost like it was a dial. He turned it.

A sound like rushing liquid emanated from the pack. Halogen light flashed at the tip of the torch before erupting into a narrow beam of plasma. The concentrated cone crackled and pulsated.

Star brought the end of the energy flames to the center of the tracker, holding it there. The plasma passed through the device without resistance. It sparked in defiance before its metal furled away from the energy and blackened. He dragged the cone of energy around the outside of the tracker, keeping close to it as well.

There was no need to scratch up his ship more than necessary.

My ship? I'm already getting attached. It's cargo. Carry it. Deliver it. Be done with it. Move on.

He completed the pass, turning off the torch before bashing its base against bits of the tracker. They shook free of their hold, and a few pieces tumbled across the ship's surface.

The Last Leaf vibrated as if in response to his thoughts, and the thrusters screamed louder.

Shit. He raced toward the ladder, shrugging free of the pack. The canyon looked to sink around him. *No, no, no.* A strap clung to his wrist still and forced him to pull it free. He twisted, hurling the torch and power source into the canyon wall.

The ship rose further.

Star doubled his momentum before sinking his weight and sliding. He skidded along the surface and passed over the wing. His lashed out with a hand, striking one of the ladder's rungs. Metal smacked against his fingers, and he lost his grip. He winced as his wrist banged against another step before he closed his fingers around it. His shoulder bore the brunt of his weight, threatening to tear the ligaments inside. His dangling position gave him a precarious view of the ship battle.

Another salvo of red lasers showered the Elan's vessel, the lavender shields flaring in response. Each flash was less pronounced than the last.

The shield was about to give way. Star winced, fighting to keep his grip on the ladder as the ship climbed. It was a good thing Ahiko didn't pull up the landing gear. All he'd have to do to get rid of Star was a press a button, and he'd be a free man. The fact he hadn't spoke volumes about the pilot in Star's mind.

Soft purple energy plumed from the ship's bow, cascading along the vessel's body like rain before dissipating. The next attack would cut right through the front. They were done.

His eyes widened as the Epyon-class ship's thrusters increased in intensity. *They're going to jump—from in atmosphere? It's suicide.* His heart somersaulted. *Suicide is sitting above the canyon chancing a nuke.* Star rolled, using *The Last Leaf's* momentum to aid him. His ribs banged against the metal ladder, but he grabbed hold with his other hand.

Don't be stupid. He glanced at the boarding ramp before looking at the Elan's ship. *Stupid's come and gone. I miss this, I die. I don't do it, I die.* He shut eyes for a moment, tensing his body.

His ship tilted as it maneuvered through a narrower part of the canyon.

Dammit. The ramp seemed to sway in front of him, taunting him. He jumped as the ship steadied its climb. Star's arms flailed as he sailed down toward the ramp. The inner parts of his biceps and forearms screamed as they hammered into the unforgiving metal. He clawed the ramp, trying to find a better hold.

The distant sky was eclipsed by verdant green that grew to wash out any other color in the horizon.

The Elan were letting everything go on this last chance before they scuttled. He watched the Epyon vessel's thrusters throb further as they built a final surge of propulsion. *Don't want to be around for this.* He screamed, kicking his legs and using the momentum to climb onto the ramp. It wasn't a time for reprieve. Star scurried forward, clasping a hand to one of the thin beams that held the ramp to the body of the ship.

The Last Leaf rose from the mouth of the canyon.

Star turned and used the last bit of energy to rush through the boarding hatch. His body overwhelmed his will as fatigue won and he collapsed against the metal frame of a nearby shelf, clinging to it with a hand.

The ship's hatch began to close.

A flash of light rippled through the canyon, making its way into the sky. Fire blossomed across the sky and washed out the sight of the Elan's ship. Rolling thunder echoed from the gorge and across the horizon. The fire rolled toward *The Last Leaf* like a wave.

Oh, hell.

CHAPTER FOURTEEN
THE LIGHT

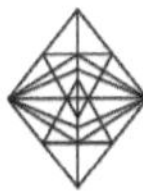

The hatch snapped shut, and the world rushed by him as his grip broke on the shelf. Star tumbled like a ragdoll into the door. The side of his body and skull throbbed, his vision cutting out for an instant.

Deafening screams from the thrusters reverberated into boarding hall.

The ship accelerated, trying to pull them away from this mess. Star couldn't blame Ahiko for pushing the vessel as hard as he was. He didn't know if *The Leaf's* shields could take that in flight, and Star wasn't sure he wanted to find out either.

The metal around him shivered like it was afraid of the coming blast. Star sympathized with the ship before realizing what he was doing. *It's cargo. Don't get attached.* He repeated the words before turning to trudge into the central hub of the *Leaf.*

Drums pounded outside the ship, sounding like

they'd shake apart *The Leaf* from their force alone.

Was always a guitar man myself. Never did fancy drums. He lurched into the central hub, teetering as the ship banked. Star blinked several times as his mind urged him to shut his eyes.

Not yet. He lumbered on, keeping his eyes fixed on the hall leading toward the cockpit. His hand went to the side of the passage to help brace himself. An incoherent stream of shouting, tinged with profanity, graced his ears as he drew closer to the front of his ship.

"—damnable, sky-on-fire, cocky Shepherd…"

Star guessed it was too much of a hope for Ahiko's mouth to have learned to stay shut after all of this. He made his way into the cockpit, plunking into the copilot's seat.

Ahiko ignored him. Sweat beaded his forehead, droplets rolling down his brow. He refused to wipe the rogue bits going into his eyes and chose to blink through them.

Star mentally applauded his focus. He opened his mouth to speak, cutting himself off as Ahiko's brows knitted together. The last thing he needed was someone nagging. Star yanked the harness around him, fastening it. Unsure of where to look, he focused ahead until the horizon looked bend and warped at the edges.

A man can go anywhere—as far as he wants—so long's his eyes are on the sky. Don't take them off. Just look and go. His father's words played through his head without stopping as *The Leaf* rocketed through the air. The trip hammer guiding his heart slowed, and the screaming in his mind followed. He repeated the words until everything quelled inside him.

The thundering overtook the sounds of the ship. A tint of orange cast itself onto the sky before them, looking like it would roll back and cling to *The Leaf*.

Ahiko swore.

Star shut his eyes, unable to escape the glare making its way through his eyelids.

The Last Leaf quivered like an insect caught in a gale. An alarm blared, picking up in volume by the second.

Ahiko's voice fell to a muddled string of grumbling.

Star peeked to see what the pilot was doing. He wished he hadn't.

The man's hands danced along consoles before brushing by a navigation monitor. His eyes scanned the screen before pecking several keys at once.

Star glanced at what Ahiko had. "Wait!" He lunged to smack the man's hand away.

The pilot slammed his palm into the throttle, taking a page out of the Elan's intended playbook.

"Don't jump us from in here!" Star held firm to the armrests.

The world outside the cockpit skewed like a hand had pulled it to the side. Colors and the distant landscape blurred like they were made from water.

Star's head snapped into the seat's rest as everything warped from view.

***

He had always found it odd how some people viewed open space as a cold void peppered with the smallest bits of warmth. They saw it as something barren, a lifeless sea to seek refuge from. So they rushed and clustered on the nearest habitable world. The only times they left was to race to another place to touch down on.

Star stared into the blackness, finding it an inviting blanket wrapped around him. It was everywhere he looked—constant—sequined with motes of distant light, some closer than others.

A shepherd's born and raised in space. Stars and skies are his guiding light. You're never lost when you've got those, even when you think you are. His father's words eased the day's weariness from him. Star's fingers went to the clasps of his harness, undoing them so he could slump easier in the seat.

Ahiko sat to his side, silent and hunched over the console.

Man's earned it.

Star glanced out the window, enjoying the simple pleasure in viewing space.

Opalescent green and blue filled the space straight ahead. It was like staring at turquoise seas harboring sets of emerald waves within them. Orange cloud, tinged with marigold, threaded the outer edges of the nebula. Portions of the astral emission raced into the center of the mass.

If this hunk of space had a set of teeth, that'd be it. And it's still so damn beautiful.

He forced himself to tear his gaze away from the pleasantry of space and looked to the monitor Ahiko had before their departure. It was a miracle they hadn't shaken themselves to bits with that stunt. Star's lips pressed together and his eyes narrowed as he shot a look at the pilot. He reined it in after deciding that

Ahiko's performance in saving them outweighed his recklessness.

And Star wasn't one to talk about being wild.

A myriad of dull aches ricocheted through his body, making themselves aware now that every reservoir of adrenaline had been drained. He felt it best to let his mind wander in the hopes it would take some of the pain with it.

Another nebula hung in the distance, silently calling for his appreciation. It looked like the last half of a rainbow had been forced into a pool before something had smeared the colors. Ethereal wisps of amethyst flitted into a tight circle. Ghostly lines of jade cut random paths through. A heavy mass of cobalt and violet swirled through most of the space.

And none of it did a thing to tell him where they were. He glanced at the monitor again. Nothing. The screen displayed a static image of where they had been.

Star's muscles felt like they were liquefying. He succumbed to their urges, reclining back and releasing a sigh.

Ahiko stirred in his seat and grumbled to himself. *And here I thought he'd shut up when sleeping.* A low, rumbling groan built in his chest, passing through his lips as he sank deeper into the chair. He glanced at the monitor again, hoping it had sorted itself out.

The monitor flickered before returning to the static display from earlier.

Damn equipment's taunting me.

The screen blipped again.

He exhaled, placing his palms against the ends of the arm rest. Star summoned what little energy he could and pushed off. His body teetered as he came to a shaky stand, forcing him to lean onto the console for support.

Ahiko released a deeper groan, muttering incoherently as he roused. He blinked several times at the view ahead. "That's something."

"It is."

The pilot let out a yawn louder than seemed necessary, going so far as to arch his back and stretch his arms. His lips smacked together, and he faced Star. "So, where are we?"

Star met his stare. "You tell me. You brought us here."

Ahiko frowned like he had issue with that train of logic. "I *brought* us out of trouble. Didn't mean to bring us *here*. Slight difference in those two actions, I'll have you know." He crossed his arms and leaned back in the chair like he was pleased with himself.

"Knowing you as well as I've come to, I have to say there's a slight difference between how you and I see those actions. They're two halves of the problem"—his stare deepened before he let the heat out of it—"thank you, Ahiko."

The pilot's face slipped into an expressionless mask, contorting like it was trying to sober.

Star had to admit, he found mild satisfaction in flummoxing Ahiko.

"Glad to know my talents are appreciated here." The hint of swagger and cheer returned to the pilot's voice as he eased out of his seat.

"They are, and, here, it's appreciated if you help solve what needs solving." Star nodded to the monitor. "Been none to compliant with giving us our whereabouts." He eyed the pilot.

"Rough guess?" Ahiko raised a brow.

Star inclined his head.

"About somewhere there and between never there and nowhere at all. Think I'm accurate as can be on calling where we be." The man's mouth quirked.

Star winced, exhaling before pinching the bridge of his nose. "I'm going to need you to be a bit more accurate on the accuracy part of your assessment. Get it working."

Ahiko snapped his forefinger and middle finger to his forehead in a mock salute. "Yassuh." He smacked the rear of the monitor, eliciting a growl from Star.

"You ever find smacking something to work?"

Light filled the pilot's eyes, making its way into a mischievous smile. "Oh, Shepherd, I could tell you the loads of ways smacking something's behind has gone in my favor."

Star stared.

The grin slipped from the pilot's face. "Right. Just needs a few hours. It's from the fallout of the nuke. Likely scrambled and needs a bit to settle."

"Fine. We'll drift nice and quiet then. If it's played hell with our navigation, chances are it did the same to the military's?" He tilted his head, staring at Ahiko for confirmation.

The pilot nodded. "Way I figure, they've got no clue if we zipped out of that blast or not. We're clear unless someone happens by this way and makes sense of who we are. Odds on that are slim-to-none."

"Good. I'll take 'em." Star moved past the seat and headed for the passage into the main hub.

"And that's it? We're going to float about? Aren't we on a timetable to get what you've got where it needs to go?"

Star didn't stop, making it halfway into the hall before Ahiko's footsteps echoed behind him. He didn't turn around when he answered him. "Sometimes there's nothing wrong with floating. You're still moving, just slower than others is all. Sometimes you need to ease up to see all that's going by. It can help you find your way again. Keeps your mind on the bigger picture." He shrugged and passed into the main hub, looking at a corridor in the far right corner.

"Uh-huh. I'm processing that slow as I can, and it still sounds like nonsense."

Star ignored him and made his way into the far hall. The footsteps grew louder behind him.

"Don't suppose I can ask where you're going, since you seem to have an idea. I sure don't."

Star snorted. "You've got questions. I've got answers. If you want 'em, that is." He drummed a few fingers along the wall, finding solace in the gentle thumping. There wasn't any sound in space. Not really. Sometimes it helped to settle a mind if one made some noise of their own. He tapped his fingers a bit harder. Ahiko's footsteps created a discordant beat along with his drumming.

"Would be nice to see a bit of what I've dug myself into. Suppose there's no going back, is there?"

Star took a breath, mulling over the pilot's words. He'd believed along those lines not too long ago. "There's always a way back. It's one of the easiest paths there is. You've just got to want it is all." Star stopped and looked over his shoulder. "So, do you? Because all you have to do is say so, and I'll drop you off at the nearest civilized place. You can find a bar and go back to being a drunk."

Ahiko blanched and had the grace to look away. "Bit harsh."

Star supposed it was. "You're right. Sorry. I'm touchy about it, and you can imagine why. I've paid a lot to get this far. Lost more." His hand fell to the revolver. He pulled it away just as fast. "I'm getting this done. I have to. I'd still like to get that done with you." He gave the pilot a brief grin.

Ahiko returned it. "Fair enough."

Star gestured with a hand and set off, leading the way in silence. He kept his fingers bouncing off the wall. The process of walking toward his destination was close to automatic for him. He lost track of the passing minutes until coming to a door. Star leaned to the side of the thin sheet of metal, staring at a blue screen. He pressed his hand against it.

The door released a weak hiss before sliding open. Cool mauve lighting spread over the room from the corners. Every metal component caught a bit of the glow, taking on a bluish-purple tinge. The area lacked most of the equipment one would expect to find in an engine room. Paper-thin frames hung along the wall, holographic displays running between them. The structure in the center dominated the room.

A sphere floated where the ship's core should have been. It looked like a fractured shell, suspended in space and the color of some moons—a ghostly, iridescent white. The orb bobbed slightly, its surface pulsating like it harbored something within. Thin lines raced along it like cracks. Nothing seeped through them, however.

Star stepped into the room, beckoning Ahiko to join him.

The pilot did and remained silent as he scanned the area.

Star moved toward the center, his skin feeling like an electric charge built over it as he approached the sphere. Star raised a hand at the device. "This is what it's all been about."

Ahiko followed his gesture, taking a single step closer.

Star lowered his hand on the railing that ran along the outside of the orb. An opening behind it filled the floor, emanating a gentle glow the color of cotton. He dragged his hand across the metal frame until it came to rest on a small screen a tad larger than his head.

"And what exactly am I looking at?"

Star pressed his hand to the screen.

The sphere stopped bobbing as the cracks along its shell appeared to deepen. Something throbbed within, deepening its glow. The metal frame quivered like it desired to shake itself apart. Light seeped through the cracks as they parted, peeled away by unseen hands.

Star reached over to the other side of the railing, snagging a pair of dark goggles hanging over it. He tossed one toward the pilot. "Might want to pop these on while you've got the chance." He slipped his pair on, blinking as he adjusted to the tinted view.

The spherical shell broke and hung frozen in air. A miniature sun, made of snow-white, radiated ethereal light throughout the room. The orb pulsed and flared like a star. Rogue tendrils of energy lanced and bowed out from its core, snapping back into its mass like they were tethered by a rubber band.

Ahiko's breath seemed caught in his chest.

Star knew the feeling. It had happened to him the first time he'd seen it as well.

"Why's that, what looks like a tiny fire moon, where your ship's engine ought to be? Shepherd, what is this?" "Our real cargo. This is The Light."

CHAPTER FIFTEEN

A THORN IN YOUR SIDE

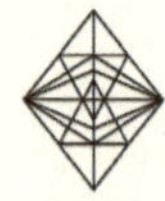

Ahiko's mouth shut before opening again, moving without sound.

Star let him work through it. The mental happenings within his head would be tangled trying to sort it all out. He'd gone through that himself when he'd first seen The Light. *Some things just need time to sit and settle.*

The pilot waved a hand to the orb. "I don't follow. We're hunted down low and high because of a giant glowing ball? It's"—he frowned—"dammit, it's not connected to anything!"

Shepherd nodded. "Beyond me too. Don't change the fact it's there. It's powering the ship."

Ahiko's eyes widened before blinking several times. "How?"

Star shrugged. "Efficiently—powerfully so, in fact. That's what I was told at least when I was hired to shepherd it to Slaydus." Star reached into his coat, drawing his revolver. He pressed a thumb to the cylinder and pushed it open. A glow, much like that of The Light, throbbed from within the weapon. He tilted it toward the pilot to give him a better view.

Ahiko eyed the gun and then the giant sphere of energy.

Star snapped his wrist, sending the cylinder back to its resting place. "Bit of that's in this. Engineers and scientists back on Autumn felt the need to make of point of The Light's power."

The pilot winced, placing a hand against his face and rubbing hard. "Why? What's the need for any of it?"

"You've seen me shoot this, yeah?" Star jiggled the revolver.

"Enough times to—" Ahiko stopped short.

"Right. Any other gun—powered or powdered— would have need some manner of reload. Not this. Wonder why?" Star stuffed the gun back into its holster, giving Ahiko a knowing look.

"That can't be right. Galaxy's been running fuel and cells since…hell, it's been so long can't fathom when it started. It's always been that way. There *ain't* nothing new, certainly nothing like that." He jabbed a finger to the weapon before snapping his hand in the direction of The Light. The pilot's limb shook as he realized what he had said.

Star couldn't tell if it was in anger, or the overwhelming understanding that came with the thought that must have crossed Ahiko's mind. "Right, and who controls all the fuel and cells? About sixteen to twenty families, if I'm counting right. Always was a bit shoddy at math, but think I'm in the park with this, yeah?"

Ahiko's face tightened and he shut his eyes, exhaling. "Yeah."

"They control every bit of anything needed to get somewhere, power something, hell, keep a man and his family warm and alive through the night. Government's just people, ain't it? They're bent over for the Oligarchy, and that makes those families mighty. They've got the goods, the power, and the money to back it. They *are* the government. Nobody pretends it ain't so." He stared hard at the pilot.

Ahiko looked away.

"So tell me, in all of that, why do you think their way's been the only way for so long you can't remember anything else?"

The pilot glanced to the ground before eyeing The Light. "Explains why they're after you—that—this." He pointed to the light. "How long's it last? What's it cost?"

"Forever. And a planet—it cost Autumn."

The words sobered the pilot, forcing him to still. "Oligarchs glassed a whole damn world"—he shook his head—"for this. I'd see why. Forever ... Shepherd, you know what this means?"

He nodded. "Wouldn't be carrying it if I didn't. This is a chance to free people. To power a galaxy on end forever. No more being led around by the few men and women with their hands on the leashes. People can have a chance to live without being told how much to pay for the 'privilege' of doing so."

The pilot rocked and sank to his knees, running a hand through his hair. "Forever." The word rolled out of his mouth like a hushed curse. "Hell, nothing lasts forever. Not without a price."

Star's lips went tight. He had to stretch his face to force them to move. "One that's already been paid. And it's going to cost us more, believe it."

Ahiko glanced at him, narrowing his eyes. "Let's hope not."

Star grunted in agreement.

"They don't know this, do they—the government? The Light is powering your whole damn ship. What do they think it is?"

He rolled his shoulders and leaned against the railing. "Not sure, and not sure I care. Let 'em think what they want so long as they're wrong. Makes it easier for us to get this where it needs to be." Star sighed, arching his back to release some of the stiffness. A series of small cracks rang out along his spine.

"Easier ain't easy, feel I should make that plain, Shepherd." Ahiko got to his feet and stared past him to The Light.

"No, it ain't."

A low, rolling laugh echoed through the space. Ahiko pressed a hand to his stomach as he bent. It looked like he was trying to keep himself from doubling over.

Star eyed him in silence, wondering if the pilot had lost it.

"You know"—he laughed hard—"I wanted to be a pilot."

Star tilted his head, staring at the man and then The Light. *Maybe it addled his brainpan.* He pushed off of the rail and crossed to the far wall, trying to put some distance between himself and the orb of energy. "You are a pilot. A damn good one." He hoped the compliment would jar the man out of his giggling stupor.

"Not like this, Shepherd." Ahiko waved a hand over his body as if the simple gesture explained what he'd meant. "Professionally—competitively."

Star shut his eyes, struggling to imagine the man as a racer. He supposed there were odder things in life. A thought crossed his mind, and he opened his mouth to speak. He shut the notion down, feeling it best to let the pilot go on. It was clear he had more to say.

A bright light filled Ahiko's eyes when he looked at Star. "It was a kid's dream, you know?"

Star didn't, but he nodded anyway.

"Didn't really think it through much. I just wanted to fly—be fast. Who didn't as a kid?" Ahiko leaned back, tilting his head as if he were staring through the ceiling and into space. A long sigh left his lips. "Used to look up and watch ships go by, wondering if I could do that. Thought the same when I watched the races. Saw them push birds like no one else could. The money never crossed my mind then, it was just fun—something pure."

Star understood that. He had nursed the same feelings about shepherding once, growing up in his father's lap staring out into open space. The universe seemed like a vast wonder to him. A galaxy was a tapestry of black splashed with cosmic colors and life. Shepherds got to see the whole of it, if they wanted. They could go anywhere, free of attachment. Life was a ship—open and able to sail anywhere. Nothing could root you down.

The laughter tinging Ahiko's voice faded, turning

into something brittle. "Part of me thinks I could've done it." The crack in his voice deepened. A glint of moisture lined the man's lower eyelids.

Star pretended not to notice.

"The whole of me regrets not trying. But, out on the outer edges, not much choice."

He nodded his head in silent agreement. It wasn't a choice he'd ever faced with living in space, but he understood the plight well enough. Everyone got handed circumstances that were none too pleasant. It didn't make life easy, certainly not fun, but it just was what happened.

"So, I did the only thing I could." Ahiko sounded like he was justifying something to himself.

Star let him. Sometimes the person a man needed to come clean with was himself. There was no harm in it.

"Joined the military." The pilot shrugged. "Wasn't bad. I travelled. Learned to fly and get my wings eventually." The dam broke, and molten metal and something ugly filled his voice. "Better I got, more I was asked to do things that didn't sit right."

Star's intestines roiled. He placed a hand to his lower abdomen, keeping quiet as the pilot continued his story.

"I was too dumb to think it through—or want to. Just did what I was told. Hell, everyone knew who pulled the military's strings. I didn't care. I was paid well and got to fly."

Star knew where the tale was headed.

"And it's fine. It's always fine, until you have to do things like bombing runs. Settlers on some world out on the edge of nowhere get uppity. You scare 'em a bit. But then some folks don't get scared. Their anger's a heavy thing. Keeps 'em fighting back. So you fight a little harder." He cleared his throat. "Sometimes you make decisions you can't come back from. That ain't saying much for the ones caught in those choices. Ain't nothing they can come back to." Ahiko's voice tightened.

Star swallowed, exhaling as lightly as he could.

"Gets bad enough that you start telling yourself little lies to bury the big truths. Things to bury the memories of what you've done. It's how you get by." Ahiko rolled his shoulders in what looked like a pained shrug.

Star could almost see the weight hanging around the man's neck.

"Long enough goes by, and it's too much. You get up to say something and you're smacked down." A fleshy *thwap* snapped out as the back of Ahiko's hand slapped into the palm of his other. "No good deed and all, you know?"

All too well.

"But when you've dragged yourself through enough muck and mud for them, they don't leave you to dry and drown it. It's bad for the image." A brittle smile made its way across the pilot's face. "*Honorable* discharge." He spat. "Ain't nothing honorable about what's going on behind their show." Heated gravel echoed in his voice.

Star stared at him, unsure of what to say to ease the pilot's ire. He decided the best course would be to splash a dose of here-and-now on the man to pull him from his thoughts. "Where's this heading, Ahiko?"

The pilot blinked several times. He cleared the stone and grit from his throat with a pointed cough, rubbing his neck. "Right. Right." He sounded like he was trying to remind himself rather than talking to Star.

"Point's this, Shepherd, I lost out on a lot of life because of the way things are—the way some folks made them to be. I thought I had a line on how to live my life the way I wanted. I didn't. I lost my dream because of this shit." Ahiko's hands balled into fists, a series of minute cracks ringing out from the knuckles.

"And I'm sorry you did, but it's never too late to get something like that back." Star gestured to the ship. "You've got a chance to be a pilot again."

"Thank you. I plan on taking it…wherever it goes." Ahiko returned Star's look, arching a brow. "Because I've got a feeling this ain't ending on Slaydus. You've got a thorn in your side over the government too. I can see that much."

Star averted his gaze.

"I mean to hit back—hard. This Light looks to be the way to do it. You've got me talking, might as well be honest. I'm not one for just seeing this package delivered. I want to—need to— know it does what you've promised me. Someone's got to see this free world of yours happen." The pilot's gaze hardened.

"Hopefully all of us." Star pushed off the wall, heading toward the panel before The Light.

The pilot grunted. "Way you said it sounds like you're expecting none of us to make it, Shepherd."

Star placed a hand to the panel. *Thought crossed my mind.*

The metal shell fell back into place. The Light vanished.

CHAPTER SIXTEEN

SOMETHING STUPID IN MIND

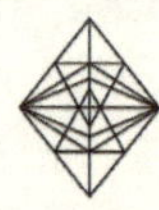

Star hooked a finger along the band of his goggles, tugging them free. A quick snap of his wrist was enough to loop them around the railing. "Come on." He turned and headed toward the door. "We've got a special package to deliver, and we're finally free of that tracker." He placed a hand on the door, prompting it to open, and stepped through. There wasn't a point in looking to see if the pilot was following him.

Star moved down the hall, listening to the thudding coming from Ahiko's boots as the man drew closer. "Glad to see you committed to this."

The pilot released a low grumble. "Got a chance to get even in the biggest game there is. It shifts a man's priorities."

That it does. Star picked up his pace, letting the metal of the halls blur until he approached the cockpit.

The navigation monitor had resolved its static

display issue, and now showed a clear reading of where they were.

Star scanned it over, mulling through his knowledge of space. He plotted out their position in relation to the nearest busy sector and relayed the information to Ahiko.

The pilot bucked, starting at him before glancing out into open space. "Why? Way I'm hearing it, we're not on any particular timetable."

We. Star fought not to smile.

"We show up on Slaydus, best we can, you do a little whistle, and your contact comes out. The Light's boxed and stocked—taken where it needs to be. What's the need in going through that bit of space to get there?"

Star opened his mouth before the pilot held up a hand. He shut it.

"I get the route. I don't get the point of it. You're taking us through a busy hub. One—I might add—that is in a pretty contentious state of being right now. Heard rumors of an embargo put in place on some of the worlds out that way. It's heavily enforced. Getting through won't be easy. Getting by ain't happening without being noticed." Ahiko stared hard at Star.

"You're looking at this the wrong way. You've got the eyes of someone in the military. Look at it my way, a shepherd's way. We're headed—if I have my way, that is—to a blockade. In all of that, there's people on worlds that need things they can't get." He returned Ahiko's look with a softened one of his own.

The pilot nodded.

"In places like that, you get people like me. Folks who want off the world to new places and can pay."

Ahiko's eyes bulged. "You're looking to risk our necks and tails to pick up work?"

Star gestured for him to calm down with a simple motion of his hands. "I'm not the only kind of person you'll find in a place like that. Just as people will want an honest way off their planet, some will want less than savory ways of getting what goods they need."

The pilot's eyes glassed over. His face tightened a moment later. "You mean smugglers." Ahiko ran his tongue along his teeth like the word left a sour taste behind.

"I do." Star eased himself into the copilot's seat, fastening the harness.

Ahiko's protests died as he sank into his chair and keyed a series of commands along the console. "I don't like this."

"You not liking things don't particularly fall into my main area of concern. It's discomforting; it's not going to kill you."

The pilot's eyes narrowed. "We don't know that." He seemed to be glowering at the console rather than directing at it Star.

He had no issue with Ahiko taking out his frustrations on his ship, so long as they remained harmless looks.

"Still don't see the need for it. We can skirt around the hubs and clear routes to Slaydus, take our time in getting there unseen." The pilot's fingers tapped against countless keys in automated precision.

"I still need to show you how to get things done, don't I?" Star forced himself not to smile. "Have a little faith."

The pilot grumbled something noncommittal under his breath before swiping a hand across the display screen. "A little faith and a lot of bad decisions are how you get into a whole mess of trouble." Ahiko side-eyed him before returning to his work on the console.

Star noted the man was taking his time in keying in their destination. He couldn't blame him. He was asking him to take them into a heavily populated area of space that a powerful chunk of the galaxy had spotlights shining on.

Sometimes the best place for a man to hide was among everyone else. It was easy to be washed out in the light, especially when it shone down on you. It had a habit of blinding anyone looking up. If you kept your eyes to the ground, you'd be fine. And you'd miss out on everyone walking by.

The logic held in his mind. He hoped it held in reality as well. Star didn't feel the overwhelming need to burden Ahiko with his thoughts. He had enough trouble convincing the pilot to take them where he wanted. Sharing the doubts wouldn't do anything but earn him another verbal sparring session. He felt it better not to trounce his employee more than a handful of times per day. It wore on their self-esteem.

Though Ahiko had enough of that for everyone in the galaxy. He could stand to be knocked down another peg or two.

Ahiko's hand fell to the throttle, resting in place. His brow furrowed, and he shut his eyes, breathing out through his nose.

Star recognized the signs of hesitation. There were moments to push someone into making a choice and leading them to make that decisions themselves. He saw it as the latter. "What happens if we take your route?"

The pilot blinked. "Worst of it is we take more time is all. Bit of an annoyance, skulking around uninhabited worlds and out-of-the-way routes. Nothing more."

He still didn't see what Star had. There wasn't an easy way for him to convince the pilot of the problems without making it seem like he were disregarding his idea. "And what happens in those vast, unoccupied, lightly traveled reaches of space?" Star left the question hanging in the air, knowing the pilot would catch on and finish the thought for him.

Ahiko's nose wrinkled and he took another breath. "Not much…"

Star remained silent and let the man run away with the question.

The pilot winced like he was trying to force an answer into his head. A low sigh left his lips, prompting him to rub a hand against his brow. "Only bit I've got is when I used to lead patrols through the open sectors at random. Boring stuff you give to freshly winged pilots and old dogs who've caused too much trouble" A crooked smile filled his face.

Star tilted his head, giving the pilot an oblique look.

Ahiko opened his mouth to speak before pausing. A light of recognition shone in his eyes. "Open space's got a habit of being prowled by smugglers and those looking to lay low. Half them"—he flexed the first two fingers on both hands like quotation marks—"'uninhabited' worlds still got some local population. Not enough to count as anything, but enough to do business of the illegal and highly frowned-upon sort."

Star gave him a knowing nod.

"And folks like me were sent out to spot them if we could. Stop 'em." Ahiko winced harder and sighed.

"Right. If we go lingering out on the edges of nowhere, we'll be seen in an awfully suspicious light. Any patrols come across our way will think to shoot first, ask later. I ain't keen on getting shot."

Ahiko stared at him.

"Again." Star raised a hand in a gesture of accepting defeat. "Not looking to be shot at anymore."

Ahiko held the stare, managing to fill the look with disbelief.

Star growled and turned to look out window. "Just get us to the Katearin Hub."

The pilot held the stare for a few more seconds before relenting. "Couldn't tell. Way it looked to me was you liked being shot at. What, with dragging me into firefights every other foot." The entire complaint had been just above a whisper, audible enough.

Star squinted at the pilot before pinching the bridge of his nose.

Ahiko eased the throttle forward, and the ship quivered.

The universe outside the glass warped and bowed along the edges like he was looking through a lens submerged in water. Space tilted as *The Leaf* angled away from the nebula and increased speed. Prismatic colors snapped into a blur racing by them as black and stretched starlight dominated their view.

Star averted his gaze, knowing the hypnotic blur would keep him enthralled and unfocused.

The pilot leaned back in the seat, shutting his eyes

and cradling the back of his head in his hands. He groaned, shifting in place. "So, what exactly *is* the plan aside from showing up unannounced in a heavily trafficked place in a spot of trouble and attention we don't need?"

"You ever lose someone in a crowd before? Faces blur. Everyone starts to look the same." Star followed his pilot's example, wriggling into the seat in what little comfort he could find. His muscles thanked him for adopting the poor posture. It'd catch up to him later, but it was an added relief in the moment.

"That only works if it's just you doing the lookin'. Not so much as when the whole crowd can be made to keep an eye out for you."

Star didn't let the pilot's reply rattle him. He released a lazy yawn, making it seem like he were brushing off Ahiko's objections. "How easy do you think it'll be for the government to turn those folks on us? Men and women whose worlds are locked down and cut from trade. People with nowhere to go and no help coming till they give back into a power that's got no love for them except for what those folk can pay up. People who just want to be free and would rather deal with smugglers to get their needs than official powers."

The pilot muttered.

"It's not easy, but you're going to have to start looking at the galaxy through my eyes, Ahiko Kohiba. And the way I see it is like this, we'd be a more welcome sight than any government or military vessel. What do you want to bet that military ain't even the ones holding the blockade? Likely private security companies owned by, who again?" Star snapped his fingers. "Right, the

Oligarchy. Odds are they're playing themselves off as just doing the bidding of the government. And we know who's pulling whose strings."

Star stopped, permitting himself a quick look out of the cockpit. The kaleidoscopic smear of colors pulled him into a near trance. He shook himself free of the lure and pressed the heel of both hands to his eyes. "Here's what I know." *You mean you hope.* "Any security ships and forces they've got will be aimed at keeping people out and in. They won't be looking for us, at least not as a priority. What else I know, being that I'm hunted and all, is that there's more words and pictures on how I look than what my ship is. As far as the government knows, the cargo's *on* the ship, not the ship herself."

Ahiko's eye's narrowed into slits. "I've got the awful feeling you're setting up to say and do something monumentally stupid. You're working another angle; I can feel it."

Star avoided the look. "Shepherds got good cause to go to an area of space like that. I could find honest work from neighboring worlds not put in a bind by the blockade."

The pilot grunted like he didn't believe a word Star had said. "Because you need the work?"

"Because any semblance of honest work and the passengers to vouch for the presumed honesty of their journey is a boon to the dishonesty I mean to use to slip our way to Slaydus." A wide smile forced its way across Star's face.

Ahiko blinked several times. "That's…horribly devious." He looked out of the window before turning back. "I like it. One problem: How do you plan on getting onto any of those worlds unseen and finding passengers—willing ones at that? And what do you plan on doing with the ship?"

Star's smile grew. "Smugglers do more than ferry goods."

Ahiko arched a brow. "And what exactly do you intend to smuggle?"

"Us."

The pilot frowned. "I knew you had something stupid in mind."

CHAPTER SEVENTEEN

AT A DISADVANTAGE

"Way your ship moves, Shepherd, we'll be there within an hour. So, do me the courtesy of explaining how this is going to work without leaving us at the mercy of the government? I'm not too fond of that outcome." Hot stone flooded the pilot's voice.

Neither am I.

"We'll set *The Leaf* down on the first planet we find that isn't under the blockade. I'll send out a call on some closed frequencies I happen to know and see who's looking to earn some coin."

Ahiko shot him a look that could have scoured old rust from metal. "Speaking of coin, I'm noticing my palms and pockets are feeling distinctively light." He made a point of patting his pants. "You've got money to hire folk apart from me. But I ain't been paid. Makes a man irritable."

Star snorted. "You were irritable before I hired you.

Bar on Terizen ring a bell?"

The pilot's mouth and nose twitched. He adopted dignified silence.

"Besides, I'm spending money to keep us from getting caught and enjoy a bigger payday. Thought that'd seem more enticing to you."

A lazy smile spread over Ahiko's face. "Hint of truth in that."

"More than a hint, I hope." Star released a heavy exhale that felt like it took more of his fatigue along with it. It was a short-lived relief. Thoughts rushed to fill the void in his mind, peppering him with possibilities to unfold ahead. He grimaced and worked to bury them all.

The blockade could harbor some military presence, though it was unlikely. *That doesn't mean impossible.* He breathed out again, hoping to flush the thought with it. It held on. *Maybe this is a bad idea.* Star rubbed a hand against the side of his head and clenched his jaw. Avoiding the military completely was out of the question. His best bet would be focusing on minimizing the exposure.

The pressure in his jaw eased, and he pulled his hand away. Following the train of thought led him to reassure himself that approaching the blockade would be the most suitable course of action to keep as low a profile as possible.

Traffic had a way of making people complacent—numb. Some folks would just want to usher people along or turn them away. Less scrutiny, more simple doing.

"You've gone quiet. That's a bad sign far as I'm

concerned."

Star let his head loll to the side as he glanced at Ahiko. "You sure you want to be making comments about talking less when you do all the talking?"

The pilot's mouth pulled to one side. He seemed to be considering his response. Ahiko's lips pursed and he looked out the window. "Fair enough, but call it a feeling—something else on your mind. I take concern with that. Your mind's done its fair bit of troublemaking for us."

He couldn't argue with that. "Hesitation. Worry. Trying to weigh things." The words fell with lead weight, dragging a silence behind them.

Ahiko's exhale was the only audible sound. The pilot looked at a loss for words.

Star committed that to memory in case he felt the need to ever quiet the man again. The way ahead wasn't clear, and all he had were broken points along the map. *And sometimes that's enough.*

He indulged the whisper in his mind, pulling along it to see where it led. His father's words echoed through him, reminding him of lessons past.

Knowing just enough is just that. It can be enough to get you to the next step in a journey, and from there, you can figure out the next bit. Rinse. Repeat. It's how great journeys are done. It's never simple. It's never straightforward. You do what you can to get where you can. When you need to rest—rest. When you need to pick up and move along, do it. Keep at it till you're there.

His father was right. Star just had to get to the Katearin Hub. He'd figure out the rest when he got there.

The blockade meant tensions were high, so the last

thing they would expect would be *The Last Leaf* and himself. He possessed authentic shepherding credentials, which could be used to pass by anyone unaware. *If they don't dig too deep and realize who I am.*

He winced and moved past the mental stumbling block. Smugglers were the trickiest option in his mind. If they got greedy, there was a chance they'd turn in Star and Ahiko. He'd have to find someone with a shred of honesty. His frown deepened as he thought that over. Honesty was a rarer currency than fuel in the galaxy.

Star shut his eyes and took a series of calming breaths. He balled his fists, bringing them down against the armrests. He peered to the side and found Ahiko staring back. "What?"

The pilot rolled his eyes, looking away for a moment. "Oh, 's'nothing. It's always a good thing when your employer loses his temper with a chair."

One of Star's eyelids twitched. The pilot was right, however. He repeated the process of deep breathing, ending it with a long exhale. "Every idea I've got has something that can go wrong."

Ahiko gave him a look, a hint of light hanging in his eyes. He said nothing however.

Star understood the meaning behind the stare and waved him off with a dismissive hand. "It wears on a person having everything you do—try and want to do—go wrong." He ran a hand through his hair, resisting the urge to grab hold and pull.

"I get that." Ahiko's gaze returned to the brilliant lightshow ahead. His voice turned distant and hollow. "Sometimes, no matter what you do right, things go wrong. I've seen enough of that in the military. Things just go wrong. Part of life. Nothing you can do about it. Get used to it. Get over it, if you can."

The people of Autumn never got that chance. They did everything right only to have everything go wrong.

The pilot was right, but that didn't mean it sat well with Star. His stomach churned as he processed the notion. "Were it only that easy." He sounded like he'd swallowed sand and ash.

"Easy's got nothing to do with it. It's just something that's got to be done. Do it or don't. Not many other options. Things are bound to go sideways, and when they do, you go with them if you can." Ahiko rolled his shoulders and gave Star a sympathetic look.

Star stared back, contemplating the shift in the pilot's behavior. Ahiko had almost sounded like his father for a moment. It was enough of a resemblance that he took the pilot's advice, settling himself in the chair. Just doing it seemed a lot simpler than would be. But maybe, sometimes things were simpler than they sounded. He looked out into space and replayed the possibilities lying ahead until the hour passed.

***

The tunnel of warped light and space snapped to a halt as Ahiko pulled the throttle.

A ring of octagonal-prisms hung in the distance. The scene reminded Star of looking at honeycombs where the warm colors had been replaced with cold silver and black paneling. Each ship kept a reasonable distance from the ones around it, forming more of a net than a wall. He turned to Ahiko, nodding out the window.

"Well, you were right about them being private security. Tigs—little ships fit for small crews and staff. No more than a dozen security officers on board, I'd say. Few personnel dedicated to ship-to-ship communications with the rest of the blockade. Makes keeping organized easy."

Star frowned, eyeing the edges of the formation. It didn't seem to end. A marbled orb of lush green and azure blue pulled his attention through the net. He peered through the gaps before glancing at the navigational monitor. "There's Martle. No way to signal past the blockade to the planet, I wager?"

Ahiko shook his head. "Way they're set up, any comms will pass through them first. As in intercepted and never passed along. It's a tight lockdown." He squinted at the ship's arrangement, turning to look at the ends like Star had.

"Unidentified ship, double Y-frame," buzzed a voice.

The pair exchanged glances before Ahiko gestured to the console. "All yours, cappun." He touched two fingers to his head as a mock salute.

Star grumbled and leaned forward, keying the communication. He took a breath and struggled for an appropriate response.

"Turn around and exit this space after identifying yourself." The unknown speaker's voice took on a harder edge.

"Can do." Star flashed a look to Ahiko for help.

The pilot seemed particularly interested in his fingernails, gazing at them like they were the most important things in the galaxy.

Star ground his teeth and looked out of the cockpit

on instinct. He reminded himself where they were, searching the blackness of space for other colors to break it up.

Deeper greens, the sort found in jungles, seeped through the far right edge of the blockade.

Star glanced at the navigation monitor. The world in question sat just outside the security ships and their net. He repeated the planet's name several times in his head. "Travelers, passing onto Lisba just out of the way of Martle. Mighty sorry to have come across whatever this is and inconvenience you."

Ahiko gave him a shrug that could have been a way of saying, "Worth a try."

Static crackled over the comms.

The pair exchanged another look before Star hooked a thumb in Lisba's direction.

Ahiko followed the gesture and inclined his head in understanding. His left hand went along the top of the console, programming a series of commands in waiting.

Star eyed the ships forming the barrier, narrowing his gaze on one in particular. He stared hard almost like the act of doing so would let him peer into the vessel.

"That's almost an attempt at identifying yourself. Name and a ship registration number." The sounds of heavy breathing flitted through the comm as the speaker likely riled themselves up making the request.

Star wondered if pushing them would lead to anything but trouble. There was the chance he could make them mad enough to overlook some things. But the possibility of them opening fire–or worse, calling the military—also existed. He pressed a button on the console, muting the comms. "Ahiko, how fast does word in the military travel?"

The pilot frowned and looked out to the net before turning back to him. "You wondering about my name?"

Star nodded.

"Can't be sure how much has been broadcast about me. I had to have caught some notice with that scuffle on Terizen. That's only if that ass reported in. With what happened on Azzip though"—his frown deepened—"can't be sure. Odds are I wasn't noticed for anything."

"Meaning you might be in good standing as far as the general public—security forces included—are concerned?" Star eyed him.

"Using my name's bound to spread. They'll run a check. Out here, it'll take a while, but it'll get done nonetheless." The pilot frowned.

"A while's better than being detained or worse now." Ahiko shrugged.

Star gestured to the console and keyed the communications back on.

The pilot breathed out a sigh and leaned forward. "Ahiko Kohiba." He rattled off his citizen identification number before pausing.

Star motioned for the man to continue.

"Um, like my colleague said, we're awfully sorry to disturbed this gathering of ships. I still remember my first ship club. We all met and hung out in a boring corner of space with our little birds, traded stories and bad food—"

Star suppressed a groan.

A different voice cut through the pilot's rambling. "Your citizenry check's come through clean. Shut up.

Answer these questions without excessive back talk." Their voice rang of cold stone and authority.

"Yes, ma'am. It is *ma'am*, right?" The pilot's mouth pulled to one corner and a hint of amusement entered his voice.

Star sucked in a breath through his teeth, swallowing a curse along with it.

"It's Hub Control Officer Sila Nepco, to *you*. Not ma'am, not sir, but what I said. Is that understood?"

Star held his breath, arching a brow at the pilot.

Ahiko nodded.

Star hoped the pilot understood the severity of the situation. Antagonizing the officer wouldn't do them any favors in getting by the blockade.

"Yessum. Understood clearly, not ma'am or sir." Ahiko lifted a hand to his forehead as a mock salute in the direction of the cluster of ships.

Star released the breath, slumping in his seat. *Well, it was my fault for asking the man to step up.* He leaned over and ran a hand along the bottom of the console near his right leg. His fingers brushed against smooth composite plastic and metal. He felt around the area until reaching a box roughly the size of his head. Star flipped a series of sliding switches, waiting for the device to respond.

The comms *blipped,* and the sounds of heavy breathing came through. "I'm going to have to run your citizen identification check again, bear with me." Sila Nepco's voice took on an edge like a sugar-coated knife. The feigned sweetness did nothing to mask the fact it'd cut, and she intended to do so.

Star flashed Ahiko an irritated look.

The pilot had the grace to shrink under it and glance away. He rolled his shoulders, keying off the communications. "What was I supposed to do?"

Star held his stare. "Not be a smartass."

The focus slipped out from Ahiko's eyes. "That's not how you pronounce *'charming.'*"

"And 'charming' ain't pronounced as 'Ahiko.' Feel that's more along the lines of annoying. Both start with an A as far I know." Star rolled his eyes and pecked the slim screen running horizontally across the box by his leg.

"There are many things I've found in the galaxy, Shepherd. Some truths and a handful of lies. Of those truths, this is the one I hold to most: Ain't nobody near as charming as me." Ahiko hooked a thumb to his chest, flashing a smile that made polished metal seem dull in comparison.

Star rolled his eyes. "Seems your truth's more the lie and the lie's the truth. Delusion's a mighty charming thing when the man's charming himself and deluding others."

Ahiko's smile slipped from his face, pulling into a frown. "Did your last pilot quit? I'm getting the feeling they might have if these are the working conditions."

Star's face hardened. "Died before even getting on *The Leaf.* Before that, was my own pilot. Never flew anything like this, though. Larger transports, things less flashy, slow." He buried his attention on the box, hoping it'd answer his prayers and divert his thoughts from where they wanted to wander.

Ahiko turned his head and coughed into the pit of his elbow. "Sorry about that. Right, right." He sounded like he was trying to convince himself of something. The man activated the comms again, leaning forward. "Hope my check's come back clean—again."

No one replied.

Ahiko's mouth wriggled, and he looked to Star for help.

Star ignored the silent plea, watching the finger-wide screen for any change. A solid line of electric-purple ran across the length of the red background. It remained static.

"It has." Sila didn't sound enthused by the outcome. "You still haven't forwarded your ship's serial number."

Star's heart performed an impressive jump and lodged itself right behind his Adam's apple. He placed a hand to his throat, rubbing the area as he tried to swallow the lump. It refused to go. He could feel Ahiko staring holes into the side of his head.

The pilot winced and dragged the back of a forearm against his forehead. "That's odd. Could've sworn we'd sent that over first thing." He gave Star another glance.

Star shook his head. Giving the serial number would surely flag them. Ignoring the request, however, would likely lead to a similar response.

I'm here, Dad, how do I get to the next part? Where's the figuring it out? Because I don't see it.

Static crackled from near his leg. Star's eyes widened and shot a glance to the box.

The purple line peaked like a mountain had formed before collapsing in on itself.

No one likes it when a dead man's right. Star smiled to himself. *Thank you.* He keyed in a series of *beeps* and long *trills.*

Ahiko clamped a hand on to his wrist, glaring at him. The pilot brought his other hand to the side of his face to mask his voice as much as possible. "What are you doing?"

"Finding us a way out of here, for the moment at least." The hold on his wrist loosened. Star continued repeating the commands, hoping someone was listening.

"What are the odds we go from trouble now to loads of it later?" Ahiko glanced to the console and the live comms.

Star reached down, breaking the man's grip on his arm and gently brushed him off. "No good options. Giving 'em *The Leaf's* serial is a problem. Chances are it's already marked to be flagged."

"*Chances.*" Ahiko rolled the word around his mouth. "Fact is they haven't shot us down—yet. They don't know *The Leaf* by description. I say give them what they want, make less trouble. Worst happens, we make like bugs and scuttle?"

Star exhaled through his nose and looked out the cockpit to Lisba. *Breathe.* He did. "All right, do it." Star reached over and entered the serial number manually, pausing with his finger over the button.

Ahiko had pulled away from him and stared at the console in silence.

A gentle static buzz informed the pair Sila Nepco remained on the line, waiting.

Star shut his eyes and pressed the button.

"Thank you, though I didn't appreciate the wait, Kohiba."

"Seems like it's a day for apologies, Hub Security Officer Sila Nepco. Any way I can make it up to you?"

Ahiko leaned closer to the comms as if he thought he could force his "charm" through.

Star gave silent thanks the man couldn't send even a wink and returned to monitoring the box.

Another garble of static crackled out. The line spiked several times. And no one responded to the calls.

Star sighed. A man couldn't run on hopes and wants forever.

"Another of your checks came back, Mr. Kohiba."

Star blinked and stared at the comms. *Mister, huh?*

"You're a former military pilot. Apologies for the delay in our system picking that up. You're clear to go on your way to Lisba, but for reasons mandated by the Oligarchy, you must stay away from Martle as well as neighboring planets: Agaran, Tanzier, and Inosil. Each is currently under trade embargo from the rest of the planets within the government. For public appearance, we've been ordered to keep the military at a distance. We don't want to give the appearance that this is a show of force."

Star stared at the blockade and the numbers of ship. He wondered what the hell she considered a show of force to be?

Ahiko's posture slumped into the chair. "Thank you for that. We'll make sure to keep our distance and head on our way now."

The comms crackled. "Keep to sublight speeds within the hub. There's zero tolerance on going faster-than-light to reach any of the permitted neighboring worlds like Lisba. Won't take you more than an hour out of your day. You're not in a hurry?"

"None. Thanks for the advice." Ahiko jabbed a

finger at the comms, turning them off. The pilot depressed a single button overhead and triggered the previously programmed commands. The console flared in a discordant pattern of repetitive lights as a line of buttons above strobed.

Everything outside of the cockpit tilted as the ship veered away from the blockade. Lisba grew in clarity, the only astral body within their realigned sight.

Ahiko eased the throttle and brought *The Leaf* into a low-acceleration close to an eighth of maximum sublight potential. "Well, that turned out fine. Maybe I should be wearing the metaphorical captain's hat. Listening to me clearly works."

Star stared at him. "Funny, I think you need to work on your listening before coming to the point of wearing any hats, metaphorical or otherwise."

The pilot huffed and pushed up on the throttle.

They accelerated to a quarter of sublight, enough of a difference that Lisba appeared to grow a fraction larger. *The Leaf* didn't have the chance to settle and coast at that speed. Ahiko increased the pace every handful of minutes until they were rocketing toward the green giant of a world.

The pilot glanced up to the navigation monitor. "Call it a small relief we're far enough of their short range comms. They made me a bit twitchy."

A bit?

"So, mind telling me what you were fiddling with?" Ahiko nodded to the box by Star's leg.

His mouth went thin and he mulled over the decision to come clean with the pilot. So far, honesty had gotten him more, so he did. Star gave the box a light tap with the back of his hand. "Secondary comms—black box."

Ahiko hissed. "You *are* trying to get us killed."

Star rolled his eyes. "I'm giving us options. Sent out a simple call of contact to anyone with ears turned away from official channels. Some folks are bit more receptive to people of the quieter sort who want no association with the powers, local or higher."

"Sounds like we're talking about smugglers again." Ahiko's eyes narrowed.

Or worse. Star kept the thought to himself. It was a simple truth of the galaxy that bad was subjective and that it came in many flavors. Most smugglers fell along those lines. Some wanted to put in honest effort but were left with nothing but dishonest work. Others wanted to dishonestly make a buck off honest folk. It was a road of gray difficult to walk. And any of the people along that path could have picked up on Star's coded message.

"Or honest trades a bit out of the blockade's way. Jumping to judgment's a sure way to get something wrong, Ahiko." Star kept his focus on the box.

Another blip. It morphed after a second into a steady stream of low peaks that occasionally spiked.

A loud crackle of static cut through the comms.

He and Ahiko stared at the box in unison.

Another garbled burst of static. "Most folk take care *not* to send out a call asking for help from our kind." The unidentified speaker's voice was forcefully neutral.

Star and Ahiko traded glances.

"See you made it past the blockade without being turned around or into ash. There's that then. So, if you're not needing our help, we'll be needing yours."

Star blinked and slid his fingers across the bottom of the box, feeling for another switch. He tripped it. The secondary comms device *pinged* in anticipation of usage. Star grabbed a palm-sized speaker situated on the side of the box and pulled it free. He brought the device to his mouth, giving Ahiko quick look.

The pilot gestured for him to speak.

Star rubbed his fingers against microphone, debating how to address the unknown speaker. "Seems you've got"—he broke off and looked to Ahiko, wondering if he should keep quiet about the man—"*me* at a disadvantage."

"Part of our job," said the speaker.

Star licked his lips. *Our.* He worked the word through his mind and all it could entail. It could have meant a large crew or more than one ship. Either possibility didn't sit well with him. "Interesting job you seem to have. And what would that be, if you don't mind me asking?"

"I do."

Star covered the microphone with his free hand, lowering it to his pelvis to keep it from picking up any sound. He turned to Ahiko. "Run a quick scan. See if you can find where they're broadcasting from."

The pilot nodded and ran through a series of commands across the console. A flashing dot came to life on the navigation monitor, pulsating like a thing possessed. Ahiko frowned and refreshed the screen. His expression deepened when the imagery remained the same. He shrugged and shook his head. "Uh, monitor must be broken. Thing's saying their call's coming from in here." He pointed to the floor paneling.

Star mirrored his frown. He pulled the microphone back to his mouth. "All right, seeing how as you said the word 'help,' mind telling me what that might mean?"

Static crackled. No answer followed.

He breathed out, wondering where the speaker was hiding. They were approaching Lisba, and the path seemed clear. No rogue astral bodies filled the space around the world, meaning they had little place to lurk.

"For now, it means just following us to Lisba. By follow, I mean exactly so."

Star blinked, searching the black expanse for any sign of them. "That's going to be a problem on account of I don't quite see you."

"You will." The line crackled again.

Star glanced at Ahiko. "Well, that's ominous."

The pilot turned away from him, gawking at a view outside the cockpit. "So's that." He pointed ahead.

Star followed the gesture. *Well, shit.*

A ship's bow broke the dark view ahead. The vessel was roughly the same width as the Elan's Epyon-class carrier. He hazarded a guess it was close to the same length. An assortment of matte black and indigo paneling made up the outer hull. The design made it nearly impossible to spot the ship without the aid of the minute, strobing orange lights running across the vessel.

Star had the feeling those were only on so he could see the carrier.

"That's not standard plating for any ship I've seen. Hell, looks like scraped junk fixed to the outside to…" Ahiko broke off and his eyes widened in understanding.

"Bastards. They *let* us see that ping." He jerked a thumb to the navigation monitor. "They were skulking below and behind us this whole time. Paneling must be radar deadening." His eyes narrowed and he fixed Star with a glare. "*Lawful* and upstanding folk don't use that on their ships."

Star turned away from the look, focusing his gaze on the ship. "No, I don't think they do."

The ship broke further head, dominating most of the view on the way to Lisba.

Static flared again. "We're going to the far side of the planet. You'll be getting a ping of coordinates. Follow them." The words came over more as a command than a suggestion.

"And if we don't?" Star held his look on the ship.

"Uh, Shepherd?" Ahiko pointed to a row of slender screens centered at the top of the cockpit window. Several horizontal bars spiked violently without stop. "Energy readings are spiking from the ship. Given that their boat's shielded, only reason we're seeing that is because they want us to."

"It'd be in your best interest. We won't fire on you, but the blockades a nice target. Given that your approach was catalogued, you'd be the first suspect. How fast can you outrun their security forces *and* the military?"

Star ground his teeth, clenching the mic hard enough to cause the composites to warp slightly in his grip. "Lead the way."

CHAPTER EIGHTEEN

HELL OF A REASON

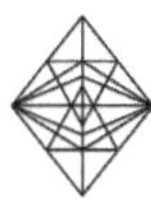

They broke through the atmosphere of Lisba as Ahiko maneuvered *The Last Leaf* toward the coordinates they'd been sent.

Star kept an eye on the moving blip on the navigation screen. The unknown ship had taken enough of a lead to be just out of sight and likely docked on the planet's surface. He figured it a safe bet they were still within the vessel's weapons and tracking range. Not something he felt should be tested.

The *Leaf's* shields could hold off any assault the ship could manage long enough for them to escape. But the battle would surely alert the security forces, and word would make its way to the military—fast. He couldn't chance that.

Star drummed his fingers along the portion of dark, composite material before the console. A hollow staccato echoed back from the dash. He kept the beat going, convincing himself it was a mounting thunder-storm.

Lisba's weather told him that his imagination wasn't needed. An explosive crack went off by the side of the ship, sounding like a bottled explosion. Water pelted the air a few inches in front of the cockpit screen. A torrent of beads hammered away as if intending to break through the shield and screen to drown the occupants.

Star shifted in his seat, eyeing Ahiko.

The tip of the pilot's tongue protruded from between his teeth. He'd bitten down on it lightly, his eyes narrowed in what looked like concentration.

Star left him to it. He turned his attention toward the planet, taking in the visual assault of greenery.

Lisba was a garden world in name only. The truth of the planet was found in the endless forests covering eighty percent of the land surface, at least he'd been told as much. Man had settled the world long enough ago to whittle the number down to near sixty percent. What remained, though, still classified as impressive. The rain served to keep the lush jungles and forests spreading with ease.

Star leaned forward, eyeing the approaching tree-tops. He shot a glance to the screen and ran through the rudimentary calculations in his head. The largest of the trees stood over two miles high. He squinted, doing his best to make out what he could through the near white-out rain.

The closest tree sported countless metal rods pro-truding from the highest and furthest out limbs. Wiring trailed from each device along the trunk, heading toward the ground, he wagered. Watermills the size of a man's head also covered the trees. They spun without pause under the rainfall.

Cheap, efficient power generation. Let the planet do the work. He wondered where Lisba's self-reliant power generation fell on the Oligarchy's priorities. *Suppose I'll just ask. If I get the chance, that is.*

An impromptu landing field came into view. Several miles worth of dark metal-polymer grating spread between the trees. The platform was suspended far above the forest floor for reasons he couldn't gather. Their forceful escort-ship sat docked several hundred yards to their left as Ahiko brought *The Leaf* down.

Star made note that this wasn't the only outpost he'd spotted during their descent. He didn't know if the others mattered or would come into play. But it meant there were more people off the grid here than he'd figured.

The pilot flashed him a quick look, arching his brow. "A bit odd."

Star gazed at the platform and noticed the distinct lack of people. The only thing dominating the scene was the other ship. "I'd say so, there's no one out there. I'm a touch fidgety when it comes to meeting another ship's crew out in the open—alone."

Ahiko shook his head. "Not what I meant, but sure, that too." He nodded toward the ship. "Take a look— close one."

Star did.

The ship didn't match the profile of any vessel he'd come across or committed to memory. Excessive paneling hung over its edges serving to break up its original shape. The entire thing looked like it had grown a mass of metal tumors. Domed protrusions dotted the surface of one side. More matte black sheets of metal jutted out to form odd geometric shapes along the bow and top.

"That ain't normal, and it sure as hell ain't efficient at anything other than mucking with radar. Heck, most of that looks like cheap scrap any military vessel would punch right through." Ahiko's eyes narrowed like he was scrutinizing the ship further. He put a finger to his lip, pulling on the bottom part of his mouth.

Star scanned the vessel and agreed with the pilot's conclusion. Something was off.

Ahiko killed the thrusters, letting *The Leaf* idle in place. "We stay here, the shields hold forever, right?"

Star nodded. "Light don't run out. Only reason there's a problem in flight is because scientists on Autumn never had time to finish the ship. Doesn't process the power right. Just has it is all."

The pilot frowned. "It's like having a pail of water that never runs out. Can keep pouring in one place and it'll never empty, but you don't ever have more than what the pail can hold to pour. That about right?"

"About so." Star unbuckled himself from the seat and rose. He placed a hand behind his lower back as he leaned, loosening the stiff muscles. "Once she's in the air, shielding goes over to cells to hold. Idea behind *The Last Leaf* was that she was made to be fast. She wasn't supposed to get stuck and have to hold to her shields."

Ahiko dragged his finger against his lip, pulling it down before releasing it. "Not much of a smart plan, to be honest."

"Honestly, not much smart men and women can

plan for. *The Leaf* was never supposed to be hunted and shot at across the galaxy. If things had gone right…this journey would've been over a short yesterday or so. I'd be unknown and back to a life of shepherding folks across the stars. And maybe…maybe people would be waking up not having to worry about powering a home or heating a meal." He shrugged and pulled the mantle of his coat.

"Fine goals, but my goals for the here and now are to walk away fine." Ahiko gestured toward the other ship. "So, way I see it—" he kicked his legs up onto the console; a light sigh left his mouth—"I sit here cozy and pretty, and there's nothing they can do about it. *The Leaf's* shields keep us safe."

Star stared out into the downpour, pulling his collar up on instinct. He didn't like the idea of getting wet again. His clothing had dried, but he hadn't bothered to change since leaving Azzip. The weariness of the journey had seen to that.

"I'd give a good deal for a moment's reprieve to sit, shower, and change." Star tugged on one of his sleeves. "But I've got a feeling that sort of idleness won't do us any favors. All they'd have to do is scarper and alert the military. We'd be stuck here or have to take back to the skies on limited shielding. Either way, doesn't look good for us."

Ahiko released a low groan, letting his feet fall from the console to *plunk* against the floor. He unbuckled his harness and pushed off the armrests to get to his feet. "I'm nursing the terrible feeling that I might get shot at again."

Star rolled his eyes and moved into the hall, walking

at a brisk pace. The pounding against metal behind him said that Ahiko was following. He kept his speed constant so the pilot didn't have to maintain his light jog.

"You planning on going out?"

Star inclined his head, one of his hands going to the butt of his revolver. He frowned in the realization that he was accustomed to reaching for the weapon. His hand remained in place, however, his fingers tapping against the metal.

"Forget shooting me, what about them shooting you? That happens, I'm back to unemployed and unpaid. Both are mighty concerning." Ahiko held up a finger to make a point. "Though, not necessarily in that order."

Star didn't turn his head to acknowledge the pilot's irrational concern. "Happens that I'm shot, forget me paying you. You'd be the captain of your own ship. Wouldn't have to cut your fee with any man."

Ahiko's eyes danced with an inner light.

"Though, that's assuming they don't shoot you next."

The gleam died in the pilot's gaze. "I mention what it means to assume?"

Star lowered his head. "You did." He hooked a thumb to his chest. "I'm the me, the U to you, and you—the ass." He didn't smile as he passed into the main hub of the ship. Star had a feeling Ahiko's face had pulled into a tight frown and the man was sputtering for a witty reply.

"I've got half a mind to leave you here, Shepherd." Ahiko's voice remained free of any hostile heat.

Star waved without turning as he headed toward the

small hall leading to the landing ramp. "So long's as a whole half of your mind's working, I'll take it." He clambered down into the narrow passage. "Keep by the console in case things take a turn for the worse."

"What?" The pilot sounded like he hadn't heard him properly.

"I made no mention of you during our brief talk with whoever they are. Far as they know, it's just me. I'd like to keep it that way. Ships like a double Y-frame don't need a crew past a pilot. Stand by, huh?"

A long pause hung in the air before Ahiko cleared his throat. "Sure thing, Shepherd. Sure thing."

Star operated the pad to the side of the door, opening the hatch to the outside world.

The rainfall hadn't tempered during their descent. It maintained the nearly all-white blanket obscuring his vision.

Star hobbled down a few feet on the ramp before pausing to wait in place. He leaned against one of the slender pillars holding the metal platform to the rest of the ship.

He glanced at the foot-sized holes running along the landing platform. They were evenly spaced and appeared to cover the entirety of what space he could see. He fathomed the openings were a part of the design.

A secondary noise, like a rolling stream barely audible in a storm, caught his attention. Star squinted at the nearest hole. Something whirred beneath it, moving in tandem with the water pooling through the opening.

More of the little mills filled the space. Everything in sight seemed designed to use the rainfall and lightning to generate power.

"No way the Oligarchy has let this slip." Verbalizing his thought helped him mull through it. Whatever was occurring on Martle had to be a larger threat to the pockets of the families in power than Lisba generating bits of its own free power. Or maybe they didn't know, and if they did, why care? Lisba didn't put out much in trade. Tourism occupied the other half of the planet.

Star exhaled as he followed the train of thought to the realization at the end. *Aw, hell. Only part of the world's settled, pumping money to the Oligarchy.* He winced and sucked in a breath before blowing it out through his nose.

A figure in the rain broke his concentration. The patchwork of black and gray clothing gave away the approaching figure.

Star figured it was a courtesy toward him. A few color changes and they'd be close to invisible in the downpour. He remained still, save for sneaking a hand into his coat to rest on his weapon. Star had only just landed and already wondered if he'd have to shoot people. The feeling grew a touch too common for his liking.

Two more figures in black appeared out of the white-out, moving at both sides of the previous figures. The trio looked like wraiths in the storm.

He narrowed his eyes, hoping to distinguish any features that would help identify them.

Their faces were obscured by dark hoods drawn up and over to fall before their brow lines. They wore thick, golden-lens goggles that reminded him of insect-like eyes. A black pyramid, the size of the average man's palm, covered their mouths. Small puffs of gas emanated from both sides of the device.

Nothing in their appearance painted them as friendly. Star tightened his grip on the weapon, tempering the itch to draw it. The longing grew until his hand tapped against the revolver.

They drew closer, their pace leisured as well as their posture.

Star eased the mounting tension in his left arm, working to appear as natural as possible.

The middle figure broke from the small pack, stepping out several feet ahead. They raised a hand in a simple greeting.

Star stared, keeping silent.

The figure folded all of their fingers, save for the index. They pointed past Star to the inside of *The Leaf.* The figure jabbed several times toward the ship.

Star glanced over his shoulder before turning back. He put a hand to the side of his mouth to help him when he raised his voice. "You'll need a helluva reason to warrant coming inside."

The figure turned their gesture down, pointing to their waist line.

Star followed the motion.

Each of the figures held a slender pistol kept low at their sides. The weapons were trained on him.

"Well, if you insist." He turned and marched into *The Leaf* at gunpoint.

CHAPTER NINETEEN
TALKS AT GUNPOINT

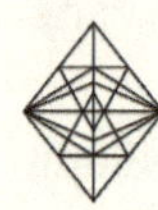

Star loosened his hold on the revolver, easing his hand out of his coat without revealing the firearm.

The figure at the center waggled their weapon to get his attention. They shook it at his sides before tilting the gun up.

He got the silent message, raising his hands overhead in surrender.

They rotated the weapon in a circular manner.

Like hell. Star took a single step back, refusing to turn around. He hoped his position was enough to placate the gunmen.

The trio stayed in place.

That ain't good.

A miniature heartbeat formed in the side of his throat, thrumming nearly in tandem with the rainfall. Any faster, and he'd choke from the thumping. Star took a series of steps back.

The figures remained still.

Well, there's that.

He backpedaled until his heels were against the bottom lip of the hatchway. *Wonder what's got them thinking I won't turn now and hop into* The Leaf?

The middle of the trio stepped onto the ramp, shaking the gun as a warning.

Star froze. *Guess now I know.* The thought crossed his mind to leap back and shut the hatch. Having his newfound "friends" alert the military wasn't as pressing as the immediate threat of being riddled holey. *And I never was much religious.*

The figures must have anticipated his thoughts. They surged onto the ramp, charging him.

He stepped back, jabbing a finger into the keypad and entering the short sequence to lock the hatch.

The middle of the trio passed through the hatch, leaving their comrades outside. They lashed out with an open palm.

Star reeled as the blow struck just below his collarbone, driving him back several feet until he fell to his ass. He scrambled away from the assailant and sent a hand into his coat.

The gunman stomped a foot in an effort to shock him.

Star pulled the revolver free, freezing as the attacker crossed the distance, and something pressed against his forehead. The tip of their weapon rested between his eyebrows. He resolved to keep from blinking and eyed them. "Most people say hello with a handshake.

The assailant offered their free hand.

Smart ass. He stared and wondered if he should take

it. An open hand was an open hand. Sometimes a man needed one to get back to his feet. Then again, it was a different story when the other hand held a gun. It didn't leave him much of a choice. Star extended his hand, waiting for the attacker to dictate what would happen next.

He winced as the gunmen's hand slapped into his wrist, digging in hard. They hauled him to his feet. Star noted the tip of the weapon had made its way from his forehead to his gut.

The remaining pair of gunmen made their way to the hatch, stepping inside and waiting in silence.

That's not disconcerting.

"I take it since you've forced yourself onto my ship—rather unkindly so, I'd note—you want to tell me about this job you're wanting me to do?" Star arched a brow, keeping the rest of his body still.

The figure in the middle placed a hand on the device covering their mouth and tugged. It came free with a light *pop* as its suction gave way. Another plume of watery mist puffed out from its sides.

What little of their face was visible looked to be human. Fair-skinned, a pointed chin that went out to a sturdy jaw. A slight sheen of moisture coated their lips.

The attacker brushed back their goggles, using the same motion to lift the obscuring hood.

Her hair hung loose to her shoulders and was the color of walnut threaded with faint lines of dark cherry. The woman's eyes were a few shades lighter than her hair, a warmer brown. She stood at his chin, looking him in the eyes.

Star figured her to be close to his age. "Don't

suppose I get a name?"

She ignored his request. "Maybe after the tour."

The tour?

The woman gestured to her companions with a lazy wave. "Stay here. Make sure no one tries to slip out while I get acquainted with the ship?"

Star frowned and decided to pull something from Ahiko in the hopes it'd help. "Just the ship?" He placed a hand over his heart. "That's awfully cold of you."

She ignored him.

I should've known better than to act like him. Hell, I give him the same look. "What makes you think there's anyone else on board?"

She eyed him then looked past him. "The fact you bothered asking me, that's what."

Star kept his face neutral. She was quick, and it could lead to trouble. He thought it best not give her cause to be on guard. Star would have a better chance at tripping her up that way.

The woman cast a look around the narrow passage before motioning with the gun. "Walk, slowly."

Star retreated up the incline as best he could while moving backwards. "This isn't the best way to hire someone to do your work for you. Professional courtesy and all that. It matters to folks like me."

"Who said we were going to be professional about this?" She arched a brow, her mouth pulling to one corner.

It was a hell of a question. Star wished he had the answer.

He backpedaled until he passed through the second hatch and into the central hub. Star waved a hand to the few seating options. "Care to sit?"

"No." Her eyes took in the room while her gun remained fixed on his abdomen.

Maybe he should have let Ahiko talk to them. The pilot could have tried to charm her. Likely he'd have ended up shot, but Ahiko wasn't Star. He preferred to come out of this as wholesome as when he'd gotten in.

"People normally discuss business seated, not standing and waggling a gun at the person they're trying to entice." Star kept his voice level. Agitating her any further wouldn't help his cause.

"You've never talked business at gunpoint then. It can work wonders for a gal."

Star shrugged. "Maybe so. Not that kind of person. I try to be *fair*." He emphasized the final word, watching to see how she'd react.

The woman didn't pause to consider it.

Fairness meant something to some folks in a galaxy where there wasn't much of that going around. It meant she was either a smuggler or something else.

"Cockpit's that way"—she waved the gun in the direction she was looking—"I gather?"

Star nodded. "It is. You planning on taking her for a spin. I'm not a possessive man, but I'm in possession of a job needing done. Timely constraints and all. No joyrides."

She stared at him before breaking the look. "I know enough about your job to want a look at this ship. Double Y-frame, not standard by any definition. She's been retrofitted, but I can't tell for what." The woman motioned with the gun.

Star swallowed the sigh and moved toward the hall

leading to the cockpit.

The sounds of heavy plodding echoed from the path ahead.

He froze in place.

"Shep—shit…" Ahiko paused in the middle of the hall, eyeing Star and the woman behind him. "I didn't know you'd let them board."

Star glanced at the gun with a mild turn of his head.

Ahiko caught the look. "Ah, right. Bit rude to turn down such a pointed self-invitation." He flashed the woman a smile.

Star didn't look, but he had the feeling she didn't return it.

"I thought no one else was on board?" She sounded like she'd received a present she'd been expecting.

Ahiko raised his hands, flashing Star a look for help. "Could be you're just imagining me. Fellas with looks like this have a tendency to only be in your dreams." His mouth spread into a wide smile.

Star fought not to groan.

"You must have dreams and nightmares confused. I'll leave it to the fact you've been running through space itching to stay a step ahead of the military."

Ahiko shot Star a wounded look.

He rolled his eyes at the pilot and ran through what he had learned. She knew about them but hadn't mentioned the bounty yet. She knew *The Leaf* wasn't standard. And she knew about the job. Or at least enough to want to dig deeper.

"When I put out that call, I was looking for honest help. I'm willing to do you a kindness in return for answering, even though you didn't help us out of that situation." Star exhaled and wondered if she'd come clean about her intentions.

"And I want to make sure you are who you say you are. Can't fault a girl for wanting to know that. Some men have a habit convincing a woman they're one thing, before turning out to be another."

Star couldn't argue that. He focused on what she had said. It implied that she knew something of who should have been piloting *The Leaf*. Did someone warn her? He sure as hell made no mention of his name. Then again, word had gone out about the ship. If she wanted to turn them in, she could have called the military.

"I've my shepherding credentials and a standard lens display in my pocket. Mind if I fetch 'em for ya, put your mind at ease?"

She let out a low grunt that he took as a go ahead.

Star moved his left hand steadily to keep her from overreacting. He dipped it into the pocket where kept the lens, fishing for the small piece of translucent polymer. His fingers brushed against a cool, slender piece of metal. He plucked both items free between his index and middle finger and gave them a gentle wag by his waist. A gentle tug threatened to pull them from his hands. He loosened his grip so she could take them. They slipped from his hands and he sucked in a breath, hoping they'd placate her.

A low hum of energy thrummed to life as the woman activated his lens. "Definitely matches your face." She didn't sound like it was a bother to have to stare at Star's visage.

He sniffed and refrained from commenting.

"Your shepherding credentials check out as well."

Star glanced at Ahiko, the two of them trading looks that led to the same silent question: What did she intend to do now?

"Okay, Star Shepherd, I'll level with you."

Star exhaled slowly, letting the stiffness leave his body along with the breath. "This means you're going to lower the gun?" Something jabbed his hand. He flinched, grabbing the thin sheets she forced into his palm. He stowed his lens and credentials and turned a fraction.

"I think I'll keep the gun until I'm comfortable you two aren't harboring any ill feelings toward my behavior." She flashed them a thin smile.

"I'm comfortable in saying that neither of us are taking any issue with your actions." Star waved a hand between Ahiko and himself.

The pilot snorted and rolled his eyes. "I am." Ahiko nodded toward the gun. "Comfortable in saying that I've got a heck of an issue with your behavior. Consider my feelings to be rather ill on the matter."

The woman blinked and turned to Star.

Star shook his head. "Don't feel too bad about it. Small blessing that I barely understand him most of the time."

Ahiko bristled. "I understand it's a blessing not to be understood. Don't feel too bad about it. Means I'm a genius." He winked at the woman before shooting Star a sly smile.

Star shut his eyes for a second and sighed. He raised a hand gestured to the woman to lower the weapon. "Might make him a tad quieter if you stow that. We've established none of us mean each other any harm. Let's aim to keep it that way. Cooler heads and all."

The woman's mouth twitched once before she lowered her head and acquiesced. She holstered the gun before extending a hand. "I can work with that. Zita Nath, free-roaming entrepreneur, negotiations expert, skillful procurer of things hard to come by." Zita gave him a lazy, cat-like smile.

Star didn't return the expression. "You're a smuggler."

Her smile deepened as if she were proud of the fact. "I feel that word demeans and undersells the vastness of my well-earned and eclectic skill set. Rule number one of business: Always upsell yourself."

"So far you're not doing a great job."

Zita's smile vanished and she faltered, mouthing soundlessly for a reply.

Star went on. "You said you'd level with us—tell us about this job. I'd like to hear it. Neither of us are in a position to dally. Military and Oligarchy are on my tail, and with you forcing us here, if things go sideways—guess where those folks will be heading? You'll get caught up in our mess. Not sure you want that."

Zita pressed her lips together, placing her hands on her hips and shifting her posture. "My job's sorting out other people's messes. Come on." She turned and beckoned him with a wave of her hand. Zita walked toward the exit hatch.

Star exchanged a look with Ahiko and rolled his shoulders in a mild shrug.

The pilot looked around the hall, mouth twitching. "Still not wholly comfortable following her out there. Can't see farther than a dozen feet or so."

Star grunted in agreement.

"What's to say this ain't an act? She's gotten you to open up *The Leaf* to her. Now all she needs is us to leave, take us out—bird's hers."

"She could've done that when she boarded. There are moments in any journey where you feel like you're pressed for options."

Ahiko stared, but said nothing.

"You can sit and do nothing. It keeps you safe, but you ain't going nowhere—certainly not where you mean to. You turn and go back. Not much chance of that for us. Or you can try to find a way to move on. Hell, ain't easy, but it hasn't been so far."

The pilot muttered something indiscernible.

Star moved after Zita, waving a hand for Ahiko to follow. "Come on. Sooner we get through this, sooner we're off to Slaydus. You want easy? I'm betting it'll come after it's all said and done." He felt it best to appeal to the pilot's sense of reward. "We'll be heroes if we do this right."

Ahiko beamed, a noticeable light taking hold in his eyes. He brought a thumb and forefinger to his chin and rubbed. "Hero, I like the sound of that. Think I'll get a statue, maybe a song?"

Star kept moving and buried the laugh trying to make its way out. "Don't think they give statues to ne'er-do-wells. Can't count on the songs either." He made his way in to the central hub of the ship where Zita waited near the ramp leading below. Star gestured with a thrust of his chin to the mask hanging off her hip. "Don't know much about Lisba but heard enough to know breathing's a pain at times. What do they do?"

Her hand fell to the mask, a few fingers brushing against it. "Breathers—separate the oxygen in the water from the rainfall and humidity. Can't go long or far here without these. Otherwise"—she touched a hand to her throat—"you end up with rot lung. Stuff's worse than pneumonia. So much moisture in your lungs and chest that you're hacking your damn organs up. Can't breathe. What little you can, you can't hold onto. You're retching water and worse. It's just nasty."

Sounds like. "This conversation's going to be awfully short if you didn't bring extras. I'm given to understand it's a courtesy to share with your *guests.*" He added extra weight to the word to make it clear he and Ahiko were still unhappy with the situation.

A wry smile made its way across her face. "Well, I was always fond of my men talking less than more." She reached behind her back and pulled free a slender rod from her belt.

The device was twice as thick as his thumb and longer than both his middle fingers put together. Slim grooves ran along the outer edges. A small puckered opening sat in the middle.

He eyed the object before arching a brow at her.

"Not as fancy as one of these"—Zita patted the breather on her hip—"but it'll get the job done. Breathe in only through your mouth." She looked past him.

Star followed her gaze.

Ahiko came to a stop a few feet behind him.

"Given how much he likes to use that mouth of his, I think he'll be just fine swallowing through it as much as he's given to spit." A wicked smile crossed her face.

Ahiko blinked several times, mouthing silently as if

trying to put together what she had said. His eyes narrowed a second later. "I consider that poor form. If there's any of that, you can be sure there's screaming to follow." He waggled his brows.

Zita's smile faded, and she lobbed the breathing device to Star before tossing another to Ahiko. "Put that in your mouth and be quiet." She glared at the pilot.

"And she's bossy; woman after my own heart." Ahiko touched a hand to his chest as he clamped his mouth around the breather.

Zita pulled the pistol free, training it on his hand. "If I wanted your heart, feel this is a quicker way to it." She matched the grin on his face before stowing the weapon.

Ahiko seemed unfazed.

Star shook his head and slipped the breathing apparatus into his mouth, taking a long drag. The sides of the object whistled as heavily recycled and filtered air rushed through the grooves. Each breath felt dry and tinged with a cool metallic taste.

Least it works. He pulled it free so he could speak freely. "This client…"

Zita tilted her head, waiting for him to continue as she unfastened her own mask.

"Can you at least tell me something about who they are? Not keen on walking into meetings blind." Star placed the breather back in his mouth, sucking on the raised edge to form a tight seal around it.

Zita turned and moved down the ramp like she hadn't heard the question.

He followed, doing a quick check to see if Ahiko stayed close. The pilot did much to his relief. Star didn't like the idea of dragging Ahiko into possible danger, but should it happen, he would rather have the man by his side.

The two figures from earlier remained by the hatch leading out. They stood like eerily still fixtures.

Rain continued to fall without sign of pausing, drumming loud enough to almost drown out any other sounds.

Zita plucked her mask free and looked over her shoulder to him. "They're part of the resistance—Liberation Movement. They've been waiting for you."

CHAPTER TWENTY

A WAY OUT

Star sucked in a sharp breath, causing the ridges along the device to whistle and shriek in response. *Someone from the Liberation Movement, here?* He looked out into the rain and ran through a thought for nearly every drop striking the landing pad.

It didn't sit well with him. Lisba was too far out of the way from the fringe worlds the resistance preferred to keep to. And it was too close to well-traveled hubs to lend them any safety from the military.

But then, that's why he was there. To hide out of sight in the crowd. He slid back to reality as the sound of Zita descending the ramp filled his ears. Star followed, ignoring the two figures standing at the exit hatch. He passed through it and onto the final ramp, letting the droning of the rain take hold of his mind.

The two figures fell into step behind him, hanging just at the edge of his peripheral vision.

They weren't willing to take chances between him and Ahiko. Star couldn't blame them. He grimaced as he stepped out from under *The Leaf's* cover, and the rain plastered his hair to his skull. Each drop looked more welcoming than it felt—peppering him like globules of liquid glass. He winced as each one struck exposed bits of skin. It was like being showered in needles.

Star weathered it in silence, taking slow, long drags through the breathing apparatus. Each breath came through smoother and moister than they had in the ship. *Least it works.* He reached up and pulled the collar of his coat high to protect his neck from the stinging downpour. His eyes found little respite until he bothered to raise a hand to shield them. The skin of his fingers ached with cold, and he wagered it wouldn't be long till the throbbing made its way to his bones.

Zita led the way at a brisk pace. She'd drawn her hood up to shelter herself from the torrent.

Star hadn't paid her clothing much attention at first. Water ran off it in sheets to join the drops streaming through the channels in the landing pad.

A series of disgruntled grunts managed to cut through the storm.

He looked over his shoulder to find Ahiko stomping through the occasional pool of water that hadn't successfully drained into the channels.

The breathing tool twitched between the pilot's lips as he grumbled and kicked another puddle. His clothes clung to him like a second layer of skin.

Star nursed a hope that Zita found them shelter fast. Otherwise, the pilot was likely to lose what little cool he had left. He recalled their first meeting and how the inebriated Ahiko had assaulted soldiers. Star didn't want a similar occurrence when they were outgunned and held hostage.

Zita led them through a series of close-standing trees forming something of a hall of wood at their sides. Intertwining branches and mats of foliage spread high above them, creating a natural blanket from much of the rainfall.

Star looked around and noticed there were a handful of similar rainless pockets created where the trees grew in the same fashion. *Handy.*

Arches fashioned from flattened metal hung several dozen feet above the landing pad, held in place to the trunks of trees. They acted as simple gutters and diverted the rainfall to their sides.

Star peered under the metal fixtures and understood their need as he sighted on openings beneath them, carved deep into the massive trees. It all made sense. It was hard enough to do anything on this side of Lisba when the other half of the planet was where all the action and money was. With the rain and tree cover, one could hide out here for a long while. They might as well have set up shop and home within the tree trunks to get cozy.

He gazed at Zita's back and had a feeling about the sort of people to frequent these parts long enough to get used to them. Everyone needed a way station—a place to kick up their feet and knock back drinks. It'd be a good place for information as well.

Zita motioned to one of the openings to their right. Warm light, a color caught between pale orange and soft yellow, radiated out from hollowed portion of the tree.

Star squinted to get a better look into the opening but couldn't make anything out. He rubbed his eyes with the heels of his palms in hopes of clearing the blur that had settled in them from staring out through the whiteout of rain. The ache in his eyes from the cold hadn't subsided. He exhaled and trudged forward so the weariness wouldn't have time to build.

Sometimes keeping moving was the best way to forget about all the pain. One step at a time. He fixed his gaze on the opening and followed behind Zita. The glow softened, and he couldn't tell if his vision was recovering or he was simply close enough to make things out.

A small bar came into view. Bright varnish of orange-brown coated the bark walls of the establishment. It added the darker coloring to the glow generated by the high-powered yellow lighting. Fist-sized orbs hung around the place randomly spaced out, generating light and warmth like miniature suns. A ghostly ethereal aura seemed to hang around the radiating fixtures, making them seem more magical than pieces of technology.

The entire bar carried a theme reserved for something out of old fantasy stories. A wooden counter began at the right edge of the entrance, curving to run straight to the far end of the place. Every bit of furniture was carved from similar wood, likely from the tree itself.

Zita entered the bar, lowering her hood and motioning for Star to follow.

He did, casting a wary eye to the onlookers who made no effort to look him over subtly. Star abandoned what little tact he'd been using and returned the favor, eyeing them without bothering to hide it.

The patrons were a motley assembly of people garbed in similar clothing to Zita's.

That meant they'd made a habit of coming here and being prepared for the weather. They were at least in the know of who and what Zita was. Star's gaze went to the smuggler. The people in the bar could've been her folk—crew—or just people here for simpler reasons. He didn't need to go looking to make people into something they weren't. That's what the government did. Star believed he was better than that.

He dragged the back of one of his wet sleeves across his eyes, rubbing them. The idea of viewing everyone as the same didn't sit well with him. It was a slippery slope too many folk fell down and few came back from.

It was how the Oligarchy got people and the government under their heel. That and money. If one could make people see you as their savior, even when you meant them harm, they'd rally to you. Done long enough, and it didn't matter when the people learned the truth. They'd accept things anyhow. And they'd demonize anyone you wanted.

He shuddered as he thought over the painful truth. It was the same tactic the government used to label the people of Autumn a threat, their work a danger. The same sort of blanketing belief that made him a wanted man in the eyes of most people. And the same sort that made it so easy for him to judge an entire room based off of his thoughts on one woman.

Star winced, purging the thoughts from his mind as he followed Zita to the furthest corner of the bar counter. He took a seat beside her and leaned forward to prop himself up with his elbows. "Everyone's staring."

Zita brushed some of her hair aside. "No more than you are. They haven't seen you around. Newcomers make people twitchy."

Twitchy. Out here that meant people having a hand on a gun or something sharper. Star shifted on the stool, eyeing as much of the bar as he could without turning his head.

Ahiko lingered just within the entrance. The pilot gave the place the same look Star had, summing up the patrons and possible threats. His lips went thin, and he nodded to himself. Ahiko looked over a shoulder to the figures who had accompanied Zita before walking toward Star.

Star sighed in relief as the pilot drew closer. *Relieved one person's watching my back in here.* The muscles along his spine loosened at the thought. Star wasn't fond of his last bar experience with the pilot. He wasn't looking for a repeat.

A hollow *plunk* echoed from the counter before him. Star stared at the thin-bodied stainless steel cup then the source.

The barman had a weathered face of deep lines, likely a combination of stress and age. He was dressed in canvas clothing that looked like it'd weathered heavy wear and years exposed to the elements. His dark hair was short cropped in a fashion that looked like it'd been done with a jagged edge. The yellow lighting did odd things to his umber skin, giving him an undertone of gold that brought out a bit of the brightness in his amber eyes.

Star glanced back to his drink. "What is it?"

The barman rolled his eyes. "Water."

Star's mouth twitched and he stuck a finger into the cup, pulling the digit back to his mouth. It tasted odd, like it carried notes of earth and a few things he couldn't make out. "What's in it?"

"Hydrogen and oxygen, idiot," said a voice carrying a metallic echo.

The barman turned toward a door behind the counter that presumably led into a storeroom. "Be nice. Don't need you scaring off a new customer the second he sits down."

The door opened, revealing what looked like a poor attempt to mimic a man, if that man's skin was made from tarnished silver. The heavily patinated metal sported minute dings and scratches that caught the light and refused to wash out under it. It had a domed head with mechanical eyes too bulbous to resemble anything human. They gave it an insect-like appearance. The vertically-streaked grill where its mouth should have been didn't help it come off any more human.

The automaton turned and tilted its head toward the barman. "You don't pay me to be nice. In fact, it's worth noting you don't pay me at all. A serious labor law transgression. For what good the laws are out here."

"That's because you ain't human. And what little bit you try to be, well, you're an ass."

Star watched the exchange and debated downing the contents of the glass in a way to recuse himself from the conversation.

The automaton sucked in a dramatized breath,

raising its armor-like chest plate in indignation. "Perhaps if you weren't so cheap, you could pay me to care."

Zita groaned and rubbed an index finger along the side of her nose. "M34, stop. I just risked getting spotted by a private security force running muscle on the embargo on behalf of the Oligarchy. And I did all that to drag him"—she jerked a thumb to Star—"here. I'm tired."

The mechanical man turned to face her, its eyes seeming to grow more bulbous as it stared. "Well, that was terribly stupid. So, I'm not surprised *you* did it."

Zita's hand blurred. She snatched the cup from in front of Star, snapping her wrist and sending it tumbling through the air.

A loud *clang* rang out as it struck the automaton's head, showering the contents over the walking annoyance.

"This is why no one likes you, Zita." The machine dragged a hand along its face as if trying to wipe the water away.

She snorted. "Everyone likes me. It's *you* they don't like."

The automaton blinked, its eyelids working like shutters as it gave her a look like it was confused. "*I* don't like you. That means your statement is false."

Star exhaled drumming his fingers against the table to get everyone's attention. "Like she said, I've been dragged out of my way, out of my comfort, and notably, against my will. I'd appreciate some answers. The bickering can stop."

The automaton faced Star, acting like it had just registered his existence despite the earlier reply. It took two steps toward him, making an exaggerated effort in each movement. The machine bent at the waist and brought itself down to stare at him eye level. "My name is M34N, not M34." It gave Zita a look that could have passed for a glare. "*I* am the owner of this establishment."

Star opened his mouth to speak.

"*You* don't matter." M34N waggled a finger in admonishment at him. "Your name doesn't matter." The automaton turned to Zita. "Who is he?"

Star's groan was matched by Ahiko, who ran a hand through his hair and grabbed tight in the center. He squeezed excess water free and shook the limb clean of the remaining droplets. "Awfully sassy for a toaster, no?" Ahiko flashed the machine a smile.

The automaton turned and stared back, its eyes blinking and rotating. M34N rose and took a step toward Ahiko before the barman cut it off.

"You're not the owner. You work here, remember? Stop antagonizing people. If you can't do that, go to the back, shut up, and wash something." The barman's tone could've peeled chips of wood from the counter.

The automaton's shoulders sank, and its voice followed. "I'll be the owner when you die. I'll live forever."

A loud snort came from the barman, the sort of noise that seemed impossible to make without agitating the insides of his sinuses. "When I die, the cat's getting this place."

The automaton shot every person watching a single glare before turning on a heel and retreating behind the door it'd come from.

Star cleared his throat as the door slammed shut. "What was that about?"

The barman released a heavy sigh. "Hospitality and service automaton. Got him cheap—too cheap. Should've known."

Star arched a brow. "Why's that?"

"On account he's about as hospitable and enjoyable as a venereal disease." The barman bent at the waist to recover the cup, snatching a small towel from the counter to clean the mess.

"You would know. I've counted that you've picked up at least six over the years." M34N's voice echoed and warbled from the back room like it was agitated.

Another loud knock sounded off as the metal cup bounced off the door. The barman made a fist in the air, shaking it in the direction of the automaton. "Shut up!"

Star looked to Zita for help.

She gave him a lopsided, apologetic smile and shrugged. "You'll have to put up with a bit of this."

Ahiko sat down beside him, shaking more water free from his hair. "For how long? We'd like to get on with what we were doing. We're in one of those positions where patience is a good virtue and all, but not much in the way of practical here."

"Mhmm." Zita drew out the sound, rolling her tongue along with it. "Sometimes there's practicality in patience. Like, maybe waiting for the person you've been brought to see?" She pointed a finger past them.

Both men followed the gesture.

Another figure stood between the two who had escorted Star and Ahiko along with Zita. They wore long, flowing robes that were clearly oversized. The material could have been spun from gold thread. It shimmered as light rolled over it, making it stand out against the melancholy and washed-out scene outside the bar. Their hood was drawn over to obscure most of their whole face, save for their mouth and jaw.

Star's ribs throbbed as something bounced off of them. He stared at the elbow that had prodded him, then to Ahiko.

A small smile spread across the pilot's face. "That there's a woman—a beautiful one. Mark my words."

Star sighed. "Consider them marked. And here's some words to consider back."

The pilot arched a brow.

"The few times a woman's come across our path and come for us"—he tilted his head towards Zita—"it's meant trouble." Star smiled as Ahiko's slipped away.

The pilot grumbled to himself and signaled the barman for a drink.

Star turned on the chair, leaning with one elbow on the counter as he stared at the yellow-robed figure. There was no point in playing dumb. She knew who she was here for. He raised a hand, waving at her. He may as well try to play nice. Maybe he'd learn more that way.

The figure reached up to lower their hood, proving Ahiko right. Her skin was the color of soft fawn, taking on a bit of the golden hues of her clothing due to the light falling over her. The trend carried to her hair, tresses of spun wheat bound into a neat and out-of-the-way bun. A few rogue strands hung at the sides.

Star recalled every memory he could of his time on

Autumn. The planet's population had been an eclectic mix of people, but the ones he'd spent the most time with all carried a certain look in their eyes. A heaviness that came with dedication—tirelessly working toward something. He gazed into her eyes.

They reminded him of oceanic worlds, distinguished by their blend of soft blues and darker greens, vying for dominance over the other color. What was left was a blur somewhere between the hues, which changed with the light.

She held his stare, but Star didn't find what he had been looking for. Her eyes carried a gentler light than he had found back in the people on Autumn. It wasn't a look of commitment. It was a look of kindness, maybe sympathy.

But for whom? People didn't walk into this life easily…and they didn't walk out gently. It felt like a pair of hands raked through his guts. He pressed a palm to his stomach in the hopes of easing the queasiness. Something didn't sit right with him.

The robed woman moved toward him as if she were gliding. She stopped within arm's reach, giving him a smile he felt had to have been practiced. "Star Shepherd?"

The background murmuring and guttural exchanges within the bar died. No one blatantly turned to look at him, but Star felt all eyes were turned his way—again.

The pilot groaned as Star had finished his thought almost as if Ahiko had heard it himself. "I'm going to need more than one drink for this."

Good to know he's expecting trouble too. Star forced a smile similar to the woman's. "That's me." He managed to look her in the eyes while keeping his awareness on the people behind her. One wrong move, and the place would go up like fire and fuel. He inched a hand into his coat.

She reached out and placed her hand on his wrist. "Do not worry. No one here will turn you in." Her voice was like powdered steel, soft and firm at the same time. She cast a look around the bar as if the simple gesture would drive the point home to the occupants.

It worked.

Most looked away and returned to their conversations. One figure, hood still up, mumbled something about being tempted to, but he heeded the woman's words.

She had enough clout to make people listen. Or the money. Maybe both? Star did her the favor of easing his hand back out from his coat.

"My name is Savi Ur." She folded her thumb against her palm, splaying four fingers before touching them to her heart. "I've been waiting for you."

Star noted the formal gesture, trying to pin down its origins and meanings. It didn't strike him as religious or tribal, and he didn't know of anything like it this close to a trade or travel hub.

Savi must have picked up on his confusion. "I'm a monk from Gornan. It's far from here, closer to the outer edges, and secluded."

Star grunted. He'd heard stories and passing rumors of the place. For a world so out of the way, its inhabitants did uncannily well. Benefits of not being political and having the government backing for your order.

Savi extended her hand to him.

He eyed it before taking hold and giving her a gentle squeeze. "What's a monk doing out here?"

She flashed him the same smile from earlier.

He wondered if they taught monks how to do that. It was damn near believable. But he'd seen enough people and lies in his life to know a fake smile when he saw one. He matched her expression.

"I told you: waiting for you."

"And why's that? Zita said you're part of the Liberation Movement." Star's smile thinned, and his stare hardened. He felt it the smallest bit of politeness to invite Savi to sit, motioning with a hand for her to do so.

She shook her head. "I am. I know what you want to ask: Why am I out here, so far away from my order and anywhere you'd expect to find someone like me?"

"Glad to see we're on the same page."

"Not quite." Savi ran both hands against her torso, smoothing out some of the folds in the robes. "I'm not the only one waiting for you. The Movement sent out dozens of agents along all the suitable and likely routes you'd travel. I happened to be lucky enough to get word you'd come this way. I paid Zita to bring you by."

It made sense. There was way to know where they'd pass through heading toward Slaydus. He narrowed his eyes as something came to mind. "Why bother?"

"Because we were told to give you an option, an out."

Star blinked, looking to Ahiko.

The pilot shook his head and took a swig from his cup.

"What's that?" said Star.

"You're hunted with your face on every lens with a bounty tempting enough for normal folk to want to hitch up and chase you. I'm here to offer you a way out. You don't have to run anymore. This is where you get off, if you want. Turn over your ship and let me deliver it. You can walk away, Shepherd."

CHAPTER TWENTY-ONE
STAKES AND CHOICES

"I'm sorry?" The tangled mess within his stomach knotted tighter. Star looked back to Ahiko.

The pilot had perked up at Savi's offer, spinning around in his seat and pausing mid-sip. "That's something, isn't it?" He glanced back to Star over the lip of the cup.

"It is." Saying it over and over to himself wouldn't help him believe it any more. It *was* one hell of an offer. He bet it comes with some equally mighty and weighty strings. Ones that would end up getting pulled on someday. He turned his attention back to Savi. "What's the catch?"

"None." Her voice didn't waver. "I've been instructed compensate to Zita and her party should you take my offer, which I suggest you do." Savi gave him a smile that brought some light to her eyes. "You'll be given new identities and passage to any world of your choosing. Start over, Shepherd. Your job's done."

Done. There's a word I've been waiting to hear for a long time. He rubbed his forehead before running the hand through his hair. "Done." He rolled the word around his mouth, drawing it out. "I'm a shepherd. Work's never done. There's always someone or something to ferry somewhere."

She brushed it off with a thin smile. "Not if you walk away right here and now. There will be one last trip—wherever you want it to be. Think about that."

Star exchanged a look with Ahiko.

The pilot's furrowed brow and pressed lips told Star he was thinking along the same lines.

What would he be if he put away the shepherd's life for something else? He'd always brought people and things to the places that needed them or they needed to be. His work had mattered, to others and to himself. He frowned. How much of that was just ego? His desire to just wanting to keep on with life as he knew it. Star pictured *The Last Leaf* and its cargo.

Life as he knew it was what brought things to where they were. Him, and a former military pilot, the galaxy wanting to cash them in like they were nothing more than a reward. Star exhaled and ground the palm of a hand against the side of his face. Fingers wrapped around his and squeezed reassuringly.

"It's frustrating, the choice in front of you and everything it's taken to get you here. I understand." A sympathetic light filled Savi's eyes. "There's a part of you that can't part with the journey. You have to see it through to the end." She squeezed his hand again. "It's brave—admirable—to want to do so. You don't want to drag anyone else into the mess." Savi pressed again.

Star became acutely aware of the five points of pressure around his wrist and jerked his hand free from the monk's. He glanced at Ahiko.

The pilot focused on the monk. "I think we can decide for ourselves, thanks. His brain might be a touch addled given some of the decisions he's made, but he doesn't need it nudged by a monk, especially the sort that knows how to manipulate a person." Ahiko inclined his head toward Star's hand then tilted it to Savi.

Her face became an expressionless mask. "What do you mean?"

"I mean, in all my years of service, I've come across some of your folk that leave the monastery. I know what you're trained to do. You learn how to 'ease a person's tension' and all. Convince them of things. The right smile at the right moment. A perfectly timed hug. Heck, squeezing someone's hand or shoulder over and over right when you say something you want them to agree with. That's before your lot loses subtlety and tries to get the message across other ways." Ahiko's gaze trailed along her body before he looked back up.

Star blinked several times, flexing the hand she had touched.

Son of a bitch. She's been pushing me toward this. Who wouldn't want a way out, an easy one at that? Just walk away and let her take The Leaf. *But why does she want it so bad? What's her problem with me taking it as is?*

He gave voice to the question.

She was unfazed by it, glossing over the accusation Ahiko had thrown her way. "Truthfully?"

The pilot glowered at her. "It'd be a nice start."

Savi went on as if Ahiko hadn't spoken. "You've drawn—and continue to do so—far too much attention to yourself. The Liberation Movement wants the package delivered. The end. They don't much care who or how at this point. We need it. We don't, sorry to say, need *you*." The light hardened in her eyes as she stared at Star.

"Now, Savi, that's no way to get a man to agree to your terms." Zita raised a cup in her direction before downing its contents.

Ahiko jerked a thumb in her direction. "What she said."

Savi raised both of her hands to her shoulders, splaying her fingers in a gesture of peace and resignation. "I didn't come here to force you into anything." She glanced toward Star. "You don't have to take the offer, just consider it. You know what's at stake. Ask yourself this: Are you okay with failing? Are you comfortable with the military taking hold of the package?"

He tried to brush off the questions off but failed. They clung to his mind like a film, refusing to back off until he answered them. Star gritted his teeth. *I won't fail, how's that?* The reply wasn't meant for Savi. He gave her a look that got the message across.

She inclined her head. "I'll let you think about it. No more pushing, promise. Just weigh everything carefully. Lives will be changed by your decision. You know that. Choose carefully—selflessly. That's why you were hired." Savi stepped back while keeping her eyes locked with his. She turned gracefully in a single step and moved to a corner on the opposite side of the bar.

He guessed it was too much to ask for her to leave altogether. She was going to stay here till they make up their minds.

He shifted on his seat to face Zita, giving her a sideways look and gesturing to Savi. "I take it your job's done now? You brought us to her and we've heard her out. Are we free to go?"

Zita moved her cup. "I guess." She didn't seem convinced.

"You guess? Might not be my place to suggest it, but I think you should guess a bit harder." Ahiko's voice sounded like he'd swallowed hot gravel, rough and heated.

Zita stopped fiddling with the cup and looked at him. "That sounded more like a threat than a suggestion." The heat from Ahiko's voice entered her eyes as she narrowed them. "As far as suggestions go, let me *suggest* you speak a bit more kindly to me."

Star chanced a glance around the room. The barman had vanished, likely behind the door and the safety it offered. Most of the patrons had frozen, eyeing the exchange between Zita and Ahiko. Star's hand returned to the side of his coat. He rubbed his fingers against the material, debating whether to brush it aside and reach for his weapon.

The rest of the occupants must have had the same thought. Hands went to their sides, some noticeably resting atop powered blasters. A few trailed their fingers along the grips of more antiquated projectile weaponry.

Star hoped those were more for show than show stopping. He looked down at Zita's waist. She'd drawn her pistol, keeping it at her hip and aimed at his groin. Star shifted and crossed his legs.

"Another piece of advice"—her face morphed into a neutral mask—"when threatening people, make sure those around you like you more than the other person." She waved her free hand to their surroundings. "In case it wasn't obvious, I'm rather well-liked here and you're...new."

Star shut his eyes and exhaled before easing his hand away from his coat. "Fair point. Don't suppose we can remedy that? I'm all for going from new trouble to old friend."

Zita snorted. "Just like that?"

"Just like that." He gave her a thin, lopsided smile.

She blinked and tilted her head as if weighing his offer. The end of the gun wavered, dipping to point at his thigh. Zita looked past him to where Savi sat before returning to stare at him. Her lips pressed together before she waggled the weapon in her grip. "Sure, let's talk."

He opened his mouth to start before she waved a hand, cutting him off.

Zita turned her head a fraction and glanced to the door behind the bar. "Molan, I don't suppose you'll be kind enough to let me borrow your back room for a private chat?"

A low groan warbled out from the backroom. "Are you holding a gun?" The barkeeper's voice carried a slight drawl that hadn't been there before. Some of the words slurred and ran together.

He must have turned to a bottle to cope with his bar turning into a firefight waiting to happen.

Zita looked around the room before settling on the space just above the door leading to the room where M34N and Molan hid. She aimed the weapon and squeezed. A bolt of viridian energy trilled through the air, burning through the wood and scorching an area the size of a man's fist. "I'm holding a gun."

The door creaked open, and Molan's head popped out to fill the gap. He glowered at Zita before turning to glance at the spot she'd fired at. "That'll cost ya."

She flashed him a smile, one she seemed to have had a habit of giving him. "Put it on my tab. Privacy?"

"Sure, sure." The barkeeper pushed the door open. "Since you asked so nicely and all." He stared at the burned spot again before stepping out and moving toward the bar counter. "All yours." He rolled his hand through the air with a flourish.

"Such a gentleman." Zita quirked a smile, shaking the gun at Star, then pointing it to the room. "Let's go talk. Privately."

He frowned. "I've got a feeling I'm not going to enjoy this conversation."

CHAPTER TWENTY-TWO
UNINVITED GUESTS

"You'll enjoy it less if you don't get up." Zita gestured to the surrounding patrons with a tilt of her head. "What's the worst that can happen?" A wicked smile crossed her face.

Plenty. Star sighed and raised a hand, eliciting a series of twitches from the nearby customers. He watched them to see if they'd react further. Reassured they'd reined themselves in, he placed a hand on the counter and eased himself to his feet.

Ahiko moved behind him before Zita clicked her tongue against her teeth.

"No. You stay here. I'll keep an eye on the shepherd." She gestured to Star before waving a hand to the patrons. "They'll keep *you* honest, pilot." Zita rose from her seat and beckoned Star to follow as she hopped over the counter.

The barkeeper's face pulled into a tight mask, his

knitted brows and clenched jaw the only visible signs of annoyance.

Despite the situation, Star decided not to add to the man's irritation. The barman seemed to be the only person not embroiled in their situation or the many sides that comprised his customer base. He was a man caught in the middle of everyone's problems while trying to get to tomorrow. Sort of what Star was like before he doubled down on this mission.

He crossed the length of the counter, going around the bend until he came to a waist-high door between the wood. Star placed a hand against one side of it and pushed it inward. He stepped through and moved to meet Zita near the door to the back room.

She gave him an oblique look. "That was a bit pointless."

"Less of a point in jumping the man's counter. He's got to clean that, you know? My way's not so much pointless as it is politeness. Words sound the same, but a world of difference in meaning, if you know what I mean." He answered her look with a crooked and self-satisfied smile.

She bristled, making no reply as walked to the door, driving the heel of her palm into it.

Star glanced at Molan. "Something I said?"

The barman looked at Zita as she passed into the back room before turning back to Star. "Word of advice?"

Star inclined his head.

"Don't antagonize her. She's not much on patience. Her life's lived up there." He pointed to the roof.

Star understood it to mean more than that. The

barkeeper meant the stars.

"She's got it hard, always on edge and having to fly and lead by the seat of her pants. Smuggling's not an easy life. Don't give her reason not to trust you any more than she already doesn't. She can be a great help." Molan snagged an empty cup from the counter, pulling a cloth rag from his pants to wipe it.

"Your friend's 'suggested' I talk with her in private. That came at gunpoint, mind you. Her level of trust doesn't seem that high." Star stared at the door.

"She did. And it's not. Don't make things worse. Whatever she's got to say, hear her out. Don't trust her on it, trust me." Molan pursed his lips as he raised the glass to eyelevel to inspect it. "Or don't. But going on and through life without trusting anyone is no way to go on at all. Especially not with what trouble you're in."

Star opened his mouth.

"Everyone knows. No one's stupid enough to do anything about it, though. Relax. Go have a talk." Molan set the cup down on a small shelf behind him.

The barman had a point. If Zita meant to hurt Star, she could've done so by now. The room made it clear she had enough friends here to pull whatever stunt she wanted. Maybe she did just want a hint of privacy to say something she didn't want others to hear. Which meant what she had to say was especially meant for Star or about him.

He blew out a breath and went for the door, opening it and stepping inside. His skin prickled and formed rows of minute bumps as a chill rolled over him. Cold fog plumed before his mouth as he exhaled.

The room was a jarring departure from the bar. He

couldn't see anything reminiscent of the tree they were inside. The walls were a textured white the color of egg shells. Little swirled patterns covered their surface and looked to be caused from the material used. Cheap metal wire racks lined every bit of free space along the sides of the room. Various bottles of alcohol, and likely stronger things, filled them.

A heavy condenser unit sat along the top of the far wall, shuddering in place as super-cooled air blew out from between its grates.

Zita stood near the middle of the room, leaning against a standing metal shelf filled with the inventory expected of a bar. A stool sat several feet in front of her. She waved a hand at it in a gesture for him to sit.

Star made his way over and plunked himself onto it. "So, now that you've got me all alone—" he bowed his head toward her gun—"don't suppose that's necessary, is it?"

Her mouth twitched, but she stowed the weapon. "No, it's not."

Star waited, intertwining his fingers and twiddling his thumbs.

Zita remained silent, however.

"This is awkward."

Both of them turned to the source of the voice.

M34N stood a dozen feet to their side, looking out from behind a large shelf by a wash basin fixed to the wall.

Star had nearly forgotten the robot.

The automaton's eyes spiraled within their sockets as if it were adjusting them to focus better. Its lens spun and locked in new configurations and what would have been its pupils extended from their base like telescopes. "Why are you two here?"

Star and Zita opened their mouths in unison.

"Wait, I don't care. You shouldn't be back here. This is for employees only." M34N pointed to an empty place on the wall.

Both Star and Zita stared at it before turning their gazes back to the machine.

"Hm." The automaton traced a finger under its chin like it was perplexed. "Maybe I shouldn't have discarded that sign."

Zita huffed a breath out. She snatched her pistol free, training it on M34N's torso. "Tell me, M34, you ever been shot in the chest...repeatedly?"

The automaton's eyes turned counter clockwise a few degrees. "I have not."

"Would you like to?" Zita flashed the robot a feral grin that showed too much of her teeth.

"Not particularly, no." The machine raised one of its index fingers. "However, let me take the moment to point out that you are exhibiting psychopathic tendencies."

Zita slipped her finger inside the trigger guard and shut one of her eyes, tilting her head like she was sighting in on the robot.

M34N threw its hands into the air. "I'm leaving, but only because I want to." The automaton plodded toward the door, looking over its shoulder to the pair of them. It reached out with a finger and tapped a series of commands on a small keypad by the door before stepping out.

The condenser unit shivered with renewed intensity

before belting out a stronger stream of cold air.

Star glowered at the door.

"Don't mind M34. Thing's got a few screws loose. Not its fault." Zita slipped her pistol back in place and crossed her arms. "About what happened back in the bar, I needed things to be forced out of hand. Or look like it at least."

Star arched a brow. "And why's that?"

"Because, otherwise, it'd look awfully suspicious. Savi paid me to get you to her. She didn't hire me to talk your ear off and make suggestions."

"And you've got something to say? Something you don't want her overhearing?"

Zita nodded. "And an opinion, if you want it."

"I'll hear it. Can't promise I'll heed it."

"Fair enough." Zita ran a hand against one of her legs, tapping her fingers against it. "Where do I start?"

He remained quiet. Star figured there was enough on her mind that made it difficult to open up and start somewhere. She probably had as many questions to ask as she had things to tell.

She exhaled, running the tip of a thumb against the corner of her mouth. "Don't take her offer."

The muscles in his throat locked, and swallowing air became an effort. It felt like he had an ice cube lodged in his gullet. The decrease in temperature was partly to blame. He worked a bit of saliva down to help him clear the blockage. "I'm sorry?"

"Don't do it." Zita's voice was harder and colder than the metal she leaned against.

He didn't know what to make of the smuggler's request. "Savi hired you."

"She did."

"And she says you owe her one." Star gave Zita a knowing look. That sort of thing always came back to cause trouble. Favors owed became favors called, and when they were, people were forced to do all manner of things they wouldn't otherwise.

"I do."

"Those aren't much for answers." Star held his look.

"They're not. Still doesn't change what I said. Don't take Savi's offer. Don't let her have your ship." Zita stared past him like she was looking through the wall and into the bar where the monk sat.

"Why not?" He rubbed the back of his head, asking himself the same question. "It's a tempting thing, having her take the heat off me and deliver the ship."

"Temptations don't always pay off. Take it from this girl." She tapped a hand against her chest. "Gotten myself into my fair share of trouble chasing things I shouldn't have. Take my advice and don't let her take it. I know I've got no room to ask you to do that, not after what I did forcing you to the planet and especially here." She gestured to the room around them.

Star sat in silence, watching her. He'd seen enough people over the years pass through on his old ship to know when someone had something more to say.

People always had those little tics. It was in the way she wrung her fingers before realizing she was, the quick brush of a hand against her pants. Her mouth twitched like she was on the verge of saying something she might regret. Or she had no idea of how to spit it out.

He'd seen enough people as a shepherd. Talked to them. Learned their pasts and their futures—things they wanted to do and the places they wished to see. He'd learned to see through them too. And what he knew told him Zita was struggling.

He reached out with a hand, tugging gently on the edges of her sleeve.

Zita paused and stared down at him like she remembered he was there. She brushed aside his hand with a light touch. "Right. Thanks."

Star said nothing.

"What you're doing—whatever it is—it means something to people like us." Zita's face twisted, and her throat visibly constricted like she was close to choking. Every word came out cold and grated.

This is hard for her. "People like us?" He worked to keep his voice neutral, not trying to inflect any tones of judgment. "What do you mean?"

She huffed and pushed off the metal shelf. "Not just smugglers, but yeah, us too. People"—she jabbed a finger in the direction of the bar—"normal people with not much but what they've got to call their own. Everyone's heard or is hearing about the shepherd on the run. We don't know much and doubt you'll tell us, but we know someone's pushing back. You've carried something they want bad, and you haven't given it in." She broke eye contact, staring at the far wall.

"Damnable robot." Zita gnashed her teeth as she stomped toward the keypad near the door. She jabbed it until the cooling unit shivered and the clouds of foggy air lessened. The smuggler turned and leaned against the wall, looking at her feet. "It's not just about you, Shepherd. Not anymore. What you're doing has impact out there." She waved a hand dismissively through the air.

"Don't let her take that from you—from us." Zita tugged her collar before balling a hand into a fist. "You did the work. It won't sit well with folks to see someone in the Liberation Movement come in and do the last leg of the journey just to take the credit. If that's how they want to act, what makes them so different from the Oligarchy? You do it all and they get the credit—the rewards?"

Star exhaled and rubbed his eyes. There was truth in that he couldn't deny. He held a hand to his head, trying to assuage the mounting throb just behind his right eye.

It didn't right with him to let Savi bring The Light home. Then again, it wasn't his choice to let anyone decide, was it? The job was given to him by her folks. If they made the call to finish it, who was he to say no? He looked to Zita and reconsidered.

So long as it got there, what did it matter who ferried it? But did he just get to walk away clean like that? Given a chance and taking it were two different things. Star rubbed harder until he felt a few lashes break free and tickle his palm. "Then what do I do?"

"Finish it. It's what people want to see. Just don't let Savi do it. It's not that I don't trust her, but no one wants to see that happen. It doesn't change anything— not to common folk. We're trading one elitist for another." She clenched her jaw and released a heavy puff through her nostrils. "It's doesn't matter if what you're carrying ends up with them anyhow. People would rather hear the shepherd did it and stuck his finger in everyone's eye while doing it."

He rose from his seat, trailing a finger over the lip of the stool as he circled it. "That's what it's about, though, the people."

Zita tilted her head, regarding him.

"What I'm carrying could change everything for common folk, level the field a bit." He gripped the side of the stool until his knuckles ached. Star let go and took a breath to calm himself, wondering how open to be with Zita.

"And you're wondering whether you want to tell me or not?"

Star stared at her.

She gave him a small, lopsided smile. "I've met and learned to read just as many people as you likely have, Shepherd. Smuggling's good for that. I won't push, but can't say I'm not curious. It's riled the Oligarchy. It's got to be something good."

"Depends on where you're standing. From their point of view, what I've got is as bad as it can be and threatens to shake their foundations. They're not overly fond of that."

Her smile deepened. "You'd be surprised how little people out here care what the Oligarchy's fond of. You've got something to hit them hard? Good. Drive it all the way to their gut and let it sit there. Folks could use that."

"It'll sit there for a long while—forever likely." His words fell with enough weight to mute the condenser's noise, which ceased shaking.

"That's…long." Zita's mouth pressed tight, and she swallowed before looking to the door. "Part of me wants to tell the crowd out there that much."

Star took a step toward her, hand outstretched to stop her before he reined in the impulse.

"Don't worry. None of us would let that word carry out of here. Turning you is stupid. You think the military would reward a bunch of smugglers? They'd take you and parade you around and shaft us. Why pay a bounty when you could take us for all we're worth and get the shepherd for free?" Zita pushed off the wall and placed a hand on the door. "Thanks for the talk, Shepherd. It helped clearing all of that out."

"Wait, dammit." He reached out to her before pulling back and making a fist. "Just wait." Star flexed his fingers, trying to stop the fidgeting. "You ought to hear all of it. Half of me thinks I'm stupid for wanting to tell you."

She quirked a smile. "And the other half?"

"Thinks I'm just as stupid but is willing to let me go ahead with it." He matched her grin. "You told me the truth about Savi. Feels like I could return the courtesy. You had no cause to open your mouth. You did. Thank you."

Zita opened her mouth then shut it just as fast, nodding instead.

"I'm trusting you with his because I might need a favor, and I'm hoping this is worth that. That fair enough?"

"I'll let you know, Star Shepherd."

He told her truth.

Her eyes widened, and she sucked in a breath. "I can't head to Slaydus, but I'll do what I can and put out eyes and ears nearby."

"Thank you, Zita."

She shook her head. "Don't thank me. Hell, no wonder the military is after you." A series of beeps shrilled from her hip. Zita twisted and wrenched a palm-sized card from her side, holding it out before her. "Speaking of"—she flipped the lens display in her grip—"we've got uninvited guests heading for Lisba."

Star swore. "The military."

CHAPTER TWENTY-THREE

OUT OF TIME

"Damn, how'd they find us?" Star gestured to the door, motioning for Zita to open it. *Was it the blockade checkpoint?* They had run Ahiko's credentials and not bothered with anything more than a cursory search. *Did they go deeper?*

Zita spat and swung the door open. "Not sure. But I had a few lurkers out in passenger shuttles doing honest and approved trade work between local planets. They pinged the military's arrival a few minutes ago. They'll be here shortly. What I'm getting's not good."

"Never is." Star followed her as she moved into the bar and he scanned for Ahiko. "What are they bringing?"

Zita glanced at the screen. "Not enough firepower to waste the planet."

"But?"

She bit the corner of lip and traded looks with Molan. "More than enough to slag our safe haven."

"That's not their game. At least, it won't be up front. They won't chance destroying *The Leaf* if they think it's here. They'd rather have it than wreck it."

The smuggler frowned, holding up her lens for everyone in the bar to see. "Means they won't want to fire on the planet. They'll deploy troops, detaining and fighting on the ground." Her voice carried through the small room, cutting through the conversations.

The clamor died. All eyes fixated on the images displayed on Zita's lens. Mouths moved silently, as if trying to find the right words to voice and failing.

Zita capitalized on the quiet. She jabbed a finger at the screen, keeping the patrons' attention on it. "We've got minutes at best before the military and its might descend on Lisba with fierce intent. That's just enough time for some—some—of you to make it to your birds and scuttle. Likely you'll get airborne and out before this section of the planet's quarantined. The rest of us are faced with a choice. A hard one." She gazed around the room, narrowing her eyes and giving each person a steady look.

A handful of patrons bolted from their seat and made their way out of the bar at full sprint.

He couldn't blame 'em, and he couldn't ask the rest to stay and help. Star stepped up to the counter, brushing past Molan. He fixed the crowd with the same look Zita wore. "It's the smart move"—he pointed to the exit—"running. Can't say if it's the right one, but it makes sense. I won't fault a single one of you for running. This ain't your fight, but this is your out, if you want it. And it's closing." He looked outside.

Several members followed his gaze. Savi remained

seated. He pushed her out of his mind and waited to see if anyone else would turn to leave. They didn't.

Well, that's something. He balled a hand, burying it in the palm of his other and cracking his knuckles. "What's coming is my fault." Everyone held his stare. They weren't scared. So, they were okay with this, or they were stupid. "I'm shepherding something that can put a serious hurt on the backs and wallets of the Oligarchy. I don't know how it'll all play out, but if it goes right, we could be waking up to a new world and lives not too far off."

A few patrons rose to their feet, leaning over to support themselves on the tables.

Guess they're interested. "I've got no call to ask you to stay, risk life and limb to fight with or for me. But I'm going to ask you anyway because I need help." Star glanced to Ahiko, who raised a glass in his direction. It was nice to know the pilot found it appropriate to get drunk. Star shook his head and focused. "What's in my hold is something that will make this"—he fished a card-sized plate of metal from his coat—"useless." He sent the stamped currency tumbling through the air with a snap of his wrist.

It struck the counter with a *clang* that muted all other noise. Every pair of eyes homed in on the rattling bit of metal until it settled.

"Maybe tomorrow, the day after that—next year— soon, you won't need that to pay to keep you warm. The folks who say how much power your home gets won't make those calls any longer. You'll be free to do a bit more with your lives, and if not you, maybe those you care about. But people will be free from those yokes." Star banged a hand against the table, jarring some of the patrons.

"This ain't just about me or you. It's something more, something not all of us can see or will live to. That's the truth. But, damn if it's not something we've all thought of at one point or another." He gripped the lip of the counter until pressure built in his knuckles, making his skin feel tight.

"Two minutes, people." Zita stole the attention and gestured to the screen. "Not long enough to scuttle and break past what's coming. Do or die time. Choose. I'm standing with the shepherd. People like us don't get much choice as it is. Now we've got one. I'm no fan of the government, and I'm willing to wager neither are you." She smirked.

A chorus of soft laughter echoed through the room.

The self-satisfied expression vanished from her face as it hardened. "Truth is, this is going to get dirty. Any of you taking to the air are taking a risk. They might shoot you down. But if you go in numbers, it'll be a great mess to sort through. It'll buy the shepherd some time." She flashed him a look. "He's not getting airborne, likely. They'll want to land troops and come for him and his ship on foot. Those of you who can take off, get yourselves to Slaydus."

Star's heart leapt without pause, feeling like it would continue until it failed from exhaustion. He shot Zita a glare.

She matched his look and threw a hand to her side to gesture to the crowd. "They've got every right to know where you plan on going to next. If we're going to risk our necks, we ought to see this done all the way.

We want to be there."

Some of the visitors murmured in agreement, trading looks.

Zita used their mumbled agreement to her advantage. "You don't know the shepherd, but you know me. I've heard his tale, and I believe him. He's not lying when he says this'll change the galaxy for us. I'm staying. I'm making sure he gets to Slaydus. This is bigger than all of us." She jabbed a finger toward the sky. "It's about taking back everything we can. Our free skies. Our ways of earning a living, keeping warm, fed—all of it!"

The bar erupted into screaming as men and women pulled their weapons free.

Star glanced at Zita's lens. *And just at the right moment.* "Time's up."

CHAPTER TWENTY-FOUR

PREFERABLY ALIVE

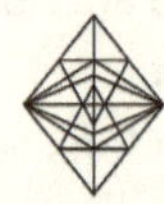

A steady rumble of thunder filled his ears, an irregular stream synonymous with only one thing. "They've broken atmosphere. Coming in!" Star leapt over the counter, drawing his pistol and grabbing Ahiko's collar.

Several patrons roared and rushed toward the exit.

"Get to your ships and take off. Keep low. Flood their radar. Make it hard as hell for them to spot the shepherd's bird." Zita turned to him, drawing her own weapon. "Does she ping when powered off?"

Star shook his head. "They won't be able to find her with the storm and everyone taking to the air." *I hope.* "Only shot they've got is with their own two eyes and hitting the ground."

"You hear that?" Zita brought the lens to her lips. The screen flashed and cut to a hooded figure dressed identically to her. They nodded in silence. "Good. Make it happen. Get anyone at every outpost to get airborne.

Tell 'em Zita's calling in favors owed. And for the ones that's not good enough for, tell them I'm paying out." She gave the screen a feral grin.

Ahiko rose to his feet, blinking as he eyed the counter uncertainly. He teetered in place despite resting his hands atop the bar. "Whozzat?" The pilot leaned forward and narrowed his eyes on Zita's lens display.

Star groaned.

"You caught sight of the other outposts on this side of Lisba, right?" The smuggler gave them both a sideways look.

Ahiko put a hand to his mouth as a high-pitched *hic* left his lips. Another hiccup rocked him, forcing him to swallow a fistful of air. "They're all smugglers?" The man squinted at the screen and his smacked lips.

Zita inclined her head. "That and other things. Don't know how many bothered to stay. We'll find out soon enough, I guess." She dragged a finger in front of the holographic display, forcing it to slide to a new live image.

A two-kilometer-long supercarrier dominated the view. It descended without resistance through the hive of smaller ships rising to meet it. None engaged in weapons fire, keeping to obscuring the already muddled view its pilot likely had.

"There's no way they're planning to land that thing." Star turned to Ahiko.

The pilot exhaled and blinked hard. "They could, but it'd be pointless." A slight slur tinged his speech, making the last word drag out. "Carrier's got enough bang"—he smacked a fist into an open palm—"to be an annoyance. They'll keep her hovering close by. Eyes and guns on the scene. Troops will drop from there. They'll be pretty shoot-to-kill over this by now. Don't expect people getting by okay, save for you, Shepherd." Ahiko gave him a knowing look.

He sighed, exhaling through his nose. "I was afraid of that." Star turned his attention to Zita. "You still up for this?"

She gave him a look that answered his question.

"Alrighty then." Star raised his revolver and glance to Ahiko. "Ready to get out there?"

The pilot took a series of deep breaths like he was trying to steady himself. "Don't think ready's got a thing to do with it, Shepherd." He jerked as a strong hiccup racked his body. "I'll do what needs doin', but…" Ahiko squinted at the screen.

"But?" Star followed his look, uncertain what the pilot made out of the images.

"Something's wrong. The military's sent too little— at least to me—to capture you. If they knew you were here, they'd have quarantined the whole planet. Hitting a quarter of the world just to screen some outposts?" Ahiko shook his head. "I think they were tipped off. They're coming to do a check, a nasty one, but they're not sold."

Star moved toward the exit. "Works for me. Let's get out of here—"

Zita cut him off, gesturing behind him.

The remaining patrons flipped over tables, using them like makeshift cover. Molan hefted a shotgun fashioned from black polymer plated in metal blends Star couldn't identify. M34N pulled an odd-looking pistol from below the counter, a skeletal frame of a weapon with a barrel lined in rings. The automaton looked it over before tapping the butt.

An electric current wound through the coils before a high-pitched whine emanated from the gun.

Power-stripped pistol. That's illegal. Star frowned and eyed the pair.

Molan gave him a toothy grin. "If I die here, he gets the place?" The barkeeper hooked a thumb towards M34N.

He, huh? Star stared at the bot.

M34N looked back to Molan. "If I die, I don't get the place." He lowered his head and sulked.

"You didn't turn and run." Molan grabbed a glass from the counter and downed its contents. A heavy sigh escaped his mouth. "You could've left us here to face the might of what's coming. You didn't. We make it out of this, people are going to talk."

He hoped so. Word needed to spread. "I'm doing this for people like us. Don't have much choice, not really." Star glanced at Ahiko, pointing to a corner of the bar to take cover in.

The pilot shook his head. "Doorway's a funnel. Use it." He motioned to both sides of the way in. "Can cause a nice mess if you and I set up there. Knock a few down, let the fine patrons of this establishment do what they do best."

Star squinted at the pilot and noted the distinct lack of inebriation. The pilot was tilted seconds ago. Either he recovered far too quick…or he wasn't as much of a drunk as Star thought. He filed away the quirk for later, deciding it best to heed the man's advice.

Star rushed to one side of the door, pressing his back

against the wall. He cast a glance at the revolver on instinct.

Ahiko took up position on the other side of the door, staring at him. He took long, dragged out breaths, like he was working to calm himself.

Good idea. Star followed suit, shutting his eyes and focusing on each breath.

"Touch down."

Star jerked back to reality at Zita's words, eyeing her lens. He spotted the supercarrier hovering just above the treetops. Countless troops flooded from its sides, all dressed in gray-white patchwork clothing meant to shed water. Their hoods were drawn, sheltering most of their faces. The rest were obscured by masks similar to those Zita and her crew had worn. Intermittent bursts of fire spouted from packs on their backs, slowing their descent. Dozens of soldiers hit the ground, fanning out in near insect-like rows. Several lines headed in their direction.

An eerie silence filled the bar, leaving only the sounds of the rainfall. Everyone in the bar had receded behind their cover to create the illusion the place was empty.

A heavy weight fell outside the entrance to the bar, disturbing the pooling water with a *splash*.

Right. Right. He reassured himself and took another breath. Star tapped his fingers against the gun's grip before tightening them around it.

A rifle barrel broke through his vision before the first figure stepped through the entrance, sweeping to his right with mechanical efficiency. The man sighted on Ahiko and raised a fist. "Con—"

The pilot didn't let him finish, pulling the solider to him with a quick yank on the weapon's strap. Ahiko seized the advantage and grabbed hold of the off-balance soldier's shoulder. He wrenched, pulling him harder. The man staggered forward allowing the pilot to get behind him and shove.

Soldiers rushed into the room, breaking off alternately between left and right.

Star sidestepped, ramming his shoulder into the first person he could and sending them toppling. He followed up by squeezing off a pair of shots and striking two men in their sides.

They dropped near the middle of the bar, breaking up the momentum of a few of their compatriots. The toppled soldier near the entrance caused a minor break in the flow of troops trying to enter.

Smugglers burst out from cover, unleashing a salvo of ballistic and high-energy powered shots. The military returned fire in the form of screeching tendrils of electric blue. Violent light filled and arced through the room.

Star winced, shying away from the opening.

Troops fell in the doorway, forcing others hobble over others in an attempt to get in. Their attempts were short-lived. Someone barked an order, prompting them to form up outside the entrance. Soldiers fired in overlapping bursts from the sides of the entrance. A few well-placed shots standing directly in line of the smuggler's' view outside the place.

It was risky but effective. The military had them pinned, and they knew it.

One of the fallen troops recovered, fishing something from his pocket.

Star aimed at the soldier and fired.

The soldier rolled to their side, pulling free a lens display of their own as Star's shot burned through the floor beside them. Holographic images sprung to life and filled the air above the lens. The soldier jabbed a finger at Star. "It's him! It's the—"

A bolt cut across the bar, striking the soldier's chest and silencing them.

Star turned to the source.

M34N's pistol crackled with minute threads of current. He glanced at Star. "If he reported you, we'd be in more trouble."

Star rubbed a palm against his face. "He did. He screamed it loud enough for them to hear."

"Should I have shot him sooner?" M34N tilted his head, waiting for an answer.

It never came. Star swore and stepped away from the doorway, moving closer to the corner. He gestured to the roof above the entry.

Ahiko caught his meaning and nodded before sinking to his knees. The pilot dropped his elbow into the base of the neck of a soldier trying to get to their feet. He pulled the soldier's weapon free, slinging its strap around himself and looked to the ceiling. "Bring it down?"

A trio of lances raced through the bar, disappearing through the doorway out into the mass of troops outside. No cries echoed outside.

Star pushed away thoughts of the soldiers just beyond the entrance. "Yeah, collapse the roof and bury the doorway."

"Collapse the what?" Molan pumped a shot through the door, shooting Star a heated glower. "Like hell"—he loosed another shot—"this is my establishment!"

M34N fired in quick succession. "I must agree with that sentiment. In the increasing likelihood that I will be inheriting this business, I would prefer to keep repair costs to a minimum."

Ahiko snarled something incoherent, leveling his newly acquired rifle toward the ceiling. The weapon rattled like a clunky wheel spun inside it. Star-bright orange light crackled at the barrel's tip before pluming into a large cone. An electric whistle shrilled without stop as a torrent of superheated rounds hammered the roof like hail.

Wood splintered, showering the entrance in particulate debris. Larger pieces of former roof and tree fell as well.

Ahiko swept the weapon in a slow arc along the entirety of the roof near the entrance.

Shit. Star sprinted the short distance to the bar counter, grabbing it with his free hand and mantling over the top. His knees ached and absorbed the impact as he landed on the other side. He spun in place, firing a round without looking at the opening. The lance of light rocketed through the entrance, glancing a soldier's shoulder.

Ahiko dragged the weapon's firing path further inward along the ceiling, bringing down more of it.

The sides of the doorway sagged toward each other as more debris littered the opening.

"Everyone, get your asses in here!" Molan jerked the door to the back room open, gesturing into it with his shotgun.

No one objected. Every patron leapt to their feet, scrambling for refuge as rooftop bits crumbled and rained to the ground.

"Think you overdid it." Star glared at the pilot.

Ahiko must not have heard him. The pilot fixated on a spot several feet above where the top of the entrance had been. He stormed the spot with the torrent of weapon's fire until another pile of tree chunks rained to block the way. The tip of the rifle glowed the same color as the salvo it had fired. A slight whine came from near the stock. Ahiko threw it to the ground. "That'll buy us some time. Not much; they'll be able to blast through that just as easily as I did."

Star arched a brow.

"They won't fire blindly into here, not now that they know you're in the midst of it. You're wanted alive, preferably."

Ahiko dropped to a knee, brushing aside a fallen soldier's coat with a callous swipe of his hand. He reached in and pulled a slender pistol free. The pilot ejected a cell, eyeing it before snapping it back in place. He fished within the soldier's clothing and found another two power cells. "Right, let's go before they decide to do as I did and bring this whole place down."

Star grimaced at the thought but moved toward the door, flashing Molan an apologetic look for the state of the bar.

The barkeeper didn't seem the least bit troubled by the outcome. He ushered Star in while barking at Ahiko to follow.

Star stepped into the room, instinctively pulling his

arms in tight in the crowded space.

The patrons were spaced out as best they could be within the storeroom's confines.

Ahiko brushed past him and looked back.

Star followed the glance as Molan stepped in, shutting the door behind him.

The barkeeper reached to one side, grabbing hold of a metal rod as thick as his arm and slid it across the length of the door. "That'll hold 'em a bit longer if they get this far."

Star pursed his lips as he looked around the room. "One problem. There's no way out."

CHAPTER TWENTY-FIVE

A LEAF IN A NET

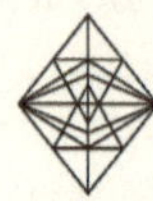

The low muttering ceased, and everyone turned to stare at him.

Star bristled under their collective gaze. "Look around. Where's our out?"

Molan shouldered his way past him, gesturing to the opposite wall. "How many of you ever take notice of all them lightning rods and paddles we've got running 'round this side of Lisba?"

A soft chorus broke out of people mumbling.

"What of it?" Ahiko scratched the side of his head, casting a wary glance to the door like he expected someone to break through at any moment. "Power generation. Cheap, damn effective, and good on you for doing it. What's the point?"

Molan moved toward the center of the room, pausing to place a hand on a metal shelf. "The point's what you're missing. What do you think all that power generation's for?" He arched a brow, turning his head slowly like he were posing the question to everyone in the room. "Think it's all for, what, scant bits of bars and rest stops likes this?" The barkeeper shook his head. "We've got pads and minor establishments scattered all over this half of the world. Do the math. That much power, it has to go somewhere, no? We don't refuel out here or affect repairs."

Another round of murmuring rolled through the small room.

Ahiko frowned, eyeing Star.

He returned the look and mulled over what the barman had said. It clicked after he thought it over in depth. "That power's not being run off; that'd be a waste." All eyes turned to him, but Star brushed off their looks. "Means you're using it to keep the lights on somewhere…else. You led us into a room with no way out. Dumb call, and you don't strike me as stupid. Meaning"—Star fixed the barkeeper with a level stare—"you've got a means of escape."

Molan flashed the mob of smugglers a toothy grin. "That I do." He trundled past the tightly packed crowd toward the far wall. The barman tapped the tip of his foot against a few of the tiles where the floor ended.

Screeching lasers sounded from outside, muffled by the door to his back. Star glanced over his shoulder and frowned. "Might want to hurry up with the tap dancing."

Several patrons turned to face the door, training their weapons on it.

The noise from the various weapons intensified. Stone crumbled under the ballistic barrage.

The barkeeper tapped his foot against a single tile

before stomping it several times. "Right." He fell to his knees, his face twisting in discomfort as a small grunt left his lips. Molan pressed a hand to the tile.

Blue light seeped through the space between the tiles around it as the far portion of the room tremored for a second. Three tiles groaned in protest and slid back over the ones behind them. The process continued until a narrow opening, six feet high, stood before them.

Molan made an exaggerated bow and flourish with his hands in the direction of the passage. "Way out. Single file, folks. No pushing. No talking. Get your asses movin'."

Star moved through the crowd with lengthy strides, reaching out with a hand to grab someone by the back of their shoulder. He twisted and forced them to turn around.

Savi tilted her head, giving him a cold, immobile look. "Is this really the time for this?" She looked back to the line of people bustling down the steps of the passage.

"Figure now might be the only time." Another salvo of high-powered blasts jarred Star, causing him to shoot a glance at the door. "You've been taking this awfully calm."

Savi opened her mouth to speak, but Star waved a hand, cutting her off.

"You didn't so much as make a peep or budge when Zita broke news of the military's approach." Star's gaze hardened.

"Was I supposed to?" The monk's face remained a frozen mask, betraying no expression. "Hm. Next time, if it makes you feel better, I will. But we wouldn't be in this situation had you heeded my advice and let me take the cargo. I gave you a choice. You chose wrong."

Star snapped out a hand, grabbing her by the wrist. "It ain't right. I've traveled around long enough to know when things don't add up." He narrowed his eyes. "Or when people are hiding something. Do us all a favor and come clean. We—"

Thunder erupted within the bar.

Savi tugged his arm. "Let go. Now is not the time."

He relented, breaking his hold and eyeing her. "You're right. Move."

The monk turned and hurried to the opening, flashing Molan a cold look, which the barkeeper turned Star's way.

Star shrugged it off and descended into the passage.

The walls were layered in a cheap, white plaster, spread in a thin and mottled coat. Bits of run-off left splatter marks and drops over the wooden flight of stairs. Weak, amber lighting illuminated the way. Each step was just shorter than the length of his feet, making it difficult for the group to make their way down in a smooth fashion. Every bit of progress down the stairs was accompanied by jabbing elbows and sudden stops.

"Could've built this place a bit better." Ahiko rapped a knuckle against the sidewall, cracking loose a chip of weakened plaster.

Star looked to Molan, who ignored the pilot's comment.

The barkeeper pressed his hand to a panel on the wall. Tiling above shook as it slid back into place. Molan reached out, grabbing the uppermost corner of the staircase where it met the now-closed tiles. He wrenched on the piece of wood before releasing his hold. The woodwork juddered before sliding forward. He backpedaled as a two feet thick block of wood sealed itself against the opening.

"It's built fine." Molan slapped a hand against the solid block above him. "Now they can look and tap all they want, they won't know where and what to look for. Thing's big enough to block any handheld scan."

Star eyed the barkeeper askance. "You've really thought this through." He turned his gaze past Molan to the mixed crowd of smugglers and folks alike. Their expressions ranged from neutral masks of professionalism, taking it all as it came to tight masks of concern. "None of them knew, did they?" He nodded to the patrons. "Everyone here thought of this place as nothing but a stop to recover and hide out when needed."

Another layer of quiet blanketed the passage. Everyone turned to stare at Star and Molan.

"I didn't know either, if that helps." M34N shambled up a couple of stairs, bumping his way past a pair of people.

"It doesn't." Star held his gaze on the barkeeper. "What's really going on? Military attacks, you're ready with a place to go and power generation to supply more than stars and darkness knows."

Molan's mouth twitched, and his shoulders sagged as if he'd been carrying an invisible weight that became too much to hold. "I'll tell you about later. Move now."

The muffled sounds of laser fire filtered into the passageway.

"They're cutting through the door, and sound

carries. Chances are if we keep arguing here, someone *will* pick it up on a handheld scanner. Move." The barkeeper broke his look with Star and shoved a few patrons unceremoniously as he moved past them.

Star exchanged a glance with Ahiko, relenting to follow behind Molan.

The motley group ambled along with the sort of quiet one would expect in a graveyard.

His back knotted as faint taps emanated above and behind them. The sounds of soldiers setting foot back in the storeroom. And they were right beneath their noses—feet. Star shut his eyes and took in a slow breath.

The descent continued until the steps ended onto level ground. Molan flipped a switch with a callous flick of his hand. White lighting the color of sunlight flooded the room.

Star winced, bringing a hand to shield himself from the momentary, jarring brightness. His eyes adjusted and he looked down the length of the hall.

The portions of the walls closest to him were what he would expect to find inside the giant trees of Lisba. As the passage stretched on, the sides morphed into craggy stone that looked like it was artificially attached to mimic reptilian scales.

"I think we're due that explanation 'bout now, barkeeper." Star hoped the man would come clean. Too many factors had come into play for Star to juggle and sift through. He didn't want any more surprises but felt they'd come nonetheless.

Molan slapped a hand to the stony surface. "Walls here are like the block near the stairs, protect these passages from being scanned as well."

Passages. More than one. Star pursed his lips, replaying the scenery from when he and Ahiko had broken Lisba's atmosphere. He recounted the forms of power generation and tree coverage that would allow for places like this, and the likely distance they had travelled.

He slipped through the crowd, moving by as they parted for him. "There's a network, right? Tunnels and ways connected through the trees and below the docks on this half of Lisba? Zita's got people monitoring government traffic for smugglers, and you cater to them. So, I have to ask, who are you here to monitor, barkeeper?"

Star swore he could hear the pulse of every person nearby quicken.

Molan licked his lips, shying away from the looks falling on him. "Reckon you've got an idea of what this is and who we are? Big galaxy after all. Hard to make a difference lingering on the edge of nowhere. Sometimes it pays to have a bit of yourselves everywhere, if you catch my meaning." He gave the crowd a weak smile.

Star caught the truth and winced. *We. Yourselves.* He brought a hand up to cradle his forehead that felt like it was nursing a heartbeat of its own. "Hell, should've seen it."

"For all the light and things supposed to be seen, I ain't seeing shit, Shepherd. Mind shining a bit of that our way and not keeping us in the dark?" Ahiko gestured with a waggle of his pistol to the crowd of patrons.

Zita cleared her throat loud enough to draw attention. "Pressed as we are, I'd like to know too." She focused her narrowed gaze on the barkeeper. "Been coming here long enough only to find out it's not quite what I thought. Makes a girl a tad uncomfortable. Not to mention, irritable." Her finger's twitched against her weapon.

Molan lowered his head and sighed. "Savi, a little help?"

And there it was: a bit of the reason she was really here and why she took everything all in stride without a hint of worry. Savi knew there was a way out. She was ready.

Zita bristled, her hand wavering and the tip of her weapon inching its way toward where Savi stood. The smuggler caught herself, getting control and stopping the gesture.

It didn't go unnoticed by the monk. "It's as you think. This, along with every other outpost scattered around this part of the planet, is part of the Liberation Movement's resistance efforts. We've long since known Lisba is frequented by smugglers and people of similar occupation. The Liberation Movement decided half a century back to give you all somewhere better equipped to do that. You kept a wide eye on the government and their movements—laws—and we could use that. So, we did."

Star's intestines felt like looped ropes tightening around themselves. He knew what would come next.

Savi stepped toward the middle of the group, seizing their silenced confusion as a stage to continue. "We used your information to better coordinate our efforts. The funds you shared with us went to the Liberation Movement. And Lisba isn't the only world where we have operations like this. The pertinent questions are answered. Anything else you want to know can wait. Now, I suggest we move before the government's dogs nip any closer to our heels."

Icy needles pricked the skin along the base of his neck as he stared at the monk. Star narrowed his gaze on Savi, thinking back to something he'd heard earlier. *Can't be.*

The monk moved to the front of the crowd and picked up her pacing.

Ahiko slipped by his side, nudging him with an elbow. "Odd turn of phrase, no? She seems a touch heated. Not normal for a monk in my experience."

Star pursed his lips. "You've got much experience with monks, have you?"

The pilot opened his mouth to speak, but Star waved him off.

"You're right. Something's off with her. Hear what she said?" Star gave Ahiko a knowing look.

"Caught it, yeah. Don't know what to make of it past that she really hates the government." Ahiko looked around. "In this crowd, who doesn't?"

There was a limit to hate, though. If one went past it, it became something else—something worse. Star held onto the thought but pushed it to the side. He shook his head and motioned for Ahiko to follow as he broke into a jog to catch up to the departing group.

Zita had lingered behind and fell into step with them. "Don't suppose you want to hear the bad news?"

Star swallowed a groan. "Suppose there's not much choice, is there?"

"Military's taken to firing on some of the smuggler ships keeping formation in lower atmosphere and just over the treetops." Zita's face tightened before softening. She looked away from them and turned to stare ahead. "Some of my friends have already gone down." She cleared her throat harder than necessary.

He focused on breathing calmly, controlling his pacing as he jogged. *Think.* He inhaled through his nose, holding onto the breath longer than necessary. *And how'd you feel if it were one of your own?* He blew out the breath, sucking down shorter, ragged ones to compensate. *I've already lost some of my own.* His fingers curled and dug into the soft tissue of his palm, jarring him back to reality.

"We'll hit 'em back, Zita." Star gave her a quick look of reassurance. "We get to Slaydus, and we'll level a blow that'll be heard through the whole galaxy."

Zita sniffed and flashed him a weak smile. "It's going to be harder than you might think."

Star knew that to be true. He buried the doubts clinging to his mind and focused on catching up with the group ahead. They'd stopped a dozen yards from him, heads craned to glance at something casting a flickering light above them. He slowed his pace as he closed in and walked the remaining steps to join the crowd.

A two-foot lens hung at an angle on the wall, displaying a scene from the surface of Lisba. Heavy rainfall obscured much of the imagery coming through the feed.

Ahiko and Zita came to his side, glancing at him. Star grimaced. "This just got a helluva lot harder."

"Why's that?" The pilot nudged him to prompt for answer.

STAR SHEPHERD

Star gestured toward the screen.
A net of thick cables covered a familiar ship.
"They've got *The Leaf*."

CHAPTER TWENTY-SIX

NE'ER-DO-WELLS

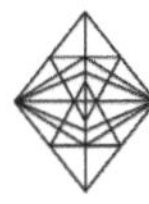

"It's over." Ahiko's voiced sounded worlds away to Star.

It felt like a copy of Lisba's storm broke out inside his skull. Stinging drops pelted his mind, and electric bursts crackled through his vision. He winced, trying to subdue the onslaught of thoughts. His heart hammered in tandem with the rainfall.

"Shepherd, you hear me?" Ahiko stepped in front of him.

Star ignored him and took a breath. His heart refused to calm itself. *Focus on where you are. Lisba. What's happened? They've got* The Leaf. *And what can you do about it? I don't know.* Dull throbbing spread through his gums the harder he clenched his jaw. "Dammit!"

Ahiko and Zita stepped back from him, exchanging looks. The rest of the crowd turned to face him and eyed him the same way.

A figure dressed like Zita broke from the group and stepped toward Star. His features were hidden behind a visor and hood. "That's it, then? That's the ship we were supposed to keep clear till you could scurry, yeah?"

Every pair of eyes weighed on Star, waiting for an answer. "Yes."

The crowd broke into low murmuring tinged with profanities. Some glanced at one another as if expecting a silent cue for what to do next.

Star stared at the screen, watching as troops tightened the net around *The Last Leaf*. *Think*. There was always a way out—a way to win. You just had to look for it. If you didn't know, ask. Star pointed to the screen again, hoping someone would tear themselves from their reverie and look. "What is that thing?"

"Ferrous net," said Ahiko. "It's made from industrial-grade cabling. Stuff can support the weight of any ship near about. They're used to capture and haul dead or non-cooperative vessels. Anchor a holding point to the top of the net and fix the end to a big enough ship. After that, just haul."

"So they've got to call in something beefy enough to tow it." Star kept his gaze on the screen.

Ahiko scratched the side of his head. "The supercarrier they've got out in orbit could do it, but it'd be a bad move. Can't haul a ship like that and leave it exposed—dangling—it'll be shot clean first chance someone gets. Normally, they're pulled into a dock onboard and left to sit till they can be cracked open safely. The cables run a continuous high-voltage charge through 'em to pop through any shield."

Star gave him a knowing look. "Not any shield." He

turned his attention back to the screen. "So, they ain't getting *The Leaf* out just yet. Means we've got a moment or two to get top side and maybe stop them."

Members of the crowd muttered amongst themselves, trading looks.

He didn't need to hear what they said to get the underlying message. They didn't feel it was worth it. They'd risked enough staying and firing on the military. Now *The Leaf* had been captured. Any further action was akin to suicide in their eyes. Star scanned the few unobscured faces, searching their expressions.

Hollow stares and sunken looks that came after the adrenaline had faded. The smugglers and misfits didn't want anything more than to run, hide, or avoid the fight ahead.

It sure as hell looked like it was over. Star had promised the people a win if they fought. He gave something more, something harder. It seemed the right thing to do for him to do his part to fix it. "If this is where any of you want to get off, do so."

People looked up at him.

"That's my ship. I'm not letting it go without a fight. And, hell, if by some manner the military does take it off-world… I'm getting it back. This is our chance to hit back for all the times folks like us have been knocked down. There's a time when people are sick and tired of having to bend a knee, run, and cower from those sitting comfy with power. This is that time. I'm a shepherd. I gave my word I'd ferry that cargo to where it needs to be. I mean to keep that word." Star raised his weapon and sighted on the lens. He fired a shot of light.

The bolt passed through the display, blowing clean through the masonry and wood behind it.

Zita put her hand on his weapon, pushing it down. "Nice speech. Hate to ruin it and the rousing effect, but—" she lifted her handheld lens—"one of my people hanging on the edge of the blockade just caught this passing by."

An octagonal prism of stone gray floated through space. The ship was an imposing, solid structure lined with long barrels that moved on a swivel. It dwarfed the supercarrier, coming in at what looked to be three times its size.

Star's eyes widened, and it felt like they were squeezed by a pair of vices. The pressure built until it resembled piercing pain more than dull agony. He'd seen ships like the one in the display before. And he'd seen what they could do to a planet.

Ahiko sniffed and spat. "I should have drunk more when I had the chance." He shook his head as if regretting the fact he hadn't done so. "It's a capital destroyer—a planet glasser. Sort of ship that destroyed Autumn."

Star bristled. "Yeah." He narrowed his gaze on the screen, purposing the fear at seeing the vessel into something else. Heat seared his nerves, and he clenched his fists. "You think it's good odds that's what's going to take *The Leaf*?"

Ahiko nodded. "Not so much worried about what it's going to take so much as what it's going to leave behind."

A fist-sized block of ice formed in Star's throat. "You think it's going to slag the planet?"

Mixed strings of profanities and panicked declarations echoed through the hall.

"I think there's a chance this half of the planet won't have to worry about the rain in the near future." Ahiko grimaced, running a hand along his jaw. "Whatever you've got in mind, best get to it and fast."

Star gazed at the screen as the cables constricted around *The Leaf* and the ship rose. Another series of braided metal wires ran from the top of the net to the base of the supercarrier in atmosphere. The vessel ascended, heading to break out of the atmosphere and take *The Leaf* with it.

"Guess they're not planning to wait for the destroyer to show up. They're going to deliver the ship in orbit." Ahiko sighed and ran a thumb along the side of his pistol like he was itching to use it on something.

Star clenched his jaw and his brows furrowed as he stared at the image of his departing ship. "Then we go out to meet them." He turned to Zita. "You got something small, fast, and strong enough to make a dent in a ship that size?" He jabbed a finger at the capital destroyer hovering in her lens display.

Zita's lower lip curled, and her eyes lost their focus for a second. "I think I've got something, though it's not punching any dents anywhere. But it'll make any existing holes bigger. We just need to find one—a soft spot—if those beasts have any?" She cast a look to Ahiko.

"Yes, maybe. It's not something—hell, you just don't attack something like that." Ahiko waved the pistol at the image of the destroyer. "Technically? Yeah. You hammer about here"—he pointed to a position closer to the middle of the ship and near the upper portions—"with enough firepower, and you might be able to make a hole large enough to squeeze something small through. It's not close to where *The Leaf* will be kept. And you can be damn sure the deck will be sealed off seconds after being exposed to space."

Star arched a brow at Zita. "Works for you?"

She nodded. "I'm not fond of this plan, if you can call it that. But if we don't do something, that thing'll waste what we have here. I don't see the government ambling by just because they have what they want." She shot a glare to the crowd. "Do any of you? After all you've been through, who wants to suffer through anything more. We have something here. Something they want to take. Are you going to let them?"

Three of the crowd shied away from her look. One of them turned back to glance at her while keeping the majority of their gaze fixed on the floor. "Sorry, Zita. Not this time." Her voice wavered like she struggled to get the words out. "We've done enough and riled the military to the point they're not forgetting this. That's what we want—need—to be forgotten. We're bugging. Sorry." She tapped two fingers to her forehead as a way of simple salute before turning and leaving with the pair by her side.

Zita frowned and turned her stare to the rest of the crowd. "Molan? Savi? Flix, Spaen, Jerrow?"

Molan's shoulders slumped, and he gave her a resigned nod. "Yeah, sure, kid. M34's in too."

The automaton swiveled his head around as if it weren't properly attached. "I am? I made no such commitment."

Molan pumped the shotgun.

"On the other hand, it seems I overlooked some details in my risk-reward ratio and, therefore, conclude it is in my best interest to go along." M34N didn't sound enthused by the prospect.

The monk shut her eyes and raised her hands in a gesture of exasperation. It was the closest thing to emotion Star had witnessed her exhibit. "This could have been avoided had the shepherd heeded my advice. But we cannot let the Oligarchy claim the ship and what's on board." She bowed her head in what he took to be agreement.

"Well, that settles that," said Zita. "Molan, which way through here's the fastest to the lower decks? I've got a few retrofitted birds down there. They'll carry just enough of us." She gestured to him, Ahiko, Savi, and herself with her weapon. "Rest of you, get to anything you can that can be of annoyance to that destroyer." She dragged a finger against the lens display.

The screen warped to show solid turquoise with intermittent streaks of white racing through. "This is Zita, and I'm putting out a call for every ship willing to break from running interference down here. Tag that supercarrier. It's hauling one of our ships to an inbound destroyer." She paused, drawing in a slow breath and waiting.

The line crackled and white peaks formed along the screen. "Sorry, must've misheard that, what with the being shot at and all while engaging a supercarrier. You say something about a destroyer—big ole ships that'll turn a planet into a floating glass bauble?" The speaker sounded like he didn't want Zita to confirm what she had said.

"That's what I said. You in?" Zita's mouth pulled at the corners, restraining a smile. "Let me rephrase before you open your mouth and say something stupid. You're in."

A raucous snort came through the line and turned into guttural laughter. "Yeah, sure. I'm in. It's stupid, hell, but I don't see anyone else complaining. You want us to be a pest and just pepper the thing?"

Zita swiped the screen, bringing back the image of the destroyer. She traced her finger around the spot Ahiko had pointed to earlier. A glowing white circle highlighted the area of the ship she marked. She flicked her finger upward. "Any and everyone seeing this, that's our target. Open fire on that section of the ship. Don't worry about aiming for anything past that. Just hammer it fast and hard as you can. We need to make a hole, doesn't much matter how much of one." She looked to Ahiko. "That about right?"

The pilot inclined his head.

"Think you lot of ne'er-do-wells can manage that?" Zita's face broke into a full smile. A chorus of enthused cries and cheers reverberated through the lens and hall. "That's that then. We need to get to one of my passenger shuttles. Molan?"

The barkeeper grunted and pointed with his shotgun to a path on the right. "A hundred yards down that way. Bit of the tunnels open up just above the next deck; you'll have to drop about ten feet. It'll rattle your knees. It's wet too. Don't slip. I don't want to clean that up." Molan took several steps down the direction he'd gestured.

A thunderclap roared through the tunnel, and the sound of falling stone and debris echoed behind.

Star looked over his shoulder. "Shit. Think they blew through the floor?"

"Dunno, and I don't want to stay to find out. Move." He took the lead, marching down the tunnel.

M34N swiveled his head to look at Molan, then the party, before turning back and following behind the barkeeper.

The remaining members of the group quickly fell in line.

Star lingered behind as Ahiko and Zita passed him by, joining the departing crowd. He watched the way they'd come from until a sharp, red light flickered into existence at the other end. His fingers drummed against his pistol.

If he loosed a shot, they'd know he was there. If he didn't, he could slink away. But they're going to be close behind.

He aimed the revolver down the length of the hall, waiting to see what broke through the red illumination.

A series of minute lights flared into existence. Each ball was just larger than his thumb, about the size of a rifle barrel. Powered weapons with charged shots.

Star lowered his gun and sprang into action. He sprinted after Molan and the others as the lights at the end of the tunnel lanced toward the spot he'd been occupying.

Prismatic streaks of energy streamed through air, blitzing into the wall. Scorched stone and wood exploded through the area.

Star resisted the urge to return fire, instead keeping

his focus on the tail end of the group as they rounded a corner. The gunfire must have given them a bit more cause to hurry. He doubled his pace, making his way around the same turn while casting a quick glance behind him.

The path he'd come from remained empty. He caught sight of Ahiko lingering a few steps near the back of the crowd.

The pilot's lips pulled together, and he tilted his head as he tapped a finger to his ear.

Star understood the silent question, answering with a quick series of gestures. He pointed to his revolver then jerked a thumb in the direction he'd left behind.

Ahiko's steps faltered, and he turned fully to face him. His face carried an expression that needed no translation. The pilot spit to his side and beckoned him to hurry up.

Star peeked past the corner he'd turned.

Red light washed over the area where the lens display had been. A trio of soldiers investigated the spot they had blasted.

He knew more men and women were lingering just out of the light's range. An itch developed in his right palm. It grew by the second, no matter how much he tried to assuage it by rubbing the rough grip of the revolver. A sharp *hsst* snapped him back to reality, and he glanced at Ahiko.

The pilot had fallen lengths behind the group. He gawked at Star like he was an idiot. Ahiko waved a hand, signaling him to stop dawdling and move along.

"There!" said the soldier holding the red light, jabbing it in Star's direction.

Shit. He bolted toward Ahiko. A series of electric shrieks rolled through the hall as blaster fire tore bits of the wall away from the corner. He used the grating sounds as a fear-inspired fuel source to pump himself harder, catching up with the group after a handful of seconds.

Ahiko ignored him, pointing his pistol behind them. He fired off a pair of shots blindly.

Several pulses of energy answered back, sailing high overhead to strike portions of the roof. Fragments of burning tree roots and splintered wood trailed behind them like confetti.

Star waited until Ahiko shot again, filling the gap between with three blasts from his revolver.

The group ahead found the strength to increase their pace further. They put more distance between Ahiko, Star, and themselves, reaching the far end of the hall.

Star swore and fired without pause, hoping the frenzied and aimless assault would pressure the soldiers to keep behind cover. A cord of pain shot up the side of his left ankle and buried itself in the tissue of his knee. He stumbled, reaching out with a hand to try and balance himself.

Ahiko helped steady him. The pilot slowed his pace, shooting over his shoulder as fast as he could. "Damn." Ahiko's face went tight as he looked at his pistol then tossed it to the side. "Charge is dead."

Star pulled himself free of his friend's hold, firing three times in two-second intervals.

No return fire came.

"How much longer?" Star's lungs felt like they had been kneaded and caked with sand. Drawing breath grew a harder chore by the second. He looked to the end of the hall where the crowd had gathered by a break in the wall wider than a standard doorway.

Molan's face twisted into a grimace as he sank to his knees. The elderly man placed a hand on the ledge and pushed himself forward, vanishing into the opening.

Star reasoned it must've been the drop he mentioned earlier. The deck was just below. The ship lay beyond that, then leaving Lisba, and finally taking back *The Leaf.*

He hobbled another few feet, gritting through the mounting pain in leg. Star took in a breath, firing behind himself as he worked to settle his mind. He pushed Ahiko with a thrust of his palm. "Don't slow down on my account. Go!"

The pilot looked past him to the bend the soldiers hung around. "Can't do it, Shepherd. We lose you, we lose what we've come this far for." He snaked a hand out, wrenching the revolver free from Star's grip.

Star protested as Ahiko closed his free hand around Star's collar and hauled. He stumbled forward, looking back to the pilot. "The hell?"

"Go, Shepherd." Ahiko sank to a knee, holding the revolver in both hands as he fired twice in quick succession.

Bits of the corner wall blasted away under the assault.

Star spat a curse and hurried toward the crowd, shouting for Ahiko to follow.

The pilot got to his feet and backpedaled, shooting randomly behind himself.

Star swallowed the pain and made it to the break, glancing down at the drop. The rest of crowd had already made the fall and proceeded along the deck.

Only Molan and Zita waited for him below. He turned and dropped, holding onto the ledge to prevent the full fall. His throbbing leg came back to mind, and he winced as he prepared himself for the hard impact. Star released his grip.

A band of electric pain went up his leg and forced it to buckle as he impacted the unforgiving metal surface. He tumbled to his ass, blinking at the world above.

Molan's face came into view as the man doubled over to look down at him. "What'd I say about slipping? Come on." He extended a hand.

Star reached out to grab it when Ahiko stepped into the break above.

A swath of laser fire lanced past the pilot. Ahiko's body jerked once as a bolt struck him in the chest by his left shoulder, and he fell into the break.

CHAPTER TWENTY-SEVEN

STARS AND SKIES

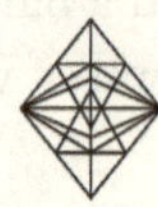

Star kicked his feet against the metal platform, scrabbling and pushing himself back.

Ahiko tumbled once before striking the hard surface with a resounding *drumf*.

Star pushed himself to his feet and scrambled over to the pilot. He grabbed Ahiko by the shoulders, twisting to turn him over. "Ahiko?" He shook him gently. "Hey?"

The pilot groaned, lifting his head to blink several times.

"Kohiba, are you all right?" Star cast a cautious glance to the opening above, calculating how long before the soldiers would advance to the spot.

"Ow." The pilot's face pulled into a strained, taut mask.

It could have been the rain and wind, but the pilot's skin looked paler than normal. Star slipped his hands under Ahiko's pits and grunted as he worked to lift him.

Ahiko howled. He sucked down a series of ragged gasps. "Shepherd, I think I've been shot." He rolled to the side, reaching for the wounded area. The tip of the revolver touched the wound. Ahiko screamed out, dropping the weapon and pawing at the area.

Shit. Star snatched his weapon up and gestured for Molan and Zita to help. "Get him up. Look him over. Come on, we don't have much time." He grunted as his leg continued playing up. Star took a wide stance, putting more of his weight on the good limb as he aimed into the opening above.

Molan came to his side looking Ahiko over. "Dunno what's worse, the shot or the fall. Zita?"

She scanned him over. "Shot's just above the heart, more in his shoulder and collar. He'll live, but he'll wish he died for a while. His face is already bruising from the fall. Betting the rest of him is too."

"So long's as it's not the important bits." Ahiko coughed, and Star imaged the man was smiling through it. "And they're all important." The pilot coughed harder.

"His brain's still working, I think." Zita slid one of Ahiko's arms over her as Molan did the same. "Let's get him to my boat. We'll patch him up best we can on the go. No point lingering."

Star breathed a sigh of relief. Ahiko would be seen to. *One problem down.* He fixed his sight on the ledge above and fired at the lip several times.

Light tore through the stonework, leaving jagged, crumbling edges that could not serve as proper holds.

If anyone wanted to follow, they'd have to jump from the top or take a risk and slide. He fired along the wall leading up to the break. Stone tumbled with each blast, jeopardizing the integrity of the structure. He hoped it fell to bits for the next person parking their ass on it.

A flash of red light broke past the opening.

Hell. Star leveled his revolver near the light and fired again.

A glowing barrel protruded from along the side of the wall.

Star took two steps back before diving as a torrent of blaster fire cut through the metal deck behind him. His hands slipped as he fought to haul himself up. He got to a shaky stand and fired at the opening again.

One of the soldiers tried to navigate the drop. They turned and grabbed hold of a large chunk of stone, fighting to find a foothold in the newly formed craters. Their hand slipped, and their ankle caught in one of the small holes. The soldier tumbled, smacking their head against the wall before landing in a crumpled heap.

Star resisted the urge to fire on the fallen troop. As long as they were there, no one would drop down on them. They served as an obstacle and an injured companion. He shot twice more into the opening then turned to lumber after Zita and Molan.

The pair had made their way to what he thought was a comically small ship in comparison to everything else he'd flown. The matte black husker-class vessel looked like a raindrop turned to its side. It had room for eight people, by his guess. The front portion of the ship was a bulbous design with a series of mini-guns attached near the bow below the cockpit windows. It gave the appearance of the ship having whiskers. The rear portions tapered into something like the wings of a fly that ended in eight independently mounted thrusters. Each sat in a rotating frame that would allow the ship to maneuver in any direction.

Zita hadn't exaggerated when she said the vessel had been retrofitted. The thing was unrecognizable from what it had originally looked like.

A bolt of halogen green passed overhead, forcing him to duck. The shot zipped between two of the ship's thrusters.

The round galvanized Star into action, and he increased his speed, ignoring the throbbing in his leg until he reached the vessel.

Zita leaned out of the middle, holding onto one of the sliding doors while extending her other arm for him to take hold of. Her eyes widened, and she looked past Star. The smuggler pulled her hand back, drawing her pistol. She aimed it close to where his head was.

Star shifted to the side as she fired. Heat and blinding light washed over his face, causing him to wince. He stuck his hand out, eyes still shut, in the hopes Zita would take it and guide him on board.

Her hand clasped around his wrist, and she hauled him up. The door slammed shut behind him. Star blinked and cleared his vision, adjusting to the inside of the vessel.

A pair of small seats, wide enough for two people, were mounted on each side of the entry to the cockpit. Savi and M34N occupied one spot each opposite one another. The remaining bench spanned the length of the opposite wall, leaving enough room for five people to cram together. That would have been had Ahiko not been lying outstretched and bound to it via the restraining belts.

The pilot's shirt had been pulled free to expose the wound. His flesh had turned an angry red and puckered around the spot the blaster had struck. The round's heat cauterized the wound, but that wouldn't do much to abate his pain.

A mechanical whine filled the air and morphed to a supersonic keen that threatened to pop his ears. Star placed his hands to the side of his head to muffle the sound as the vessel rocked.

The thrusters doubled in noise, and the shaking increased.

He looked out the window as they took off. Several soldiers had navigated down the crumbling drop to their prone companion. The ship rocked to one side, forcing Star to shift his position and steady himself. "Somebody check on Ahiko. I've got nothing in the way of medical training."

M34N rose from his seat and made his way over to the bench. "I can help, though it doesn't mean I want to."

Star glared at him. "Can you or can't you?"

The automaton cocked his head. "Of course. I was a medical assistant before being forced to undergo new outfitting to serve as a hospitality bot."

Course he was. Here's hoping his bedside manner is better than his hospitality protocols.

The bot bent over, his eyes whirring as gears interlocked and the mechanisms extended. M34N poked one of his forearms with a finger, prompting a panel to flip open on the limb. He removed a lens device and brought it to life with a tap of his thumb. A snap of his wrist caused a wide, ghostly blue light to wash over Ahiko. "The wound looks worse than it is."

The husker shook again. Star braced himself against the door and eyed the pilot. "How do you figure?"

"The charge didn't blow out of the other end." M34N held the lens of Ahiko's chest. "That means the power on the blast was dialed down. They were likely shooting with the intent to maim, not kill. He's lucky."

"Screw you, tin can!" Ahiko shivered atop the seat, managing to shoo the automaton a glare before his head lolled to the side.

"He is also an ass." M34N pulled the lens away from the pilot. "One who'll live—shame."

"I can see why you were kicked from the doctor's side, but thank you." Star turned and made his way to the cockpit as the shaking worsened. A hand closed around his wrist. He looked down to Savi.

The monk shook her head. "Sit. It's about to get worse."

"How do you figure?"

She tilted her head toward the door. "Notice how we're not being fired upon from the ground?"

Meaning someone's taking to the air to bring us down. Oh, hell.

His fears were confirmed the next instant.

"Get buckled. We've got A-slings incoming and itching for a fight," said Zita.

Star gripped the sides of the entry into the cockpit and fought to not topple over as the husker angled to one side. He stumbled into the cockpit, eyeing an open seat near the back right behind where Molan and Zita sat. Star smacked a hand against the headrest, digging in with his fingers as he pulled himself into the seat. He fastened the belt, leaning to the side as much as possible to get a view ahead.

He counted a pair of A-shaped vessels rocketing toward them. If he squinted, he'd likely see some semblance of the pilot inside the domed cockpit protruding from the middle of the diminutive fighter. They were sleek, fast, had room for one, and had the punch of three similarly sized ships.

"I hope this boat of yours is shielded." Star looked to one of the instrument clusters to see if he could be of any help.

"She is." Zita flashed him a quick, wolfish grin before flipping a trio of switches to her right. "Molan, you've got the welcome gifts."

The barkeeper grunted and brought both his hands to a flat screen nestled within the dash in front of him. "This is not how I wanted to spend my evening."

"Deal with it, old man. I had to send my crew to take my ship off-planet first word we got of this. Now I'm stuck piloting a scout bird." Zita grimaced and reached overhead with her left hand, dragging a switch horizontally through a groove. "Guns are primed. Give them a nice hello, Molan."

The barkeeper keyed the comms, a static crackle answering him as thumbed a button to broadcast. "Hello."

Mini-guns thundered to life, peppering one of the incoming fighters. A sound like endless stones hitting a metal wall filled his ears. Star glanced back to the gauges and screens to his side.

Each displayed a secondary set of readouts mirroring what the pilot could scan herself, were she not occupied with being attacked.

Star wasn't fond of sitting on the side being useless.

The A-sling screamed by, flashes of red coming from its front.

"Damn thing shrugged that off like it was nothing." Molan scowled, and his fingers went to work over the screen again.

Strobes of carmine emanated from the second fighter. Blasts struck the husker-class ship, jarring everything.

Star rattled in his seat as the object felt like it'd tear loose from the floor. His body strained against the belts as their edges dug into him. He winced through it.

"We're not going to last long in a fight where it's just us against two of 'em. I'll need to break into space to join the rest of them." Zita's hand went to a lever between her console and Molan's. She slammed her palm into it, pushing it up.

The husker accelerated and screamed toward the atmosphere. They broke through the clouds, hurtling upward as howling red light arced by.

The ship shook again.

"What was that?" Star glanced to the monitors. A single screen at the top had his answer. Against the green background, a white outline of their ship flashed near the rear. "Rearward shields took a nasty hit, but they're holding."

"Let's hope they hold long enough. There's worse happening in orbit and beyond. Military's taken to shooting down any ship they can. It's straight murder.

People are fighting back. It's getting nasty." Iron and grit filled Zita's voice.

Star swallowed a curse as they passed into the dark expanse.

Prismatic beams of all colors cut through the black canvas of space. Various vessels shot past and traded shots with legions of A-slings, painting a dizzying blur of laser fire.

"Oh, damn." Zita gestured ahead with one of her hands.

Star nursed the same thought.

The capital destroyer hovered within weapon's range of Lisba. Smaller fighters zipped by, making it through the crowded formations of A-slings to fire on the supersized vessel to no avail.

Half a dozen orbs of lime green flared to life along the destroyer's sides. Each ball dwarfed their ship and pulsated. The destroyer's bow flashed once, triggering the collapse of every orb throbbing at the ready. Light streaked through space and vaporized any ship in the way. Each beam hurtled through Lisba's atmosphere and struck the surface of the planet's half they'd been on. Explosive plumes washed into the sky, visible from where they sat.

Star gazed at a monitor showing the damage. "Stars and skies…"

CHAPTER TWENTY-EIGHT

FLOATING DEAD AND QUIET

Horrendous waves of light washed over the planet's outposts and forests, leaving nothing but oceans of ash and glass. Everything as far as he could see had been reduced to dunes of gray and black.

Star shut his eyes, fighting to keep from reliving Autumn's fate. He clenched his fists, eliciting pops as his knuckles cracked. Dryness spread through his throat and made the tissue inside feel like it'd been rubbed with coarse sand. "Tell me you see a way through this mess, Zita."

"Huh?" The smuggler's mouth trembled as she looked to a screen. "They just… Half a planet. I mean, I've heard stories, but to see it. I…" She exhaled and shut her eyes.

"Too many people stayed." Molan hung his head, shaking it. "Damn fools. If ever there was a sign to scarper, government coming knocking would be it."

Star couldn't blame them for being out of sorts having witnessed that. But if he didn't say something—do something—they'd be taken down by a pass from A-slings.

Star cleared his throat as loud as he could.

No effect.

"Zita. Molan!" He clapped his hands together.

Both of them snapped out of their trances, staring at him.

"I know what's going on in your heads, believe me. I've seen this before, and it never sits easy. Hell, trust me when I say you'll never be free of those images. Never. But now's not the time for it. We sit here and do nothing, we're bound to join any folks that stayed down there. Do something!" Star slashed the air with a hand to accentuate the urgency.

"Right, the destroyer, punching a hole somewhere along it. Right." Zita shook her head and stared hard at the ship. Her right hand flipped a series of switches at her side before turning a dial. She licked her lips, leaning closes to a finger-length microphone protruding from the dash. "This is Zita, calling in anyone harboring these skies outside Lisba."

No response.

Her brows furrowed, and she released a piercing whistle into the microphone's receiver.

"What in the cold and frighteningly dark, ass-end-side of space was that?" cried a voice through the comms.

"Got your ears now, do I?" Zita cast the husker vessel into a turn that rattled the insides of Star's skull. The smuggler grimaced and brought the craft to level.

"I need everyone who's listening to this to do me a favor."

"Hell, Zita. Did you see what happened? We're doing ourselves a favor trying to get out and survive this," said another voice.

"And run to do what? You hide, and they'll come again and again. They just glassed half a planet. The hell do you think they'll do next time. You think the sort of folk who can do that, wield power like that, use it how they see fit, care?"

Silence.

"That says it all, doesn't it?" Zita grunted and put the ship through another series of sharp turns and dives to avoid incoming A-slings. "Look around you. We're already fighting. We've got every sort of ship out here, and I know for a fact that you're all damn better pilots than any one of them. Prove me right. Fight back. For what was ours. For our home, our sanctuary. For Lisba!"

A garble of overlapping cries blared through the comms, echoing Zita's scream.

"Now, where the hell's my ship?" Zita scanned the scene outside.

A purple ring of light flared on the navigation screen before Star as well as the one above Zita. The blip pulsed several times then vanished off the far corner of the display. It surfaced seconds later. An unidentified voice crackled over the comms, "Might want to take a gander at the far side of Lisba's moon, captain."

Star leaned to the side and followed Zita as she turned her head in the direction advised by the stranger. A ship's bow broke out from behind the planet's moon. Picking out the vessel was a hard task against the darkened backdrop, and the multitude of obscuring panels along its body didn't help.

Zita made a fist and pumped it in a small gesture of triumph. "Knew you lot wouldn't leave me here all by my lonesome."

A chorus of laughter rolled through the comms. "Heard the chatter about hitting the destroyer hard." A dry cough rattled over the speaker. "We managed to catch sight of a bit of what they did to Lisba. Give us the word, boss, and we'll make it happen."

"We've not got much in the way weapons on that boat. Be smart about it, Rett." Zita exhaled and gazed at the destroyer in the distance. "I'll give you a mark, and you let go with everything she's got at once. Then, turn tail and get my ship out of here. That's an order."

"Done. Just say the word, Captain," said Rett.

Star flexed his left leg, working through the cramp that had settled during the escape from Lisba. It was something for him to do as he sat by the side. He ran over the monitors before him once again, committing each one's function to memory. A particular one caught his eye.

A row of digital gauges ran along a small arc over the screen. Each displayed a measurement to monitor industrial tools: temperature, charge, power, and speed modulation.

They were smugglers; how much of stretch was it to assume they were thieves as well?

"What's this for?" Star gestured at the screen.

"Ship's got a military-grade torch mounted below. Monster's set in a gyroscopic frame and can cut about any which way you want from any angle we're at." Zita sounded like she didn't much care to answer his question.

"Strong enough to cut through a chunk of shielding on a destroyer after it's been hit with every ship out there?" Star arched a brow.

"Yeah." Zita flashed him a grin and accelerated the ship. She pulled her lens free, holding it up before another screen, tapping the device against the larger display. Both screens flashed before mirroring each other. An image of the capital destroyer dominated both displays, a single area sectioned off earlier by Ahiko. Zita thumbed a button on the side of the monitor. "Everyone got that?"

A multitude of affirmations came through the comms.

"Hit 'em!" Zita pulled the husker into a sharp turn, avoiding a pair of incoming A-slings. She pulled back on the throttle and ran her left hand along a console.

The ship pulled up, space spinning before them as she righted the turn and brought them out behind the twin ships that had soared by.

Molan worked the commands before him, unleashing a torrent of fire from the mini-guns.

Rounds cut through space and showered the closest of the A-slings. Its shields flared as it repositioned itself to gain a clean firing path on them. The fighter's shields waned, collapsing on themselves the next moment. Countless bullets drilled into the vessel. The ship fell apart with no sight of the pilot.

The second A-sling fired twin pulses of green energy toward them. Each bolt washed over the husker's shields, rattling the ship.

"Forget him, Zita." Molan jabbed a finger toward the destroyer. "Look, we've got people getting through this mess of fighters to punch the big boat. Let's get there."

Star clenched his jaw and watched the secondary navigation monitor. The fighter passed overhead and swooped around their back. The vessel's image on the screen drifted past the central axis line like it was trying to steady up for the perfect shot on their rear. "Send what power you can to the rear shields, now!"

Zita's hands blurred.

The ship's shields strobed, but held.

"Nice call." Zita turned to Molan. "Maybe you're right about us bowing out of this one. We keep it up, a fighter's bound to get lucky." The smuggler captain directed the ship toward the destroyer. "Molan, anyone comes too close for comfort, scare 'em off or take them down."

The barkeeper grunted.

Zita maneuvered the husker through a throng of A-slings moving in a net-like formation, leaving little room. She brought the ship within weapon's range of the destroyer. "Everyone who's got a bead on that boat, hit it!"

Countless ships of all makes zipped over the capital ship, sending a barrage of projectile-based and energy weapon's fire at the spot Ahiko had mentioned earlier. The destroyer's shields shimmered. A ripple rolled through the entirety of the translucent field of protection, settling in the same pocket where the smuggler vessels fired.

Half a dozen other ships made a first pass overhead,

blitzing the area with another salvo of fire, some going as far as launching missiles.

Another flash of light in resistance. The shields held.

Zita leaned over and faced the comms. "Someone blast that sucker with something strong. Whatever you've got."

A trio of A-slings broke from a nearby squadron, diving low and out of sight.

Shit. Star tracked the three fighters as they zoomed along the screen, heading toward the belly of the husker. He had no choice but to do it and find out what the torch was really capable of. He scanned over the console for the cutting tool, familiarizing himself as fast as possible. They were just controls, and he was a shepherd. There wasn't a ship he couldn't learn. Star thumbed a switch to the side of the screen.

The display flashed, images vanishing to be replaced by a live view of space below the ship. A-slings closed in from the distance. A viewing lens must have been mounted somewhere along the torch. A light *fwlip* sounded off near his seat.

He looked to the source to find a slender side-stick protruding from the floor paneling and resting by his right hand. Star gripped it, running his fingers over the small insets around it. His thumb trailed a silver, ridged dial near the top of the stick. A crescent-shaped trigger sat comfortably where his index finger rested. Another smaller trigger sat below.

The closest of the three A-slings fired twin streams of red energy toward the bottom of the ship.

Star watched the beams hurtle toward them. Instinct took hold and used the side-stick like a gun, pulling on the trigger.

A flash of amber light, tinged with hints of gold, lanced between the ships. The pulse faded as quickly as it had come.

Star frowned as the A-slings shots impacted their ship, eliciting an erratic beeping from the screen monitoring shields. He slid his thumb across the dial and squeezed the trigger, holding it down.

A sustained burst of light shot out of the torch. *There we go.*

One of the A-slings angled away from the blast of cutting energy. Another passed close enough by for the beam to wash over its shields. The ship's defensive barrier crackled in response, losing the intensity in its color as it zipped by.

Damn thing's strong if it dropped a shield that much. Star wrenched on the stick, swiveling the torch's head to follow the A-sling he'd just clipped. The beam trailed behind the fighter and inched closer as Zita maneuvered the husker through the battle.

The third A-sling used the momentary lapse in awareness to swing by and clip their shields with a pair of shots.

His right arm felt like the sinews were steel cable going taut. He fought through the spasm and kept control of the quivering side-stick. *Come on.* Star tracked the weakened fighter as it swerved to the left before twirling twice to the right. *Man knows if I get a bead, I'm taking him down.* Star hunted the fleeing A-sling until it slowed its pace to avoid another of its squadron.

Gotch ya. He pulled up at an angle on the stick, sending the cutting laser across the center of the ship.

The beam dragged along the A-sling and burned through its shield before reaching the cockpit. Bright light passed through the vessel and out the back, leaving the bisected ship floating dead.

If it could punch through a small ship that quickly, they had a real shot of cutting through the destroyer. Star's clenched his jaw and set his sight on the capital ship ahead. He'd soon get *The Leaf* back.

The capital destroyer grew closer.

Star swallowed what little moisture remained his throat. His fingers tapped against the control. He glanced at Zita, wondering what the pilot had in mind.

She leaned near the mic. "Anything else you all have left, let it go. Hammer that bastard till you're dry, then bug out."

"But—"

"That's an order, Rett!" Zita reached overhead, thumbing four switches up in a row. She looked to Molan. "That's everything primed. It ain't much on this bird, but it'll be something extra. And right now, that'll count."

Molan set his shoulders and fired the mini-guns.

Bullets rocketed through space, peppering their designated spot on the shields. Seconds later, nothing. "We're out." The barkeeper glanced to Zita.

Zita toggled the previously flipped switches back down. Ribbons of azure lasers arced out from atop the husker, soaring up before crashing down against the destroyer's shields.

"The hell was that?" Star watched the blasts spread out and dissipate against the destroyer's protection. Tendrils of residual energy crackled and waved along the vessel, drawing strobes of resistance from the shielding.

"All but one of the overcharged cells we've plucked and plundered from military salvage and the like over the years. I always keep one saved and stored just in case I need it later. Things take forever to build up a decent shot, but they're close enough to ship killers on small boats. Illegal, but worth the price." Zita shot him a quick glance. "Stuff ends up like plasma and sticks to shields—pounds them good." She leaned back to the mic. "Rett, you ready yet? Clean off the dirt, will you?"

"You sure?" Rett's voice shook in a way Star felt had nothing to do with the static plaguing the comms. "That's going to be awful messy. Going to play hell with any ships nearby the biggun."

"That's what I'm hoping for. Pop them off," said Zita.

Light flashed from countless panels along Zita's larger smuggling ship. Bright silver strobed over the cockpit as metal cylinders soared overhead. "Dirty bombs." She looked over her shoulder and flashed a crooked smile at him.

Star gawked, watching the missiles hurtle toward the destroyer.

"Made of radioactive waste and other explosives. Stuff's been cobbled together. Nothing remotely close to the real things. But what little radiation's in 'em will play hell with the shields for a bit." Zita's smile widened. "The destroyer will take the hit unfazed, but it'll scramble the A-slings hovering around it. They won't be able to do squat with instruments. Floating dead and quiet. Life support's all they'll likely have."

Star matched her smile. "Works for me."

"Everyone out there still in this fight, that's your cue. Drop what you can and scuttle!" Zita switched the comms off as every smuggler vessel in sight fired off a mixed salvo of weapon's fire, explosives, and improvised blasts Star couldn't identify.

The shots passed the slower moving dirty bombs, showering the destroyer. Its shields pulsed with every impact. The color and brightness faded from the defensive barrier until it was barely visible against the black backdrop of space.

The first of the silver missiles struck the destroyer, detonating closer to the bow than the intended target. A miniature version of the explosion that had glassed Lisba plumed out from the ship. Two other clouds of fire and light sprouted along the vessel until the entirety of the destroyer was engulfed by the fallout from the blasts. Waves of energy rolled out, rippling through a hive of A-slings and heading toward them.

"Oh, hell." Zita let out a growl and wrenched on the yoke, pulling the husker up. She failed to respond in time.

A cocktail of explosive and radioactive energy buffeted the ship. Various screens and systems elicited muddled electronic cries as they faded out. Some displays recovered only to wink out just as quickly.

Star held onto the stick to keep himself from rattling around in his seat as the world spun without sign of stopping. He shut his eyes, focusing on his breathing as a way to orient himself and his thoughts.

"We're spinning out of control and heading for something worse." Zita's voice was barely audible over the blaring from the systems within the ship.

Star raised his voice to overcome the electronic cacophony. "What's that exactly?"

"The destroyer—and fast!"

Star opened his eyes just as the husker impacted the destroyer.

CHAPTER TWENTY-NINE

DIRTYING UP THE PLACE

An ear-splitting howl of twisting metal and crunching composites drowned out the screaming monitors. Star jerked to the side with enough force he feared his bones had shifted out of alignment. But everything stopped spinning.

He blinked several times, more out of weary-driven instinct than choice. The world cleared, and he stared out of the cockpit into a black void littered with gray paneling.

Several overlapping groans came from ahead of him.

Zita's head lolled to one side, and she brought a hand up to push against it. A soft crack rang out before she swore. "Ugh, what the hell?"

Molan released another drawn-out groan.

Star's extremities tingled like they'd fallen asleep during the crash, but he worked them regardless. He fumbled while unfastening his harness and pushed off the chair. Star toppled to the side as he came to his feet, and he grabbed hold of the edge of an instrument cluster to keep from falling completely. "I think our plan worked." His ribs ached, forcing him to exhale slowly through his teeth.

"How's that?" Zita cradled her head, working with one hand to free herself from her seat.

"I'm no engineer, but looks like we're inside the destroyer. Part of it, anyhow." Star released his hold on the panel, stumbling to the side. "Oh, and you parked crooked."

Zita snorted, cutting it short to moan. "Don't make me laugh. Not yet." She unbuckled herself and lurched to one side. Zita smacked her hands against the consoles, fighting for purchase. She found none and collapsed against the floor. "Damn. That one hurt. Tell me again, you said we're in the ship?"

"Yeah." Star plodded forward, reaching out for the torch's side-stick. "And not far enough. Looks like we're wedged in the exterior panels. Not sure how deep. Can't tell if this part of the ship's exposed to space or not."

Zita spat and slammed an open palm against one of the consoles. "Damn." She clawed at the lip of one of the instrument panels, pulling herself up. "Fine, let's see if we can get farther in. A ship like this will likely have interior seals mounted along the panels. They'll clamp down and run a low power shield to keep the air in." A silence trailed after she'd finished speaking.

Star got the unsaid message. Zita hoped she was right about the insides of the destroyer. So did he; otherwise, their trip would be a short one. "Find us a way through. I'll check on the folks in back." He released his hold, fighting the canted angle of the ship to leap toward the door. His aim was off.

Star crashed into the side of the doorway, banging the edge with his shoulder. A throb rolled through his joint to settle in his elbow. Static tingling swarmed the area. He gritted his teeth and slapped a hand to the doorway's lip, hauling himself through it.

He pressed his back against the side of the doorway, fixing his sight on Ahiko. "You okay?"

The pilot remained silent and immobile.

"I'm fine. Thank you for asking. I note that you didn't. But I didn't expect a human to worry about *my* safety. Oh, no." M34N tilted his head, eyes whirring without stop. "Nobody ever asks about the automaton." He turned his head to look away.

Star ignored the griping bot and turned to Savi.

The monk's head rest against the panel behind her. She sat limp, arms by her side and loose like there was no strength left in them.

"Savi?" Star inched his way toward her. "Savi?"

A soft murmur passed through her lips. She jerked as if coming to consciousness and raised her head. "What happened?"

Star told her.

She groaned, bringing both hands to the sides of her head and massaging her brow. "So, we succeeded?"

He shook his head. "Not quite. We're in the ship, but we're not *in*, if you catch my drift."

"I don't." She groaned and rolled her neck.

Star moved by her, working around the side of the ship and clinging to any handhold that would allow him to close in on Ahiko. "The short of it is this: We're going to have to punch more of a hole. No idea if our ass end is hanging out in space or what we'll find once we blow through. Could be a host of soldiers waiting to pop us."

The monk narrowed her gaze. "Your optimism is rather terrible."

"That's because it's pragmatism." Star grunted, the muscles in his arms straining as he pulled himself past the side door. He sank to his knees and braced against the panels. Star just needed one good push. He eyed the base of the bench Ahiko rested atop. Part of the metal frame protruded near the bottom to serve as a curved base. Star kicked against the side wall and jumped.

He lashed out with a hand, grabbing onto the frame and pulling. "Ahiko?" He reached up and grabbed the man's leg, shaking it.

The pilot's body quivered once before going still. He groaned. "Shepherd?"

"Yeah, it's me."

"Oh, damn. I thought I'd died and gone to heaven. I hate being wrong." The pilot coughed twice, shuddering.

Star sighed, but silent relief ran through him that Ahiko had made it through fine by all appearances. "How do you feel?"

"Like I've been shot and just went through one helluva crash. What happened?"

"You've been shot and just went through one helluva crash." Star pulled himself up, coming to rest on the edge of the seat. He grabbed one of the straps binding Ahiko to keep himself from falling from his perch.

The pilot groaned again. "This is why you shouldn't fly things."

Star shut his eyes and exhaled. "I'm a shepherd. I can fly just fine."

Ahiko let his head loll to the side, thrusting his chin to the front of the ship. "That why we crash?"

Star's mouth twitched. "Zita was flying."

"This is why I should do the flying." Ahiko turned back to stare at him before wincing. "When I'm recovered, that is."

"Is it fair to say you'll be recovered soon?" Star eyed him before glancing back toward the cockpit.

"Why's that? The hell's going on?"

Star told him the same he'd shared with Savi.

Ahiko blinked several times. "Right. Seems about what I'd expect our luck to run like. I guess I'll have to manage. Help me up, gimme a gun, and I'll follow along…notably a fair bit behind the rest of you."

Star stifled a laugh and unfastened the pilot, holding out his hand for Ahiko to take.

The pilot shifted, rolling his shoulders and grimacing through whatever likely pain coursed through his body. He lifted a hand.

Star grabbed hold and leaned to the side, serving more as an anchor for Ahiko to pull against. He didn't want to wrench on the injured pilot and hurt him further. With an extra grunt of effort, he brought the pilot up to a sitting position.

Ahiko breathed like he'd run through a series of halls avoiding gunfire. "I'm fine. Need a minute. Find us a way out of this and let me get to my feet on my own."

Star nodded, releasing his hold on the seat and stumbling toward the doorway. He caught the edge of the frame to stop his descent and swung through the opening of the cockpit, aiming for his seat. The chair passed him by as he overshot, forcing him to snap out a hand. His fingers clamped around the side-stick and forced the control to lurch in his direction. It fell forward, catching on its stop.

The ship shuddered and metal ground like everything had shifted.

Star shook the stick. Everything rattled in response.

Zita looked back at him. "The torch is still functional, barely. See if you can get it to cut our way through. I'll see about firing up any sort of thrusters we might have working."

Star nodded and wrenched on the lever, praying it wouldn't give way under his weight. He managed to claw and pull his way to the base of the seat, smacking his left hand around the metal mount holding it fixed to the floor paneling. Star clambered up into the chair and took hold of the control once again, giving it a more delicate turn.

A low, nearly guttural drone of twisting metal sounded off as the torch moved within the mangled portion of the destroyer. No screen input came up for him. He'd have to operate by guesswork.

Star squeezed the trigger. The stick vibrated like it was threatening to shatter. He imagined the small bones in his hands rattling away from the violent shaking of the stick. Star clenched the device tighter and held the trigger.

A horrible screech echoed around them before the familiar sound of a high-powered laser overshadowed the sharp keen. Orange light bored through the metal ahead, strobing back off the reflective surfaces.

Star shut his eyes and held firm to the trigger, sliding his thumb across the ridged knob on the side. The vibrations doubled in strength, and his wrist throbbed from the renewed effort he exerted.

A cavernous echo filled his ears as the torch grew louder. The beam increased in intensity and width, peeling apart the interior works of the destroyer. Metal turned to slag, forced out of the way by the husker's bulk as it crashed through the final portions of the hull.

Star yelped and clung onto his seat, and the stick as the vessel tilted.

Panicked shouts rolled through the ship from the passenger compartment behind.

He sucked in ragged breaths as the husker wedged between the corridor walls within one of the levels of the destroyer. Star gazed out of the cockpit screen, peering down the antiseptically clean white passage.

The walls glinted like they'd been recently polished.

Bit of a shame we dirtied the place. Don't want to be the fella sent to clean up after us.

"Shepherd, ahead!" Zita jabbed a finger to a corner down the hall ahead.

Black armored figures spilled out from the side, rounding the bend and coming down the passage toward them.

Star's heart lurched, and his mouth went dry. He remembered the last encounter he had with similarly clad troops. "Fire something!"

Five troops near the front of the pack stopped and dropped to a single knee, leveling rifles at them.

I wasn't talking to them.

The remaining soldiers set up position behind the kneeling men. They opened fire.

Star hit the floor, flattening himself as the cockpit screen shattered. If this kept up, they'd blow through the back paneling and risk hitting Ahiko. Star turned his head as much as he could.

Zita lay on the floor too, using the angled structure of the console to hide beneath and shield herself from the bulk of the fire.

They traded glances.

"Do something. Fire back!" he said.

Zita's lips peeled back in an almost animalistic snarl, showing too much teeth. "We've got nothing left but small, charged rounds. They're dead from the crash."

Hell with it. He reached into his coat, snatching free the revolver. Star raised the weapon overhead and fired four shots.

The laser fire ceased.

Star leaned up to peak out the cockpit. *Not what I wanted to see.*

The armored soldiers repositioned themselves, three of them setting up a tripod. A pair of troops lumbered toward the stand with what looked like a comically larger version of their rifles.

Star shimmied to his side, rolling onto his back and sighting in on one of the soldiers carrying the heavy weapon. He squeezed off two shots in their direction before turning onto his belly. He clawed his way back to the torch's lever.

"What are you doing, Shepherd?"

"Saving us." *I think.* He twisted to pop off another shot. Star wondered if he'd gotten one of the soldiers carrying the monstrous weapon. A whirring screech racked his ears, prompting him to turn. He glanced down the hall at the mounted turret. *Guess that's a no.*

The turret screamed, carmine lances shooting out in an incalculable burst with no sign of stopping. Streams cut through the remaining bits of the cockpit. Rogue blasts burned through various parts of the ship, slagging panels.

Star fired off a panicked shot, hoping to frighten the soldier behind the turret. He scrambled forward, swinging his free arm wide to grab hold of the stick. His fingers closed around it, and he squeezed the trigger.

The torch belched in disdain, but no flash of light fired from the device.

Star pulled the trigger again.

The tool and ship juddered in unison, but nothing came of it.

Dammit. He slapped the stick in a fit of frustration and squeezed.

The machine flared to life, screaming like it was exerting itself to the point of failure. A beam of energy rocketed toward the troops.

The soldiers dove out of the way, a few falling in place and flattening themselves against the ground as the torch burned through the turret.

Star pulled on the lever until the cutting beam angled toward the floor. *Come on, come on.*

"Shepherd, you trying to get us killed?" Zita pulled herself to her feet, drawing her blaster and firing at the prone soldiers.

He ignored her, focusing on tracing a path against the floor.

Metal groaned below.

"Ahiko, can you hear me?"

"Sadly, yes. Why?"

"You might want to buckle back up." Star thumbed the dial along the stick, increasing the beam's intensity.

"Why's that, Shepherd?"

"Because this is going to hurt!" Star winced as screeching metal cried out.

The ship rocked before the inevitable. The floor paneling gave way with a last moan of protest, and the world sailed away from him.

Star clung to the stick as his body rose, threatening to slam into the roof as they fell.

The husker crashed onto the level below with a sound that Star was sure carried through the entirety of the destroyer.

He struck the floor, his chest bouncing off the unforgiving metal. Star felt like he'd have to learn how to not breathe for a while. The injury would smart for a while. He released his hold on the stick, rolling onto his back and pressed a hand to his ribs.

The urge to lie there and shut his eyes grew. Dull pain rolled through his chest and back, some making its way to the base of his neck. His eyes felt weighed down by lead. If he fell asleep here, he'd likely wake up in a cell. If he were lucky. And Star was never lucky.

He groaned and pushed himself up. "Zita? Molan? You two okay?"

The pair gave him varying disgruntled sounds he

took as an affirmative.

"Ahiko!" Star got to his feet, relieved that the ship no longer sat at an awkward angle. He shambled toward the doorway into the passenger's compartment. "Ahiko?"

The pilot lumbered into the doorway, blocking his path and glaring at him. "There's something mighty wrong with whatever goes on in your skull, you know that?"

Star inclined his head. "Might be. But for now, we've got to go. We're lucky we haven't been sucked into space. Guessin' we were inside the shields the whole time. Best we get a move on before heavily armed and cantankerous folks get here."

The pilot gave him a lopsided smile that faded into a thin, pained grin. "Yeah, works for me." He pressed a hand to his chest. "If I die—"

Star waved him off. "You won't. You're too irritating to. Way my life's been going, universe has seen fit to have you hounding my ass and ears till I croak. Now, move." He gestured to the broken cockpit screen.

Ahiko chuckled and lurched past him, still nursing his wound.

Savi and M34N made their way through the doorway, moving by Star without saying a word.

Guess they're mad.

He turned and walked after them.

Zita and Molan had already clambered out and stood several feet from the ship, scanning the hall.

Star leapt out from the cockpit, wincing as the impact sent another rattle through his body that agitated his already aching bones. He looked over his shoulder to survey the ship, pursing his lips.

"Shame to leave the old boat here. Been through a lot with me, and I'd hate for the Oligarchy to get what's left." Zita came to his side, eyeing her ship with something close to fondness. "Wish the bird could have done more than just punch a few holes in this ship."

Star blinked, eyeing the husker's torch and thinking back to what Zita had said earlier. "You mentioned something about an overcharged cell?"

The smuggler tilted her head. "Yeah, and?"

"What happens if one of those things gets more charge than it can handle?" Star's mouth spread into a hungry smile.

She arched a brow. "What do you mean?"

Star gestured to the portion of the torch protruding from the ship's crumbled frame. "I mean, we run the torch's power supply into charging the cell until it has but one end. The explosive kind."

CHAPTER THIRTY

BAD PLANS

"That's crazy." Zita looked around to each of the crew members as if seeking their agreement.

Ahiko shied away from the look.

Savi shrugged.

Molan acted as if he hadn't heard a thing.

"I find it a wholly appropriate response given the Oligarchy and military glassed half a planet. Not to mention, the possibility of me inheriting the bar." M34N traded glances with Zita and him.

Zita sighed, cradling her forehead with a hand. "Of course the sociopathic automaton agrees with you."

M34N sniffed, making a sound like wind blowing through hollow metal tubes.

"Got the idea from some Elan Ahiko and I ran into back on Azzip. They rigged an old drive core to blow. Don't know exactly how, but they had the thing go nuclear." Star shrugged, jerking a thumb in the direction of the torch. "Thing's still got power. Run it to the cell, we could overload it."

Zita huffed a breath and shook her head. "You have any idea the kind of damage that'll do?"

He shook his head. "You?"

"It'll punch a hole several levels deep…at least. Can't say more than that. If I'm wrong, it could take out this entire level, not counting what's below. In case it's slipped your notice, we're on this level." Zita fixed him with a level stare.

"Best get moving then. Someone give me a quick rundown on how to make it happen. I'll stay back and do it. It'll be worth the damage and distraction." Star moved toward the torch.

"Aw, hell." Zita shouldered him aside, crouching and reaching for the cutting tool. "I'll do it. Watch my back."

Star opened his mouth to speak when he caught movement near the edge of the hole in the ceiling. He raised his revolver and fired at the lip. The round blasted the paneling away.

An armored helmet peeked over the deteriorating edge, sticking the tip of a rifle into view.

Star unloaded a volley of shots in a circle to trail the hole and deter any soldiers from getting too close. "Any time now."

Zita swore at him as she wrenched cabling free from the hose and scuttled under a portion of the ship that wasn't flush against the floor. She emerged seconds later, panting. "Give me a second to go in and trigger the torch." She hopped into the cockpit, sprinting toward the lever.

Star watched as she squeezed the trigger, pumping it harder than necessary.

She released another string of profanity before snatching a bit of cordage from her hood, tearing it free and lashing it around the stick to hold the trigger in place. The smuggler turned and ran.

Star gestured to the rest of the crew to move as he backpedaled, popping off a few more shots. "How long do we have?"

Zita shook her head. "Minutes at best. It'll be a slow charge. Couldn't do more, rigging it that way. Torch is barely trickling out power as it is. Chance they figure out what we're up to and cut the power."

He grimaced. It was a chance they'd have to take. Star's torso throbbed with every step. His ribs felt like someone was bouncing a mallet against each one. He clenched his jaw, burying the pain and focusing on the mounting pressure in his gums.

M34N broke out ahead of the group.

The hell?

The automaton swiveled his head both ways, settling on a path to the right. He waved a hand and beckoned for the rest of them to follow as he lumbered down the side passage.

Star exchanged a look with Zita and Ahiko.

The pair shrugged.

Star didn't know where to go, but he figured anywhere was better so long as it was away from the bomb-to-be. He pushed himself harder, making his way to the passage and turning into it.

M34N stood at the end of the short hall by a curved doorway.

Star made his way over to him, checking over his shoulder to ensure the rest were right behind him. "What's going on?" He paused to lean against the wall and catch his breath.

The automaton pointed to the curved surface. "It's a lift. It will be faster than looking for service stairs.

Star looked back again, nursing the worry soldiers would round the corner any second. It was a dead end until the door opened. His hand flexed against his revolver.

The rest of the crew came to a stop by him.

Zita glanced at him, then M34N. "Why are we stopped?"

The automaton gestured to the lift once more. "Elevator."

"Doesn't do us any good if we can't open it." Zita scowled, looking over her shoulder as Star had done.

M34N jabbed a flat button nestled into the elevator's frame. "It's a transport system on one of the largest vessels in the Oligarchy, not a vault."

The lift responded with a soft chime and opened.

M34N turned back to stare at them all. He managed to shoot them a look of self-satisfaction, which Star found quite the feat considering the bot's face was made from metal.

Ahiko slipped by them all and entered the lift, scanning its inside. He waved at them to follow.

Star waited for the rest to board before he stepped in. *Damn.*

Two unarmored soldiers, dressed in gray service uniforms, ran by the hall. One stopped, staring down the length of the passage at them, then went for the weapon at his side.

Star pointed and fired.

The shot went lower than he'd hoped, striking the man in his thigh and dropping him. The man howled in agony.

His companion backpedaled and froze.

Star aimed at his torso.

The lift door shut.

He raised the weapon and pulled away from the elevator's front. "What was that?" Star glanced to Ahiko.

The pilot ignored him, one finger held to a button while he scanned a translucent panel littered with tracks of light.

"You making any sense of that?" Star arched a brow, drumming his fingers along the revolver. They could find themselves in more trouble the second the door opened again. Soldiers teemed within the ship. There were bound to be some waiting on the other side. He stole a breath to calm himself, pushing aside the line of thought keeping count of his climbing heartbeat.

Ahiko grunted. "I served, remember? It's a live-time layout of the levels, occupancy rates, and floor statuses. Any emergencies change the light coloring. Quick, efficient, hard to read for those who shouldn't be on board." He turned slightly and flashed them all a knowing look.

"I've made a habit of going places I shouldn't." Star gave him a lopsided grin. "Don't see why I ought to stop now."

The lift shuddered, and the lights flickered.

Everyone eyed various parts of the elevator.

Star turned to the pilot. "That's not good, is it?"

Ahiko gave him a hapless shrug. "When's it ever? So long as it doesn't stop before we reach here." He pointed to a spot on the illuminated panel. "Reclaim hangar lower in on the ship. Used for, you guessed it, storing seized ships and the like. They're out of the way, which is good for us." Ahiko licked his lips and looked away from the display like there was something else he'd wanted to say but cut short.

Star picked up on the abrupt and lingering silence. It was the sort that came along when a person weighed if what they wanted to say would help or be a detriment. He felt it necessary to push for the information, no matter how Ahiko felt about it. "What else do you have to say?"

The pilot frowned, turning his gaze back to the panel like he were trying to burn holes through it with his stare. "It's out of the way, but that doesn't mean it'll be a ways out from protecting, if you get my meaning."

Star did. He rubbed a hand across his face, going through the possibilities that waited ahead. "You're saying it'll be guarded and well?"

Ahiko nodded. "Given *The Leaf's* the most wanted thing in the galaxy right now? Yes. Don't much know what to find down there, but it'll be bad. Know even less about how we'll snag her back."

The elevator jerked to a halt.

Star's gripped his weapon harder.

The lights died. Bands of faint white flickered to life along the back edges of the elevator, giving off enough illumination to make out the crew.

Star shut his eyes, taking a quick series of breaths. Only one thing lay ahead now. He had to think clearly, aim cleanly, and shoot first. Something bumped his shoulder, prompting him to open his eyes and glance around.

M34N had shouldered Molan and Savi up ahead, forcing himself against the back wall. He gave Star a level stare. "The more mass between me and them, the less likely I am to be shot." The bot's voice stayed chillingly neutral.

"Considering you're not one to feel anything, I'd prefer you be shot and I remain wholesome." Star hooked a thumb to his chest.

The automaton sniffed and turned his head as if he'd taken umbrage at the comment. "It's a rather limited opinion to think because I'm mechanical I don't feel things."

Well, we're about to find out. Star ignored the bot and gazed at the door.

It vibrated, sliding open an inch before shutting.

Star couldn't think of a worst place to be stuck when a bomb hung overhead. "Ahiko, how far down are we?"

The pilot frowned. "About twenty levels. Another fifteen to go."

Star blinked. They'd moved quicker than he'd imagined. "Zita, any idea when that bomb's going off?"

The smuggler shook her head. "I've got no idea if it even will. Been rigged to, doesn't mean it'll work. Chance that soldiers scoped out the ship and found what we'd done." She exhaled, pausing before opening her mouth to speak again.

A thunderclap roared through, shaking the lift with enough force Star worried it'd break from its supports into a freefall.

Zita grabbed hold of him, shouting and failing to compete with the sound of the explosion.

Star fumbled with his revolver as he tried clapping his hands to his ears. The elevator rocked harder, sending him crashing into the door. His ribs cried out as the impact sent the inside of his elbow bouncing off the row of bones. He winced through the agony, fighting to grab hold of the lip around the door.

Soft metal paneling quivered along the elevator as the sounds of the explosion echoed on.

The door opened, and Star shook himself free of his thoughts. He grabbed his weapon with both hands, sighting down the passage. A small breath of relief left his mouth when he found the hall ahead empty. It was short-lived as the elevator jerked back into motion, descending. Star reeled from the open door.

The lift jerked to a halt.

He stumbled forward, the mantle of his coat going tight around his shoulders. Zita and Ahiko held onto the jacket to keep him from slamming face first into the elevator shaft's wall. The pair hauled him back to an even standstill. He gave them a quick nod of thanks before glancing to the panel Ahiko had been staring at earlier.

It flickered with a momentary burst of life before fading.

Star couldn't make anything out of the intermittent display. He frowned, eyeing Ahiko.

The pilot squinted at the display like he was trying to stare through it. He held the look for several cycles of the panel flickering through colors and nothingness. "No joy. Panel's coming and going, and what little I can make out says we've still a long way to go." He pursed his lips, cradling his chin in one hand. "Thinking the explosion cut through the floor we entered on. At least enough to damage the elevator. I figure we're hanging by emergency brakes, and secondary power isn't up yet for this area. Lift's probably running on its own stored reserves."

Star exhaled, staring at the exposed shaft before glancing up. It wasn't too far that he couldn't climb out. He could pull the rest up and out and go on foot.

The elevator lurched.

Star backpedaled from the opening, grabbing hold of Ahiko and yanking him back as well. The pair tumbled into M34N and Molan.

Metal moaned around them.

The lift plummeted, air rushing into the opening like an invisible pair of hands promising to grab hold and rip him free from the elevator.

Star sent a hand behind him, fumbling to grab hold of the automaton. The automaton weighed a decent bit. Enough so that Star could hold on and let him be an anchor. His fingers closed around cool metal, and he held tight.

M34N offered no complaint.

The world ground to a halt as if the elevator hung from a chain that'd gone taut.

Star stumbled to all sides, trying to find his balance as every possible member of the ragtag crew barreled into each other. He let it go and resigned himself to being battered. His attention turned back to the open door.

The lift had come to a nearly level stop, its bottom

hanging a couple of feet above the next floor.

Star took the chance and leapt out, hitting the floor and letting his momentum carry him a few feet farther. He waved a hand to beckon the rest.

M34N shuffled by Savi, shouldering aside Molan and breaking free of the small crowd. He jumped, landing with a *thunk* that caused the paneling below him to flex. The automaton tilted his head, regarding Star. "I weigh the most. It made sense for me to be the first to exit."

Yeah, nothing to do with you being a self-preserving hunk of metal. He kept his thoughts to himself, looking down the hall with a slight turn of his head.

The passage remained blissfully empty.

It came as a small relief. He figured the place would be crawling with soldiers by now. They likely had other concerns. That tended to happen when a bomb went off on your ship.

A series of *smacks* filled his ears, and he turned to find the rest of the crew recovering from their landings. The kind thing to do would have been to give them a moment to settle. *Sometimes kindness kills.* Star broke into a brisk walk, putting several meters of distance between himself and the group in the event he did find trouble.

Footsteps echoed behind to let him know they followed him.

The aches and throbs of the journey felt like they had doubled as he moved down the path. It was like walls closed in on his mind the harder he fought against the mounting weariness and pain, working to squeeze him until he collapsed. Star clamped his jaw. Focusing on something else would get him through it. Anything else. Once he had *The Leaf* back, he could lie down and relax for a bit.

His teeth felt like they'd grind into powder, but the constant pressure kept his mind away from the agony creeping throughout his body. Star closed in on the corner and sped up to round it.

A pair of footsteps grew louder and faster.

Star ignored the person closing in and turned left into the new hall.

"Shepherd, wait. You've any idea where the hell you're going?" Ahiko sounded like he'd swallowed a fistful of ash and grit.

"No, but moving beats standing around waiting. They've got *The Leaf.* If they figure out what's really on it—what they're looking for—it's over. They may not have an idea of what The Light is but, hell, there's only so much of the ship they can search before they find it." Star picked up his pace, listening in as Ahiko matched his.

"I know"—the pilot shouldered him, wincing and forcing his way ahead—"and that's why I ought to lead. I know my way around." He broke off and nodded to a split in the paths ahead. "Up on the right. We'll be coming up on another lift." Ahiko looked over his shoulder. "We've got a straight shot to the reclaim hangar." The pilot stepped onto the path on the right and increased his speed.

Star looked back to the following crew before sprinting to catch up to Ahiko. He moved behind him, eyes scanning every inch of the hall to the point of bordering paranoia.

Ahiko stopped in the middle of the hall, slamming

the base of a fist into a panel on the wall closet to him. A strip of the panel glowed a faint amber in response. He gestured to the curved doorway. "It'll be here in seconds unless it stops to pick someone else up."

Star gave him a level look. "Let's hope not." He glanced down the way he'd come.

The group headed toward Ahiko and him.

He sighed in relief and leaned forward to rest a hand against the wall by the lift.

The elevator chimed, hissing as the door opened.

It wasn't empty.

Star stared at the black-armored trio occupying the lift. His hand leapt of its own accord, instinct driving him to bring the revolver up to waist height.

The far right soldier blurred into action while the other two stayed fixed in place.

Star squeezed the trigger, sending a bolt of light into the side of the middle soldier's hip.

The shot struck the armor plating. Ripples of light spread over the soldier's torso as the energy drove them back into the elevator wall with violent force.

Ahiko surged past him, reaching out to take the armored troop on the right by the shoulders.

Star traded a look with soldier on the far left.

The armored soldier didn't draw their weapon as he stepped toward Star and swung an open palm at him.

The blow struck the side of Star's head and left one ear ringing. He blinked and reeled to the side. Sharp pain washed over his other cheek and brow as another slap rocked. The skin felt stretched and raw. He backpedaled a step, fighting the seesawing world. Star raised the revolver.

The soldier sank to a knee and swung an arm in a downward blow like an axe. They clipped the revolver's barrel, knocking it free from his grip.

Star stepped out of the elevator and pressed a hand to the side of his head to stop the blaring bells inside.

The soldier rocketed to their feet, charging him.

Ahiko remained in a contest of strength with his grapple hold on the other soldier. They kept each other's hands locked to prevent either one from going for their weapons. Ahiko's face stretched tight in a barely masked display of effort and pain. One of his arms quivered visibly like it would give out under the strain.

Star swallowed and braced for the impact of the oncoming charge. A cannonball connected with his shoulder, knocking him aside. He stumbled before falling.

M34N had shoved him and took his spot.

The soldier raised his profile, arms going wide as if they planned to wrestle the automaton to the ground.

The bot sent an arm snaking out and grabbed the soldier by the throat. He yanked them close, lifting them from the ground with ease. "You're in our way. We have a ship to steal back. Thank you." M34N slammed the soldier against the wall twice, ensuring their head banged against the structure before throwing them to the ground with just as much force.

Floor paneling warped under the soldier's weight and momentum. The automaton felt it necessary to pause, staring at them all, then sinking to the ground to deliver a fatal blow to the soldier's head. M34N walked past Star and entered the lift. Similar sounds of *thuds* and flexing metal echoed from inside.

Star scrambled to his feet, snatching his revolver and rushing into the lift.

The soldier Ahiko had been struggling with now lay atop the one Star had shot.

He eyed the automaton. "You're pretty violent for a former medical and hospitality bot, you know?"

M34N blinked, eyes working like mechanical shutters. "I thought I was rather reserved in my treatment."

If that's reserved, I'd hate to see him angry. Star took a step away from the automaton.

The rest of the crew followed, slipping into the lift.

Star gestured to the two unconscious soldiers occupying the elevator. "Thoughts?"

Ahiko stared at him then sank to his haunches, stripping one of the soldiers of their sidearm then their rifle. "Toss 'em out, though I know what you're thinking."

Star grinned and shrugged out of his coat. "Get the lift going." He raised a leg, yanking one of his boots off.

Savi stepped in front of him, giving him a look like she thought he'd gone crazy. "What are you doing?"

"Blending in with the locale. If we're going to storm a hangar and take back the ship, figured it best to have a little extra protection. Maybe look like the sort of folk you don't want to question." Star pointed to the soldiers. He stripped out of his other boot and pulled his pants free.

Savi's eyes widened, and she turned away from him. "You know this only works in stories."

He ignored her, letting his clothes fall into a pile by

his feet. Star kneeled and wrenched on the helmet, twisting it free. He looked to Ahiko and followed the pilot's example as the man showcased an easier time in removing the armor.

"I hope you two know what you're doing." Zita shook her head and thumbed the elevator button.

CHAPTER THIRTY-ONE
NOT EXACTLY INCONSPICUOUS

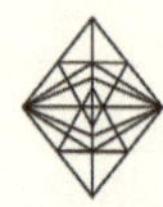

Star wriggled, grunting under the added bulk from the armor. The world took on a darker tint through the helmet's visor. Everything looked narrower, like his field of view had been pinched in a thin band. *No wonder these bastards can't hit anything.* He winced as a minor prickle rolled through his cheek, reminding him of the soldier's slap. *Didn't stop 'em from clipping me good, though.*

A ribbon of light moved through the display panel on the side.

He looked to Ahiko. "We close?" His voice warbled, coming out like he was submerged under water.

The pilot nodded, rolling his shoulders as if the armor bothered him. "Few more floors. Few more seconds. Everyone ready?"

The crew murmured what he took to mean agreement.

His breathing felt heavier in the suit, but he convinced himself it was nerves and paranoia. Star had abandoned the soldier's rifle, giving it over to Molan. He chose to stick with his revolver as well as the diminutive pistol he'd plucked from the soldier's holster. *Small breaths. In—out. Breathe.* His heart ignored the advice to steady itself.

The elevator stopped, but his mind kicked into supersonic speeds. Star abandoned the calming techniques and welcomed the oncoming surge of adrenaline. The strain would burn him out, but he had to get *The Leaf* back.

The door slid open with a soft hiss.

Star raised both weapons, eyeing the passage ahead with hyperawareness.

Waist-high consoles ran along both sides of the darkened corridor. The walls were fashioned from transparent material that Star figured were military grade and designed to withstand energy and projectile weapon's fire.

He stepped out of the elevator, taking two longer strides before sweeping in a semi-circle. His heart refused to relent the jackhammer-like pace. *It's empty. Why?*

Ahiko came to his side, cocking his head to one side. "Well, this is odd. If I had just nicked the most important bird in all the galaxy, you could be sure I'd have a damn sight more people guarding the way to it." He moved past Star, leaning to stare out of one of the clear panels. Ahiko let out a long, high whistle.

Star turned to find the pilot gesturing with the rifle he'd taken. He gazed to where Ahiko pointed.

The hangar went on farther than he could see. A

ship nearly took up the entirety of the space he could make out. It looked like a series of gargantuan boxes all crammed within another, and the long boxy design didn't seem practical by any means. It was painted a soft white that had faded with time. Red streaks arced over the bulk of the ship.

Not exactly inconspicuous. "What is it?" Star cast a wary glance around the passage. No one had come barging in yet. *The hell's going on?*

"It's a Karion generator ship." Ahiko took a step closer to the glass. "They…they never produced 'em. Damn things were prototypes. They're space-worthy power cells pretty much. Not much good in a fight, but land one somewhere and you've got a ship that can generate a world of power for any sort of equipment. Hell, Shepherd, they can power other ships if you can set up a space link."

Star stared at the ship. It sounded much like *The Leaf.* "Why'd the Oligarchy and military shut down produc-tion?

Ahiko pulled himself away from the panel and shrugged. "Don't know really. Rumor mill said some-thing about too costly. Though, after meeting you and *The Leaf,* I'm thinking the idea of ships generating that much power scared the Oligarchy. Word gets out mobile power on that scale exists, even if temporary, it'll rile a mess of people."

That it would. And now they had something that would never die. Some that could power the galaxy. It didn't do the government much good keeping this stored and quiet. "And what better place to keep one of these hidden than on one of the galaxy's most powerful ships." Star lowered his weapons and moved to one of the nearby consoles.

"Right," said Ahiko.

Star scanned over the console, looking for a way to bring it to life. He grunted in what he hoped Ahiko would take a sign to come help.

The pilot made his way over. He jabbed a lengthy, flat key with his index finger.

Weak green light flashed from the embedded lens display within the console's frame.

Star looked it over, frowning as he tried to make sense of it. "Awfully tempted to shoot the thing."

Ahiko snorted. "Using your fingers"—he waggled his digits—"does you loads of good more than shooting a load."

Star imagined the pilot was winking at him through the helmet. "Find me something."

Ahiko nudged him with his hips, moving over to take the console. The pilot keyed in a series of commands and hummed as he worked. "Huh. Well, good news first?"

Star sighed. "Means bad news will follow. Shoot."

"Your boat's here." Ahiko gestured with a jab of the weapon down the hall. "Two hangar lengths down. There's a small mobile transport buggy to get us there." He pointed to a small length of carts farther ahead.

Star gripped his weapons tighter for a moment before loosening the hold. "And the bad?"

"Uh, there are two elevators sectioned off to come directly to this floor with no stop. They've been locked out by an authority command that's signaling it's an admiral. Lifts have been scheduled to descend in five minutes. So, someone's busy, important, and coming here in minutes." Ahiko pulled away from the console.

I've got a good guess who that admiral is. Star looked behind him to the crew. "Let's go."

Savi and Zita picked up their pace, falling in behind him. Molan lingered and moved at a brisk walk. M34N broke ahead of them all to come by Star and fix him with an odd look.

"How important are your clothes?" The automaton sounded like he was genuinely curious.

"Very. They're what little bit I've got left that I can truly call my own, especially my jacket." Star fixed him with a glare he knew the machine couldn't see.

M34N raised the bundle of clothing, looking at it like every piece was just as confusing to him as the last. "Oh, so you would be angry if I dumped them here and left them behind? I wanted to do that."

Star held his glare. "Very angry. Enough so that the military would find bits of automaton scattered around my clothes." He waggled both of the guns in his hands.

The automaton clutched the assortment of clothing with new resolve.

Star shook his head and moved on, heading toward the row of carts ahead.

The diminutive train of cubes ran the length of the foreseeable passage, kept to one side, and nestled into a deep track. Each cart sported a single seat with a harness assembly much like that on any ship.

Star approached the one closest to him, taking a step back as the device hissed and part of its sidewall retracted. He stepped up into the opening and plopped into the seat.

The rest of the crew followed his example.

Star buckled the harness around himself and waited. Nothing happened.

He looked to Ahiko, signaling with a wave of a hand.

"Gimme a sec. Look down, it's not complicated." The pilot waved him off with a dismissive hand gesture.

Star did as he was told. A small, translucent panel sat wedged within the front of cart. He tapped a finger to it, holding it in place as a kaleidoscope of colors spread out from the point he'd touched. Various blips of static light flared to life and dotted along a singular path on the display. Star looked ahead and realized the lens was a representation of the passage. He trailed his finger along the path, stopping at the closest blip.

A short message scrolled across the lens detailing the hangar and what occupied it.

No Leaf.

He repeated the process but skipped certain blips, recalling what Ahiko had mentioned about *The Leaf's* location. Star had guessed correctly and was rewarded with a train of text indicating *The Last Leaf* sat in hangar he'd chosen. "Now what?" He leaned in the cart, glancing at Ahiko and waiting for an answer.

"Click the dot." Ahiko mimed jabbing a screen in the air with one finger.

Star poked the display. Nothing happened, prompting him to look over his shoulder and put a hand to the side of his mouth. "Press the purple one." He watched as the rest of the crew followed the suggestion.

The carts rattled, and a hydraulic rasp shot out from below. The train of cubes sank deeper into the groove they sat in, shimmying like they were settling in. Clamps sprang out from the sides of the tracks and snapped against the frame of the carts. An electric charge ran along the length of the train.

Star's world rushed by him as his head bounced off the seat rest. He shut his eyes despite knowing the helmet would protect him. *Stars and skies, this is all kinds of unnecessary. The hell's wrong with walking.* He snapped forward as the carts jerked to a halt. The harness held him tight, save for his head. He winced, bringing a hand up to his neck.

Ahiko leapt out of the cart and moved like he was unfazed by the bone-jarring trip.

Star glared at him. *Son of bitch could've warned us.* He blew out a breath through clenched teeth, easing his way out of the harness and then the cart. Each step left him feeling like he would topple over as the floor gave the impression of wobbling. The ride spun him worse than any set of drinks he'd ever had. He looked up to the hangar window before him.

The weariness and fatigue washed away. A gentle relief pushed through from the center of his chest to his extremities.

A polar silver-painted ship filled the hangar, looking like a bird of prey. The Y-frame had a red stripe running along the side of it.

There you are. Let's get you home. Star let the thought hold him steady, using it to anchor himself and move without succumbing to the bone-deep tiredness. He lumbered toward a military-grade door set within the clear paneling.

The entrance was fashioned from thick metal, olive drab in color, and riddled with arm-length ridges protruding from it.

Star looked it over and focused on the panel to the side of the door. There was no lock he could make sense of or any way to properly interact with the device. He touched a finger to it.

It had no effect.

He pressed his hand against it, splaying his fingers then pulling them together. Neither variation did anything. Star brought both guns up, aiming at the panel.

"Ah-ah, easy there, Shepherd." Ahiko placed a hand on Star's forearm, lowering the revolver and shooting him a look through the helmet advising him to put the other gun down as well.

Star did. "Didn't come this far to be stumped by a damn door."

Ahiko placed a hand to Star's chest and pushed him back. "Then don't let it." The pilot gave him another firm shove. "Oligarchy strengths don't lie in being efficient. Business first. That means redundancies, odd policies, things getting overlooked. That trickles into the military, believe me. Records aren't kept and updated as often as they should be. Same goes for codes. Honorably discharged soldier, likely his authentication still works some places so long as he's kept his good graces." Ahiko tilted his head in Star's direction.

He imagined the pilot was smirking in self-satisfaction.

The pilot placed his left hand over his right wrist, wrenching with a sharp twist on the armored glove. It broke free, and he slipped out of it. Ahiko placed his hand on the display, looking to his side to flash Star a smile.

The panel flashed once before emanating a raucous buzz.

Ahiko's smile vanished. "Well, I take back what I said. Looks like we're not getting in without someone cleared to open it."

Star thought back to what Ahiko had said about the incoming company. "You're right. Fortunately, someone's on their way who can make that happen."

"Shepherd, you're not thinking of—" Ahiko snorted. "You're smarter than you look."

"Thanks. And you're just as smart as I'd expect someone who looks like you to be." Star fought not to smile as Ahiko bristled.

The pilot crossed his arms and tilted his head like he were lost in deep thought. "There's a chance they might overpower us. Don't expect the admiral will be alone."

Star smiled. "I'm counting on it. Now, let's go kidnap an admiral."

CHAPTER THIRTY-TWO
AT A DISADVANTAGE

"This is a bad idea. A very bad one. Would you like to know the odds of how badly this is likely to go?" M34N turned and rested his head against the back of the cart he was squatting behind.

Star shifted his weight, grimacing under the restrictive armor and the pressure it added to his knees. "Not really."

"They're bad." M34N gave him a knowing look.

Star brushed it off. "I'm not fond of hiding behind this crate either, but Ahiko said the party's more likely to walk than take these. You see anywhere else to hide?"

Ahiko cleared his throat, stealing the attention. "Picture yourself, years of hard work, the proper placement of your lips on the right hind ends. You think you'd muss up your illustrious uniform hopping into one of these things? The admiral will take their good time making their way here all dignified like. After all, who'd be a threat on a destroyer? No one's dumb enough to storm one of these." Ahiko let out a light laugh.

Savi cut him short. "It'd be foolish to assume they don't know we're here by now. We crashed a ship into their hull, blew it up, and shot soldiers. It's a miracle the ship's not on an alert."

"Stop fighting, children." Zita glowered at them all.

Molan pressed his lips into a tight, neutral expression and said nothing.

Star tuned out his own errant thoughts as well as the comments muttered by the crew. The elevator should have touched down by now. He ran through a mental check of how much distance they'd covered with the carts from where they started. "Ahiko, how many ways to this floor are there?"

The pilot held up two fingers. "Way we came and that way ahead." He gestured down the way. "Either side will take 'em a while to reach here."

Star tallied how much time they'd spent lingering in the reclaim hangar and how long they'd been waiting. *Should be any minute now.*

His patience was rewarded by the sound of heavy footsteps. It was an awkward percussion of perfectly timed taps, as if every person walked in robotic synchrony.

He started a countdown, ticking off each step as they grew louder.

The marching stopped, sounding like the party was just on the other side of the carts.

Star looked to his side and nodded to the crew. "Now!" He surged out from behind the cart, leveling both guns at chest height.

Admiral Killian Cain stared back with his revolver trained on him. "Hello, Star Shepherd. I'd hoped you'd be stuck here." He pursed his lips in mock disappointment and looked to the door. "Shame." The admiral scanned the crew before settling on the armored pilot. "I presume that's Ahiko Kohiba under there. Yes, before you can ask, we ensured any access codes of import on this level were wiped, saved for admiralty." He raised a black-gloved hand and waggled his fingers.

"This won't play out the way you intend it to, Star." Cain waved a hand to the four soldiers to his sides.

Each pair wore armor far more ornate than the simple, near-brutish black pieces worn by Star and Ahiko. Cain's guards were clad in a burgundy material that carried a slight sheen like it was made from wet plastic. Ridged, overlapping plates covered their arms, stopping at the shoulders, which were protected by oversized pauldrons. The antiquated motif continued through the bulky chest plate and leggings reserved for fantasy stories. Their helms were lengthy, narrow domes with a single dark slit to see from.

Star noted a distinct lack of projectile or energy-based guns in their hands or on their persons. "And, what, the plastic puppets are supposed to scare us into turning over our weapons? Don't think so."

Admiral Cain smirked. "By all means, play your hand as is."

"Fine by me." Star shifted his aim toward the soldier on Cain's right. Firing on the admiral would keep them from being able to open the door to free *The Leaf*. He squeezed off a shot from each gun.

The energy bolt, as well as the lance of light, struck the red-armored soldier. Each shot fizzled from existence upon impact.

The soldier stood in place like nothing had happened.

A flash of red burst from Admiral Cain's revolver.

Star's chest exploded in electric agony as carmine light splashed over his vision. He struck the hangar panel behind him, head snapping against the sturdy structure. He sank to the ground unable to do anything more than blink.

The crew fired on Cain's party.

Star watched the blasts flash overhead, picturing them striking each guard to no effect. Bolts of red light answered back to hammer Ahiko into the wall.

The pilot sank beside him.

"You can put them down." Cain clucked his tongue like he were chiding children. He made his way to the side of the carts and into Star's view. "Interesting things, these weapons." He turned the revolver over in his hand. "You know, the military rewarded me for claiming one of these from Autumn." He pressed his lips together. "Its study has led to some fascinating research." He waved his free hand to the armored troops at his side.

I bet. Damn freaks stood through a shot from The Light. Never seen that before.

"There were many tests, of course. You'd be surprised just how much damage The Light, isn't it, can cause." Cain reversed his hold on the revolver to turn it back over. "It was a small surprise that the armor you have on now protected, if only a bit, against these." He shook the weapon. "If something like this can come from such a small thing, what then, do you imagine, will come from what you're hiding on the ship?"

Stars and skies, he doesn't know. Damn fool still thinks The Light's just shoved off into a set of guns for killin'. Star groaned and tried to flex his fingers to get them to move. His body refused to cooperate.

"We had trouble, which was to be expected given that it's *your* ship. You haven't exactly made it easy for the government to stop you." Cain loomed over him, letting the revolver dangle in his grip.

Star couldn't help but note that even in the casual hold, the weapon's tip aimed at his skull. He tried to wriggle and flex his other hand, hoping to fire off a shot from his revolver. His hand felt a world away.

Admiral Cain didn't seem to notice his efforts. "Now that you're here, though, I believe it's time we reunite you and your ship. I believe the pair of you have something to share with the government."

Go fuck yourself. He opened his mouth to voice the recommendation. A weak puff of air left his lungs instead.

"Don't bother, Shepherd. You're wasting your breath. What little you have, that is." Cain swiped a hand in his direction.

Two of the armored troops flanked Star and hauled him to a shaky stand.

His feet felt numb and uncooperative, so he let himself go slack. *Let the bastards work for it.*

If they had any complaints, they didn't voice them.

The remaining two soldiers did the same to Ahiko and brought him to his feet.

Star glanced at the rest of his crew as they dropped

their arms.

M34N clutched the bundle of clothing tighter. "He told me not to drop these. Will I be shot if I don't?"

Cain looked to the automaton like he had just registered M34N's existence. "No, bot, you will not. Hold onto the clothing. It makes little difference."

"Oh." M34N sank his head like he were displeased by the notion of hanging onto Star's personal effects.

Admiral Cain turned and took a long, single step toward the panel. He pulled a glove free and placed a hand to the display. It flickered as the door groaned in discontent. "Come along. I'd rather not tarry. We've important things to get done." Cain stepped through the doorway, moving into the hangar without looking back.

The crew followed between the admiral and the armored guards carrying Star and Ahiko.

Star shot the pilot a quick look, hoping it went unnoticed by the soldiers holding him.

Ahiko stared back and gave no indication that he took the look to mean anything at all.

A soft tingling enveloped Star's fingers before filling his toes as well. He wriggled his extremities. He balled a hand into a fist, letting a small smile work over his face. The weight of the revolver still hanging in his hand finally registered. He kept his gaze on Ahiko, making sure the pilot noticed the movement in his hand.

Ahiko made a subtle nod.

That was something. If they couldn't shoot him, he'd take them down another away. They wouldn't see it coming. He focused on Cain's weapon.

Star's knees smacked into the bottom lip of the door

as the soldiers dragged him through. He swallowed a growl and flexed the muscles in his legs. "Now!"

Cain faltered a step, whirling about.

Savi snapped out with a hand to grab the admiral's cape, pulling him close and lashing out with an open palm.

Cain stepped back, years of training showing in his movements. The blow caught him partially across the jaw and staggered him. He recovered quickly, throwing an arm in a wide arc. He brought the inside of one wrist smacking against the fabric to tear his cape free of Savi's grip. He succeeded.

Star thrashed, pulling on both soldiers holding him to upset their balance. They stumbled in their attempts to hold him steady and keep their footing. He brought his feet out from under him, planting them against the floor.

One of the soldiers released their hold and swung their forearm.

The strike connected against the back of Star's head like a hammer, driving him into a deeper squat. He ignored the rattle inside his skull and pushed off his heels. He rocketed to his feet, twisting to send his free hand into the underside of a soldier's chin. His closed fist snapped into the guard's jaw and rocked them back. Star capitalized on their loss of even footing and stepped toward them to shove with both palms.

The guard toppled to their ass.

A broad area of his back cried out like he'd been clubbed. He staggered and dropped to a knee, looking back. An armored boot lashed out and struck his head. The world flashed red tinged with white. He blinked the flare-like spots out of his vision.

A lance of crimson screamed its way between him and the soldier, burning a hole into the ground.

He risked looking at the source.

Cain backpedaled from the monk's assault, shying away from horizontal kicks and sword-like slashes from her arms. He fired in the short lulls between her strikes, putting distance between her. A few shots arced out that looked like he'd ceased aiming at times.

Star rose, watching the soldier in front of them.

The guard reached behind their back and drew a lengthy rod. They snapped their wrist, extending the device. Bands of white electrical current sprang to life and wrapped around the weapon.

You have got to be joking.

Another crackle of electricity cried out behind him.

Star glanced out of the corner of the helmet.

The soldier he'd struck moments earlier had activated their own rod.

Star shut his eyes for a quick second and braced for what was coming. He screamed, charging the soldier in front of him.

The armored trooper, paused, recoiling at Star's sudden attack.

He used the moment of confusion to aim his revolver in front of the soldier's feet. Star fired as many times as he could, blowing smoldering holes into the paneling.

The guard stumbled, cutting off their steps as they tried to navigate the holes. Their forward momentum got the better of them. They staggered out of control, falling to their knees.

Star turned to see a crackling rod cut through the air in front of him. The device crashed into his helmet. Tendril's of electricity arced over his armor and found their way through. He gritted through what felt like a softened charge. The armor must have kept most of it out. A small relief. His muscles unclenched, leaving his breath ragged. He fired a shot near the soldier's foot.

The ground blasted away, leaving a crumbling edge behind. The soldier's weight eroded the already deteriorating bit of paneling. They fell into the small hole and twisted. The guard screamed, writhing as they fought to pull their leg free and clutch their ankle.

Star turned and rushed the other fallen soldier, reversing his grip on the revolver as he did. He sank the entirety of his weight into the blow and dropped his body. The weapon's butt connected with the back of the guard's helmet. A viscous *crack* filled his ears. The material held strong, but the soldier's skull thudded against the ground.

Star exhaled in relief. He looked around to find the other soldier's had been subdued, leaving Killian Cain in a standoff with Savi.

The monk stood several feet from the admiral, hands raised and open like she was using them like blades. Cain had adopted a hunched profile, keeping his body tight and minimizing openings. One hand was balled into a fist while the other was kept open.

A revolver identical to Star's, in every way but for color, lay discarded between them. Star cleared his throat to get their attention.

The pair ignored him.

The rest of the crew lingered at the edges, wearing

looks like they didn't want to interfere.

Star knew what they were thinking: A sudden wrong move could prompt Cain into action. If the admiral recovered his weapon, they'd have a harder time of this.

Star fired between the pair. The Light howled by, causing both of them to track the shot before turning to him. He waved. "Seems like you're at a disadvantage, Admiral Cain."

CHAPTER THIRTY-THREE

YOU'VE PUSHED TOO MIGHTILY

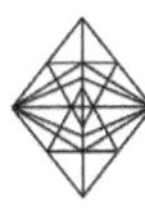

The admiral's face remained carved from stone, betraying no emotion besides concentration.

"Thanks for opening the door to the hangar. Don't suppose I can convince you to give me the hangar codes peacefully? For your own health and all." Star shook the revolver to make his point.

Admiral Cain said nothing.

"Don't bother." Ahiko doubled over, resting his hands on his knees. "Any code shot out to hangar controls opens them from the inside. It's how it works. Military never expects people to waltz in and take out their own ships. Lots of reclaimed ships, no time or too much hassle to rewrite their authentication codes to sync up with military ones. Makes flying them in and out until they're brought back to a base a mighty pain. Ain't that right?" The pilot stared at Cain.

The admiral's mouth twitched, but he held his

composure. "I should've have made it a larger priority to have you killed back on Azzip, Kohiba." His voice was cold and neutral, like stone. He looked back to Star. "Go ahead, Shepherd, kill me. Is that what you'd like, for Autumn?" The admiral took a step toward him, ignoring his own fallen revolver.

The weapon shook in his hand. *Bastard deserves it and more. And you're killing him in cold blood. No different than he did on Autumn. Hell, you've killed people your way here. Why's it different? Because being different is what it's about. You have a chance not to be like him. Be better.*

The admiral raised both hands overhead in a gesture of surrender. "You can't do it. Not like this, can you? I thought as much. I got the measure of you back on that planet. You're a good man, Shepherd."

The admiral was playing him.

"But good men can't do the hard things the galaxy needs them to. What exactly do you think you're doing by delivering a weapon to the resistance?" Cain's brows knitted together, and his eyes narrowed like he were truly curious.

Son of a bitch. Man really thinks there's something dangerous on board. "You really don't know what I'm carrying, do you?" Star tilted his head.

Cain's features remained frozen. "Word came in from the Oligarchy that Autumn was developing a new form of energy weapon, something that would render military technology obsolete. Something, that if spread throughout the resistance, would let them butcher entire worlds—upset the government."

Star's mind went numb. "Weapons? You've lost your damn mind."

Cain blinked then inclined his head at the revolver in Star's hand before gesturing to the one he'd dropped. "Have I? I've seen it firsthand. Held it, and so have you. What, then, do you think the cargo on your ship is? Have you even seen it?"

"I have." Star gritted his teeth.

"And I haven't. What I have seen is a weapon, hidden in an antiquated shell to pass suspicion, and it is capable of tearing through matter like nothing before. Something able to cut through metal and stone with an ease that baffles the mind. A blast that manages to harm those, even if lightly, wearing armor that repels anything else the military has to offer." Cain pointed to the suit Star wore.

He swallowed. The admiral had a point. A wrong one, but Star couldn't fault him for it. The admiral honestly believed it. "You're wrong, Cain. Horribly so. What's onboard that vessel ain't meant to harm a soul but free them. You remember that idea? Freedom. People not bound to a government, a set of corporations controlling it all. People having a chance to make a life of their own free from outside forces. So long as they obey the law and do what's right, what's the harm?"

Cain remained unfazed.

Star took a step toward him. "Answer me. You want to talk about weapons and danger—who just glassed half a world?" He jabbed a finger at Cain. "You did. You burned a planet. You turned Autumn to ash and nothingness. For what? For this?" He fired a shot past the admiral. "Tell me something, Admiral Cain, if this was really supposed to be for a weapon that could turn the Oligarchy and its people to dust, why didn't Autumn use it against you?"

All expression faded from Cain's face. The admiral's brows knitted together, creases formed along his forehead, and the skin under his eyes wrinkled. He seemed lost in thought.

"If they had this power—believe me, they did—on Autumn, why are you still alive? You should have been burned into space dust. I could do that to you now." The gun shook harder in his grip. Star fought to control it. "And I'm awfully tempted."

Cain pulled himself out of whatever reverie had silenced him. He looked around before stepping closer. "So, why don't you?"

Star clenched his jaw, tightening his fist around the weapon. He took a breath and loosened his hold. "I'm thinking there's a better revenge than just blasting you. The sort that comes with seeing your government crumble. The kind that comes when people go free and can live again. What will you do then? Maybe take up different job, a simpler life? Shepherding's good." Star lowered the weapon. "Make sure you live to see it." His voice hardened into something that could have cracked through blaster-proof armor.

Savi lunged for the weapon.

"No!" Star reached out, running toward her.

She fell to a knee and snatched the weapon in a smooth move, springing back to a stand and training the weapon on the admiral's back.

The crew remained rooted in place, watching the exchange.

Star raised his gun at her. "Stop."

Savi's eyes widened, and her mouth hung partially

open. "Why? So he can keep on murdering more worlds? All of you"—she glanced at the crew—"all of you saw what happened on Lisba. He was responsible. Dogs like him need to be put down."

Star jerked at Savi's turn of phrase. He thought back again to something Zheer had said, clinging to it for later. "We shoot an admiral and leave, the destroyer might forget the wanted alive and intact part."

Savi glared at him, turning the weapon on Star.

"I've got a feeling the only reason we've lived long as we have is a certain someone has taken this more seriously than we'd first thought." Star gave Admiral Cain a look. "Isn't that right?"

The admiral returned his stare with an uneven smile of self-satisfaction.

"We shoot him, word's bound to spread fast. Won't do us any favors." Star's hand steadied. Star wondered if something had to be wrong with him in that he found it easier to shoot a monk than the man who had glassed a world and more over. "Who would have thought the monk would be a murdering psychotic?" M34N shrugged.

Admiral Cain scoffed, shaking his head. "That's not a monk."

Savi turned the revolver back to Admiral Cain.

"No!" Star fired. The bolt cut past her, forcing her to recoil, her weapon aiming into the air.

Red light erupted from the stolen revolver.

Admiral Cain broke into a run, reaching into his coat.

Shit. Star turned to track him, sighting in and leading him the best he could.

Amber light flooded the hangar, and a mechanical

droning filled the air. It increased in volume, hitting the point it blared out all sound, even thoughts.

He should have shot the admiral when he had the chance. Star watched Killian Cain pass through the door, slamming it shut. He turned and gestured to *The Leaf.* "Get on board, now!"

The crew rushed into action, making a run for the ship.

Star broke into a full sprint, passing the frozen Savi, who kept her gaze fixed on the door. Star glanced at her, drawing her attention for a moment.

Her expression spoke volumes. They were going to talk, and he knew she would make sure of that.

Star decided their conversation would be better saved for the ship and when they were away from a boat that could burn worlds. He made his way up the ramp, reaching up to key the door open.

It responded.

Zita and Ahiko rushed by, brushing him aside callously. Molan lumbered by with M34N in tow.

Savi fired at the door with Cain's weapon. The bolts tore through the door, striking the paneling on the other side to warp the composite material.

Cain stood behind the clear wall, an arm stretched out of sight.

The alarm died. Faint echoes still made their way through the walls. A static crackle cut through the hangar.

Star ignored it, turning to Savi. "Get on the ship, now!"

The monk shook before turning and marching toward him. She lowered the revolver and passed him without a glance.

Star turned to follow her in.

"Shepherd." Cain's voice reverberated through the hangar.

Star ignored the call and ran into the ship, smacking the interior console to close the door behind him. He ran up the ramp, making his way through the central hub.

M34N glanced at him and then dumped his clothes. "There, I've done—"

Star didn't stay to hear the rest of what the sociopathic automaton had to say. He raced into the corridor leading to the cockpit.

"Shepherd!"

He pushed away Cain's cries.

The ship thrummed to life, the thrusters emitting a lower rate of power than he thought Ahiko would have gone for.

What's he up to? Star made his way into cockpit, falling into his seat beside the pilot.

"Took you long enough." Ahiko keyed in a series of commands before reaching up to remove his helmet. He shook his head, running an armored hand through his hair. "Need you to keep the admiral stalled. He's calling for you; keep him talking."

Star stared at him.

"He's angry—stressed. Keep him so. He gets his wits about him, and he can lock the bay down. Right now, he's only triggered the alarm for reinforcements and local batteries to fire on us."

Star held the look. *Is that all, huh?*

"He's rankled. Make him worse."

Star activated the comms broadcasting, switching them over to local area. He held off from thumbing the speakers. "How do I do that, Ahiko?"

The pilot shrugged and swiped a finger across a panel. "Don't know. Don't care. My experience? You're more than adept at pissing off people. Just be you."

He scowled and tripped the speakers. "I'm listening, Cain."

"You've made a mistake."

"I've made plenty of 'em. Got room and life to make many more." Star ripped his helmet free, turning it over to look at the empty covering in the eye visor as if staring at a person.

"I'll hunt you, Shepherd." Cain's voice hardened and sounded tinged with spittle like he was seething.

"You'll hunt me." Star had to acknowledge the truth that Cain would never stop the pursuit.

"You won't have a place to hide. I'll see to that." Cain's voice edged into something colder.

"Then I won't, Admiral."

"There'll be a point where you can't run any longer, Shepherd."

There was truth to that too. And when it came, Star would do what was necessary. "Then I'll stop and face you. But until that time, I'll run. I'll do my job. And I'll keep me and mine safe." Star gripped the helmet, fingers pressing against the visor. "And when we do meet again, keep that in mind, Admiral."

Silence hung through the channel.

Star leaned closer to the comms. "When push comes to shove, we've all got a side of us that needs letting out. And you've pushed mightily, Cain. So, here's me telling you, don't push me any further. Don't shove. Because you won't like what comes out—and you won't survive it."

Ahiko threw his head back and howled in triumph. "Got it. Cut it, Shepherd."

Star flipped the comms to dead.

The hangar door groaned and shuddered as it opened.

Ahiko didn't wait for Star's cue, and he keyed in a jump.

Star arched a brow. "You ever do that out of a hangar bay before?"

The pilot gave him a lopsided smile. "No." Ahiko pushed up on the throttle.

CHAPTER THIRTY-FOUR

WHAT CAN BREAK HOLDS

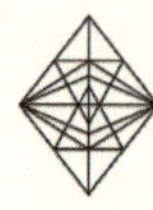

Space bowed and warped as *The Leaf* tore free from the reclaim hangar bay.

Star placed the revolver on the dash and sank into his seat, putting a hand to the collar of armor and tugging. It held fast, but he ran his fingers along the edges, loosening the inner clasps and holding it firm to his body. A series of minute *snaps* cried out as the chest piece sagged. He undid his harness and let the armor fall free, repeating the same process with the rest of the gear.

Ahiko mimicked Star's relaxed posture, letting his head fall to the side. The pilot arched a brow as he watched Star strip. "Your ship. Your rules. But, still think people are going to have a problem with a nude shepherd walking about."

Star rolled his eyes. "I'm covered"—he pointed to his waist—"partially so. It's enough. I need to be out of that." He gestured to the fallen armor.

Ahiko said nothing. He did as Star had, slipping free of his harness and removing the armor.

Star left him to it. He plucked up the revolver and made his way barefoot through the corridor leading back to the central hub. A clamor carried through the mouth of the hall as he drew closer. *Great. Just got free and there's still trouble.* He passed through the opening and into the hub.

Molan sat on one of the seats, seeming a bit too preoccupied with a small table.

M34N stood with his arms crossed and silent.

Zita and Savi had weapons drawn, pointed at one another.

Star coughed loud enough to pull everyone's attention to him. "Put 'em down. We just left that sort of thing behind. Don't need to carry that sort of attitude with us. Hold onto something like that long enough, and you start to turn into those people. It's how it always starts: paranoia, hate, simple and quick solutions. Things like drawing guns on each other. Put them down."

Both women stared at him before flicking a look at each other.

Star kept his revolver at his waist and aimed at the ground. *And sometimes you've got to lead by example.* He chose to raise his voice instead of the weapon. "My ship. My rules. Put them down. I won't ask again." He met their looks without blinking.

The pair lowered their guns, holding their locked stares.

"What's going on?" He looked to Savi then Zita.

The smuggler huffed a breath and moved to stand by M34N, turning away to run a hand through her hair. "You're awfully bossy for a man walking around in next to nothing."

"My ship, my rules, like I said." Star waited for either Savi or Zita to answer his question.

The monk turned to face him. "She took issue with how I handled things back there."

Star opened his mouth to speak, but the monk waved him off.

"You'll note my actions not only disarmed the admiral but saved our lives. It allowed us to leave with this." Savi turned her hand over, drawing attention to the black revolver.

"Consider it noted. You'll be wanting to hand that over to me." Star reached out with his free hand. "It doesn't belong to you."

The monk flashed him a dangerous smile, all teeth with nothing reassuring lingering within. "Like the smuggler said, 'You're awfully bossy for a man walking around in next to nothing.'"

He ground his teeth and moved past Savi, stopping by the automaton and the pile of clothes at his feet. Star bent, eliciting a sharp whistle from behind. He ignored it and snatched up his clothing. *Not very monk-like.* He wriggled his way back into his pants before slipping into his shirt. The boots didn't warrant immediate importance. He left them along with his coat as he turned back to address Savi.

The monk shied away from his look, staring at the weapon instead. "It doesn't belong to you either, you know? It belongs to the resistance." Something creeped into her voice at the last word. The word had come out hollow—distanced, like she had trouble recalling it.

"Funny thing about the resistance…" Star stepped closer. "I've never seen any of them act like you did back on that ship. You were pretty near crazed, especially for a monk. Thought you lot were more peaceful than that."

"Monk life and resistance life don't mesh easily." She still refused to meet his gaze.

"Few parts of life mix easily, but that's not what I'm talking about, you know. You were going to kill the admiral. And it seemed a damn more heated than something just personal." Star held his look on Savi until he felt like his gaze drilled holes through her.

The monk broke her stare on the weapon, looking up and meeting his eyes. A small fire kindled within them. "That's because it's not about me. It's like what you've said." She licked her lips and took a breath. "It's about everyone else out there. I was tempted to do what I tried because of them."

Every crazy person told themselves that until they were convinced of it. How long before they believed it? What then? That's what led people down dark and dangerous paths. They got reckless, and they swept a lot of people into their madness. "Fair enough." He didn't truly believe the words coming out of his mouth. "What do you plan to do with the weapon?" Star's gaze fell on the gun.

Savi didn't relinquish her hold on it like he had asked. "Turn it over to the right people when the time comes. I don't intend to keep it longer than necessary."

Star's mouth twitched. *Me either.* He looked to the

revolver in his hand. But what was necessary and what someone wanted weren't always the same. "Hold onto it till we get to where we're going. I expect you to do what's right then." He gave her a look that let her know if she didn't, he'd make her.

The monk nodded.

Star sighed, slipping the revolver in his holster and fetching his boots. He jammed his feet into them, wriggling until they settled comfortably. A reassuring weight fell over his shoulders and hugged him. He looked to his side to see M34N had placed his coat on him. "Thank you," Star said as he slipped into the jacket.

The bot ran his hands along Star's shoulders, smoothing out the coat. "It is a nice jacket."

Star heard a hint of longing in the automaton's voice.

"If you die, Shepherd, can I have it? I think I'd look wonderful in this coat." M34N's voice was devoid of any note of humor.

Star sighed. "If I die before you, something's gone terribly wrong in the universe." He pulled away from the automaton and moved toward the hall at the other end of the hub. "Come on, all. I've got something to show you." His voice warbled like it was leaving him. He leaned to the side and placed a hand to the nearest wall to steady himself.

"You okay?" Zita came to his side, slipping under his other shoulder to support him.

"Feel like I had my ass kicked across a couple of planets, crashed into a ship, and took one helluva beating from armored soldiers." He gave her a weak smile.

"Some men learn the hard way." She matched his

smile. "Other's keep doing things the hard way and never learn." She winked.

Star shook his head and hobbled forward. "Fatigue's getting to me, but figure I'll show you all what this has been about. Then we can all shower and pass out nice and easy till we get to where we need." *Providing the military isn't hot on our tails.*

Savi followed in tow. M34N glanced to Molan before coming along. The barkeeper placed his hands on his knees and rose to join them.

Star led the way in silence, leaning harder on Zita through the corridor. They reached the doorway, and he unlocked it. Star pulled himself away from the smuggler, waving a hand as thanks as he made his way over to the sphere at the end of the room.

"Odd lookin' room for a place that should be housing a drive." Zita slowly scanned the room, settling her gaze on him.

He shrugged it off and motioned to the sphere. "There's a reason for that. It's a rather odd lookin' drive." Star donned a nearby pair of goggles and opened the sphere, letting The Light wash over the room in all its intensity. It made more of a point without the glasses first time around. He turned to watch their reactions.

Zita sucked in a breath and placed a hand to her brow to block some of radiance.

Molan blew out a light puff, leaning against the wall. His eyes widened in something close to childlike wonder. He broke the stare, shutting his eyes to protect himself. "Well, damn. That's something to behold."

Savi's mouth hung open. She followed Molan's example and shut her eyes. The monk took a step toward The Light, moving blindly while holding a hand out like she intended to grab it.

Star touched the console and sealed the sphere. The Light faded, leaving the room to darken. He pulled the goggles free and wrapped them around the railing running around The Light's seal. "So." He let the word hang in the air, waiting for their reactions.

"What was that, Shepherd?" Molan pushed off the wall. "In all my years, something like that, that's out of dreams." He shook his head and fixed his gaze on the metal sphere.

"It is, isn't it?" Star hooked a thumb over his shoulder. "You're right. It's the stuff of dreams. It's what's going to make them real for a whole mess of people through this galaxy. It's The Light." He snatched his revolver free, holding it up for them to see. "Bit of that's in here. Powerful stuff because *it is* power." The words fell with lead-like weight.

Everyone stared at him in silence.

"That's what the Oligarchy is after. You heard Cain's speech. Don't think half or more of the people in the government even know the truth. But you can be damned sure the people in power—the ones at the top—know. They glassed a world to protect their bottom line." Star put the weapon back in his holster.

Zita took a step closer. "That's…powering this ship?" She rubbed her forehead, looking away to the floor. "Can't believe something like that exists. What you said back on Lisba, it sounded great. But…seeing it?"

"It makes it real, don't it? I was the same way when I first saw it back on Autumn." Star weighed the temptation to open The Light again, but he decided against it.

Savi came to his side, placing a hand against the sphere. "It's beautiful, like looking at a miniature star. That's what you've been carrying this whole time, Shepherd—a star?"

Something like that.

"I'm carrying the power to let people break their hold of the Oligarchy. No more being tied to a bunch of families that control every resource imaginable. Power to run your homes, tools, lives, and more. That's what that is."

Savi pulled her hand away from the sphere. "And that scares them. Good. Fear is a powerful thing. It's about time they felt it." The monk's jaw visibly clenched. Savi raised the black revolver. "This will change a lot once delivered. It could be the weapon we need—that much power."

Star placed his hand on the barrel of her weapon. He pushed it down. "This isn't meant to be the kind of weapon you're thinking of. It's meant to eliminate the need of the Oligarchy. Let people have a chance to pull themselves up without people standing by ready to kick them back down to their knees." Heat filled him and he challenged it into a glare he hoped the monk would remember for a long time. "Never forget that." Star moved away from her, heading towards the door.

Zita came to his side and nudged his side with her hip.

He looked at her as he continued to walk.

"You're just going to leave them there gawking at it?" She cast a look over her shoulder, wearing an expression like she was half torn to go back and stare.

Star shrugged. "No harm in it. Let them sit and wonder. It'll do *some* of them good. There's a hint of magic in that, the thoughts and dreams that come with what The Light can do for people, the universe."

Zita pressed her lips together and nodded.

"Not much longer now. I'm figuring Ahiko's plotted a series of jumps to take us to Slaydus. No point in hiding now; might as well make the fastest burn we can. Military's already irked to no end." Star stopped as points of pressure built inside his shoulder.

Zita held a hand on him, squeezing the muscle in a strong, reassuring grip. "You ought to rest. Heck, we all need one after going through this. Slaydus isn't going anywhere. It'll be over, soon."

He pulled her hand away, squeezing it for a second. "Showers are off the passage to the far right of the main hub. Ship's got about six bunks past that. It's tight, but they're comfortable. Tell the rest."

"About the size of a small crew, enough to pilot this bird," said Zita. A silent question hung in the air.

Yeah, about that size. Star took a few steps away.

"What happened to them?"

"They never made it off Autumn." The words fell with more weight than he had intended. Star broke into a brisk walk, leaving Zita behind. He tore into the center hub of the ship and made his way toward the showers. It would be a welcome relief to soak up something hot and wash the aches away. And the thoughts, if he could.

He stepped into the showers, turning slightly and thumbing the console to the side of the door. It *blipped* in response, and a heavy bolt clicked into place. *Won't mind having the place to myself for a while.* Star moved to the closest stall, staring into the cloudy and textured glass.

His face looked back at him as a warped and strained mess. Much of the color had faded from his skin, though he figured some of that came from the dim lighting and tinged glass. *I look about as good as I feel. Fair enough.*

He placed an index and middle finger against the small lens display on the left of the stall and dragged the digits across it. The stall clicked and the glass door drifted open. He grabbed hold of the lip, giving it a little tug. Star stripped out of his clothes, throwing them to the ground more forcefully than necessary.

He stepped into the shower, slamming the base of his fist into the side wall. Dull pain radiated through the mass and made it into the bones of his pinky finger. All of the journey's pain, hot and ugly, twisted inside him. His gut roiled, and he let out the mounting anger. Star's scream reverberated through the stall. He slammed the bottom of his fist against the hard shower wall until he felt more numbness than pain.

He leaned his forehead against the stall, sighing and thumbing the shower on with his other hand. Beads of hot water peppered his skin. He released a low groan. The warmth spread over him, making its way into his muscles. He pushed off the wall, pulling his forehead away to lean back against the opposite end. Star slid down along the stall until he rested on the floor, letting the shower rain over his body.

The hell am I doing?

He shut his eyes, pretending each drop of water washed away a bit of his worry and pain. A tremor built in his hands. He flexed his fingers, balling them into fists to try and fight the quivering. It didn't work. *Shit.* He relented, letting them shake as he brought them to his face. Star rubbed his palms against his cheeks and eyes before massaging the sides of his neck. He scrubbed the area like an invisible film of ichor clung to it.

He'd almost shot Cain, no different than the admiral had done to people on Autumn. Cold and angry. That was a good damn way to end up like the man himself. There was no point in doing any of this if Star walked out a monster like the admiral.

He rubbed harder. The action soothed some of the knots twisting through his body and mind. He stopped and let himself sink a bit lower.

A marmalade sky, tinged with streaks the color of smeared strawberries, swam through his mind. He lost himself in the memory of Autumn's sky. Beams of green light cut through the distant horizon, spreading out to wash over everything.

His eyes snapped open and he leaned forward, sucking in sharp breaths littered with bits of water. He spat out the moisture. *Hell.* He pressed a hand to the side of his head and got to his feet.

The shower's warmth held, and he gave silent thanks for the energy provided by The Light. Something built in his stomach and chest, causing him to shake. He let out the light laugh that quickly evolved into a rolling chuckle.

He imagined folks out in the galaxy having the ability to sit and scream away their pain in a shower that could stay hot forever. No more worrying about the little things. A shepherd could find a bit of warmth and reprieve even out in the dark vastness of space, run ragged by the military, and still enjoy this.

He laughed harder, sliding a hand along the stall to turn off the shower. The reminder made some of his pains and thoughts seem further in the distance. If The Light could do that for him, he couldn't wait to see what it would do for others. He opened the door and stepped out of the shower to fetch his clothes. Star slipped back into them, brushing away the thought that they were still dirty.

He opened the door to leave and saw Molan shambling by.

The barkeeper caught his look and stopped, eyeing him. "That's something else you've got on board, Shepherd."

Star remained silent.

"And you're planning on giving that up?" Molan arched a brow and shrugged. "That easy, no fight?"

"Been fighting a lot, in case you haven't noticed."

The barkeeper shook his head. "Not what I'm talking about. Not the military—Oligarchy and powers that be. The resistance. They're people too."

Star knew where the barkeeper was going, but he let him continue in peace. He needed to hear someone else give voice to the concern building inside him.

"And people—" Molan stopped and took a breath. His posture sagged—"people go wrong with time. Some of them end up twisted, extreme. That's out there, you know? Resistance has had its fair share of people go rogue and take things too far."

Star nodded, keeping mute.

"You're taking this to them in the hopes they'll do right by it, right by the common folk out there." Molan reached out and clapped a hand to Star's shoulder, giving him a gentle shake. "I get it. But how do you know they will?"

Star swallowed and looked down. *I don't.*

"I've lived long enough to see some things, some like that Light, that are still a surprise. But in it all, I've learned something." Molan gave Star a level look. "People *let* things change them. Power does that. Even that kind, the kind that's supposed to help. It's energy, power. Keep that in mind."

Star opened his mouth to speak, but the barkeeper waved him off.

"Seems to me that, so far, you're the only one doing what's right. Just doing your job. You're a shepherd, paid to deliver this. But I can also see you damn well believe in it. You care. That's important. Means what this Light can do matters to you more than the people who want it." Molan's look hardened. "Remember that, why *you're* doing this, not why others are."

Star brushed the barkeepers hand free of his shoulder. "I aim to. But I find it a tad funny someone from the resistance is telling me this. Shouldn't you be telling me to get off my ass and get to Slaydus as fast as possible?"

Molan stared down the hall like he was weighing what to say. "I mentioned something about people changing, no? Speaking from experience. There's a reason I sat on the wayside on Lisba, running a bar and trading info and favors. I could have been fighting. Spent my fair share of youth doing that. Watched my perfect looks slip away during that time." He flashed Star a toothy smile.

Star returned it.

"Ideas change with people is all I'm saying, Shepherd. Things get twisted just as easily as people. I've stayed out of them for a long while. People like Savi have stayed in too long by my estimation." Molan shrugged nonchalantly. "I'm just nursing an old man's fears is all. Sometimes two sides fight for so long they end up looking hellishy the same to the people watching from outside. Terrible and frightening thing. Just make sure at the end of the day, when it's all said and done, that you think you're doing the right thing, Shepherd." The barkeeper walked away toward the bunks without letting him say a word in return.

Star stood there, absorbing it all and trundling through it in his mind. *No pressure.* He pressed a hand to the side of his head and made his way down the hall. He had no inclination to go to bed alongside everyone else. The cockpit offered him a solace that he sorely needed.

He made the walk in a handful of minutes, entering the room and slipping into his seat.

Ahiko hadn't moved from his place, sitting in nothing but his briefs.

Star glanced at him.

The pilot didn't take note of it, acting like nothing was out of the ordinary.

He sighed. The man had an odd sense about everything.

"So, you show them what you're carrying?" Ahiko tilted his head to the side, regarding him.

Star nodded.

"Huh. It set them on their heels as much as it did me?"

Star bowed his head and slid lower in his seat. The weight from earlier returned, begging him to give in and sleep for a while. *Good idea. Glad I came up with it.* He held off on the urge long enough to give voice to a question on his mind. "You taking us straight to Slaydus?"

The pilot inclined his head. "As close to a straight shot as I can make it. Keyed in a few short pauses between the jumps. No choice. We bugged out of that ship with no clue what was ahead. Truthfully, it was a small miracle that kept us from pancaking into a planet or a star. I stopped us a while ago to get our bearings and jump us again. We'll be coming up on orbit in a dozen hours."

Long enough to make for a good sleep. And he did.

CHAPTER THIRTY-FIVE
TWISTING TRUTHS

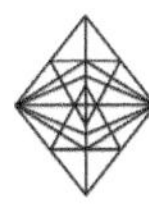

Star's body shook, tugging him from sleep. He resisted, turning to his side and burying himself deeper against the seat.

"I'm not the sort of man to ruin another's go at love, but you're fondling that seat a bit too much for my comfort. Wake up, Shepherd." Ahiko sounded like he was just coming out of sleep himself.

Star groaned. Cement clung to the inside of his skull, weighing his head and mind down. He pushed against one of the arm rests to help right himself. "Where are we?" He dragged the back of his arm against his eyes to encourage them to stay open.

"Coming up on orbit outside Slaydus."

Star released another groan, shifting in his seat to stare out the cockpit.

The planet hung before them, dominated by lush greens and rogue patches of aquamarine.

"Can't believe a world like this is sitting out here all alone, uninhabited. You think it'd be the first place the Oligarchy would've stripped or colonized. Profit or settle. Guess the distance from everything else makes it too much of a pain." Ahiko shook his head, placing a hand on the throttle to ease up on the speed. He brought *The Leaf* down to a slow cruise that almost felt as though they were drifting without power.

Star glanced at the pilot.

Ahiko had suited up in the black armor they'd stolen.

"You think you're going need that?" Star inclined his head and arched a brow.

The pilot's lips pressed thin. "Not sure, to be honest. Just got this terrible feeling is all. Slaydus is too far out of the way for the military, but same goes for any help should we find ourselves in need." He gave Star a knowing look and shrugged. "Just can't shake this itch in the back of my mind. We're going down there to hand over something the galaxy's never seen before. That's a weighty thing. Can't see this exchange going over without some tension and the possibility of threats."

Molan's words last night had Star thinking the same. He sighed and looked at the set of armor he'd discarded by his seat. His left hand fell to the butt of the revolver. He hoped this would be the last time he'd have to use the weapon. A little more, and it would be all over. He'd walk away with a ship and maybe, maybe, a crew to get back to shepherding with. He glanced at Ahiko.

The pilot remained fixed on the planet. "You know, seen many worlds in my time of service." He shook his head, a small smile playing across his face. "Never seen one that looked as untouched as this. What'd they call 'em, golden worlds?"

Star matched the pilot's smile. "You see your fair share of them in shepherding. Pass worlds like this all the time. Sometimes ferry people to 'em, people who want a fresh start somewhere quiet and out of the way. No law to touch them as they build a life of their dreams and own making. If you plan to stick around after this is done, you'll see more golden worlds."

Ahiko let out a sigh of satisfaction, reclining in the seat as he kicked his feet up onto the dash. "I could get used to that."

Ain't nothing better than sailing through peaceful skies and stars. He rose from his seat, giving the bits of armor a last look before leaving the cockpit. Star shambled his way into the main hub and headed toward one of the lockers off to the side. He fumbled with the storage unit as he fought with it.

It relented and opened.

He crammed his fingers into the crack and wrenched. The drawers slid out. Star plunged his hand in, grabbing a gold-wrapped bar thicker than his forearm. He pulled it free and shifted it to his other hand. He sent his hand back in, fishing around for a series of thinner pieces. Content he'd plucked enough of a variety, he walked to the small table.

He laid the goods out and headed toward the bunks. Star stopped when a series of footsteps sounded off ahead of him. M34N hobbled down the hall toward him.

The automaton blinked upon seeing him, making no other gestures otherwise. He moved by without a word.

Guess he's not a morning person.

Others plodded out from the bunks. Molan and Zita made their way toward him, caught in a hushed conversation he couldn't make out. The pair gave him a curt nod as they passed.

Maybe it's just me?

He waited for Savi.

The monk never came.

Star made his way into the bunk room, eyeing the beds.

Savi sat at the edge of the farthest lower bunk, black revolver in her hands. She started looking at the weapon much the way he did.

He went over to her, standing a foot away. "You sleep fine?"

She stared at him as if wondering if he were real or a mirage. Savi held the look for a fifteen-count before lowering her head. "Well enough."

That was lie. One he'd told himself a fair amount of times. Star looked at the weapon in her hands. "Looks like it's weighing you down an awful bit."

Savi lifted her head and gave him a thin, crooked smile. "More than you know. But part of that feels right."

His thoughts turned to what Molan had told him before he'd gone off to sleep. He didn't know what to make of the monk's words, but they tugged at a part of him he wanted to push away. *What's it mean when that sort of weight and power starts to feel right?* He decided to change the subject and offer the monk a break from the thoughts and pressure. "We've come up on Slaydus.

Ahiko's got us drifting out of orbit. Gives us time to get some semblance of a meal."

The monk eyed him askance.

He shrugged and brought his hands to the air nonchalantly. "Don't got much, but it qualifies as food." *On some level at least.* He beckoned her with a wave of a hand. "Come on." Star turned and marched toward the central hub, not looking back to see if the monk would follow.

He'd seen that weariness in folks before. She'd come. There wasn't much a decent meal couldn't solve, if even for a moment. Sometimes that was all a person needed. One moment to put it all away and see things in a different light.

He entered the main hub of the ship and froze.

The crew had torn the gold wrapping free of the heavy bar, breaking chunks from the brick. Dark brown, with the consistency of wet clay, the chewy bar contained a month's worth of calories in its entirety. A single bite could serve to replace a whole meal.

The bar was missing more than several bites per person.

Star narrowed his gaze, staring at Ahiko.

The pilot had torn a palm-size portion free, kneading it within a hand and picking bits free to lob in his mouth. "You'd think they'd find other flavors for these things. Only so much chocolate you can taste before it gets boring."

Zita flashed the pilot a look that said he was insane for that comment.

"This is breakfast?" Savi raised a brow and glanced at the mix of bars scattered over the table.

Ahiko snatched up a thin prism wrapped in a metallic green foil. He ripped it open, pinching a clear, gelatinous globule from within. He opened his mouth and tossed it back, biting into it. A bit of moisture trickled from between his lips, beading along the base of his chin. He repeated the process and chomped down on two more of the liquid rations.

The crew ate mechanically, tearing through what Star had provided.

He made his way to the table and pinched off portions for himself, leaning against a wall as he enjoyed the meal. The first bite compressed under his teeth before tearing apart. Ahiko had been right about the taste. It was like chewing on chocolate with the texture of dough. There was a decadence to it that he let himself get lost in.

Simple pleasures could sometimes wash away a world of complex problems. He lobbed another chunk into his mouth, swallowing it before throwing back three moisture bubbles. Each burst within his mouth, spraying carbonated droplets of orange-flavored water. He convinced himself the fizzing nature of the liquid would help energize him. The little lie did small wonders for his mind, so he ran with it.

He waited until everyone had taken what looked to be a decent fill from the food before clearing his throat. All eyes turned to him and he stole a quick breath. "We're hanging just outside Slaydus. Take it you know what comes next?"

The crew remained silent.

"I'm dropping off the ship and The Light down there." He glanced at Ahiko and relayed the exact coordinate for the drop to him.

The pilot nodded but made no move to leave.

"A lot of money's coming my way. Enough so I can buy my own ship, helluva one too at that. Didn't mean to rope you all in, but if you want, there's a place for you"—he looked each of them in the eyes—"every one of you, on it. If not, I'll part with what funds I can and get you as close as I can to where you need or want to be. Sound fair?"

Molan shrugged as if he didn't care.

M34N looked to the barkeeper then crossed his arms and mirrored the gesture.

Zita leaned over and rested on clasped hands. "My crew already knows where we were headed. I'm wondering why they're not here already, but I've got no problem waiting for them to pick me up. Keep your money, Shepherd."

He turned to the monk, waiting for her response.

Savi met his stare but chose to remain quiet.

Fair enough then. He left the crew where they were, moving toward the cockpit. Star beckoned Ahiko with a gesture as he moved past the pilot. He led the way down the hall in silence, mulling over what would come. And it could all happen—or none of it. He wouldn't know till they set down. It was best to stick to what happened as it did. Star decided there was no sense in worrying over things that weren't.

He entered the cockpit and strapped himself back into his seat. "Take us in, but do a pass over the coordinates before touching down. I want a good look at what we're landing into."

Ahiko's mouth twitched, but he said nothing. The

pilot eased *The Leaf* into acceleration, holding the ship at a steady pace.

They entered the planet's atmosphere after minutes of travel. Ahiko eased off the acceleration, lowering the ship vertically until they broke through cloud coverage.

The planet's surface lived up to its reputation of an untouched golden world. Dense jungles created an impenetrable surface of treetops farther than he could see. Something moved at the corner of his vision, prompting him to turn.

A four-count of creatures undulated through the air. They reminded him of gargantuan slugs, stretched out to roughly one hundred meters and flattened out. Flat ridges ran along their bodies, flapping as their bodies inflated before compressing. Plumes of moisture-riddled air puffed out from the gills like the creatures used the gas to float and move about.

Well, that's a sight.

They sailed off into the distance.

"Something's blipping on the nav." Ahiko stole his attention, pointing to the console.

A singular area sectioned was out on the monitor by a red square, notably absent of heavy tree coverage. He scanned over the location and compared it to the coordinates he'd burned into his mind. "That's where we're supposed to set down."

Ahiko narrowed his eyes and tilted his head. "Didn't think there'd be anything developed on a place like this. Normally you do a deal somewhere open without any sort of structures. Makes parties feel at ease."

Star said nothing, shying away from the look to stare out of the cockpit screen. He was right. Nobody had mentioned anything of the sort. His attention went back to the armor resting by his seat. If he showed up looking for a fight, might be he got one. He shook his head and decided against it. One man suited up was enough. His hand fell to his revolver, and he sympathized with why Savi wanted to hold onto hers.

A hint of stone broke up the near-endless wash of treetops. The jungle faded, clearly cut down and pulled away to leave miles of flat ground running away from the base of a stone tower. Rectangular blocks formed a flat-topped pyramid. Rows of smaller ships dotted the edge of the open perimeter, keeping close to the distant tree line.

He found it odd to keep ships so far away from the structure. Unless they figured they might end up a target.

He traded a look with Ahiko.

A single question hung in the pilot's contorted face: What were they really walking into?

Star shook his head, putting a hand to his brow to help him see. "Bring us back around and ease us in. I want to make out every damn thing I can before our feet hit the ground."

Ahiko bowed his head and brought *The Leaf* about into a slow turn before heading toward the pyramid. He brought them over a patch of land devoid of any ships and ground traffic. "Setting her down, Shepherd. You feel some of us ought to hang back, let you do the talking?"

Star arched a brow.

"Bad feeling is all." Ahiko shrugged.

Star blew out a breath through his nostrils, nodding his head in agreement. "I can't shake it either. Something's bugging me." He scanned the pyramid grounds as they descended, noting people bustling about, some lingering at the edges by their ships and some walking along the tiered stones of the structure's outside.

This wasn't just a simple hand-off-and-leave deal. It looked like he'd be the one leaving after all was said and done.

"What do you make of that?" Star gestured toward the people walking along the pyramid.

The pilot pursed his lips, watching for a handful of seconds in silence. "Like the resistance picked Slaydus for a good reason. They don't plan to scuttle after this. This *is* a resistance base and world."

Star sunk in his seat. "Yeah, felt as much. We've walked into the beehive here. And I've got a feeling the bear isn't too far behind."

Ahiko opened his mouth but shut it a second later. He lowered the ship without a word.

They touched down, the world gently bobbing once as the ship sank into the ground before recovering.

Star unfastened his harness and stood, grabbing hold of the seat as he pulled himself around it. "Come on. Figure one armored friend at my side will make 'em think twice about anything shady. Two will give 'em reason to have itchy fingers. I don't want that."

Ahiko stood up and moved into step along him.

They marched toward the central hub, passing the crew in silence and heading toward the exit hatch.

Footsteps smacked out against the floor paneling behind him.

Star didn't bother to look. He did a rough count and put together that the crew had decided to follow him.

A small smile crossed his face. *Well, at least I know who to trust.*

He opened the hatch, shutting his eyes to welcome the first breath the planet had to offer. It hit him in one swoop—fresh air, heavy with moisture and the scent of wet earth and wood. His nose wriggled as something else made its way into the smell. A sickly-sweet odor that clung to the tissue of his nostrils, threatening to burn them.

Ship fuel. It wouldn't do much for a so-called golden world. People were mucking it up with that piss already.

Time and weather had taken their toll on the structure ahead. Vines raced along the aged stone. Plant life sprouted from cracks along the pyramid, allowing untold years of moisture to seep through and worsen the damage. Water trickled down from the top along the sides in several miniature streams.

He probably wouldn't be able to blast through that stone with a blaster, but nature broke through just fine.

Star shook his head clear and resumed walking toward the pyramid.

A train of people exited the structure, rushing towards *The Leaf.* The line split, and the group fanned out.

Star's hand fell slowly to his revolver, resting atop the weapon casually. He came to a halt as the crowd increased their pace. Star looked over his shoulder to see *The Leaf's* makeshift crew fanning out.

Zita and Molan stood at either side of him and a few steps back. M34N came ahead of them to hover by Star's right, while Ahiko passed him by, standing a couple of feet before him on the left.

An armored man makes a one-pointed statement. He noted that Savi lingered too far for comfort, hanging closer to the ship than with the crew. Star narrowed his eyes to focus his vision.

The monk gripped the black revolver hard enough that her hand visibly quivered even in the distance.

Why? These are her folk. Star pulled his gaze away, turning it back to the approaching group.

The person at the head of the oncoming crowd stood a few inches short of Star's chin. Her hair was the color of light sand caught in the sun, and tufts of hair protruded from under her white cap. She dressed in loose-fitting clothing like a pilot would. Her gray shirt looked oversized at first glance by the number of folds forming in it. The leather jacket had to have been plucked from someone carrying another thirty pounds more than her. The pants were loose and shimmered like they were made from multiple synthetics.

She put more distance between herself and the following crowd, making her way several feet from Star. The woman stopped and held out a hand. "*The Last Leaf*, we spotted you coming in a few miles out." Her face broke into a smile that made its way into her dark rum-colored eyes. "You didn't have to swing over and by before landing."

Star did his best to match her smile. His face refused to stretch easily, letting him know he did a poor job of returning the expression. "Call it a precaution." He took her hand, giving it a gentle squeeze and shake.

"Fair enough. Can't imagine you were expecting to come across a resistance base." She held the smile. "Tani Stahn, resistance pilot and coordinating the defense and our assault, when ready."

Assault? He didn't remember any mention of that being made. He fought to keep his face neutral. "Right. What now?" Star pulled his hand free from hers.

She leaned to her side, eyeing the ship. "We take the ship, pay you, and wait for the rest of them." Tani arched a brow. "Where are they? We haven't heard a bit of word aside from you. Granted, you've made an intergalactic ruckus the likes of nothing else before. Noise about you's been louder than the glass of Autumn *and* Lisba."

Star lost the battle to keep his face a stone mask. "You haven't heard anything because there's nothing to hear. *The Last Leaf* wasn't just the last of the ships made for the journey; it's the last of them. Rest never made it off Autumn." He took a breath. "Least not to my knowledge."

The rest of Tani's group had made it by her side, close enough to hear what he had just said. Their faces sank in unison. Several members turned to each other, murmuring things he couldn't make out. Tani blinked and licked her lips, her mouth turning into a weak and lopsided smile. "That's wrong." She sounded like she was trying to convince herself. "That has to be wrong."

"It's not." Star's words fell with a weight greater than any of the stones making up the pyramid. "I boarded *The Leaf* as the first salvo rained down on the planet. I got her airborne in time to escape the wave washing over the area. Seconds too late, and I'd have been glassed too. Made a desperate jump to the only thing that came to mind—Terizen Station. Been running since, trying to get here."

Tani turned away from him, looking to the crowd. Her face made it clear she was searching for the right words to calm them, to give them some semblance of hope.

Good luck with that. Twistin' truths gets you nowhere fast. Best face things as they are; you'll make it further that way. He cleared his throat to pull her attention back to him. "I brought the ship. Was my understanding we're to be paid, and the resistance sets about getting The Light spread to worlds that need it, right?"

The smile returned to Tani's face and she nodded. "Right. Let's get you all inside and talk." She inclined her head toward the barkeeper, giving him a friendly smile. "Molan."

Molan returned it in earnest without word.

Tani turned to a man on her left, giving one of his sleeves a gentle tug.

He could have been a mildly warped reflection of Star. The man had a similar build right down to the height. He had the same skin, eyes, and hair color.

"Can you get a crew to run a set of siphons to *The Last Leaf* and start breaking down The Light? I don't want to disassemble the ship right now. There's not enough time. Get as many conduits on the energy source as you can, Kheelo."

Star's eyes widened, and he regarded the man. *Kheelo, that's an old shepherding call.* He traded glances with the man as Kheelo nodded to Tani and moved past Star.

"I'll take you and your crew into the base and clear some things up for you all." Tani turned and waved her hand for them to follow. The group around her broke into pairs and dispersed. Tani walked toward the pyramid.

Star fell into step behind her, his crew following without needing further prompting. He watched passersby scuttle to and from ships, some rushing toward *The Last Leaf*. Whatever they were planning, they weren't waiting about to do it. They must have been pressed for time. He reasoned something was going to happen and soon. Star gave Ahiko a look, catching the pilot's attention before gesturing to their surroundings.

The pilot inclined his head in understanding but kept quiet.

Molan might have been right about something being off. The question was: What?

"Don't suppose I can ask why one of your crew is wearing hound-knight armor?" Tani glanced at him before turning to look at Ahiko. "Some people here have awful memories of men and women in that gear doing terrible things to their families and worlds. You're lucky he wasn't shot on stepping out of *The Leaf*."

Star followed the woman's gaze to Ahiko. "Hound knight?"

The pilot sighed, running a hand against the side of his head. "Name's sort of stuck, what, with half the galaxy thinking of us as dogs of the military. Anyone wearing this"—he rapped a fist against the chest piece—"gets plastered with the title. Military went along with it not long after."

Star rolled his eyes. "Glad you weren't shot."

Ahiko gave him a look that said he agreed.

He and the crew followed Tani into a wide opening nearly the same dimensions as one of the stones comprising the pyramid. Cylindrical tube-lights hung along the walls from power cables, dangling from shoddily installed brackets. The hall went on for minutes until it broke into a three-way path.

Tani didn't stop to direct them, turning down the right and heading into the hall.

Star adjusted his weight as the path rose. The incline grew as he moved up the passage.

The walk went on for a handful of minutes that he kept a rough count of until Tani stopped outside an opening.

She turned to face him. "People considerably more important than myself would like to see you." Tani waved him into the room.

He stepped through, moving aside as she came by him. Star noted the far end of the room had two exits, one at each side.

The walls were plastered in dark paint, forcing one's attention to the circular lens stand in the middle of the room. Lines of white light formed a wire diagram of a capital destroyer floating in the air. The image faded, replaced by a structure that bore a startling resemblance to the pyramid they stood in. The top of the building had been removed to house something that looked like a cannon.

The device was comprised of three acute triangles stretched far and joined only at the ends. A flat prism sat at its base. Tendrils of light flared to life within the display, arcing between the triangular planes as they coursed along them. A beam lanced out from the cannon.

The image dissolved, once again displaying the destroyer. A stream of light cut into the frame from the lens base and headed for the ship. The energy struck the ship, passing through it as if the vessel had no defensive measures. The destroyer split down the middle as wisps of light clung to the ship and ate away at its hull.

The visual washed away to show a planet Star was familiar with. Heavily populated, a place dominated by towering buildings, threaded with skywalks, and home to tens of billions of people.

Six ships appeared on the screen, their wire frames stripped away by invisible tools to show The Light housed within each. The energy spheres were compressed into thin streams of light that were launched into the planet.

The world vanished in a flash.

Star blinked at the images, running through everything in his mind and putting it together. "Stars and skies. The Light *really* is a weapon. You mean to turn it on people." He felt the tip of a revolver press against the back of his head.

"That's right," said Savi.

CHAPTER THIRTY-SIX
A STRANGE DISLIKE

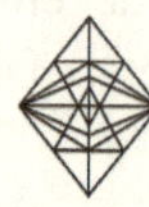

Star raised his hands slowly to his sides, slowing his breathing to ensure he didn't set off the monk.

Tani brushed her coat aside, taking a step back as she drew a blaster. The weapon looked small, even by normal standards. Its frame barely protruded from her hand, the barrel coming in a shade shorter than her index finger. The diminutive weapon didn't look like it packed a punch. "What's going on?"

Star risked turning his head a fraction, just enough to stare at Savi out of the corner of his eyes. "Part of me wondered if you'd pull a stunt like this."

Savi pushed the barrel harder against his head. "Move into the room—fast, near the display."

He did as she asked. The gun remained close to the back of his skull as he maneuvered around the holographic lens setup. Savi kept herself perfectly in line with him, matching his steps and angling herself to stay behind.

Ahiko entered the room, drawing a weapon before registering everything going on. He didn't miss a beat in passing over Tani to level the gun on Savi. "The hell?"

"Been wondering the same thing." Tani narrowed her eyes and glowered at Ahiko before turning the look back on the monk. "Why would one your crew turn on your captain?"

Ahiko's mouth worked soundlessly, like he was trying to fight for an explanation he'd never come up with.

"She's not part of the crew. Not any longer." Star bristled as the barrel of the gun ground against his head. "Captains have a strange dislike of those that turn guns on 'em. It's one of our irrational flaws."

"Quiet." Savi's voice wavered.

Star watched as Tani moved her gun a bit higher, like she were weighing whether or not she could make a shot on the monk without blasting him. He appreciated the sentiment but preferred people not gamble with his life. "You weren't even resistance, were you, Savi?"

The monk remained silent.

"Picked up on a few choice words you've said along our rather brief time together." He waited to see if she'd respond.

She didn't.

Star pushed the point further. "I've never heard them said aloud apart from a particular group of people—extremists."

Tani's eyes hardened, and her gun inched higher.

"Not many people go around calling the military

'dogs.' At least, not the way you do. An old, not-that-good-of-a-friend mentioned that to me. By the look on her face"—he gestured with the slightest raise of his chin toward Tani—"she's thoroughly confused as to who the hell you even are." Star winced as the revolver twitched against his head.

Savi's breathing grew loud enough to be heard over the low, electrical humming of the lens display. The monk kept quiet, however.

He thought back to how she had acted on the capital destroyer, the seething hatred she displayed for Admiral Cain. He could sympathize, and, yet, he couldn't have brought himself to murder the disarmed and outnumbered admiral. That took a special kind of coldness he didn't know if he were capable of. A small part of him hoped he'd never have to find out.

There was a point anger and buried feelings coalesced into something worse, something uglier. They tangled and knotted to form something that subdued other thoughts and rationality. In the end, they grew to become a person's sole or dominant motivation for doing things. It was a path that led people to whittle away the kinder parts of themselves, leaving behind only the extremist bits.

He'd seen it a few times over the course of his life: broken people who were pushed just a bit too far by circumstances out of their control. They shunned the help, consoling themselves with something easier—rage.

Savi echoed those signs to him.

He tried to pinpoint what else he could, but having a gun to his head left him with little else to do besides keeping alive. Star swallowed as Molan and the rest of the crew entered.

Savi snaked an arm around his throat, pulling him back with her as she took several steps away from the growing crowd.

Molan fumbled around his pants as if he were searching for something. His face lit up then sank.

Star gazed at the barkeeper, thinking over what he had said and how he had acted around Savi. The old man had been resistance himself, and he'd treated Savi as something close to it from what Star had seen. That meant he was a traitor too…or something else.

Zita drew a blaster. "Shepherd, Savi, what's going on?"

Molan raised both hands, silently ushering for calm.

Everyone ignored him, much to Star's dismay.

The barkeeper shifted his weight, keeping his eyes on Savi as he placed a hand on Zita's weapon. He urged her with a gentle push to lower it.

She eyed him like he were crazy but relented with a scowl and lowered the gun.

The barkeeper edged toward Savi, hands still out to his side. "What are you doing?" Molan arched a brow as he inched forward.

Star connected the other truths that had been in front of him. He stared at Savi. "You *were* resistance at some point, weren't you?"

Tani bristled, her jaw going hard. "I've never seen her, much less heard of this trash."

"Trash?" Savi's voice hardened, spittle peppering the back of Star's skull. "You've no idea what I've done for your movement. None at all."

Molan took another step. "Calm down, Savi. You

too, Tani. There's a story here that needs tellin', and the shepherd needs to know it."

Star kept his mouth shut, giving a slight nod to let the barkeeper know he appreciated the sentiment.

"Savi was resistance. Came to us long ago from a monastery." The barkeeper took another step, positioning himself between all three points of fire: Ahiko, Tani, and Savi, should she choose to aim her weapon past Star.

So, she was a monk. It was good to know there was a hint of truth in her lie. But, then, there always was. It was what made the best lies stick.

"We took her in, and she took to the resistance and what we did." Molan's expression changed into something of fondness, the kind a proud parent would make. "She took to some things better than I thought."

Star had an idea of what that might be, but he kept his teeth clamped against each other. He didn't want to talk out of turn and risk Savi losing her clearly diminishing patience.

"Namely, killing. Small girl could get into many places without earning a second look. A lot of anger in her, though." Molan looked down like invisible weights pulled on him.

Shame, regret? Star couldn't peg what it was exactly, only that the man had something on his conscience involving the monk.

"World's not a fair place, and we should never have sent a kid out to do the things we asked her to do. But, sometimes, you've got no choice. It changed her, made her more extreme. After long enough, we asked her to leave. She went back to the monastery for a while from what I heard. Wasn't long before she took to doing things on her own, using the monks for what she could learn in a neutral, safe place. Leave when she could; take actions as she saw fit. That's when I thought I'd lost her." Molan's gaze crept back up, not quite meeting Star in the eyes.

Star could fill in the rest. "She's been an extremist since. Let me guess, you heard from her around the time word spread of Autumn and the rumors went wild."

Molan looked away but nodded.

Star turned his head a just enough to let the monk know his question was meant for her. "And *you* came back, acting like resistance to get this chance, to what, Savi?"

The monk grabbed him tighter, digging nails into his coat until he felt a shadow of them squeezing against his collar bone. "Get the truth of it all. Confirm what it was you were carrying, that it's a weapon the resistance means to use, and…lead *our* fleet here to take what we can."

He blinked. *Our fleet. Oh, hell.* Star thought back to the bar on Lisba. Zita had announced his destination to the entire crowd. Word had to have spread beyond just her crew and loyal friends. Savi must have sent word to her contacts somehow.

Star shut his eyes, trying to picture what was heading their way. He had no idea what the extremist fleet consisted of, but it couldn't be good. At the very least, a fight would break out over the planet, taxing the resistance's resources. It could end up the sort of battle to attract other eyes.

M34N lumbered into the room, drawing a series of panicked glances in his direction as his heavy metal frame elicited deep *plods* from the stone below. The automaton met every person's looks before settling on Savi. "Oh, I seem to have interrupted something involving guns. Those are very bad for my health. I should be leaving now." He took a step back.

"Move, and I kill the shepherd. He's not needed now, just a bit of leverage until I get the data I need." Savi ground the gun against his head for effect.

M34N rolled his shoulders as a way of a shrug. "I have no problem with that."

Molan glowered at him. "What took you so long?"

"I became lost, eventually coming across—" a series of footsteps and heavy breathing cut the automaton off.

Kheelo ran into the room. "We've word coming in of fleets near the edge of the system. They're crawling in slow to not blip sensors. Scouts lingering on nearby worlds pinged 'em and sent word." He stopped, eyeing the situation. His lips pressed together, but he didn't go for a weapon.

Star picked up on something of particular note. *Fleets, plural.* "Just how many fleets are heading our way, and more importantly, whose?"

A visible lump formed in Kheelo's throat as he swallowed. "One's a ragtag band of unknowns."

Star figured that would be the extremist's likely motley assembly of ships.

"The other's the military."

CHAPTER THIRTY-SEVEN
A HANDFUL OF CONTINGENCIES

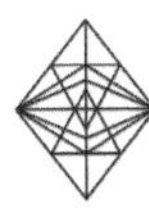

Star swore. Fortunately, it wasn't enough of a sudden shock to force Savi into evaporating his head. A firefight erupted within his mind. Thoughts lanced by like shots, making it near impossible for him to focus and find a solution.

He thought back to when he'd figured something was truly off about Savi: the reclaim hangar and the battle with Cain. There should have been a damn legion guarding *The Leaf* if what Cain had said about its importance was true. *Unless…* "Oh, dammit."

"What?" said everyone in unison.

He sighed, sinking his posture and pulling his shoulders away from Savi's chest. The maneuver loosened her hold. He hoped she wasn't too aware of it. "None of you see it, do you? *They*, the military, let us escape."

An unnatural quiet filled the room.

"How else do you think we got away? Why was the ship unguarded? They had to have had a hunch that we'd head straight for our target destination after plucking *The Leaf* back from 'em. They followed us." Star's words could have rang through the entire structure.

Kheelo scratched his chin, glancing at the lens display. "This changes things. Don't suppose I could ask you all to drop whatever business it is you've got going on and do something productive?" He kept his voice neutral, but fire kindled in his eyes and his jaw clenched.

Star opened his mouth.

The lights went out, leaving the lens as the only source of illumination. An alarm wailed to life.

Savi's grip on Star loosened further.

He seized the opportunity, thrusting his hips against hers and pulling away. He broke free, but not before one of her palms crashed into his back. Star staggered forward.

A shot sailed by him.

It was impossible to make out the source. He sank to a knee, drawing his revolver. Another shot zipped overhead, prompting him to lower himself further. He looked over his shoulder to see a silhouette close in on the lens. *Savi.*

She jabbed a hand at the display. The images flickered before collapsing in on themselves and into nothingness.

Data drive? He rounded about, leveling his weapon at her.

Red lights flared through the room, strobing and

washing across the walls as the alarm loudened.

He blinked against the sudden brightness, shielding his eyes on instinct.

Another shot cried out.

"Dammit!" Tani's snarl was barely audible under the howling alarm.

Star knew the reason behind her anger. He righted himself, scanning the red tinged room. Everyone was present save Savi. He glanced toward the two exits at the far end of the chamber. The one on the left bore a scorch mark that had to have come from Tani's blaster. *Least we know which way she went.*

An incalculable slew of questions rushed through Star's mind, but he shook his head in an attempt to put them aside. "Ahiko, Tani—somebody—what's going on?"

Tani came to his side, slipping an arm under one of his shoulders to help him up. "The alarm means the planet's been ordered to scuttle defenses. Every base here is readying up to launch a counter attack."

Every base? Just like Lisba. Everyone had a handful of contingencies but him and his crew.

"Kheelo," Tani said, "how much longer do you think we have?"

Star pulled himself away from Tani's grip, moving past her toward the exit. He waved to his crew to follow.

"Minutes at best." Kheelo rushed ahead of Star and exited the room first, beckoning everyone to follow him. "You'll want to make your way to the Ops Center downstairs." He directed his attention to Tani.

Star paused. "And us?"

Kheelo shrugged, holding his gaze on Tani. "Leave.

Don't. No time for it, and I don't care. If you're going to stay, help us. Otherwise, take your money and piss off." He turned and broke into a jog.

Tani flashed Star an apologetic smile before taking off after Kheelo.

The crew stared at him.

He'd dragged them into this, the least he could do was get them out—safely so. And hopefully paid. "After them." Star motioned to the crew and sprinted after Tani and Kheelo.

The lights in the halls had morphed to a soft red as well, making visibility in the already dimly lit halls worse. The small orbs of illumination from each bulb didn't fully overlap with the ones strung along ahead and left darkened patches in between.

He kept his eyes fixed on Tani's form ahead, repeating the direction of each turn she took as she took them. Star reached out with a hand, slapping it against the edge of a turn to grip and pull himself with. He rounded the corner faster than he would have liked, barreling into the opposite side. His shoulder throbbed from the impact.

White light flooded a room at the end of the hall.

He doubled his efforts, closing the gap between himself and Tani. Star entered the room, following right behind Tani with his crew coming in steps after him.

Lens screens hung over the far wall, the largest of which dwarfed him several times over in height and nearly just as long. A series of smaller display podiums were spread throughout the room, showcasing various images of the planet's surface and the immediate orbit scene.

A woman, who Star wagered was in her early forties, stepped into view from a lens podium at the side of the room. She had a kind face, weathered with the sort of lines that came from constant sun exposure and too much smiling. Her dark hair had been cropped short like Tani's. She wore similar clothing to the younger woman as well. Her eyes reminded Star of wet grass, a dark and rich green.

Tani inclined her head in a curt gesture. "Ma'am."

The older woman returned it, moving closer and pointing to a particular display.

It featured a similar scenario to the one in the previous room, depicting the altered rooftop of the pyramid. The same cannon protruded from the structure, building coils of energy along it that fired into space.

"What's the situation, Kheelo?" The woman didn't take her eyes off the display as she addressed him.

"Two fleets at last count. Both just entered the system and wanted to crawl in to get closer. Scouts pinged them as soon as they came in. Both fleets are far enough apart from each other that I'm not sure they've noticed or care about the others. They're heading our way; that much is given." Kheelo's mouth twitched as if he had something more to add.

The woman waved a hand. "Go on."

Kheelo exhaled before taking a deep breath. "We've got fighters rounded up and ready to scramble, but we're holding off on launch till either fleet's touching orbit. I'm hoping they turn on each other and we can launch to hit 'em hard enough while the rest escape. Conduits running to the ship are up and primed. Light cannon will be functional in minutes."

She pursed her lips, releasing a light *mmhm*.

Tani crept forward as if wanting to speak.

Star cleared his throat loud enough to steal the attention. "Don't suppose I can sneak in a word before the likely bombardment of this planet?"

The woman turned to him, staring at him like she had just noticed he was there. "And you are?" She raised a brow, looking to Tani for an explanation.

He didn't give her a chance to answer on his behalf. "Star Shepherd. The man you're supposed to pay for delivering The Light. Might make mention of the fact you didn't tell me I was shepherding a weapon of mass destruction, Miss…"

"Laren. Cassana Laren, elected official and the voice of the resistance. Representative of the free peoples of the galaxy. In charge of everything you've seen here and will see." Her voice carried an air of authority that he'd seen in career politicians. It held a quiet strength and a fair share of confidence some could call arrogance.

"Mighty impressive titles. That mean you plan on paying us rather handsomely for the work we've done?" Star tried to keep his voice steady. There was more at stake here than the money, but he couldn't let that slip. He had to find a way to stop them using The Light like that. Left unchecked, there'd be a new a power that could end up as bad as the Oligarchy—or worse.

Cassana moved toward a set of old metal lockers near the far wall. She slipped a finger into a small, plastic loop and tugged on it. The door snapped open. She reached in, removing a slender steel case as long as his forearm. Cassana brought it over to a podium and put it down.

Star stared at her before snapping it up open. He let out a low whistle. A series of flat bars filled the case. Each shone a myriad of colors like the metal was forged from crystallized rainbows. A set of names were stamped into each bar: Holder family, The Holder Raw and Alloy Materials Company.

Thram. That stamp made the reward worth more the value of the metals alone.

The metal alloy held no practical or industrial use, but it was prized for aesthetics and simple rarity. It was a symbol of wealth, and its own status artificially increased its worth. The Holder family rarely broke with their tradition of allowing the metal to be traded and sold outside their extended family.

Meaning it had been stolen. It was still worth a set of fortunes dozens of times over. And if the resistance was willing to part with it… He looked up to Cassana Laren. "Money and freedom ain't your end goals, are they?"

She ignored him, waving a dismissive hand to Kheelo and Tani. "Get to your ships and lead a counter attack *after* opening salvos from the Light cannon."

Both of them snapped quick salutes and moved off without so much as glancing in Star's direction.

Ahiko came to his side, staring at the case. "Do we really care, Shepherd? That much money, we can go to any end of the galaxy we want and eat and drink freely till we die." His voice wavered as if his heart really wasn't in the statement.

Star kept his gaze on Cassana. "Depends if you think we're doing the right thing by leaving to do that, Ahiko."

The pilot exhaled through his nose, grabbing the case and shutting it. He didn't reply.

"You'll find that I, the galaxy, and, most certainly, the Oligarchy don't care for what *you* consider to be right," said Cassana. She moved to another console, hunching over and running a hand along a curved panel.

The device whirred and displayed wires of light that shaped themselves to a view of space around the planet.

The first of a fleet that had to belong to the military came into view. Two capital destroyers, half a dozen super carriers, and the list continued to grow.

Star swallowed. That wasn't a fight the resistance would win unless they meant to make a statement and escape. He stared at the display as it reconfigured.

The images showed the cannon from earlier, except a series of command prompts hovered in digital writing above the display. Cassana touched a finger to one of them.

The pyramid shook like the ground below them was about to split.

Tendrils of energy build around the digital weapon, and a horrible thought crossed Star's mind as the building quivered some more. He turned, sprinting past his crew without word, barreling down the hall. He had no idea which way led out of the labyrinth of tunnels.

It's no different than shepherding. Running straight and true best you can, think clear, and you'll find your way.

He thought back to the turns they'd taken to get to the last room and then from there to the Ops Center. It wasn't as accurate a mental map as he would have liked, but he trusted it and ran harder.

Minutes passed before a softer light filtered in

through the end of the hall ahead.

He pumped his legs harder, ignoring the building heat and straining muscles. Star kept going until he was far enough to turn and glance at the top of the pyramid. *Aw hell.*

True to the image from the lens display, a cannon fashioned of cold metal and composites protruded from where the capstone had been. The same coils of ethereal light banded and flowed around it.

No, no, no. He clenched a fist, running his other hand through his hair. Star whirled about to gauge the weapon's target. He squinted, gazing up at the cloudless sky and the ship descending upon the planet.

One of the supercarriers entered the atmosphere, likely to drop an untold number of ground troops and vehicles.

An ear-splitting shriek tore through the air, prompting him to clamp his hands to his ears. Star shrunk away from the overhead keen and looked up to see what had caused it.

A beam of brilliant golden-white light cut through the sky, striking the supercarrier.

The resistance had just started a full-blown war.

CHAPTER THIRTY-EIGHT
TRADING POWERS

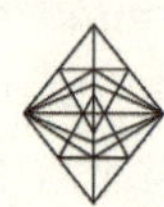

The Light washed over the ship's shield and battered it relentlessly. Amaranthine waves of light rolled over the ship as they worked to repel the cannon's bursts. The Light refused to let up, hammering away until it passed through the shields. A thin flash spurted from the bottom and top ends of the ship where the beam had cut through.

Every ship in orbit would be watching this. They would drop everything they had on the planet in retaliation. Every able body was about to come down and lay siege.

The beam held, eroding the ship around the cone of light until the inevitable. Blossoms of fire erupted throughout the carrier, pluming out of the hull as the vessel exploded.

Star shut his eyes and took a deep breath. They were trading one power for another. And the people who mattered, they wouldn't come out winning. They'd find themselves under a new heel. He opened his eyes and looked around the field.

People scrambled to the edge of the plane, breaking through the trees lining the spot and likely to the ships nestled within the jungle. A few vessels littered the area. Pilots clambered up and in, powering them up to take off.

Star ignored them, focusing on the flexible conduits snaking around the field. He followed their path with his eyes. Each of the tubes ran up the outside of the pyramid to converge on a single point—the base of the weapon. He turned around, tracing the conduits to their origin.

Sunuvabitch. Star rushed towards *The Leaf*, unconcerned with the handful of people standing before the access ramp. *I should never have turned over the ship. Dammit.* He stopped running when another ship came into view.

A second followed.

The third supercarrier came shortly after.

Each vessel descended fast, almost as if they gave no concern for crashing into the planet.

The cannon struggled to align itself and target another carrier. They were going to just hit the ground hard, unload troops, and storm the place on foot. Less risk involved than airdropping and waiting to be taken out by that weapon. He rubbed a hand over his face. *The hell do I do?*

He aimed his revolver at one of the conduits. A single shot ought to cut right through one of them. If he did that, what would keep the resistance from putting up a fight? Just because the people at the top pulled a stunt like this didn't mean he should let everyone else pay for it.

"Shepherd!"

Star turned toward the source of the voice.

Ahiko ran toward him, the rest of the crew in tow. They stopped as the cannon fired again. Each member spun around to view The Light as it hurtled from the pyramid like a comet of energy, passing out of view into space.

A variety of smaller ships took off around them before the sky above echoed like a dozen thunderclaps occurring at once. Fire spread out high above like drops of oil over the surface of water. The lightshow vanished seconds later.

They had just taken out another vessel, and he hadn't even seen it enter the atmosphere.

Ahiko made his way over to Star. The pilot swallowed a gulp, nodding to the cannon then the ship ahead. "Place is going to hell and fast. What do we do?"

Star felt the urge to shrug and admit that he had no idea. He weighed the decision as the crew closed in on him, save for one member. Star tilted his head, looking past the group in search for the odd man out. "Where's Molan?"

Zita and M34N stopped a step away from Ahiko and traded glances.

The automaton's eyes whirred and reconfigured, the flat panels and lens folding over each other like he were confused. He turned halfway around, looking to the pyramid. "Odd. He was behind us for most of the run." M34N released a low sound that could have passed for a dejected moan. "Do you think he's lost? It wouldn't surprise me. He's rather old, possibly senile."

Star took a breath to steady himself as his head pounded. *Priorities, right.* "We'll find Molan. Right now, we need a plan. Military's set down a mile down from the tree line here." Star pointed to the far end of the field. "They'll be here in twenty minutes depending on how slow they are navigating the jungle and if they meet any resistance." He looked to Ahiko for silent confirmation of the timeframe.

The pilot bowed his head.

"Right. They're not looking to take this fight to the air if possible, not with that cannon." Star waved a dismissive hand. "Got a few options—"

"Why do I feel like none of them are good ones?" Zita let out a heavy sigh.

Star rolled his shoulders. "We stay and fight"—he held up his hands as the crew erupted into a clamor—"for a bit. We help what people we can and escape. Resistance ain't all bad people. Hell, how many do you figure really know the truth?"

Ahiko shook his head. "If it's like the military, hardly any."

Star agreed with a simple grunt. "I'm not letting good people die because I'm soured by what Cassana Laren pulled over our eyes. We do what we can, take *The Leaf* back, and scarper."

The crew traded looks. Ahiko wriggled the case as a way to draw attention. "That's fine and all, but what's the other option? I'm fond of us holding onto our vast and rather rare fortune here. Truth be told, didn't expect to make it far enough to be paid."

"Now consider yourself paid in advance and

expected to stick around and do more." Star grinned. "Other option's we cut the conduits"—he pointed a finger at several of the pipes running along the ground—"and bail with the ship now."

The sound of blaster fire pulled his attention toward the jungle. Errant bolts cut through the trees, sailing across the field. He collapsed to the ground, watching the crew do the same.

Shit.

"Whatever we do, we best do it fast!" Ahiko threw one hand over the back of his head to shield himself as he buried the case under his body.

Least he's got his priorities settled.

Resistance members ran past, stampeding their way toward the edge of the field. They returned fire without any targets in sight. The strategy seemed to be bombarding the jungle with every bit of shots they could in the hope of thinning the herd before meeting them.

Hope that works for them. Star scrambled to all fours, keeping low as he turned.

Resistance members poured out from the structure, carrying rectangular frames with slightly rounded edges. They fighters stopped at staggered points, fanning out and slamming the portable devices into the ground. Each frame was nearly as long as Star and twice as wide. Fighters trailed their hands along both ends of one length of the frame, flipping their thumbs against something at each side.

Translucent light of sapphire blue leapt from the corners of the frames to meet at the center and fill it. The substance looked like a layer of gel stretched to be a membrane and serve as a shield.

Fighters continued to litter the field with the make-shift defensive barriers.

Works for me. "New plan: Take cover, fight back. Things start to get dicey, we leave." Star made sure his voice carried over the blaster fire near the edge of the field.

The crew screamed an incoherent cry of agreement.

Star pushed himself to his feet and ran toward the closest of the barriers. He narrowed his vision, blotting out the strings of energy zipping by in the near distance. Last thing he needed was one of those hitting him in the back.

He skirted around the edge of the shield, gripping the frame and using it to pull himself around it at high speed.

A bolt struck the energy membrane, causing it to shift colors. The blue warped into an agitated purple as the blaster shot dissipated, and the shield returned to normal.

He turned to the resistance member on his right.

They were dressed identically to Tani, clad in loose-fitting clothing suitable for a pilot. A helmet obscured their face, the visor preventing anyone from looking in on them. "Who the hell are you?" The resistance fighter didn't bother looking at him when they spoke. They edged out from the side of the shield, releasing two shots from his powered pistol.

"Shepherd who brought you what's powering your fancy toy up there." Star jabbed a finger toward the cannon.

The fighter pulled away from the lip of the shield and followed Star's gesture. "Huh, didn't even notice the damn thing." His voice rang with sincerity. "Didn't sign up for this. Fighting, sure, if it came to it. Didn't think we were going to hit back with weapons like that."

Me either.

The cannon roared as another pulse of light erupted from it.

Star thought back to what Admiral Cain had told him. They'd rather throw all the bodies they could, take the world at whatever cost, and walk away with The Light and a working weapon. If the military took and twisted that technology…

Stars and skies. He didn't want to imagine the military with that level of power in their hands. *So, who deserves it, and how the hell do I get it to them?*

As if he'd heard his thoughts, the fighter to his side brushed against his shoulder. "You know, we were supposed end this all in a day." He snapped his fingers. "Was told that we were close to getting a source of energy that would make the Oligarchy crumble overnight. People would wake up to new power, and that'd be the end of it. Nothing you could do to stop it." He shook his head and pulled away to shoot past the lip of the shield.

Survive this, cut the conduits, get The Leaf *out of here, and figure it out from there.* If the cannon went down too early, the military might think the weapon was a dud and chance glassing the planet. He weighed what he would do in their position, the worth of The Light, and everything else he'd learned.

Star figured it didn't matter in the end. He settled on doing what he could and following what had driven him this far. He turned around, squinting to get a better view through the rippling surface of the translucent shield.

Hound knights emerged from the jungle. The black-armored wraiths shrugged off most of the incoming blaster fire and led the way for the soldiers behind. Men and women wearing the expected fatigues, likely carrying a few armored plates under their clothing to protect their vitals, swarmed from the tree line.

Star glanced to the resistance fighter by his side. "How serious were you about that fighting bit?"

The resistance member stared at him.

"Because we're about to get it."

CHAPTER THIRTY-NINE

A LOSS OF LIGHT

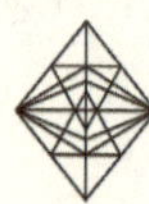

A torrent of red bolts scattered across the field, hammering into the shields to fade into nothingness. Errant shots zipped past, striking bits of stone and the trees behind them. A few overly eager resistance fighters leaned too far out of cover and caught blasts to their exposed bits.

The assault grew in intensity as more soldiers rushed out of the jungle like a wave of armor and weaponry. Powered blasts lanced back from the resistance to meet a wall in the form of the hound knights. Most of the shots struck the black-clad soldiers, driving them back a step. A few fell to their knees as their armor absorbed the energy and kinetic impact.

A clap of muted thunder went off from nearby.

Star missed the source, but he watched as a hound knight fell to his ass like he'd been struck by a sledgehammer. Black composite material showered from the soldier's chest.

Star looked to see who'd fired the shot.

Ahiko crouched behind similar cover close to a dozen yards away. The pilot had hung his cell-powered pistol from a loop on his waist and held onto a long rifle with a protruding magazine. The weapon's build was far more slender that he would have imagined. A long, thin barrel extended from a larger rectangular frame. The pilot had to shoulder the weapon, placing a hand underneath the front of the weapon to help steady it.

Antiquated rifle?

Ahiko kept one of his eyes to the lengthy scope fixed atop the weapon. One of his hands slid against part of the weapon Star couldn't see. The pilot squeezed the trigger, the rifle bucking in his grip.

Another crack of thunder sounded. Another hound knight tumbled back, armor shattering where the round had struck.

Projectiles. Of course. Damn armor's built to catch and disperse powered blasts.

Star turned, slapping the back of his hand into the shoulder of the resistance member by him. "You got a local comms?"

The soldier jerked his head in what could have been taken as an affirmative.

"Tell everyone using powered weapons to focus on the unarmored. Anyone who's got a hand on something old, projectile-based, turn 'em on the hound knights. Old rounds crack that armor. Got it?" Star rapped the back of a fist against the man's sleeve.

The fighter clutched the front of his collar, turning

his head to speak into the shirt and relayed Star's instructions.

A series of clicks and beeps echoed back from the fighter's collar.

"Copy."

"Son of—got it…"

"Now you tell us."

Star ignored the voices.

The cannon fired another brilliant beam of light.

What now? He traced the path of energy to find another ship dropping down—fast.

The cannon-shot missed the rapidly descending ship. The vessel careened to one side.

Hazardous piloting, unless they're trying to be crazy in hopes they don't get blasted to bits.

The ship was a far cry from the heavily armored and imposing carriers used by the military. It looked like a repurposed cargo frigate: a boxy vessel that had been fixed with endless and superfluous paneling, much like Zita's boat had been. The added metal wouldn't do much to deter heavy fire, but it could keep smaller fighters from tearing through and into the hull.

That must be one of the other fleet's birds. Extremists were touching down, and they were about to be fighting a war on both sides.

A second vessel, near identical to the one that had just touched down, slipped past the firing cannon to land in the jungle opposite to where the military had.

Shit, we're surrounded. All for one building. Star let out a piercing whistle as he turned to fire a four-count of shots toward the approaching horde of soldiers.

The resistance fighter to his side got the message.

"Yeah, I see it too. Our birds have been keeping low to the jungle to avoid being blasted by the bigger ships out in orbit. Command just sent out the signal to start strafing the ground and popping anything trying to land. It's about to get worse."

Star cast a look over his shoulder to where the extremist vessel had touched down. They had landed closer to the tree line than the military had, leaving less of a march for them.

And they're all after The Light, the base, the cannon. Meaning...I render it useless, it changes the dynamic now that they're all here.

Ships screamed overhead. A variety of smaller vessels, the majority of which were shaped like stretched-out triangles, spun through aggressive turns as they fired in sporadic bursts. Radiant green rays shot out from the ships in staccato bursts, peppering the ground and tearing up land.

Explosions sent handfuls of soldiers into the air, screaming until their landings stifled any sounds they might have made. The resistance fighter ships wove intricately overhead, exchanging fire with the descending military and extremist ships alike. Most of their fire was turned away by the shields on the heavier vessels. A few of the resistance squadron broke off to strafe the surrounding jungles, likely directing their fire at any ground soldiers trudging through the trees and vegetation.

The cannon fired again.

Star peeked out from cover. A bolt cut in front of him, sailing by to blow a chunk clean out of a section of the pyramid. He pulled back, glancing through the shield membrane. He rocked on the balls of his feet, timing the break from cover as he watched the incoming fire. *Now!* He surged out from cover, sprinting toward the next shield.

Scorching heat wracked his left shoulder, spreading over the muscle. The smell of burning leather and skin touched his nostrils, clinging tight and refusing to leave no matter how fast he breathed. The acrid stench burned nearly as much as the wound. He fell flat to the ground, placing the butt of his revolver in his mouth and clawing his way to the next shield. Blaster fire ripped through the air above.

Star made it behind cover, letting his weapon fall from his lips. He rolled to the side and brought a hand to the injury. Sharp pain radiated as his fingertips brushed the wound. He winced through it and the tears, kicking at the ground to push himself closer against the protective barrier.

Damn. This complicated things. He fumbled with his weapon, recovering it in a single-handed grip. The gun wavered in his hand as he trained it on one of the conduits running over the ground. He clenched his teeth and tightened his hold on the weapon to steady it for a moment. The shot struck the piping he'd aimed at, disintegrating a section and taking a chunk out of the earth below.

He gazed up at the cannon, putting a hand back to his wound. The injury still burned, but he endured the pain.

The weapon atop the pyramid sputtered for an instant before firing.

Star spat a curse and fired without pause at every

conduit in sight. A few shots went wide, doing nothing but blowing away the ground. Eventually, he tore through the power-carrying lengths of tubing.

Another series of currents built and wrapped around the cannon. They faded from sight an instant later. The weapon continued to whir about, tracking incoming ships but failing to fire.

That'll change things, and I've got a feeling it's for the immediate worse.

People broke out from the far side of the jungle opposite the military.

Me and my mouth. Star couldn't make out the extremists as well in the distance, but he noticed enough. Swaths of mixed projectile and energy fire came their way. He flopped to his side, burying his revolver into his coat and scrambling best he could along the ground.

"Ahiko!"

The pilot ignored the call or didn't hear it.

Dammit. Star cupped a hand to this side of his face. "Ahiko!"

The pilot pulled away from the sniper sight, looking over in Star's direction until he spotted him. "What?"

Star gestured to the cannon before making a horizontal chopping motion along his neck. "Killed it. Defenses are going to crumble at this rate. We need to take the ship back and leave!"

Ahiko didn't argue, inclining his head before looking away from Star. He called out something indiscernible that elicited a series of cries back.

Star managed to pick out bits of the sounds and voices, attributing them to the crew. *Glad to know they're around.* He leaned to the side to get a view of them. He caught sight of Zita and M34N huddling shoulder-to-shoulder behind another shield.

The pair fired without breaking cover once, shooting with just their hands edging out from behind the safety of the membrane, using the shots more like deterrents. *Smart.*

They rallied to Ahiko's cry, rushing toward him then turning their attention to Star.

He jabbed a finger towards *The Leaf.* At the rate things were going, the military would be on the ship and pass it in a handful of minutes. If Star and his crew didn't get there and lock it down, this would be over for good.

Star gripped the frame of the shield, using it to haul himself to his feet. His hands went back to his coat to retrieve his weapon. *Right, just one good run. That's it. Simple.*

He stole a quick breath. *As if anything's ever that simple.* Star turned, slipping out from cover and broke into a sprint. He didn't look to see if the crew had followed him. He knew they had.

Star squeezed off more shots than he could count, blanketing the air before him in golden light. He didn't care much for what his blasts were hitting, so long as they headed in the right direction and stayed clear of his ship.

A small group of four people huddled within the safety of *The Leaf's* access ramp, occasionally peeking out to fire at the approaching soldiers.

Not fond of what I'm going to have to do next.

He picked up the pace, storming the area before them and the ramp.

The Liberation Movement soldiers exchanged quick

looks and trained their weapons on him.

"This is my ship!" He waved a hand to the side, drawing their attention to the revolver. He squeezed off a shot to make his point.

All eyes followed the flash of light as it erupted from the gun.

"Things are about to go further to hell than you expect. You've got a few choices. Stay here, fight, likely die. You can turn and make way to the pyramid, find cover. It's got to have an underground bunker."

A few of the freedom fighters nodded.

"You can try to get off-world on your own. It's a smart move." Star gave them a knowing look. "Or…you can get out of my way, and you're welcome to board *The Leaf*. I'll take you anywhere you want, sure as hell away from here." He held his look.

Odds were that some of the fools wouldn't take the offer. There was a point where idealism became a death wish, though, Star had done a fine job of toeing that line himself and dragging others across it.

Star gritted his teeth, losing patience with the deliberating group. *The Leaf* sat unpowered, having filtered The Light to the cannon until he'd cut it. He didn't know the science behind the power source, but he hoped it would respond just as before. *That was the idea, anyhow.* He took a pair of steps up the ramp, causing the soldiers to jerk and steady their aim on him. Star's lips peeled back, and he bared his teeth in a snarl. "We don't have time for this!"

The soldiers traded looks, each of them flinching as a rogue energy bolt struck the ground by the ramp.

Hell with it. He shouldered one aside, reaching up to

open the small panel fixed into the ship's body.

"What are you doing?" One of the soldiers pointed a rifle at his face, going far enough to jam its barrel against his cheek.

Heavy whining filled the air, the sound of a screaming engine fighting failure. Something hurtled by the edges of his vision.

Star looked without turning his head, lest he jar the twitchy soldier into a sudden and rather unfortunate reaction.

An ivory-white-and-red-streaked fighter glided too close to the ground. Its nose warbled up and down like it was struggling to keep level at best. It failed. The ship struck the earth, crumpling a bit before somersaulting along the field. It was like watching a piece of scrunched-up cloth tumble across grass. Every possible piece hit and deformed against the soil until the ship slammed into the pyramid wall. Thunder and fire rolled out from the point of impact to shower the area with debris.

It wasn't an isolated occurrence.

Another ship crashed to the ground, repeating the sequence.

Angry, white-blue bolts rained down on all sides.

Black ships, shaped like sideways hourglasses, hurtled by.

He had never seen anything like those in all his life. Their looks made it clear they were military vessels, which meant the situation grew worse by the second.

Star let the betrayal, frustration—all of it—pool into heat that he channeled into a glare. "If you're going to shoot me, then go ahead and save me some time. If not, get the damn hell out of my way and let me save some people." He twisted his hips, bringing his good arm up to slam the butt of the revolver into the rifle's side. Having batted the weapon away, Star jabbed his finger into the keypad to prime *The Leaf's* thrusters.

A low whine built around him before sputtering out. *Oh...*

He spat and let loose a string of obscenities that drew the stares of the soldiers and his crew lingering behind. He turned around, chest heaving. "Ship's possibly dead."

The group flashed him looks that spoke volumes.

The Leaf was their only way off-world and, at the very least, their only safe harbor.

They had left the cannon—his fault. Without it, Slaydus would be overrun soon. And if what the military had come for was gone, and they caught wind of that... He swallowed at the realization. "They're going to glass the world and wipe out the resistance in one go. Or as much of it as they can." He hadn't noticed he'd spoken aloud until he caught the varying looks from the people around him.

Ahiko stepped onto the ramp, grabbing hold of the collar of the nearest soldier. "You keep standing here, you die here. Move!" He jabbed a finger to one of the shields nearby. "You heard the shepherd: Ship's dead, your cannon's dead. Got nothing left but your lives. Fight for 'em, keep 'em."

The resistance fighters scattered. Some ran toward the various shield placements, returning fire to both sides as they ran, targeting the military and extremists alike. Other fighters headed toward the pyramid, taking off at full sprints with little regard for the incoming blasts and crashing ships.

The world was falling to pieces, and if they hung around any longer, they'd crumble with it. What the hell was he to do?

"Thought you told me The Light don't work like that?" Ahiko raised a brow.

Star blinked, reeling from the pilot's question. "What?" He didn't have time to figure out what he had meant, instead moving toward the open hatch and stepping into the ship. He summoned the crew with a wave of a hand, lingering by the door with the intent of sealing it behind.

Zita rushed the ramp, passing him without looking back.

The automaton stopped by his side and blocked the way for the pilot. M34N exhaled, lowering his head. "Molan hasn't returned." The machine hadn't said anything else, but the words carried enough within them. Despite the automaton's nonchalant and, at times, brusque attitude, he cared for the barkeeper.

Dammit. Old man went after Savi, no doubt. Plain as day there was something left unsaid between 'em. Chance that the monk shot him. She seemed the sort. He gave M34N a steady look. "I'll wait for him as long as I can, promise."

The automaton seemed placated, shambling off behind Zita.

Ahiko checked Star with heavy shoulder thump to his good side, fortunately. "I'm swinging by the engine room before hitting the cockpit. You might want to, too." He sped up the ramp into the main hub of the ship.

Star winced, finger hovering over the keypad to shut the door. He stuffed the revolver into his coat in a fit of frustration. His breaths left him harder than necessary. He took a long, slow one to calm himself down. *Shit, promised the damn tin can I'd wait.* Star raced up the ramp, ignoring the lockers in the hub as he passed by.

He felt it best to wait to dress his wound. If he didn't find a way to get *The Leaf's* shields up before things escalated, he wouldn't have to worry about the shoulder injury.

Ahiko stormed by him, heading toward the cockpit. The pilot nursed a giant smile.

Star narrowed his eyes and doubled his pace to the engine room. He made his way in, sucking in a breath.

Golden waves flooded his vision. The sphere housing The Light hung open, pulsating and glowing like normal.

Star grimaced and worked through what had caused the ship to falter in starting. Someone had killed something in its systems. The resistance likely knew every damn thing about the bird. They had commissioned it—which meant they had an idea he might try to take it back. Star found his sympathy waning.

He hurried from the room, heading toward the front of *The Leaf. Hope Ahiko figures out how to get us airborne— fast.* Star tore through the halls, a momentary pang returned his attention to his burning shoulder. He entered the cockpit and came to stand behind the pilot.

Ahiko was doubled over and wriggled under a console. He muttered colorful phrases that Star felt deserved to be remembered for future use. "Ruttin' resistance—heads up asses—can't believe they hobbled propulsion."

Star hovered over the pilot, clearing his throat to get the man's attention. "Not to trouble you—"

"But troubling me is what you do. What, Shepherd?" Ahiko flailed a leg like he were trying to kick Star without looking.

"We're mighty pressed for time, and I'm out of ideas. Tell me you've got something." Star hoped the pilot had even a shaky plan at best. It would be better than waiting around for them to be surrounded—or worse, the planet to be glassed.

Ahiko grumbled something before slipping out from under the console. He leaned on his side, looking up at Star. "Yeah. Plan's fix the ship and *vroom vroom* out of here fast as we can and don't look back. We did what we set out to do, even got paid, handsomely so. Let's not try to be heroes and go down for it. Money's no good if you can't spend it, and it's clear nobody means to use The Light for proper reasons."

Maybe that's more of a reason for us to. He blinked as the thought crossed his mind, shaking it away. That idealism was what got him into this mess. He wasn't sure it'd get him and his people out. Instead of following the musings, he fixed Ahiko with a flat look. "My ship don't ever *vroom vroom.*"

Ahiko snorted, pulling himself back under the panels. "I can make any girl make those sounds, believe me. Give me a few more minutes underneath her, I'll have her screaming and wailing every which way and sounds alike." He sounded rather pleased with himself.

Star stared out through the cockpit screen.

The military had advanced to fifty yards from the

bow of the vessel. Soldiers closed in, ignoring the bulk of the ship in their way.

Or they've got orders to leave it alone till they can take it. Another thought crossed his mind as he glanced up.

One of the supercarriers hurried up into atmosphere like it couldn't escape fast enough.

They should have been dropping more forces down with the cannon gone, not pulling them up. Unless…they were evacuating because something worse was about to go down. A terrible notion tugged at the back of his brain. "Ahiko, we got any semblance of power at all?"

The pilot groaned, inching out again from the console. "Might be. The Light's up and firing, ain't it? Got a feeling only thing that's been cut is drive systems. Get her on at the very least."

Star flung himself into a seat, taking care to avoid brushing his injured shoulder into the chair. He ran his right hand along the consoles in front of him to bring the ship to life.

A low hum coursed through *The Leaf.* Monitors responded, winking into existence with various flashes. Every readout worked as intended.

Minor relief. It was short-lived as he turned his attention to a screen hanging above his right.

The monitor showcased endless throbbing blips closing in on the pyramid from both sides.

Extremists were coming in, and by the numbers, they brought a lot more of their folks than the military. And then the resistance bases scattered over the planet added to math. The ship leaving… He put it together a moment too late. "They're gonna blast the surface of the planet and wash out anyone in the way—own people included!"

Ahiko rocketed to his feet. "What?"

His heart jackhammered, building up to a rapid, percussive beat that pushed away the pain and weariness. Only the frantic drumming within his body remained. He felt like he'd have to raise his voice to compete with the thundering sounds inside him. "How strong do you think *The Leaf's* shields really are? You're military, give me a guess?"

The pilot looked away for moment, his face pulling into a tight mask. "Dunno. You told me yourself they can last forever. You wondering if they can take a certain kind of blast…" Ahiko's mouth hung open the second he finished the sentence. "Shit, the glassing, right." He licked his lips and breathed out in a sigh. "All I can think of is turning every single system off save for life support."

Star arched a brow.

"Have The Light, all of it, dedicated to holding the shields. Drive any power cells you've got to that too. Leave life support because it's mighty hard to breathe when the world goes that hot. This is all assuming that we don't leave if and before they decide to do this." Ahiko matched Star's expression.

"Then get to work either getting us airborne or shielded." Star gestured out the cockpit to another departing carrier. "Because they're pulling out now, and I've got a feeling they'll cook us all along with their own folk."

The pilot's eyes widened, and he dove beneath the console.

Star turned and ran back to the central hub, giving the room a quick look.

Molan hadn't returned…

Dammit. He couldn't hold to his promise. Not if it meant the death of everyone else. *Sorry, bot.*

He rushed by and hobbled down the first ramp, coming to stop by the side of the hatch. Star glanced out the opening to see if anyone else was headed toward the ship.

Various resistance members either pooled out from the pyramid or headed into it for refuge. None seemed particularly interested in *The Leaf* at the moment.

Good. He started keying in the command to shut the door.

Five iron rods clamped around his wrist, squeezing with enough force he worried the small bones in the joint would give way. The metal hand pulled his away from the keypad. M34N stared him hard in the eyes, each socket staying the sort of still only machinery could manage.

It was like looking into a statue's gaze—unmoving. After a point, he wondered if the automaton was even online.

"You promised me you would wait for Molan." M34N's voice warbled, carrying more a heated inflection than perhaps even the machine had intended.

Star tried to pull his hand free of the automaton's grip but failed. "Look around you. The planet might be glassed. I can't let the rest of you die for him. None of us gets to make that call concerning other's lives."

The bot's eyes swiveled and narrowed.

Star's injured shoulder ignited in hot agony as the

bot clamped his other hand to the injury.

"I am capable of making that call. He risked enough for you. He lost his home for your cause. And I lost mine." The robot fixed him with a look Star didn't think possible for a machine.

Great, a robot with a conscience and an idea of what friendship means. He picked one hell of a time to learn all this.

The world around him screamed like a million shrieking birds.

Star froze. He'd heard the sound before. Star glanced out of the corner of his eyes to catch the distant sky become caked with a sickly green tinge.

M34N's grip loosened as the bot looked back.

Star slammed his forehead into the machine's domed skull, regretting the heavy throb that spread through his head. He winced and broke free of the hold, turning to shut the hatch.

A wave of horrible light rolled toward them as the hatch closed.

I brought The Light out to the wrong people only to lose it. Star shut his eyes.

CHAPTER FORTY

OLD MEN AND STUPID THINGS

Heat made its way through the hull of the ship, reminding Star of his time on Azzip. The temperature climbed. Sweat beaded on his skin, and his vision swam. He fell to his knees, scrambling forward.

M34N grabbed the back of his collar, hauling him to his feet.

He had no idea how the heat made it through the shields.

The rumbling sound of thunder grew closer until it overwhelmed him. The ship lurched and rocked like it was a leaf caught in a storm, the force of which would tear the vessel apart.

"You killed him." The automaton's words were flat, a statement of fact. He trundled forward and balanced himself through the shaking ship.

Star backpedaled from the approaching machine. His hand twitched, and he repressed the urge to draw and fire on M34N. The automaton had every right to be mad, but Star had just as much to place the lives of Zita and Ahiko over one man's. Doubly so when that man ran off on his own.

The machine thrust an open palm out, slamming it into Star's chest. It drove him into the ramp leading up into the hub. Star's back cried out as it banged into the metal walkway. His head bounced off a low railing to the side. If the world hadn't been shaking enough before, it was certainly doing so now. He blinked through the spinning insides of the ship.

The sounds outside picked up into an ear-splitting keen through the bellowing storm-like roar. It was like the entire sky had begun screaming in protest to the superheated blast from the glassing. Star imagined it to be the voices of the poor souls caught directly in the wave.

It didn't help him process it.

M34N bent at the waist, pulling Star back to his feet, slamming a metal fist into his gut.

Air fled his lungs, leaving him feeling like they'd been wrung dry. The assault didn't cease. Another blow cracked into his ribs, just hard enough to bruise him without breaking anything. A follow-up caught him behind his left ear and rocked him to the side. The bot's fist crashed into the bottom of his chin, lifting him to his toes and blurring the world. His hearing followed.

He teetered in place, breathing ragged and waiting for either the ship's shields to fail or the bot to kill him. One or the other seemed the likely outcome. The taste of salt and copper rolled over his tongue. "You done?" The simple question taxed him, but he managed to get it out despite the blood pooling in his mouth.

M34N's eyes snapped closed and opened like shutters several times.

The world shook harder while Star waited for his answer. *If I die in anticipation for a machine's words, I'm doing my damnedest to come back a ghostly something and haunt his tin ass forever.*

The automaton's shoulders sank. "I'm done. I'm not entirely sure what happened." He sounded sincere.

Star ran his tongue along his teeth, tasting more blood than he would have liked. He spat and held onto the rail behind him to endure the shaking. The persistent rattling made its way through his muscles and deep into his bone, making the pangs and pain more pronounced. "You acted human, that's what. Good for you. And for what it's worth"—he spat again—"I'm sorry."

The world stilled and quieted.

M34N turned his head farther than Star would have imagined, glancing at the hatch. "Do you think he survived that?"

Star blinked. *Stars and skies.* The automaton held onto a hope that Molan lived through glassing. There might have been more wrong with the machine than just its hospitality protocols. He was acting human—childlike. Star let out a series of weak coughs, deciding to give the automaton what it needed to hear. It felt right. "Only one way to find out. We open the door and check."

Footsteps plodded nearby, the sounds drumming in his ears along with a rattle that caused him to wince.

Half regretting not having died in the blast about now.

Ahiko swung around the lip of the upper doorway,

staring at them through the opening. "Good news or bad?" He sucked in a breath, looking Star up and down.

Star winced. Breathing out through his nose sent chilling waves through the area that stung. "Your pick."

"Good news: We're alive, if you haven't noticed. Don't know how long that's going to last." The pilot's lips quirked at the edges, pulling into a tight and uneven smile. "Bad news is that you look like six miles of bad road and the road kill along it. Oh, and from what little I can see out the cockpit, planet's glassed. Not to mention these." Ahiko held a hand up. Two bundles of wires hung from his fist, each ending in a wide, rectangular clip with holes meant to be jacked into a console port.

Star's brain refused to stop tumbling, but he worked out enough of what they were.

"Subspace transmitter, military"—he gestured to the black wire bundle—"it's how they tracked us. The worse news is I don't know who put the second one in…or what it's for."

Star eyed the bundle, wondering the same thing. "Why's your face telling me you've got even worse news than that?"

Ahiko's smile waned. "Ship's still grounded; doing what I can. Won't be long, but resistance really mucked about. I know, none of us are keen on hanging about with military ships and who knows what else in orbit. But…I only *just* pulled the transmitters."

Star picked up on the hidden meaning. "There's a chance, with the glassing, a ship could have pinged us. We might not be alone for long."

The pilot nodded. "Our monitors can't pick up a

thing. Can't say the same for military vessels. But the shields held, if only. Every cell we've got is dead. So once we burn through atmo, we best not get into any fights. Or it's over."

Star sighed, leaning harder against the wall for support. "Got it. Do what you can. I'm heading out."

Ahiko opened his mouth like he wanted to protest but shut it when Star flashed him a glare. He pursed his lips. "I'll let Zita know and keep her with me. I could use the help." The pilot turned and made his way back inside.

Star shambled over, brushing aside the automaton's hand it had offered in a gesture of aid. His fingers were remote bars of ice, cold and unresponsive as he jabbed the keypad.

The hatch opened.

Star stared at the scene before him. Words escaped him no matter how hard he tried to grab for something to say.

The lush field and dense jungle had been cleanly erased, giving the impression they had never been there. An untouched expanse of cloudy gray went on as far as he could see. The sky mirrored the ground, looking like it would break into a storm any moment. Tendrils of lightning crackled above, the flashes painting the grim scene all the better. Black smoke wafted from random patches of land.

A garden world turned to ash.

The air gripped his nostrils, hot and sterile, refusing to let go. It smelled antiseptic and wrong for a planet that had been teeming with life and bathed in endless greens.

The inside of his mouth felt like he'd swallowed a fistful of the ash around him—dry. Star's mind numbed as he fought to process the change in the planet. It was like looking at a colorful painting replaced by one in grayscale.

He lumbered down the ramp, driven by something deep in his brain outside conscious thought. The process was automated and mechanical as he stepped onto the soft ground, kicking up a cloud of dust.

The only sounds touching his ears were those of the minor ringing from the automaton's beating. It didn't sit right with him to be in a place so quiet. *Just dust and echoes. Stars and skies. Never seen something more wrong in my life.*

He trudged forward to where he estimated the pyramid had been. Stone had been eroded into noth-ingness from the base of the structure up. Nobody could have survived this.

Something *thudded* nearby.

Star spun to the spot, kicking up a column of dark ash. He ripped his revolver free, releasing a small hiss in pain as his torso ached from the sudden twist.

Thud. Thud.

M34N came by his shoulder, eyeing the spot Star was. "Something is buried under the ash. Correction: Something is buried beneath what is already under the ash."

Star slowed his breathing, still keeping his weapon aimed at the spot. *Damn pyramid was a maze, but if I were behind building that thing, I'd make sure there were just as many ways down as there were up. Smugglers—* He stopped himself short, realizing what the source of the sound could be.

Star stumbled forward, not breaking into a run despite wanting to. "Help me!" He made a feeble wave with the revolver as he staggered to the spot. Star dragged a foot across where he heard the thumping sounds.

M34N fell to his knees and brushed away ash as fast as he could.

Star winced, sucking in a breath through his teeth. The simple motion of dropping to a single knee sent pain rolling through his muscles and joints. He refused to stow the weapon, instead leaning over and shoving aside the dust with broad swipes of his forearm.

Thud.

Yeah, I hear you, pal. Just hope you're someone friendly—familiar.

Thud, thud.

Star banged the tip of his revolver against where he thought the sound was coming from, eliciting a series of light taps.

The thudding stopped. The ground shifted below them, raising before collapsing.

He traded a glance with the automaton. "I've got an idea." He rose to his feet, taking some steps back.

"Given that everything since Lisba has been a consequence of your ideas, Star Shepherd, please forgive me for being unenthused over any ideas you might have." M34N fixed him with a look. "Wait, that almost sounded like a sincere apology. It wasn't supposed to be."

Star frowned. "Got it."

"I meant it to sound offensive because it was, and your idea is likely rather stupid."

"I got it."

"It's very likely what you're about to do will go as well as everything you've done before, which is to say poorly." The automaton held its look.

Star raised his weapon. "If I shoot you in the face, you stop talkin', right?"

The automaton took the hint and moved away from the area.

Thud. Thud. Thud-thud-thud.

Star racked his throat for whatever moisture he could find. "If someone's down there, stand back!"

The ground tremored. Ash particulates bounced, and a wave of the material lifted before flattening.

Star fired a shot at the edge of where the ground had moved.

Something snapped and cracked like thin stone breaking.

He fired again, watching as ash sank into the spot. *Knew it.* Something was down there, an opening. "Keep back!" He hoped whoever was under there had heard him. Star fired a volley of shots along the edge of the stone slab, tearing chunks of it away.

"Damnable, *rargle-urgle,* Shepherd!" The voice came over muted from beneath the earth and ash. Star didn't need to make it out to know who had spoken.

M34N surged toward the stone before Star could say a word. The automaton doubled over by the jagged lip Star had created and hooked his fingers against it. The machine heaved, pulling on the heavy slab. It rose until the automaton stopped, holding one end steady several feet above the ground.

A grimy hand emerged from the opening, slapping

onto the ashen earth of Slaydus. Molan climbed out and kept to all fours as he collapsed.

M34N lowered the slab an inch, looking ready to drop the whole thing.

"Wait!" Molan turned over, holding out a hand.

The machine held the heavy block, its arms quaking much like a person's would under the sustained load.

Someone dressed in resistance fighter fatigues hurried out from underneath the stone—Kheelo. He turned over, snaking half of his upper body below the slab. The man reached in with an arm, hauling something.

Tani clambered out, leaning heavy on Kheelo.

"That's it." Molan released a heavy sigh, collapsing.

M34N dropped the block with an earth-jarring *slam*.

Stone shattered, and it had nothing to do with the slab impacting the ground. A fist-sized chunk evaporated, the area crumbling around it as a crimson ray shot out. The blast passed through the side of M34N's mouth, shearing the metal away clean.

The machine dropped to the ground.

A barrage of violent red reduced the stone to a deteriorating heap that fell in on itself.

Star hurried over to the fallen machine as fast as he could. He leaned over, surveying the damage.

M34N's face had burned away on one side, leaving him with a macabre and aggressive expression—a permanent one, by the looks of it. The metal where his upper lip would be had deformed to form a series of low hanging and sharp edges, like fangs. The area around it up to a small patch beneath his left eye was singed black. The automaton jerked spasmodically. His eyes whirred out of focus, the mechanisms fighting to stop.

Star looked back to the cracking stone.

Savi Ur pulled herself out, chest heaving and a wild light hanging in her eyes. Powdered stone and grime clung to her cheeks, mixing with what looked like thin streams of tears. Ash matted her hair to her scalp. She raised the revolver at Star.

Tani and Kheelo fumbled on their sides, no doubt reaching for their weapons.

Star raised his revolver at Savi. "What now? We kill each other on an already-dead world?" He gave her a grim smile. "Not much point in that, is there?"

She spat. "*You* ruined everything. Look at this world. Look at what *you, you*"—she articulated each worth with a jab of the black revolver—"let the military do. This is your fault, Shepherd. You led them here. You took that cannon down. You could have let me take the ship and The Light back on Lisba. Our cause would have had it."

"Yeah, and I've seen what your cause is willing to do. Mighty similar to the military's. Hell"—he glowered at Tani and Kheelo—"throw yours in there too."

Savi quivered, stilling her hand so it remained steady. "You don't know a rutting thing! The military would never have found this world. With The Light, we could have done something like this a dozen times over to their planets." Her voice dropped to a harsh whisper near the end.

"That's what I was afraid of." Star sighed. Out of the corner of his vision, he caught Molan inching forward. *Don't do something stupid, old man.*

The barkeeper grunted before clearing his throat, drawing the angered woman's attention to him. "Savi…" He held up a hand. "Savi, it's over. Let it go."

She turned the weapon on him in a snap-twist of her body. "Don't. Don't start, not here and now after what's happened." She threw an arm to the side, waving at the world around them. "*Look* at what happened. I warned you all those years ago it would. The shepherd wrought this. It didn't have to happen. The resistance is dead. And if it isn't, it will be soon. But it's not over. My people are still out there. The Light is. It's right there"—she gestured to *The Leaf*—"in arm's reach."

Molan took a pair of steps closer.

Savi took a series of slow and heavy breaths.

Star recognized the gesture. They were the kind of breaths one took to steel themselves before doing something hard and frightening. *No…* He sighted in on Savi, fighting the mounting pain catching up to him. His vision blurred; the aching throughout his body intensified. The gun shook in his hand, his arm refusing to raise it higher than the woman's midsection.

"I'm not letting you talk me out of something else, Molan. Not when I know it's right." Her jaw hardened. A dark look settled into the woman's eyes.

Molan gave her an honest and fatherly smile. "I know Savi, I—"

A bolt of crimson struck the barkeeper's chest, stopping him cold. A second drove through his ribcage before the third passed through his gut. The old man held the smile on his face as he fell to the ground, burying his face in the ash.

Star squeezed the trigger and sent a golden ray

through Savi's side, following Molan's trip to the earth. He fell hard and let exhaustion take its toll.

The screams echoing around him sounded distant, almost like he might have imagined them. They warbled and carried a series of metallic notes. Star turned his head to one side.

He found the source of the screaming.

M34N had righted himself to sitting position, staring at Molan. The automaton's mouth hung open at a canted angle. Loose metal rattled as he continued howling.

CHAPTER FORTY-ONE
MESSAGES

Hearing the machine make such a noise, one filled with so much pain and racked with heaviness broke Star. He shut his eyes, squeezing them as hard as he could to ignore the moisture lining his lids. Ash stuck to his face and mixed with the tears to form a paste on his skin. He managed to drag his good arm up to his cheeks, rubbing the sleeve of his coat against the area.

It only served to drag more ash over him.

M34N's cries echoed through the skies of Slaydus, managing to drown the rumbling of thunder above.

As loud as the world around him was, it felt like a thick blanket had been cast over him, sheltering him from the noise.

A numbing silence filled him.

The sky roared with a violent snap of thunder. Rain followed, beating down on him and drawing small a *plup-plup-plup* as it struck his leather coat. It was the only sound that didn't hurt to hear.

He lay still, watching as Tani and Kheelo finally got to their feet, making their way to Molan.

"Don't touch him!" M34N rose to a stand, trundling toward the barkeeper. His body spasmed like his components were failing and refusing his commands. The machine marched forward regardless.

A pair of hands grabbed Star by both arms, lifting him to his feet. His injured shoulder screamed out in renewed pain despite his fatigue and creeping numbness. *I ain't meant to catch a break.*

"We…heard the shots and the screams, Shepherd." Ahiko's face went through a series of expressions before he looked away.

Zita kept her gaze fixed on him, tears marring her face. She twitched for a second to face Molan's direction before bristling. The smuggler composed herself, holding her look on Star.

He didn't know what to say. Star knew she had been close to the barkeeper. Death changed lots of things, and sometimes, not for the better. She looked on edge—ragged. To go through all this and lose a friend. Then there was how her band of friends had never showed. She knew it all deep down. He bit his tongue and kept from saying anything about that.

"Shepherd…" Ahiko trailed off, breathing hard and clearly fighting to control it. "We've got to go. Clocked something small-hitting passing orbit and into atmo. They'll be here soon. Managed to ping some semblance of a registration from it—capital shuttle."

And I know who'll be aboard it. I mean to look him in the eyes if I can. He gently shook off Zita and Ahiko's hands.

"Help get Molan on board."

Ahiko started protesting.

"Get him on board!" Star staggered a step, taxed from the sudden shout. He waved off the pair's help.

Ahiko nodded, taking Zita by a hand to lead her toward the machine and fallen barkeeper.

Star gritted his teeth and trudged toward Savi.

The woman convulsed.

Star clenched his jaw harder. He came to a stop just beyond the woman's reach and looked down. Star focused the sight of the weapon, convincing himself he was already staring at a dead woman. Another shot wouldn't matter. His hand shook.

Savi coughed. A chunk at the side of her stomach was missing, like it had been scooped neatly away. The edges were cauterized by the blast, the skin blackened. Blood trickled from between her pressed lips. A weak sigh followed. Savi lifted her hand, the weapon hanging limp from her grip. The limb fell flat against the ground.

"You killed a man, someone who looked at you like a child from what I could see. And for what? Anger, your want to hurt the military? Hell, I've got that too, more than you can know. I won't kill a man in cold blood. No matter…" Star clenched his hand hard against the revolver until his knuckles ached. The growing cold and rain didn't help.

Savi didn't reply. In truth, he hadn't expected her to. The woman kept her hand tight to the weapon, letting her head loll to the side to stare at it. The Light, the weapon, and what it represented, clearly meant every-thing to her.

More than an old friend's life and love, apparently. "Keep the damnable thing for a few moments longer." Star lowered his gun, refusing to shoot her. "You're dying anyway. Best you hold onto the last and only piece of The Light you'll ever see again."

Savi had the strength left to shut her eyes. A thin smile spread across her face. Her grip visibly weakened on the weapon as she sighed.

Star stowed his revolver, bending to snatch up the black one. "This belonged to a great captain—lady—damn sight a better person than you." *Even me.* Star turned, watching Ahiko, Zita, and M34N carry Molan into the ship with every bit of dignity they could spare. *Man deserves as much.*

Kheelo and Tani stood off to the side, watching him.

He returned their stares. "I ain't gonna give you a speech about what to do next. Come with me or stay here with your damn resistance. I don't care." He turned and marched toward his ship.

A sharp whine rolled through the sky, building into a scream.

Star kept moving as he glanced up.

A cold, gray-white shuttle zoomed through the distant horizon, heading their way. The vessel looked hawkish: small, narrow, with angled wings hanging down as well as a sloping bow. It couldn't have fit more than ten people.

Star stopped as he took the first step onto the ramp, grabbing one of the beams holding the metal platform to the ship. It had grown cold, chilling him further. He ignored the discomfort.

Tani and Kheelo walked by him, keeping their gazes low but shooting him a passing look. The pair made their way through the hatch and onto the ship.

Someone plodded toward him.

He looked back without turning to see Ahiko lingering by the entry.

"Ship's good. I'm priming thrusters soon as I get back, and we're *vroom vrooming* out of here fast as we can." The pilot's face split into a small smile that was trying too hard.

Star appreciated the simple teasing. He returned the grin and nodded. "Take her, slowly. Something I need to see. I'll page you through comms when I want you to hit it."

The pilot nodded and disappeared.

Seconds later, *The Last Leaf* roared to life and climbed steadily into the air.

The military shuttle landed. A ramp descended from the side, and red-armored soldiers fanned out over the ground. They fell to their knees, training long rifles on Star as the ship climbed.

He ignored them. *Come on, bastard. Show up.*

Admiral Killian Cain stepped out of the shuttle, not bothering to survey the ground. He looked up at the vessel, waving a hand to the troops beside him. They lowered their weapons.

Star couldn't make out the man's face perfectly, but he imagined he was smiling. He pulled his hand away from the beam supporting him and fought to keep himself balanced. Star fired off a single bolt from the black revolver.

The shot struck several feet from the admiral, doing nothing to perturb the man. The soldiers by his side held their gaze like nothing had happened.

Star pictured the man's smile widening. *Just a message. Next time I'll do what I should've.* He clamped back onto the beam and used it to steady himself before making his way into the hatch. He shut it behind him, keying the pad again. The comms crackled. "Ahiko, take us out—hard in while we're in atmosphere."

The pilot said nothing, just blipping the comms as acknowledgement.

Star collapsed against the hatch as the ship lurched into a jump. He shut his eyes and let darkness take him.

CHAPTER FORTY-TWO

A SHEPHERD'S FAREWELL

He woke in warmth and bright light, low voices muttering around him. Star blinked and groaned.

A world of unmarred white greeted him. An arched ceiling above, upward curving walls, all of which were illuminated by thin strips of dotted white lights running overhead.

Gentle heat radiated from below him, spreading through his legs and back, easing his aches.

It took him a moment to realize he was atop a hard metal surface blanketed in something soft—plush. He put his location together. Star lay in the med bay atop one of those things they passed off as a recovery table. His limbs weren't bound by leather straps, a small plus in his mind.

He'd been stripped of his coat, boots, and socks, leaving only his shirt and pants. Both had dried from the heat coming from the table. It made sense to remove his wet socks, allowing his extremities an easier time of warming up. Despite the comforting temperature around him, his injured shoulder tingled and felt cool.

Antiseptic. Someone had treated and patched the wound. He groaned again, touching a finger to the area to brush against gauze. Star looked to where the voices were coming from.

Zita and Ahiko sat on the edge of the nearest bed. M34N stood off to the side, storing medical supplies that had no doubt been used in cleaning and dressing his wound. Kheelo and Tani sat on the floor between the crew, arms around each other. The pair's eyes seemed to carry a distant and hollow light.

He grunted, his sides going tight as he twisted to get up. Star propped his good arm under him to support his weight. "What'd I miss?"

Zita and Ahiko looked up at him, both giving him weary smiles.

Ahiko leaned over, clasping his hands and resting his chin atop them. "We bugged out of Slaydus, hit empty space, and have been drifting since. Out here, it's nothing but cosmic storms and gas nebulas. Things are pretty mucky and dangerous, but we'll be hidden."

Star's mouth twitched. "How long will the shields last out here?"

Ahiko ran a hand through his hair, puffing his cheeks and blowing out a long breath. "Hopefully, forever."

Star arched a brow.

"I put *The Leaf* to sleep, so to speak. She's mostly off but for critical systems. Tricked the shields into behaving the way they do when the bird's idle. Means we've got no control, but we should be safe."

Star picked up on the unspoken words Ahiko had wanted to say. *For now.* He filed it away as a future concern.

Zita caught his attention, turning her head and motioning quietly towards M34N.

Star got the subtle hint. He slid off the bed, hitting the ground harder than he expected. His knees wobbled like they'd forgotten how to handle his weight. He placed his hands against the frame for support until he was steady. "M34." He left off the N, hoping the machine would notice.

The automaton froze, turning his head. He said nothing. Half of his mouth was still a mangled mess.

"I'm sorry, for what it's worth…about Molan."

The machine's mouth moved soundlessly, his eyes spinning as they readjusted.

A moment of silence passed.

"So am I, Star Shepherd." M34N held his gaze for countless seconds before turning away. The automaton marched out of the room, unceremoniously dropping the large of roll of gauze in his hands so it unfurled over the floor.

Star sighed. He rubbed a hand over his face and searched for his belongings. His coat and effects lay in crumpled heap to the side of his bed. He didn't bother donning the clothing or retrieving his weapon. Instead, he picked up the black revolver, stowing it in his pants, letting the band hold the weapon in place. He then followed after the machine.

"Where are you going?" Zita moved into step with him. Ahiko followed behind.

Star stopped, turning a shade to look at Tani and Kheelo. "Get up. Follow. My ship, my rules. You two can feel sorry for yourselves later. There's work to be done."

The pair got to their feet, leaning on each other for support. His words had rocked them into some semblance of awareness. They took a few steps until they were in line with Ahiko.

Good enough. Star set after M34N, knowing where the automaton was headed. The short walk went by to the sound of plodding footsteps as they headed to the central hub.

Molan's body rested on the floor paneling, arms crossed over his chest to hide the bulk of the wounds from the black revolver. If Star looked at an angle, the blast through the ribcage was hardly noticeable. It felt callous, wrong at first, to have the man lying where he was in that shape. He hadn't been washed or changed.

The automaton must have read his mind. M34N eyed him and shook his head. "He wouldn't care much about what he looked like dead. Dead is dead." The machine delivered the words like fact, but something shook in its metal tones.

Guess not.

"He'd want his funeral to be the same—honest, simple, like he was." M34N kept his look up.

Star understood the silent request. "I can do that." Despite what his body had been through, he made his way over to one end, grabbing Molan by the ankles. "Everyone get in and help."

Nobody offered a word of protest, coming to Molan's side to help lift. M34N could have done it himself, but Star didn't feel it right. They carried the barkeeper overhead in silence.

Star gestured with a hand on occasion, leading the way via finger points as they navigated the ship to come to a lengthy, narrow hall.

The wall to the right nestled a dozen domed protrusions—the hatches to escape tubes should the crew be forced to abandon the ship. Each clear hatch revealed the pristine white interior of the small vessels: padded walls made from foam that conformed to the occupants' shape. An adjustable harness hung within.

Star touched an index and middle finger to the side of one of the hatches. He dragged the digits along the curvature of the hatch. Green light trailed behind his fingers.

The lid hissed and snapped open.

"Ease him in," said Star.

They did as he asked, lowering Molan into the tube.

Silence returned, lingering for several moments.

Star decided to break it. "We should all say words. Figure we've got enough to say, even those of us who knew him the shortest."

M34N didn't need further prompting. The automaton stepped in front of the hatch. Incoherent sounds left his mouth like his speech protocols had failed. He shouldn't have been faltering. It was near impossible for an automaton to struggle that way. Language had been hardcoded into him. M34N placed a hand against the lip of opening, leaning against it.

Star gave him a moment before grabbing the machine gently by a shoulder, leaving his hand there as a reassuring weight.

"He was a simple man, a good one. He didn't care about things like title and wealth, where you came from, or if you were even human. He only cared about how you acted—your heart. He ran a bar and didn't want for much outside that. Maybe a little more fairness in life for others less fortunate than him. That's the Molan Edolin I knew, not the one of the resistance." M34N stepped away from the hatch.

Zita sniffed and looked away. Her eyes had reddened, tears not quite falling yet. She refused to say a word.

Star couldn't blame her.

Ahiko stood where he was and cleared his throat. "You were gruff, tough, could shoot damn well. I think if we'd gotten more time to hang around, I would've gotten to like you, old man." Ahiko snapped rigid, adopting a perfect military posture and saluted. The look on his face showed he meant it, jaw clenched, eyes hard.

Tani made her way over. She brought two fingers to her lips, kissing them before reaching into to touch them to Molan's forehead. "You've known me long enough to hear everything and anything I could say to you now. You'd know I'd mean it, and I do. I'll miss you."

Kheelo remained the definition of a statue, unmoving, lifeless. He stared.

Star ignored him and decided to be the last to speak. "Didn't know you, I would've liked to. Truth be told, I've done far too many funerals of late, more than enough to last me forever. I'm sorry I dragged you into this." He licked his lips, feeling the eyes and weight on him.

"Don't know what to say, so I'll say what I've done for others—captains, shepherds not by blood and trade, but by the choices they made and the way they've come." He cleared his throat and reached for an old poem buried in his memories. "Among stars and skies, no shepherd of the path truly dies. Through darkness, by the grace of starlight, you'll make it home to rest tonight. Every shepherd finds the way, today, and every day—"

Kheelo cut off Star. "We'll see each other soon. In the endless black, we're one family, one sun, one star, one moon. Kheera nai," he said.

Star held off on what he wanted to say, deciding to address the surprising outburst after he was done. His shepherd's sendoff wasn't harmed by another man's words. Star pulled the black revolver free, thumbing the cylinder open. *Seems fitting to use the thing that cut him down to send him off in grace.*

Light pulsated from within the weapon like it held a miniature red giant star. The innards of the weapon were comprised of a singular housing mated to the cylinder and segmented into six pieces still joined to The Light's container.

Just a piece of what you fought for to send you off. Star tore at his shirt, pulling free a thin strip that he touched to the red light. It ignited into flames the same color as the energy source. Despite the speed of the fiery tendrils licking their way up the clothing, he took his time and care in leaning over to drop the fabric onto Molan.

The fire spread, engulfing the man in seconds and bathing him in brilliant, carmine light.

Star shut the hatch, locking it. He gave the crew a

long look, settling on M34N.

The machine nodded.

Star jettisoned the escape tube, watching through the transparent frame as the fire burned bright in space. The insides of Molan's vessel flared strong until all light vanished.

***

Star gave the crew several hours to compose themselves before calling them to the central hub.

They seated themselves where they could. Both he and M34N elected to stand.

He stared each member in the eye, giving them a hard look. "I know most of you don't have a clue what comes next. Been there myself. I've got an idea but not sure if you want to hear it." Star let the words hang, waiting to see if anyone had something to say.

"Yeah," said Ahiko. "I want to hear it because from where I'm sitting, it's dead—mission, something to believe in, what you convinced me to believe in. Not an easy thing to do, by the way. What now? Tell me, Shepherd."

He expected the comments from the pilot. He was only surprised no one else had echoed them. Star wagered they were all thinking along those lines. "Mission ain't dead. The Light's not gone, just the people who we thought would do right by it, us. That hasn't changed. We've got each other to look to. We can do what needs to be done with The Light. And I mean to." He narrowed his eyes, finding every trace of anger he had in him and letting it flood his voice.

"Molan died for that. Good people along this way, folks back on Autumn, died for this. Their lives don't go to waste by shucking this off and going to spend our money and make merry. Hell no." Star pulled the revolver free, waggling it to draw their attention. "This, The Light, they're the last gifts of what are now the ghosts of Autumn. The hopes and dreams of countless people who wanted to see a freer galaxy and people. I mean to honor that."

Zita finally spoke up. "You want us risking our lives for ghosts? And do what exactly?"

"We become ghosts. No one looks for those. We drift. Get our bearings, search for a means to get The Light out to every world in this galaxy and strip the Oligarchy of its power. Who's with me?" Star knew the answer before he'd asked the question.

The ragtag crew smiled and threw in their agreements.

"I'd enjoy all the cash we earned a damn sight better if I knew we'd stripped the Oligarchy of theirs. Hell, maybe when it's all said and done, I'll sleep on a pile of money to celebrate," said Ahiko.

"I'd love nothing more than to have the military's ass handed to them by smugglers and common folk alike." Zita flashed him a feral grin.

"Molan died for it; I plan to live for it." Tani gave him a hardened stare.

Kheelo inclined his head in silence.

Star turned to M34N. "You in?"

The automaton tilted his head, spreading his damaged mouth into a shark-like grin. "The Oligarchy owes me a bar. So, yes."

Star smiled. "Good. Let's go topple a government."

If you liked this book please consider leaving a review

ACKNOWLEDGEMENTS

To my editors, Michelle Dunbar, Cayleigh Stickler, my publisher, Bolide, and everyone who alpha read this and pushed me along thinking this was a good idea. And to the readers who come along this with a love for space westerns and witty and weird dialogue. Thank you.

ABOUT THE AUTHOR

R.R. Virdi is the Dragon Award—Nominated author of The Grave Report, a paranormal investigator series set in the great state of New York. He is also the author of The Books of Winter series. A portal urban fantasy series set in the same world as The Grave Report. He has worked in the automotive industry as a mechanic, retail, and in the custom gaming computer world. He's an avid car nut with a special love for American classics.

The hardest challenge for him up to this point has been fooling most of society into believing he's a completely sane member of the general public.

Follow him on his website. http://rrvirdi.com/

www.ingramcontent.com/pod-product-compliance
Lightning Source LLC
Chambersburg PA
CBHW060938190726
48286CB00005B/1320